THE WICKED BEST MAN

ERIN SWANN

This book is a work of fiction. The names, characters, businesses, and events portrayed in this book are fictitious. Any similarity to real persons, living or dead, businesses, or events is coincidental and not intended by the author.

Copyright © 2024 by Swann Publications

All rights reserved.

No part of this book may be reproduced, stored in a retrieval system, or transmitted in any form or by any means, electronic, mechanical, photocopying, recording, or otherwise, without the express written permission of the publisher. Reasonable portions may be quoted for review purposes.

The author acknowledges the trademarked status and trademark owners of various products referenced in this work of fiction, which have been used without permission. The publication/use of these trademarks is not authorized, associated with, or sponsored by the trademark owners.

Edited by Jessica Royer Ocken

Proofreaders: Rosa at Fairy Proofmother Proofreading, Jen Boles, Victoria Straw, Jennifer Herrington of Fresh Look Editorial

The following story is intended for mature readers. It contains mature themes, strong language, and sexual situations. All characters are 18+ years of age, and all sexual acts are consensual.

Erin can be found on the web at https://www.erinswann.com

❦ Created with Vellum

ALSO BY ERIN SWANN

Why romance? Because we all need a chance to escape doing the next load of laundry.

We deserve a chance to enjoy love, laughs, intrigue, and yes, fear, heartbreak, and tears, all without having to leave the house.

If you can read my books without feeling all of these then I haven't done my job right.

Standalone Novels:

Devil in a Tux – Available on Amazon

(Evan and Alexa's story) They called Evan McAllister the devil in a suit. The saying is that dancing with the devil changes you. Alexa was about to find out.

The Wicked Best Man – Available on Amazon

(Travis and Adriana's story) Seeing him at the engagement party sent a chill through her. He wasn't on the guest list, he shouldn't have been there. When he was introduced as the substitute best man, Adriana had no idea how much her life was about to change.

Protecting Serena – Available on Amazon

(Duke and Serena's story) After being run off the road, billionaire heiress Serena Benson needed protection. Daddy wouldn't approve of, Duke, the panty-melting, tattooed, wall of muscle who is now her bodyguard. When Duke's overprotective nature cramps her style, she needs to either punch him to get her way or kiss his grumpy ass senseless. Then, she is attacked again.

Covington Billionaires Series:

The Billionaire's Trust - Available on Amazon, also in AUDIOBOOK

(Bill and Lauren's story) He needed to save the company. He needed her. He couldn't have both. The wedding proposal in front of hundreds was like a fairy tale come true—Until she uncovered his darkest secret.

Chosen by the Billionaire - Available on Amazon, also in AUDIOBOOK

(Steven and Emma's story) The youngest of the Covington clan, Steven, avoided the family business to become a rarity, an honest lawyer. He didn't suspect that pursuing Emma could destroy his career. She didn't know what trusting him could cost her.

Previously titled: The Youngest Billionaire

The Secret Billionaire – Available on Amazon, also in AUDIOBOOK

(Patrick and Elizabeth's story) Women naturally circled the flame of wealth and power, and his is brighter than most. Does she love him? Does she not? There's no way to know. When Pat stopped to help her, Liz mistook him for a carpenter. Maybe this time he'd know. Everything was perfect. Until the day she left.

The Billionaire's Hope - Available on Amazon, also in AUDIOBOOK

(Nick and Katie's story) They came from different worlds. Katie hadn't seen him since the day he broke her brother's nose. Her family retaliated by destroying Nick's life. She never suspected where accepting a ride from him today would take her. They said they could do casual. They lied.

Previously titled: Protecting the Billionaire

Picked by the Billionaire – Available on Amazon, also in AUDIOBOOK

(Liam and Amy's story) A night she wouldn't forget. An offer she couldn't refuse. He alone could save her, and she held the key to his survival. If only they could pass the test together.

Saved by the Billionaire – Available on Amazon, also in AUDIOBOOK

(Ryan and Natalie's story) The FBI and the cartel were both after her for the same thing: information she didn't have. First, the FBI took everything, and then the cartel came for her. She trusted Ryan with her safety, but could she trust him with her heart?

<u>London Billionaires Series:</u>

Return to London – Available on Amazon

(Ethan and Rebecca's story) Rebecca looks forward to the most important case of her career. Until, she is paired with Ethan, the man she knew years ago. Mutual attraction and old secrets combine to complicate everything. What could have been a second chance results in an impossible choice.

The Rivals – Available on Amazon

(Charlie and Danielle's story) He was her first crush. That ended when their families had a falling out. Now, they are forced to work together on a complicated acquisition.

Mutual attraction is complicated by distrust as things go wrong around them. A second chance turns into an impossible choice.

Benson Billionaires Series:

Caught by the Billionaire – Available on Amazon, also in AUDIOBOOK

(Vincent and Ashley's story) Ashley's undercover assignment was simple enough: nail the crooked billionaire. The surprise came when she opened the folder, and the target was her one-time high school sweetheart, Vincent Benson. Choices must be made when an unknown foe attacks.

The Driven Billionaire – Available on Amazon

(Zachary and Brittney's story) Rule number one: hands off your best friend's sister. With nowhere to turn when she returns from upstate, Brittney accepts Zach's offer of a room. Mutual attraction quickly blurs the rules. When she comes under attack, pulling Brittney closer is the only way to keep her safe. But, the truth of why she left town in the first place will threaten to destroy them both.

Nailing the Billionaire – Available on Amazon

(Dennis and Jennifer's story) Jennifer knew he destroyed her family. Now she is close to finding the records that will bring Dennis down. When a corporate shakeup forces her to work with him, anger and desire compete. Vengeance was supposed to be simple, swift, and sweet. It was none of those things.

Undercover Billionaire – Available on Amazon

(Adam and Kelly's story) Their wealthy families have been at war forever. When Kelly receives a chilling note, the FBI assigns Adam to protect her. Family histories and desire soon collide, questioning old truths. Keeping ahead of the threat won't be their only challenge.

Trapped with the Billionaire – Available on Amazon

(Josh and Nicole's story) Nicole returns from vacation to find her company has been sold to Josh's family. Being assigned to work for the new CEO is only the first of her problems. Competing visions of how to run things and mutual passion create a volatile mix. The reappearance of a killer from years ago soon threatens everything.

Saving Debbie – Available on Amazon

(Luke and Debbie's story) On the run from her family and the cops, Debbie finds the only person she can trust is Luke, the ex-con who patched up her injuries. Old lies haunt her, and the only way to unravel them is to talk with Josh, the boy who lived through the nightmare with her years ago.

Clear Lake Series: The Clear Lake books follow the small town Bensons of Clear Lake as they deal with a disappearance in town. The tranquility of their community is shattered, and they are now in the cross-hairs of the local police chief.

Temptation at the Lake – Available on Amazon

(Casey and Jordan's story) Shot in the line of duty and on temporary disability, Jordan leaves the city for Clear Lake to recuperate. Getting back to one hundred percent was supposed to be hard, but she didn't count on the irresistible Casey becoming the devil pushing her to the breaking point. A fling with this devil becomes complicated when she gets pulled into the dangerous town feud.

Desire at the Lake – Available on Amazon

(Waylon and Anna's story) Things quickly spiral out of control for Anna when her boss disappears. Suddenly out of a job and with no place to stay, her only refuge becomes Waylon's garage. The undeniable chemistry between them explodes. Everything changes when Waylon is arrested for her ex-boss's murder.

Passion at the Lake – Available on Amazon

(Boone and Angela's story) Angela's planned escape from the hell of her life in Boston goes awry when she is stranded in Clear Lake. Things go from bad to worse when her fate depends on her personal devil, Boone. She has no intention of falling for the beast again. But, the sparks between them result in a fire that can't be controlled. With her computer talents, Angela uncovers a clue in the disappearance of Lee Pollock.

Heat at the Lake – Available on Amazon

(Blake and Priscilla's story) Blake arrived in town to help his Gramps. A chance to work for the local police force was just what he needed to further his career goals. When he hooked up with the feisty little bombshell, he had no idea she was one of the prime suspects in a local murder case. Then, he discovered she was on the other side of the duplex he'd leased. Undeniable chemistry was about to complicate everything.

CHAPTER 1

*A*DRIANA

Friday afternoon, just as my to-go order was called, I drank down the last of my cup and reread the final line of the chapter.

"I want to see all of you, feel all of you, enjoy all of you."

My phone, open on the table, flashed with a message. Closing my book, I read the Google alert—another drowning, this one in Alabama. Earlier this morning, it had been Florida. Life didn't promise the happy endings books did.

Putting the phone away, I rose and deposited my empty cup in the trash. I then brought the two piping hot to-go cups back to my tiny table.

"How do you like that book?" the lady at the neighboring table asked.

"I'm just getting started," I answered as I stuffed my paperback copy of *Secretary to the Bazillionaire* in my backpack.

"The cover is such a departure," she noted. "I wasn't sure I wanted to get it."

She seemed to be waiting for me to say more, and I decided she looked like someone who wouldn't judge me. "So far, it's great, and I'd recommend anything by this author."

That made her smile. "Thanks."

It was a romance novel, and a steamy one. Thank God some of my favorite authors had changed from the traditional bare-chested man on their covers to more discreet designs. Now, I could read in the coffee shop or on the train without being embarrassed.

Outside, I buried my chin in the collar of my coat against the cold January wind. I turned left, holding a coffee in each hand.

When I reached the intersection, I saw him at the end of the block, directly in my intended path to the left. I went straight instead and crossed the street quickly. It had already been a long day in the classroom, and I wasn't finished yet. An encounter with my ex, Simon, would be the shittiest way to end the week.

A block later, I reluctantly put down one of the coffees I was carrying. The hot coffee was the only thing keeping my hands from freezing in the January chill. But I'd heard two messages arrive and needed to check them.

CHELSEA: Reservations all set.

My best friend, Chelsea Hobbs, had moved up her wedding to next weekend—or rather, her mother had—which had meant a rush to arrange the travel.

I thumb-typed my reply.

ME: Great

The second message was annoying.

RACHEL: Hurry

What is her problem? I was ahead of schedule for the meeting.

I put the phone back in my purse, picked up the coffee, and continued on. Rachel Schwartzman didn't believe in long explanations by text—or any explanations, actually. It wouldn't do any good to call and ask, particularly since I wasn't about to run with two drinks in my hands, and I couldn't talk and carry the coffees at the same time either.

Her message meant I'd have to take the direct route and walk by the Carlyle Plaza. When I reached it, I hurried past the tall monstrosity that had ruined Daddy's life four years ago. It belonged in Manhattan, not Queens, and it made me want to puke every time I saw it.

Four blocks later, I turned into the doorway of the long, squat building that was the Astoria Community Center. This was a part-time gig for me, but my passion. It was so fulfilling to help these kids after hours. They had the deck stacked against them, unlike the entitled, rich brats I taught at Hightower Prep, a well-known Ivy League feeder school.

As always, Rachel was behind the lobby desk. Despite the anxious message she'd sent, she greeted me with a smile and an outstretched hand. Her sweater today was cat-themed, as it often was. "I love it when you have a meeting with Benjamin," she said.

These were the days I brought her a Starbucks mocha if I had time to stop on my way from school. Personally, I considered four o'clock too late in the day to have coffee, but that was just me. "And I love bringing you this." I handed her the double-sleeved paper cup and adjusted my grip on her husband, Benjamin's, caramel macchiato. "Why the hurry-up message?"

"One of the men from the bank arrived early, and I have a question for you after," she said. "The guy just went up. Benjamin said you were going to join him, and I didn't realize how close you were."

I checked my watch. "Just one?" One person was at least two people shy of a typical bank team. Bankers were wimps and preferred group decisions. "You sure he was from the bank?"

She shrugged. "He was in a suit and asked for Benjamin by name. If he was an interview candidate, Benjamin didn't mention him." She raised her cup. "Looked like a banker to me."

"Thanks. I'll be back for that question." I dutifully headed down the hall, glancing up at the sign above the pool entrance as I always did. The Katarina Xenakis Memorial Pool was, in my opinion, our most important asset.

I hurried up the stairs because these meetings had taken on a new urgency. A month ago, Benjamin had started searching for someone to replace him. Soon, the center would lose his knowledge and talent while he and Rachel toured the world. Benjamin Schwartzman had been the manager here since the center's founding. He and Rachel were fixtures in Queens. They were ready to retire, though, and it would be tough losing them. Rachel was already getting Social Security payments, and Benjamin's would kick in soon. As he put it, they wanted to walk Rome's seven hills while they still could.

Upstairs, I stopped outside Benjamin's office when I heard a conversation. With a stain on my top from a science experiment gone wrong today, I needed to change it before the meeting with First Atlantic Bank. Corporate donations to the community center were vital.

I waited for the right moment and strode past to my office, where I quickly changed into my spare Hightower Prep polo shirt before checking my lipstick and hair. Yes, the casual, dark-red shirt clashed with the lime-green pencil skirt I'd worn today, but it would have to do. I returned to Benjamin's office door.

From the back, the man talking with Benjamin looked both tall and built, with broad shoulders and a trim waist. His suit was expensive and fitted to his body, probably not off the rack. Proper banker attire, I decided.

Benjamin didn't sound like his normal, effusive self, but that's what the macchiato in my office was for. I'd planned to get it to him before the meeting, but it would have been rude to bring it along in front of a guest, so I'd left it behind.

"Since I'm retiring in a few months," Benjamin said, "I may not be the best one to have this discussion with."

I didn't care for schmoozing rich dudes for donations. But I reminded myself of Benjamin's words the first time I'd verbalized that complaint: *"Get used to it. They're the ones with money to spare."*

Benjamin had emphasized that it didn't matter whether donors did so to make a difference, to make themselves feel good, or just for a tax deduction. It took money to run the center, and no matter the source, we needed it. *"Their money is the same color as yours or mine."*

I can do this. I plastered on my best smile and waltzed into the room, ready to sell the hell out of this place as a great investment in the future of Queens and its residents.

Benjamin lifted his bulk from his chair as I entered. "Andy."

"Sorry I'm late," I said. "Hope I didn't miss anything important."

When the visitor turned toward me, he took my breath away. He was more than fit; he was gorgeous—strong chin, chiseled cheekbones, an engaging smile, and those eyes… They were a pale-blue that held me captive for several seconds.

I'd thought of bankers as pudgy old men who would be lucky to hit four on the ten-point scale, and this man was a solid eleven.

"Travis," Benjamin said. "This is Andy Moreno, our director of education."

Travis stepped forward and offered his hand, a large one with long, sexy fingers.

Why am I noticing that? I was in a dry spell, but I was more of a butt girl than a hand girl. I blinked away that thought and stepped in for the handshake. So what if he was gorgeous? He was a banker.

I felt the spark when our hands met. Maybe it was static electricity. But the goose bumps that formed on my arm said it wasn't—I had dubbed him an eleven, after all. And in short sleeves, they showed.

He took a deep breath as we shook. Had he felt the spark too? Was I lucky enough to have caused goose bumps under the sleeves of that impeccably tailored suit?

His grip was not painfully overpowering but still extremely firm—a real man's handshake that reminded me to tighten my fingers in return.

Right. He was a banker, and we were playing by male-dominance rules here. Goose bumps or not, this was a serious meeting. I would not let a hot guy fluster me. And, being obviously rich knocked him down a few points, in my view.

I didn't pull my hand away, go limp like a girlie girl, or meekly avert my eyes. No, I stared him down, or rather up, and matched his visual intimidation. He had to be six-three or four.

He released my hand. "Andy?" he asked in a deep baritone, turning his smile up a notch, a glint in those blue eyes. "Is that perhaps short for something?"

A donation from the bank was important, so I couldn't lose focus. Straightening my spine, I answered, "Adriana." My hand still tingled from our shake. I subtly wiped my palm on the side of my skirt to get the pheromones off.

Benjamin sat back down.

"Suits you," Travis said with a smile that telegraphed the words I knew would come next.

As soon as I'd arrived at college, I'd decided my given name was too delicate and switched to Andy. It stopped the pretty-name comments that always annoyed me. Nobody ever told a Brett or a Clint that their names were strong or manly.

"That's a positively beautiful name," he said, adding additional wattage to his smile. *Positively beautiful* was a surprising change from *pretty,* but I was still being assigned the pretty-girl category instead of the gender-doesn't-matter competent-person one. Intimidation had morphed into condescension.

I ignored his comment and got back to business. Like hyenas, I knew bankers traveled in packs. "Should we wait for the rest of the group?"

He pointed at the writing on my shirt and changed the subject. "I went to Hightower too. Did you have Smedley for science? He was tough."

"I teach there," I corrected him. "Smedley is still tough as shoe leather, but I'm tougher."

That garnered me a raised eyebrow and a nod. "You sound like you're proud of that."

The kids needed to learn that life wasn't a bed of roses. I was most proud of how many parents of the rich brats I taught called to complain about how unfairly tough I was. But I wouldn't admit that to this smug ass.

Travis had probably been as entitled as the current crop when he attended Hightower Prep.

Benjamin cleared his throat, getting my attention. "Andy, Travis isn't with the bank."

It was my turn to be confused. The expensive suit had led me astray. Did that mean he was an applicant for Benjamin's job? "I'm sorry. I thought—"

"Travis is giving us a heads-up," Benjamin explained, "that his company is under contract to purchase the building."

I stopped breathing, waiting for details. How much was the rent going to increase? Would we be able to handle it?

"I thought the early notice would allow you extra time to search for a new location. Extra time for us to—"

"They want to force us to move and replace us with a skyscraper," Benjamin said with a sneer.

Shock rendered me speechless, but it didn't stop me from imagining my eyes boring laser holes into this jerk.

Travis raised a finger. "To assist you, I was going to say."

"We're not moving," I insisted, getting my breath back.

"It wouldn't be right away," Travis said, taking a step back. If he thought I might hit him or kick him, he was right. "We're trying to smooth the transition as much as possible by giving you notice and offering—"

"Who is *we*?" Benjamin asked.

Just like that, this Travis asswipe intended to close us down and end the services we brought to the community.

6

I stared fuck-you eyes at him, waiting for the answer.

"The Carlyle Heights Group."

My blood boiled. Once again, a Carlyle was screwing up my life.

CHAPTER 2

Travis

The beautiful Adriana's mossy-green eyes turned instantly murderous. "You work for the Carlyles, as in the Carlyle Plaza monstrosity?"

The words formed a question, but she spit them out with the venom of an accusation. People didn't take that tone with me, not even people who'd known me forever. My family name had always afforded me privilege, and I'd never considered it a liability until this moment.

Anger radiated from the woman. She'd gone from short, curvy temptress to fire-breathing dragon in seconds. "Kicking people out and insulting them with your *compensation*?" She added air quotes to the last word.

I held up my hands. I knew it had been a mistake to let Luca negotiate the compensation packages on the Plaza. "Before you take a swing at me, I was not involved in that part of the Plaza project. If I had been, things would have been diff—"

"Right," Schwartzman scoffed, not letting me finish. "I've heard that song before."

I judged him as the pragmatic one of the two, and the curvy brunette as the hothead. She'd jumped to two immediate, erroneous conclusions about me without asking questions. I didn't work for a bank, and I wasn't anybody's flunky.

Schwartzman had the extra eighty or so pounds that came from riding a desk for decades but also the keen eyes of experience under that horseshoe ring of graying hair. He would be the one to pitch to.

"I don't trust a thing that Carlyle jerk sends his flunkies to say," he continued. His opinion of my half brother, Luca, was crystal clear. Now they had both jumped to incorrect assumptions.

"Yeah, and *vaffanculo*," Adriana added, crossing her arms over her chest. I had no idea what she meant, but her tone said angry.

She shook her head. "You developers are all the same, locusts looking to devour a neighborhood so you can shit on it and leave behind a glass-and-steel monument to your own egos."

This was going south fast. "It's not like that," I countered.

"Is that why the Carlyle name is plastered on that monstrosity you call the Plaza?"

I sighed and waited for a moment of calm.

"Just what are you going to name the new building?" she demanded.

"We should get back on topic," I suggested.

She pointed an accusing finger at me. "You can go tell the high and mighty Mr. Carlyle to take a flying—"

"Andy," Schwartzman cautioned.

She held back the f-bombs she'd likely been about to hurl. "Tell him this means war, and it's happening over my dead body—probably his dead body too, if he sets foot on this side of the East River."

Schwartzman leaned back in his chair. "And after the last time, we're better prepared for the war."

Adriana nodded. "We've got an email list that's forty thousand strong now, and we know people on the city council. Tell that fu…" She clenched her teeth. "That dirtball Carlyle, he won't be able to buy off the politicians this time, once we mobilize the troops."

I swallowed hard. *"Keep it from blowing up,"* Dad had said when giving me this assignment. I was as far from that as possible.

Although my heart sped up, I willed myself to stay calm—something I excelled at. Fighting emotions with emotions wasn't a winning strategy. That email list would be dangerous opposition, but I tried not to let that show in my face. "I assure you, things will be different this time, more than fair."

"Why don't you call that Carlyle slimeball?" she coated the words in derision. "Call him right now and tell him it's checkmate and he'd better call off the deal."

"I am the Mr. Carlyle you're dealing with in this situation." I didn't add the qualifier, *as of today*. I hadn't created this mess, but it was now my responsibility to fix it.

She looked at me in disbelief. "You don't look like a Carlyle."

This was true. I didn't look anything like Luca.

"You dealt with my half brother, Luca, last time," I explained. "He's irrelevant. You'll now be dealing directly with me."

Schwartzman steepled his hands. "And how much assistance would the Carlyle Heights Group be willing to supply?"

Now that he knew I had real monetary authority, he'd decided to test the waters. But I knew better than to start that sort of negotiation at the first meeting. "Today, I only mean to put your fears to rest and make you aware of the purchase taking place. We can discuss specifics a little later."

Adriana frowned at Schwartzman. "I, for one, can't be bought. We've got the perfect location for the center now. It's right on the train line and three bus routes, for Christ's sake, so it would be better for everyone involved if you vultures moved on to some other property."

She'd hit the nail on the head. Proximity to the station that allowed tenants quick and easy access to Manhattan had been the driver for choosing this location for Carlyle Towers. I shifted my stance to her. "Like I said, we can be very generous in backstopping you. As for the details, we'll discuss those later." Talking to her while she was this agitated could screw everything up.

It appeared I had Schwartzman's interest. He saw me as an opportunity to pad the center's bank account in a big way. Good for him. That was the point of this visit.

Adriana, however, gave me a slow shake of her head. "You're wasting your breath." She was going to be harder to deal with—a lot harder, and it sounded like she was the key to smoothing things over. But I wouldn't be able to gauge the cost of that smoothing until I had her in a calmer state of mind.

Men in suits appeared outside the office—most likely the bank group they'd thought I was a part of. Four white shirts, four ill-fitting charcoal two-piece suits, four potbellies—yup, bankers.

This was a high-stakes game, and I didn't have a winning hand yet. I whipped out a card and handed it to Schwartzman. Better to retreat and regroup.

He took the opportunity to call a halt to the sparring. "Mr. Carlyle, I'm afraid we'll have to continue this later. I have another meeting scheduled, and I see our guests have arrived." The diplomat had spoken.

"Thank you for making time for me, Mr. Schwartzman. I assure you we want to avoid any unpleasantness and can be very generous," I said before turning to the feisty lady. "It's been a pleasure, Adriana." I offered her a card as well. "We should have dinner and talk. Sooner rather than later. Just let me know when you're available." For a second, it looked like she might refuse the card. Adriana wasn't into diplomacy.

"Don't hold your breath," she mumbled as she yanked the card away.

"It sounds like a splendid idea," Schwartzman said.

Now it was a battle between them.

"A very beautiful name for a positively beautiful woman," I said with my broadest smile before leaving.

"Kiss my ass," was her whispered comment as I left.

Her ass wasn't where I imagined kissing her as I descended the stairs. I texted George to pick me up and banished all thoughts of Adriana.

But as I waited on the street, the gorgeous woman forced her way back into my consciousness. I guessed Schwartzman would talk her into the dinner invitation after I left. She'd resist, but he'd cajole her. He was too invested in learning how generous we could be. It was his job.

With sinful curves and tons of attitude, Adriana was the opposite of the women I normally dined with. The women in my Manhattan orbit were all socialite chameleons wanting to use me to their advantage. They molded themselves to be who they expected me to desire.

Those women all dreamed of becoming Mrs. Carlyle, or failing that, getting some tabloid exposure out of dating me. They thought adding my name to their list of prior boyfriends would make them more appealing to the next potential rich husband. Although, *hook-up* was probably a better term than *boyfriend*. It was a game I was all too familiar with and one I played willingly, so none of them lasted. Just as I liked it.

This was going to be an interesting negotiation. It would be refreshing to be across the table from an honest woman for a change—even if she'd voiced her desire to kill me. When George pulled up, I was still thinking about her and that smile. It had been captivating, while it lasted.

"Your father requested you call," George said as I slid in and closed the door.

As he pulled into traffic, I dialed Dad's number, afraid something serious had happened to him or my sister.

"Come to my office as soon as you get back," Dad said, without bothering to ask if I had anything else on my schedule. "We need to talk about your meeting, but not on the phone." He hung up.

While relieved that it wasn't an emergency, I remained confused because this was completely out of character for Dad. He didn't ask for immediate meeting feedback like some insecure teenager.

CHAPTER 3

Adriana

Benjamin stood. "Gentlemen, come on in. Let me introduce you to Director of Education Adriana Moreno."

I collected four business cards and shook four hands, all of which were limp compared to Carlyle's, two of which were sweaty, and none of which gave me a spark. *Why am I even thinking that?*

The meeting with First Atlantic went by in a blur. It pissed me off beyond belief that another stupid Carlyle was going to take something away from us. I said the appropriate things when Benjamin prompted me, but all I could think about was how he had offered me up to Satan in a Suit. Benjamin was willing to trade me like a piece of meat. *"It sounds like a splendid idea,"* he'd said. Dinner with asswipe Travis Carlyle? I'd rather get a root canal without anesthesia.

At the end of the meeting, I swallowed my anger and escorted the bank guys downstairs to see them off. This had netted us a commitment for only two thousand dollars. *Stingy bankers.*

Back upstairs, I stormed into Benjamin's office and closed the door behind me. "How could you?"

He looked up from his monitor. "Pardon? How could I what?"

"Prostitute me like that."

He honestly looked perplexed.

"You said dinner with him was, and I quote, 'a splendid idea.'"

He shrugged. "Maybe you're right."

Maybe?

"We might miss the opportunity to find out how deep his pockets are, but so what?"

I sighed and sat down in his visitor's chair. "You're trying to make me feel bad."

"We can't wish any of this away. But you're the smart one. You went to college, so you tell me what our options are."

I snort-laughed. "Isn't that your job?"

"You're the one he wanted to talk to, so you're the one in the driver's seat here. The fate of the Astoria Community Center is in your hands."

I laughed. "You've gotta be kidding."

"The fact is, not only am I a short-timer who might not make the right trade-offs for the center, but Rachel has us scheduled on a two-week cruise starting next week." He tapped the little plaque on his desk that read *Astoria Community Center Manager*. "This says I get to delegate, and I select you."

"You can't put me in that position. It's not fair." I could barely breathe with the weight of the responsibility he'd laid on me.

"Life's not fair, and it's not me forcing this on you, it's Father Time. Let's face it, these old bones are getting tired, and I won't be here much longer. I promised Rachel I'd get us out of here and around the world before we're both in walkers."

"You're not that old," I argued.

He ignored me. "So, what are your options? That includes doing nothing, because even that is a choice. Why don't you start there?"

I preferred it at school, where I gave out the instructions. Unfortunately, he was right. We had to be proactive instead of letting the fucking Carlyles dictate things. "If we do nothing, being the jerks they are, the Carlyles will provide little to no compensation, and we have to move."

"Where to?" he asked, prodding me along.

I wasn't a real estate expert, but I had walked a lot of Astoria and beyond in Queens. "Probably a smaller building, and definitely one without a pool." I cringed at that, because it would mean giving up swimming instruction and the aquacise classes for the oldsters. I owed it to Katarina to do everything I could to keep the pool.

Sure, the seniors could exercise in other ways, but youth swimming classes required a pool. New York State averaged more than a hundred drownings a year, and many of those deaths were preventable with swim training.

"Maybe no indoor courts either," I added to get my mind off of losing our pool. We also had the space here for year-round indoor basketball instead of just the outdoor asphalt other centers relied upon.

"Not very appealing, huh?"

"It sucks."

"Next option?" he asked.

"We fight them." That had been my knee-jerk reaction, and it was clearly better than doing nothing. "If so, I think we'd win. The history of the battle over that last building gives us extra power. We took them down a notch for sure, and we have grown the email list since then. If we go at them strong enough early on, they'll back out of the purchase."

He nodded. "They might. And then what?"

"We get to stay."

He circled his fingers for me to go on.

I'd stated the obvious, but I needed to flesh out the alternatives, just as I made my students do. "This location sits on transit, which makes it both easy for Queens residents to get here and also perfect for getting the residents of their stupid high-rise into the city." I paused, forced to acknowledge the inevitable. "So it will only be a temporary win."

Benjamin nodded again.

I continued. "We now know that if the price is right, the building will be sold. So, it will only be a matter of time before another buyer comes along and sees the same potential." Now I saw where Benjamin was going. "And we won't be able to fight off somebody else as easily."

He waited for me to finish. It made me depressed that he'd found no fault in my logic.

"And we have no idea if the next one would even consider giving us any help."

He nodded. "Your conclusion regarding that option?"

I shook my head. "It's pretty awful. If it isn't Carlyle now, it may not be long before it's somebody else. And, without the bad history the Carlyles bring, I don't know if we could convince the city to shut down the sale a second time."

"Which leaves?" he prodded.

I twisted my face in disgust at the prospect of talking to Carlyle. "Having dinner with assface, Satan in a Suit Carlyle is the least-bad option. The threat of negative publicity gives us some leverage, I guess."

"Exactly," Benjamin agreed. "Otherwise, he wouldn't have come to see us this early."

It was odd that the Carlyle Plaza, which had brought such pain, was now the aid to this predicament. "How do you suggest I handle it?"

"That's for you to figure out. Let me know what you two agree to at dinner."

Professor Markowitz's Principles of Negotiation class I'd taken in college came back to me. *Send the underling so additional concessions can be gotten when the boss disapproves of the settlement the underling agreed to.*

"I can't tonight. I have an engagement party I have to go to."

"Fine. Doesn't have to be tonight. Make him think you're playing hard to get. Remember, he asked for the meeting, not you."

"Should I get Isabel and Paula involved to gang up on him?"

Isabel Sanchez and Paula Garcetti had joined me in rallying the community against the Plaza project—not because they were affected directly, but because of a hatred for gentrification in general.

"Not if we want to accomplish anything. They'd just be looking for a fight, and it would put us back at option number two."

"Yeah." He was probably right about that. The next step was up to me. Through the glass door, I saw Loretta waiting. She was the only tutoring session I could fit in before tonight's party.

I stood. "My appointment's here. I'll let you know how it goes with Satan in a Suit."

"One more thing," Benjamin said. "I don't know how long it will take to find a suitable building, and my time is short. So, locating the new building is another thing I'm delegating to you."

That was the only part of this that sounded remotely positive. A new location opened up all kinds of possibilities, like a theater for talks and presentations. "I know somebody who works in real estate and can help." Working in real estate was exactly the right way to describe Chelsea. She *owned* a ton of real estate in Manhattan.

"Okay then, keep me up to date."

Before heading out, I found Carlyle's card in my pocket to send him a text. Since I despised the man, playing hard to get wouldn't be difficult.

With that task done, I ushered Loretta into my office and silenced my phone. This was a rule for both me and the student.

CHAPTER 4

Travis

As I approached Dad's office, I imagined the nameplate transforming to read *Travis Carlyle*. I hadn't always been the one the office was destined for, but now I was determined it would be mine someday.

"Xavier is in with him," said Deena, Dad's longtime assistant, pulling my gaze away.

"Thanks." When I looked back over, it was Dad's name on the nameplate, as it always had been.

While I waited outside, Xavier Breton's voice came through the open door. Xavier was our CFO, and a frequent visitor to this office. In our company, you came to Dad; he didn't go to you.

"I'm sorry to be the bearer of bad news, but this is not pennies," he informed my father. "This could cause us some trouble at the March audit."

"Thanks for bringing it to my attention," Dad said. "I'll take a look when I get some time."

"Okay. We have until the quarter ends," Xavier said on his way out.

"My schedule should free up after the shareholders' meeting. I'll deal with it before quarter's end."

I stepped back.

Noticing me, Xavier nodded. "Hi, Travis." His signature plaid bow tie bobbed as he spoke.

I returned a chin tip. "Xavier." I closed the door behind me as I entered the office. *Which will one day be mine*. I was the oldest, and hard work and dedication always paid off.

Looking paler than usual, Dad shook his head and slid some papers off the desk and into a drawer. Unsurprisingly, they were the green shade of paper Xavier preferred. Dad motioned to one of the two chairs in front of his desk and lifted an Evian bottle toward me. A few months ago, he'd removed the whiskey decanter that had once been a fixture in his office.

I shook my head and sat. "No thanks."

He poured himself a glass of the water and turned to take a single potato chip from his half-eaten lunch on the credenza behind him.

"Tell me about your meeting." He said this like a challenge, without even a *How are you doing, Son?* to start off.

"It could have been better," I admitted. I had to ease him into the idea that we should probably abandon this endeavor rather than risk a very public brawl with half the population of Queens.

He crunched on the chip and followed it with a sip of water. "Tell me everything. Leave nothing out." This officially put us in uncharted territory. He'd never needed instant feedback before.

"I met with Benjamin Schwartzman—"

"What the hell?" With a deep breath, Dad closed his eyes for a second and probably stopped himself from adding the *"Leo would have known better"* comment that always stung.

I ran my nails over my forearm. It itched at times like this.

"He was one of the agitators against us the last time we built in Queens," Dad ranted. "Why the hell would you alert him?"

Schwartzman's role in the Plaza debacle was news to me. "You asked me to handle this, and he is the manager of the community center. There's no way to avoid him," I said calmly. I'd done nothing wrong, and Dad had only given me this assignment two hours ago with a single instruction: *"Keep this from blowing up."* Dad knew the parking lot and two small hotels on the property would not be a problem. Demolishing the community center was the only thing likely to cause a stir. That's why he'd sent me, to smooth things over.

"Go on," he said impatiently.

"Then we were joined by another member of the staff, Adriana Moreno, the center's director of education."

"Fucking hell," Dad yelled. "I sent you to keep it from blowing up, not to convene a meeting of the opposition. She was the fucking ringleader of the crazies trying to shut down the Plaza."

This conversation had gone from unusual to scary. Dad almost never swore. He considered himself above it. *"It is a sign of weakness to have to resort to four-letter words to express yourself,"* he always said.

"It wasn't my choice," I explained. "She works there and invited herself."

"You should have made up an excuse to leave rather than get trapped in a room with both of them."

"I couldn't." Maybe Dad could get away with shit like that, but it didn't mean I could. It also wouldn't have been professional or honest.

"Did you even read the folder?"

"What folder?"

"The one with all the background material on the Plaza debacle that Deena printed out for you."

"I didn't get a folder."

"You should have waited for it."

What the hell? "You told me to fix this and didn't mention a folder of material to wait for." *Take that. This is not my fault.*

"Continue."

Of course, there was no apology. As king of all he surveyed, Victor Carlyle didn't apologize.

"What's going on, Dad? Why is this such a big deal?"

"Continue," he repeated, ignoring my question.

"She went off the rails immediately, and it wasn't the right time to broach any specifics."

He let out a loud breath. "This is getting worse by the second. How much will it take to buy her off?"

"I said we didn't get into specifics. I'm going to meet with her separately to scope that out."

"Do it soon."

I now had to bring up the distasteful elephant in the room. Dad might have to tell Luca to kill the deal. "I'll find out before the contingency period expires." We always had multiple contingencies in place with real estate purchases to handle issues that came up during due diligence. I could advise Dad to pull the plug to avoid the reputational damage that would come from this fight.

"There are no contingencies," he said.

"How did that happen?"

"That is no longer the question." The rise in Dad's tone indicated I'd stepped over the line.

But it wasn't a rhetorical question. Nobody did deals of this magnitude without purchase contingencies in place. I was at a loss for words. In the Plaza project, instead of easing into conversations with the affected tenants and offering compensation, Luca had sent letters telling them we would start tearing down buildings as soon as possible after the purchase closed. He'd also mentioned that we would be providing zero support. *Idiot.*

Now, Luca had graduated to next-level stupid by committing us to a purchase that could end up without the ability to build the towers we'd planned *and* destroy the company's reputation in the process.

"What matters now is keeping it from blowing up in our faces," Dad emphasized.

In other words, stop whining, stop bitching, and head off the opposition.

"We can walk away from the deposit," I pointed out. It was usually a small, single-digit percentage of transactions such as this, just enough to make the contract legal. The lawyers called it earnest money.

"It's forty-five million," Dad said glumly.

It wouldn't help to point out how insane that was or to ask who had let Luca commit the company to that amount without contingencies. Xavier should have required that Luca check with Dad first before releasing that much cash. Had Luca gone around Dad? Was that why Dad had thrown me into this mess?

"I'll work on it."

He nodded. "Find a solution quickly."

"Does Luca know I'm doing this?"

Dad sighed. "I'll take care of Luca." At least he hadn't suggested I broach this with my half brother.

Luca was territorial by nature, and I didn't even work in his branch of the business anymore. Dad had moved me over to ventures and acquisitions.

"What latitude do I have?"

"I have faith in you," Dad said after a moment. "Use your good judgment. Anything within reason, I suppose, outside of canceling the contract. The Fontana Group are one-quarter owners, and I don't want to piss them off. I'll leave you to it." That signaled the end of our discussion.

I pointed out the other option. "If we hit a rough patch, don't you think Xavier's brother can still get us through the planning department?"

Since Yannick Breton worked in the planning department, Xavier could get us an occasional advantage. He had helped us iron out issues before the opposition solidified within the department twice before.

"I suppose so, but if it becomes a fight, we've failed. We don't need any more hits to our reputation. I want to have an article in the *Times* by Tuesday that says the Astoria Community Center is delighted to be moving to a new location. That would be a success for us. Understand? We can't allow any time for opposition to form on this one."

I understood perfectly. He'd said if it became a fight we would have failed, but he meant it would be my failure. My marching orders were clear enough—keep this from blowing up, backing out was not an option, and finish it all over the weekend.

How had Luca managed to screw this up so royally? And why did I feel like I was the one being punished? Before I reached my office downstairs, the first problem developed.

UNKNOWN: I can't make dinner tonight - maybe next month
UNKNOWN: Andy

I added Adriana to my contacts. I hadn't suggested tonight, as I wasn't available either, but next month wouldn't do. We needed to move quickly, so I sent a reply telling her so.

An hour later, I still hadn't heard anything else from her.

CHAPTER 5

Adriana

On my way out after finishing my tutoring session with Loretta, I plopped Benjamin's macchiato on his desk. "Sorry. You can blame the Carlyle interruption for it not being hot."

He grumbled something unintelligible as I left.

I unsilenced my phone on the way down the stairs and checked it when I reached the bottom, only to find a text message waiting. Apparently almost running into Simon hadn't been the worst thing that could happen to me today. The message was from Carlyle.

> SATAN: This can't wait that long. We'll meet tomorrow over lunch.

I stopped by Rachel's desk before leaving. "What was it you wanted to ask?"

She cocked her head. "What has you making that face?"

"What face?"

"Like a bee took a left turn up your nose."

"It's nothing." I put my phone in my coat pocket and made a point of smiling.

She narrowed her eyes for a split second, then dropped it. "What do you think I should do about Comet's food?"

"I dunno." I'd never owned a cat. "What's the problem?"

From what I could tell, the cat was training the owner, not the other way around. The cat tormented Rachel every other week it seemed, refusing to eat unless she changed its diet yet again. The smart feline knew how to get variety.

"She's spending more time than usual licking her butt," Rachel explained. "I think the salmon isn't sitting well with her, and I'm going to have to change her food again."

"Sounds like a good plan." I had no interest in learning how much butt-licking was normal for a cat.

"Maybe if I go back to the pheasant for a while…" she mused.

"Maybe." Who was I to judge that she cooked salmon and pheasant for her cat, while her husband was lucky to get a hamburger? At least that was the story I got from Benjamin.

I was smart enough to take two relevant lessons from this. First, don't get a cat. On second thought, that was the only lesson. I was going to say watch out for someone who treats their pet like royalty, but I liked Rachel too much to take that one to heart, and Benjamin seemed happy.

I checked my watch—not behind schedule yet, but about to be.

Rachel waved me off. "Go, girl. I know you have that party tonight. We can talk about Comet next week."

I nodded. I knew we would talk about her cat again.

And again.

Before I made it to the door, Rachel asked, "Don't you think it's odd for your friend to have her engagement party so close to the wedding?"

I stopped. "If you met Mrs. Hobbs, you'd understand. She's been planning the wedding and insisted Chelsea and Spencer have it at the same location where she and Mr. Hobbs, as well as Chelsea's grandparents, had theirs. This date only just became available, and it was either now or next year. I'm amazed they're still fitting the engagement party in."

"It should be the kids' choice, if you ask me."

"Tradition, I guess," I said as I backed up to the door. I was firmly in Camp Rachel on this.

Out on the street, I retrieved my phone and forced myself to deal with the source of my annoyance. Fate had dealt me a cruel hand today. I texted Carlyle and kept on walking.

CHAPTER 6

Travis

I exited the elevator on the fifty-second floor and marched straight to my office.

My assistant, Mindy, held up a folder. "Deena brought this down and suggested you read it."

"Of course she did." I took it. "No interruptions until I finish this."

Mindy gave me a mock salute and closed the office door behind me.

I knew the Plaza project in Queens had turned into a total shitshow, but I'd been working two West Coast acquisitions from the San Francisco office during the few months it had played out. I'd kept my distance and my opinions to myself.

If Dad had wanted me to get involved, he would have yanked me back to New York in a nanosecond. My time was always his to control.

As I started through the articles, all I could do was cringe at the magnitude of negative press coverage we'd received and the way Luca had totally fucked up the process.

After a few, I paused to count the clippings. There were thirty-seven in total about the opposition to our Carlyle Plaza project in Queens. In the end, it had taken months of lobbying the city council to keep the project from getting killed. The delays had cost us millions.

And that was before considering the lost revenue in lopping ten floors off the height of the building. That change had been necessary for the politicians to show their constituents that they'd accomplished something. Even Dad's pull downtown hadn't been able to avoid that.

Through all the early articles, I noticed the same four names showing up as the main community activists opposed to the Plaza project: Garcetti, Sanchez, Moreno, and Schwartzman.

I'd met Schwartzman. He would probably be pliable once the compensation was adequate—it was the nature of his job. The articles referred to community activist Andy Moreno as him—probably a mistake. Journalists in the internet age were herd animals, copying and modifying each other's material at light speed and not as concerned with accuracy as much as they used to be.

Then I got to an article that highlighted the plight of one of the tenants, Mario Moreno—Andy's father, according to the writer. His auto repair business had been devastated by the eviction. He'd lost his location, and because of that, his approval for city vehicle repair. The bitterness was palpable. It explained why his daughter had become the fire-breathing dragon I met in today's meeting.

That article was followed by a copy of the letter Luca had drafted to the tenants after purchasing the property. It was so badly done I almost couldn't finish it.

All the vitriol directed at us and all the damage to our reputation could have been avoided if Luca had followed our normal process of working with the tenants. Carlyle Plaza could have been a cherished landmark in Queens instead of an embarrassment.

Two later articles described the loss in the next election for all three of the Queens city council members who'd voted to allow even the reduced-height Plaza to move forward.

I closed the folder and swiveled to look out the window.

The Plaza rose in the distance across the river. Having the Carlyle Towers join it looked like a much more difficult task than it had a half hour ago.

Dad's comment that Adriana had been the *ringleader* last time presented a problem. She was not going to be easy to deal with anyway, and there was no telling how her position might harden if I gave her time to conspire with the two I hadn't met yet, Paula Garcetti and Isabel Sanchez. Time was definitely of the essence.

Her father's business had been destroyed, the article said. That was going to be the biggest hurdle. I picked up the article again but was interrupted by a text message. The screen showed the name I'd been waiting for.

> ADRIANA: Can't - I have a date
> ME: Then dinner.

It took longer for the next message to arrive.

> ADRIANA: Dinner date too

I growled loudly at the phone. She was exasperating.
"Everything all right, in there?" Mindy asked.
"Yeah, just dealing with an annoying woman."
"Try flowers."
"Good idea," I said after a few seconds. If pragmatic didn't work, perhaps flowery words would.

> ME: A very lucky guy. I can see I'm not the only one in the city who thinks you are as positively beautiful as your name. If not lunch or dinner, when can we meet over coffee to talk?

I'd laid it on thick, but she was sexy and beautiful. To distract myself, I turned the phone over on my thigh and looked out the window again. *Get a grip. This is business.* My phone vibrated with a reply.

> ADRIANA: I'll think about it

Since flattery wasn't working, it was time for something stronger.

> ME: I thought the future of the community center was important to you.

This time she responded right away.

> ADRIANA: Maybe two o'clock
> ME: It's a date.
> ADRIANA: It is a meeting not a date
> ME: Agreed.

I set the phone down and went to Google on my computer. It took me three tries of the spelling to find out vaffanculo was Italian for *fuck you* or *fuck off*.

Yes, she was a different kind of woman. Feisty. And coffee with her tomorrow would be a refreshing change.

CHAPTER 7

Adriana

I gazed at the opulent decor of the hotel's grand ballroom, surrounded by vapid conversations. The who's who of Manhattan society—a group I didn't fit in with at all—were in attendance this evening. After today's encounter with Travis of the pillaging Carlyles, my dislike of entitled, rich snobs had gone up a notch.

I followed Chelsea and her fiancé, Spencer, to the next couple. Since Chelsea and I had become fast friends at college, I didn't hold it against her or her future husband that they were from Manhattan…and rich.

Anyway, tonight was just what I needed to forget today—an evening of dressing up and plenty of champagne.

Like the third wheel I was, I stood there nodding as the happy pair thanked the Windsors for coming to the event. Another plate of appetizers went by without a chance to grab one. When I was introduced as the maid of honor, I smiled and shook hands again. It was my job.

"When is Seth coming?" I asked Chelsea. She'd said the best man was supposed to be doing this meet-and-greet with us. I'd been looking forward to meeting Spencer's brother in person. She said I would like him, and it stood to reason that he'd be normal since Spencer was certainly nice. At least that was my logic.

She laughed at something Spencer said and didn't hear me over the din of the raucous party. She waved at someone in the far corner.

I didn't want to embarrass Spencer by asking about his tardy brother again, so I didn't follow up. Instead, I stopped a passing server.

Server Guy wasn't subtle about checking my cleavage as he held out the tray of champagne flutes.

I took one and almost called him on it, but decided to take the high road. "Thank you." *See? I can fit in.*

Plus, it was the dress's fault. I felt positively naked in this silver scrap of fabric that Chelsea had helped me find at a consignment store. Even on consignment, it had set me back more than a whole paycheck. Why was it they got to charge more for less dress?

The server nodded. "Later." Then he wandered off.

Later wasn't happening. Tonight I had a job and responsibilities. That was me, Miss Responsible Maid of Honor.

But then I sipped the bubbly and decided what the hell? I should own this look tonight. Between the plunging neckline, the slit practically to my hip, and being backless, it had garnered me more than a few lengthy looks. It felt good, almost like I belonged. I had them fooled.

"Chelsea." The scream came from behind us.

I turned to see Alexa Borelli, another Alpha Kappa sister, barreling toward us in a yellow gown, arms wide. Alexa was from Brooklyn and, like me, was one of the poor girls attending NYU who had gotten into the Alpha Kappa sorority with Chelsea's sponsorship.

She bowled Chelsea over, wrapping her up in a hug. "You look gorgeous."

"Look who's talking," Chelsea replied.

I became Alexa's next hug victim. "Andy, you look smashing."

I managed a polite, "Thank you. Where's your fiancé?" She'd gotten engaged ahead of Chelsea, but her process was unfolding at a more normal pace.

"He has to learn to say no. He got tag-teamed by the Martin brothers at the door." She shook her head. "Something about preferred shares." She pivoted back to Chelsea. "How's Talia doing?" Talia was Chelsea's sister.

"Bitching like hell about being cooped up and researching how early a C-section can be performed." Talia was on doctor-imposed bed rest for the remainder of her pregnancy, which is why I'd gotten maid of honor duties.

Talia's earlier cancer, which she was now free of, had been the impetus for

Chelsea to start the Three Sisters Fund cancer charity. That's what had bonded Alexa and Chelsea together in the first place.

In fact, Alexa had been fundraising for the charity when she fell for Evan McAllister, Wall Street's Shark in a Suit and a perennial playboy. Tonight, she sported a monster ring to prove she'd tamed him. It hadn't been a match I saw coming, because their families hated each other.

Based on what the McAllisters had done to the Borellis, I would have cut his balls off instead of marrying the guy. But she didn't need my approval and was very happy, which in the end was what mattered.

I'd only met Evan a few times, but he seemed genuinely nice. Alexa had pointed him my way, and he'd given the community center a generous donation.

Wendy Breton, one of the bridesmaids, arrived in a scarlet red minidress with a neckline open down to her belly button. She had to be using tape.

Alexa flashed her a smile and a wave before beginning a discussion with Chelsea on the difficulties of wedding dress shopping.

Spencer looked at me and lifted his glass. "I need to refresh this. You?"

"I'm good," I assured him.

He had the manners to check with Wendy as well before leaving in search of scotch.

It was in my job description to be polite to all the bridesmaids, so I offered Wendy a smile. "Hi."

She looked me up and down before the sneer hit her face. "Thrift store shopping, I see."

With that, politeness went out the window and I tapped my teeth. "At least I don't have spinach stuck in my grill."

She huffed and hurried off, in search of a mirror, no doubt. Wendy and I had been the polar opposite of friends after I got a better grade than her in English our freshman year at NYU. She'd retaliated by stealing my boyfriend.

I turned away from the retreating bitch. I could be an adult and not obsess while I waited for an opening to spill a drink on her. It would be a science experiment to see if she dissolved like the witch I knew she was.

Instead of joining the conversation about wedding dresses, I turned toward the entrance to see if I could pick Spencer's brother, Seth, out of the crowd as he arrived. But there were too many guys in tuxes, and nobody stood out as looking like Spencer.

When I saw somebody who shouldn't have been here, I almost spit out my champagne. It wasn't logical. His name wasn't on the guest list. I was sure of it, yet there he stood, impeccably tailored, the hottest bachelor in Manhattan.

"I've got to go rescue Evan from the Martin brothers," Alexa said, "so I'll catch up with you two later."

When she left, I locked eyes on the intruder again. It was unfair how devastatingly hot Travis Carlyle looked in that tux. I could see why the gossip press called him the Lion of Lower Manhattan. Rumor had it he was charming the panties off a different woman almost every week.

But they only had half the story. He deserved to be Lucifer of Lower Manhattan for all the destruction he and his family caused.

He didn't have a woman on his arm tonight, but his reputation indicated that he never left an event like this alone.

I'd googled him and devoured all the tabloid drivel I could stand once I knew I'd have to meet him tomorrow. Travis Carlyle was the definition of gossip site fodder. He was constantly photographed around town with a rotating cast of arm candy.

One reporter—if that's what you called people who chased down gossip about people like Carlyle—had interviewed several of his numerous ex-girl-friends. Wickedly cold and calculating had been the character summary I'd gotten from it. The thing that stuck out most was how coldly he'd dropped them. Two of the women had described waking up one morning to find him mysteriously gone from bed. After that, they'd never heard from him again. Talk about cold. What kind of man didn't even tell the woman it was over and face the music, be that wrath or apathy?

Spencer returned with a glass of manly amber liquid. "Miss me?"

Chelsea pretended not to hear him. "Pardon?"

As much fun as it would be, it wasn't my place to point out that Carlyle wasn't on the guest list, so I turned to scan the room. Which woman would he choose tonight? Which poor, defenseless lady would become his target?

I hadn't finished sizing up the field of women when Chelsea's voice grabbed my attention. "There's Travis, Spencer's new best man."

I turned to see my personal nightmare approaching. *Best man? Him?* "I thought Seth..." Words failed me as Travis freaking Carlyle drew nearer.

Chelsea grinned. "Seth can't make the wedding on the new date. So Travis was nice enough to fill in for him."

What I'd expected to be a fun evening of experiencing how the one-percent lived had just turned to shit.

31

"Hey, Travis. You're late." Spencer embraced him in one of those one-armed, backslapping buddy hugs guys did.

Travis released him and took Chelsea's hand. "You look gorgeous tonight." He brushed a kiss across her knuckles. *Snob.*

Chelsea ate it up and blushed. "Travis, this is Andy," she said. "My maid of honor."

Travis turned a fake-as-hell smile in my direction. "I certainly would have gotten off the call with the president earlier if you'd told me this lovely lady was going to be here."

Chelsea laughed.

My cheeks heated, though the compliment was over-the-top silly. "President?"

Spencer slapped him on the shoulder. "Now that you're done solving the country's problems, we can party."

Spencer loved his parties.

Travis's pale-blues traveled from my cleavage up to my eyes. "Adriana, it's wonderful to see you again. You look positively radiant."

No doubt he could teach a class on how to be a two-faced jerk and look good doing it. *Ass.*

I didn't return the pleasantry or offer my hand. "Carlyle." I nodded. No knuckle kissing for this low-class girl.

"You two know each other?" Chelsea asked.

"We've met," Travis said. "I told her how beautiful her name was, as I recall."

My blush intensified a notch, and I nodded again rather than open my mouth to clarify.

"That's great." Chelsea squealed. "A best man and maid of honor who already like each other. What could be more perfect?"

I felt like puking but nodded along with Carlyle instead. I felt naked as his eyes traveled the length of me again. His gaze seemed intense enough to turn my gown into a pile of ash at my feet.

He took my hand. "Adriana, we are going to dance."

The ominous tone of his voice warned me not to refuse. But the fact that he'd worded it like a command made my blood boil—I was not a marionette on a string. Then I noticed the smile on Chelsea's face. I wouldn't ruin her night by fighting with Spencer's new best man. "Sure," I said, like the risk-taker I imagined myself to be in my dreams.

Carlyle had no idea who he was dealing with. I was the one woman in the room aware of his true nature and immune to his charms.

He took my hand. In no time we were on the marble dance floor near the speakers. "We need to talk."

I hated that I was caught between the bad alternatives of doing a deal with this scumbag or fighting him in the press and at city hall. "There's a perfectly good balcony outside," I yelled over the music.

He shook his head.

Another principles-of-negotiation lesson I'd learned was that she who stated the first position usually lost. "Then talk."

He pulled me toward him, and we started moving to the song. "You look positively stunning, Adriana." Apparently *positively* was one of his favorite words.

"Cut the crap, Carlyle. I'm here to support Chelsea and Spencer, not to listen to your stupid pickup lines."

He moved closer, and I caught a whiff of something woodsy and masculine. "What are you doing?"

His mouth quirked up. "Dancing with a lovely lady."

When his hand slid to meet the bare skin of my back, I nearly ignited. This wasn't the mild zing of static electricity. It was like a lightning bolt scorching me. I should have pushed away, but my hands refused the logical command and instead slid up his lapels to his shoulders.

It wasn't supposed to be like this. I didn't like him. I hated anyone involved with the gentrification that was destroying Queens one neighborhood at a time. Most of all, those with the last name Carlyle deserved to be burned at the stake for destroying my father's business, his life.

He brought me closer. "Neither of us wants people listening in."

"Uh-huh," was the best response I could manage as we swayed to the music. I was hyper aware of my nipples hardening as my breasts brushed his chest with every movement. What took over my insides wasn't the subtle flutter of butterflies. It was a crazed flock of damned condors, demanding to be noticed. The rest of the room dissipated into mist as my senses noticed only him, only his touch, only his gaze, only his lips.

Hello, brain? Anybody up there notice what's going on?

He pulled me closer. "Relax. You don't want to spoil the illusion."

I considered resisting… Until I caught sight of Wendy Breton sneering at me again. Then I melted into Carlyle's embrace with a megawatt smile directed at Wendy. Take that, bitch—the most eligible bachelor in the city is dancing with me.

He lowered his mouth to my ear. "I won't bite."

The image of several places I wouldn't mind being bitten by this man forced their way past my defenses.

"Much," he added.

How can I get so horny so quickly? If one minute with this devil did this to me, what would four days at the tropical wedding venue be like?

He was a mutant that secreted superpheromones. That had to be it. I looked up. "You try and I'll drag your worthless carcass into the sunlight and watch you turn to ash."

"Adriana, you can put the wooden stakes away. I'm one of the good guys."

My heart thundered in my chest. I willed myself to ignore all the bodily signals and breathed through my mouth to avoid the pheromones.

His hand slid an inch down my back, and none of my mental gymnastics helped me ignore the tingles that ran to the ends of my limbs. He was the fucking devil.

I hated him and everything he stood for. I couldn't even say his last name without feeling ill. Silently, I repeated that I hated this man.

A few seconds later, he added, "I have bad news for you."

CHAPTER 8

Travis

She stiffened in my arms.

I took in a lung-full of the lemony scent of her hair. "I'm going to make you agree with me." It was that simple. I always won. It was how I'd gotten where I was. "By giving you what you need." Good negotiators worked toward win-win, mostly, and I was a damned good negotiator.

She tilted her head back to look up, pressing her soft tits into me. "Listen to me, butthead. You can't make me agree with you on anything more than how cold it is outside, and you have no idea what I need."

I laughed. "Butthead? Are we in middle school? Nobody has called me that in forever."

"Not to your face maybe," she shot back.

Wow. I had no comeback to that.

"Look, I don't swear because I work around kids all day. Now let me give you the adult version. See if you can follow." She'd riled herself up. "Fuck that, assface."

Two nearby couples looked over.

"You really said that to him?" I asked loudly enough that those couples could hear. Into Adriana's hair I softly added, "Quiet, darling. We don't want to spoil the party for Chelsea and Spencer. And don't you mean *vaffanculo*?"

She shook her head and smirked as we moved to the music. "You figured that out, huh?"

That slight curve of her lips was the closest she'd gotten to a smile. It gave me hope. "Google. It's the first time anybody's sworn at me in a foreign language."

"With your personality, I'm sure it won't be the last. And I'll tell you what I need," she added after a moment. "It's to be away from you." She pushed against my chest.

I gave her space but didn't let her escape completely. Not yet. Even after our bodies parted, the feel of her tits against my chest lingered, just the right combination of warm and soft. "Don't you want to know what I can give you? At least the headlines?"

She stopped struggling. "If you say *a good time*, I'm going to barf on your very nice tux. Now let me go, or there'll be a headline tomorrow morning all right. It will be about my foot colliding with your balls."

I released her. "That might be the headline, angel, but the bulk of the story will be about how the maid of honor started a fight and ruined her best friend's engagement party."

She sneered and stepped back. "If you'll excuse me, which I don't give a flying fuck if you do or not, I've had enough of your company."

I followed. "Darling, aren't you even curious about what I can give you?"

Her only response was to raise a middle finger over her shoulder.

I focused on her nice ass as she walked away. Adriana was no emaciated, size zero skeleton of a woman. She had a body built for sin. It made it difficult to come up with my next argument.

Focus. You have a task to accomplish, not a woman to win.

She made a beeline for the happy couple, so I stopped at the edge of the dance floor. My hands had balled into fists, a reaction to her intransigence. She could leave for the moment. The warning about not making a scene and ruining the night for Spencer and Chelsea applied to me as well as her.

I spied the bar along the wall. Having failed in my attempt to start the negotiation on the relocation of the community center, it was time for a Macallan. Patience was essential, and I was wound too tight. One drink would take the edge off. Then I'd get her alone and complete the task I'd been given. We would come to an agreement. She and Schwartzman would issue a press release about the voluntary relocation of the Astoria Community Center, and the bomb Luca had lit would be defused.

As I watched, I couldn't get over how entrancing she was, even from this

36

distance. If we didn't have business to conduct, I'd pursue her for entirely different reasons. She would put up obstacles, but I could be persistent, if need be. The woman had spunk, and she'd make it a good chase—but, business trumped all.

"Spunk and a body built for sin," I murmured under my breath.

"You look like you could use another dance." It was Wendy.

CHAPTER 9

Adriana

I walked off the dance floor, briskly enough to not be caught by Carlyle, but not so fast as to look like I was scared. I hadn't left only to avoid the evil effects of his touch. It was the first move in our negotiation—avoiding the talk he wanted to have.

It wasn't a discussion I was looking forward to. None of the outcomes Benjamin and I had brainstormed were good for the community center. The fact that I only had bad alternatives to choose from infuriated me. Therefore, Carlyle was going to have to chase me, and he was going to have to stake out the first position. At least that would get us a *better* bad outcome for the center.

When I looked back, he had already found another dance partner—Wendy. Instead of watching that disgusting sight, I headed for the bathroom.

Chelsea and Alexa were talking when I returned. The men had wandered off. I figured I'd be safe from Travis with them.

Chelsea grinned. "You two looked cozy."

"You're imagining things. I hate him."

She raised an eyebrow. "Really? Well, he certainly likes you."

"He's just saying that." I laughed. "We only met this afternoon."

"I agree with Chelsea," Alexa said, nodding her head to my left. "He didn't get the message. He's still watching you."

I turned.

Travis was by the bar now, and staring directly at me. He didn't even have the decency to avert his eyes when I caught him. Instead, he raised his glass.

Goose bumps overtook me, and I was the one to look away first. So what if he was handsome beyond measure? That didn't make up for destroying people's lives.

"Sure you hate him," Chelsea said glancing down at my goose-bump-covered arms. "It shows."

Alexa nodded along.

I rubbed my arms. "I'm cold. I positively do not like him." *OMG, seriously?* It was infuriating that his vocabulary had seeped into mine. "I'd flip him the bird, but I don't want to embarrass you."

"He plays poker with Evan and the guys," Alexa said. "I've never seen anything to hate about him. He's quite the catch. Actually, I'd be interested if I wasn't already…" She held up her left hand, and the diamond sparkled, finishing the sentence for her.

I shook my head and avoided the temptation to see if Travis was still by the bar. "Not interested. Not one bit."

Chelsea scanned over my other shoulder. "If not him, what about Randy?"

Apparently, we were playing the time-honored game of pairing up the single bridesmaids and groomsmen. Randolf Thurgood Wilmont III was a frat boy who had yet to grow up and according to Chelsea had an aversion to doing any real work.

"No thanks," I said. "I dated him once." A lie, but good enough to keep them from pushing him on me. He was good-looking, but I wasn't interested in anybody right now, and a lack of ambition was a turnoff.

"Really?" Chelsea questioned. When I didn't say anything, she moved on to the next candidate. "I'll do you a favor and skip over Ed."

I rolled my eyes. "Thanks." Edgar Thorpe, according to the gossip rags, had broken up with his long-term girlfriend, Mathilda, for what seemed like the tenth time. Their breaks never lasted long. I didn't know which of them was so high maintenance, but I didn't care.

"I'd skip Harry too," Alexa said.

"Yeah, been there done that," I agreed.

Alexa's brow rose. "You dated him too? I didn't know."

"It was short," I mumbled, not interested in elaborating on why I'd agreed to a series of dates with Harry. I'd kept it from everybody at the time.

"Melissa said he wasn't that bad," Chelsea responded.

I laughed. "Yeah, because she's a black belt and shows every guy her pepper spray on the first date."

"Why did Spencer pick him to be a groomsman anyway?" Alexa asked.

Chelsea shivered. "He didn't have a choice. His dad and Harry's dad work together so…" She trailed off with a shrug.

This talk of being forced to pick Harry as a groomsman convinced me that Chelsea and Spencer had let their parents get way too involved in the wedding planning. If it were my wedding, I'd be making the timing, location, and bridal party choices without my parents.

At college, nobody knew the truth, but word at NYU had been that fat envelopes of his father's money had gotten Handsy Harold Hornblatt out of serious girl trouble not once but twice. Even worse, I knew for a fact that one of his girlfriends since then had been a sophomore at Hightower. Once he got you alone, he had the manners of a goat and was risky with a capital R. I wished the parents of that poor girl had wanted to pursue charges, but apparently Harry's wallet had persuaded them otherwise.

"Aw shucks," I said, pointing to the corner. "It doesn't matter. It looks like I'm too late."

Ginny Montgomery, another one of the bridesmaids, was chatting him up, or he was chatting her up. Whichever it was, it got me out of the fix-up attempt. Harry would probably have his hand up her dress before I finished my next drink.

"Ginny never did have good taste," Alexa lamented, rolling her eyes. "But at least she'll be staying warm tonight."

When Chelsea had first mentioned a wedding in June, I'd pictured it being local, like the Plaza or the Four Seasons. A simple Uber to the event and then back to my place at the end of the day—but no, that had changed.

Instead Chelsea's mom had changed the date when the venue in the Bahamas became available—to keep with tradition. And a single-day wedding had become a four-day excursion. Admittedly, a few days in a tropical setting, away from the cold New York City winter, was appealing.

Equally appealing was the fully paid airfare to paradise.

This would be the Caribbean getaway I couldn't afford on my own. My passport hadn't arrived yet, but I'd started the expedited application process last week when Chelsea told me about the change. I'd bet I was the only one on the guest list who didn't already own one of those little blue books, filled with stamps from faraway locales.

I went back to doing my job for the evening and trailed Chelsea as she greeted more guests. Spencer yukked it up with some of the guys across the room. Between introductions, I slipped in my request. "Chelsea, I could use your help."

She turned. "Sure. What do you need?"

"I'm a complete novice when it comes to leases and anything real estate. Could you help me locate a new space for the community center to lease? We may have to move."

"Of course." She pointed to the left. "Oh. You've got to meet the Sprigs. She used to be a teacher like you."

I hurried to follow her. And just like that, I had a lifeline and somebody I could trust in my corner.

Four couples later, I'd decided that this dress and the thirty minutes I'd spent on my makeup allowed me to fit in with this crowd, but only as long as I kept my mouth shut.

I was used to heated arguments about the Jets, the Knicks, or who had the best pizza. There was no way I could mimic the inane conversations these people had about the theater, this gallery or that, esoteric fashion trends, their golf handicaps, or their country club menus. They could eat Spam for all I cared.

I chanced a glance toward the bar.

Travis Carlyle was talking to some guy, looking as uncomfortable as I felt. He had probably filled his passport pages with stamps from Monaco, St. Barts, and sunny Spain. He fit in with this crowd, so what was his problem? *And why do I care?*

I smiled to myself when I decided it had to be the stick up his ass. Now it made sense. I cared because he was uncomfortable, but only one one-thousandth as uncomfortable as I wished him to be.

He ought to try out having his father lose his business and spend months worrying that losing the house would be the next step. That was the anguish this wicked best man deserved.

Chelsea said something I hadn't caught, and I angled myself to nod along with the couple we visited with. But I glanced back over in time for Satan to look straight at me, ignoring his conversation partner as he raised his glass to me.

He crooked his finger, gesturing for me to come over to him.

I froze, unsure how to respond. Then I heard Professor Markowitz in my ear. *"Show less interest in the negotiation pace than the other party."* My first instinct was to stick out my tongue and flip him the bird, but that would embarrass Chelsea.

He gestured again.

Chelsea moved a few paces forward to the next guests.

I settled for wiping the side of my nose with my extended middle finger. See? I could be subtle and sophisticated. No tongue necessary.

When Carlyle smiled in response, I broke eye contact and followed the bride.

CHAPTER 10

Travis

I stood next to the bar and pretended to take another sip of the Macallan I held, as a prop. I'd been watching Adriana, looking for the right opening to approach her again. With her body, it was an easy task.

Because of our unanticipated roles in my friend's wedding, neither of us could leave this party early. The setting should have made having a few words with her in private easy, but she wasn't cooperating.

We played visual chess, me trying to catch her eye, and her attempting to avoid looking directly at me. She also stayed glued to Chelsea's side as an obvious stay-away message to me.

"They make a cute couple, don't they?" Spencer's mother asked. She and his dad had snuck up on me.

"The cutest," I agreed.

"What are you drinking?" Spencer's dad pointed at my half-empty glass.

"Macallan."

"I'm a bourbon man myself. Want another?"

"I'm good for now. Pacing myself." It was true. I wanted a clear head when I finally got Adriana alone.

We chatted for a few minutes before they moved on.

Spencer's parents were a nicely suited couple. I'd been over for dinner at their house twice and not sensed any of the tension that pervaded our family table because of Dad and Nadia.

Over the next half hour, seven different women, including two I knew, took my standing by the bar to mean I was looking for a dance partner. I declined them all with a modicum of delicacy. This was a working evening, as far as I was concerned, and I had to watch for my opening.

We couldn't talk about the purchase of the center's building with an audience. And Adriana's behavior didn't make any sense to me. She needed this conversation even more than I did. How were we going to come to terms on how to move forward without talking through the options?

Adriana tried to be casual as she looked my way every so often—eleven times now, by my count. She always pasted on a fake scowl before looking away. I wasn't buying it. She couldn't dislike me that much.

My only transgression was being related, through no fault of my own, to my stupid half brother. It was him she should be mad at. He was the one who'd bought the building out from under her precious community center.

"You're interested in our Andy?"

I turned to find Spencer approaching. "No. She's not my type." I wasn't interested in the way he meant it. She intrigued me, but we had business to conduct.

He scoffed. "Right, she's not a dumb, emaciated, stick-figure blonde with no opinions about anything, who preens for selfies rather than talking. A woman looking to get a ring, or failing that, to add you to her bedroom conquests while on the hunt for a man with a good enough prenup to marry."

"That's not my type," I assured him. "Those are merely the available ones in this city, and I prefer it when they don't talk." *The Kardashians* and *The Real Wives of Beverly Hills* didn't qualify as topics of actual conversation anyway.

"Uh-huh. You've been watching her all night."

"She hates my guts," I added.

"Then why is she the only girl you've danced with? This is a party, for God's sake. And why are you the only one she's danced with?"

Just as he said that, I watched another guy leave Adriana with a disappointed look after talking to her for a few seconds.

"She's quite a girl, Travis."

"Why the hell are you watching me?" I asked. "Don't you have a pretty bride you should be paying attention to?"

"Touché. Why are you such an ass tonight?"

44

I took in a breath after being appropriately called out. "Sorry. Just have a lot on my mind."

"She's a tough one once you piss her off, but you've got the touch. Go talk to her and apologize." He wasn't going to let go of this without the truth.

"I need to talk to her. Privately," I confessed. "It's a business thing."

"You want to give her the business, huh?"

I shook my head. "It's not like that."

"Come with me, then." He headed for my quarry, and I followed.

Chelsea's face lit up when we reached them. Adriana's did not.

Spencer held out his hand to Chelsea. "I think it's time you agreed to a dance."

"I think it's time you decided to ask," she said, giddy as a schoolgirl.

This was perfect. I'd finally have Adriana alone.

I held out my hand. "Would you grace me with another dance?" When Adriana didn't respond, I added, "Please."

"I'm going to freshen up," she said before hurrying away.

Like a doting boyfriend, I said, "I'll wait for you."

My phone vibrated in my pocket. The text was not good news.

> DAD: I hear the news of our Queens acquisition is going to hit the papers on Monday or Tuesday. You need to have a resolution before then. Do not let this blow up on us. Get it done.

I was tempted to throw the fucking phone. It was so like Dad to send an ultimatum rather than call me for a calm discussion of our options.

Before I could launch it, Xavier and his wife walked up, and I was forced to pocket the device.

Xavier had chosen a gaudy, pink-plaid bow tie to go with his black tux, probably to keep people from noticing the uneven bald spot on his head.

"Travis," exclaimed Olivia, his wife. "Loosen up. That look of yours could freeze ice. This is a lovely party—lots of beautiful single ladies. Including..." She pointed to a statuesque blonde a short distance away. "Our daughter, Wendy. She's one of the bridesmaids." Whereas Xavier was as reserved as you expected an accountant to be, Olivia was the opposite. "Let me introduce you," she continued.

"We've met. Even danced." Only my phone ringing in my pocket saved me from another dance with the vapid blonde. I raised a finger. "Just a sec. I've got to get this." I pulled it out quickly and answered. "Yes, Dad?" I turned away.

"Did you get my message?" he asked.

"Yes. I got the message." I waited while Dad coughed.

"Ask him," Olivia said behind me.

"Damned crackers," Dad choked out. "Give me a sec." My stepmother's latest health craze for Dad was half a box a day of the driest, most bland flaxseed crackers on earth.

I'd given up after two of the awful things.

Olivia was still working on Xavier. "You should ask him about the move to operations that you deserve."

Xavier had brought it up once already, and I'd given him the honest truth. It wasn't up to me since he worked for Dad.

"Later maybe," Xavier told her.

I wished he'd shut her down more forcefully.

His wife didn't take the message well. "That's your answer for everything."

I moved farther away from the not-so-happy couple as Dad continued to hack. His two marriages hadn't been beds of roses either.

Would Spencer and Chelsea end up like my dad and stepmother, or Xavier and his wife? Or would they beat the odds and be like Spencer's parents, still in love, with none of the drama or tension?

"Dad," I mouthed to the couple and wandered away for some privacy.

Dad's voice on the phone brought me back to the present. "Sorry about that. I hate those damned crackers."

"Then toss them."

"Can't," he explained. "The price of domestic tranquility." When I didn't respond, he continued, "If you can't wrap up this Queens business quickly, we do have another option."

"What is that?" I asked, willing my previous anger to subside. Why hadn't he started the conversation with this?

"We play the long game and handle it like we did the Peabody building." Three years of rent increases had gotten that tenant to leave on his own— later than we wanted, but with none of the acrimony the Plaza project had created.

"Thanks, Dad. I'll keep that in mind as a secondary option."

"Just in case," he agreed. "But, since you understand how critical it is to defuse this situation and get the Towers underway, I doubt you'll need it."

Before I could reply, Dad hung up, so I pocketed the phone and searched the room for Adriana. We needed to have that talk.

I located the bride and groom and made my way over to them and out of Olivia Breton's reach. More Wendy was the last thing I needed.

Chelsea looked around. "Where's Andy?" Her brow creased. "Did you scare off my best friend?"

I held up my hands in innocence. "She went to the restroom."

Spencer wrapped an arm around his bride's waist. "Probably avoiding him."

"Why?" Chelsea asked, prodding me in the chest with a sharp finger. "Are you interested in her?"

"No," I said at the same time as Spencer answered, "Yes."

Chelsea narrowed her eyes. "She may be unattached, but I know how you cycle through women. She's off-limits. I will not be happy with you, Travis Carlyle, if you toy with my friend."

"As your groom so astutely pointed out earlier, she's not my type," I answered.

"He wants to talk to her," Spencer said. "But she's mad at him for something or other."

Chelsea stabbed me with her finger again. "What did you do?"

I backed a step. "Nothing. I just want to talk to her."

"Hmm…" she said. "You should try cheesecake."

The song changed to a slow one, and Spencer dragged his bride away. "This is one of our songs."

From across the room, I saw a woman's eyes on me.

She kept her hungry gaze on me as she approached. She was tall, blond, absurdly thin, and wearing a very revealing designer dress. As she came closer, I could see she was adorned with expensive jewelry. In other words, she fit Spencer's exact description of my type.

Her makeup was immaculate, and not a single hair on her head dared to escape her perfect twist. She could have passed for half the women I'd dated in the last few months.

When had I become so predictable?

"Hello there." She held her hand out palm down, high enough that it was clear she expected me to kiss it. "I'm Virginia, one of the bridesmaids, and I hear you're the best man."

"Yes." I decided to kiss her knuckles since she was in the bridal party. "Travis Carlyle, and you look very nice tonight, Virginia."

I kept checking the room for Adriana as Virginia asked how I knew the happy couple.

When I was too distracted to formulate an answer, she looked me up and down. "You're even more handsome in person than…" She giggled. "Anyway, this must be fate. You and me both here."

"What?" I scanned again for Adriana.

"We both went to NYU, and here we are in the same bridal party. Our destinies are meshing."

"Uh-huh."

"We should dance." She grabbed for my hand.

I didn't care how pushy she was, I wasn't budging. "I told the maid of honor I'd wait for her." Then I caught a glimpse of Adriana leaving the ballroom. *Damn.* I should have watched the hallway more closely.

Virginia tugged my hand again. "Let's dance while you wait. Get in a little practice for the wedding."

Extracting my hand, I told her, "No thank you."

"Come on. Just one."

"I have to use the restroom," I said and turned away.

She ran a hand down her side. "I'll wait."

She would have a long wait. When I reached the restroom hallway, I veered away and toward the exit.

Adriana had a thing or two to learn about how I conducted business. It wasn't without cost to walk away from me like that.

CHAPTER 11

Adriana

After ten minutes of hiding in the powder room, I knew one thing for sure. I wanted off this assignment of negotiating with a Carlyle. I yanked my phone out to text Benjamin.

> ME: I can't do the negotiation with Carlyle. I can't stand to be around him for two minutes.

Another woman entered, and I busied myself in front of the mirror. Benjamin's reply came quickly.

> BENJAMIN: Call me after your party.

I put my phone away, still pissed at Carlyle, and checked outside the powder room, just in case he'd decided to stake out the hallway.
He wasn't there.
I'd been at the party long enough that it wouldn't be an affront to Chelsea and Spencer if I left now. And I wasn't chancing another encounter with Satan himself. All I had to do was slide along the wall a short distance to the door. That would lead out to the hotel entrance.

At the end of the hallway, I made the mistake of looking over to where he'd been standing. There he was, and so was she.

I watched as he kissed freaking Ginny Montgomery's hand. Yup, a player.

I'd wondered earlier which woman he would choose to take home. I should have figured it would be a girl like her. An hour from now, she'd be ass up in his bed, begging for it. Or they might only make it into his car, or even a closet somewhere. That girl had zero self-esteem. Hell, I'd seen her coming on to Harry.

I hurried to the exit and scooted to the coat check, where I handed over my chit. It felt good to be out of that room full of idiots, so mistakenly self-assured of their own importance.

"Sorry," the girl said when she returned. "That hanger is empty." She wasn't the pimply teenage guy I'd handed my coat to when I arrived.

I stood there, mouth open like a beached trout. "You lost it?"

She shrugged. "What does it look like? I can check the other hangers."

"Black wool, midlength, with a red belt." The original black one had been lost at the dry cleaners.

"Red?"

I nodded.

"Very trendy." She returned empty-handed. "I'm so sorry. Doric must have given it to someone else. He's color blind."

What did color blindness have to do with it? The numbers on the tickets were in black and white. With a mismatched belt, how could anybody else have accepted it as theirs?

"If you want to wait, we could see if somebody returns it."

"Maybe tomorrow." Sticking around with Carlyle here was out of the question. Pulling out my phone, I requested a rideshare as I walked to the door.

Some event had to be getting out at the MET because the map showed a feeding frenzy of cars up north on Fifth Avenue. A lone car icon traveled south on Central Park West. A few seconds later, I had a ding, and that lone car heading south had claimed my ride to Queens. He would be here in four minutes.

I stood near the door and rubbed my arms, wishing a special hell on pimple-faced Doric for losing my coat. I was officially done with the party, so I dialed Benjamin.

50

"Hi. That was quick." A television was on in the background. "It's just Andy," he said to the side.

"I can't take it. This thing with Carlyle isn't going to work. I'm sorry, but you need to find somebody else."

"No can do, Andy. You're the one. You've had the class, remember?"

A woman entered the hotel, and I turned toward the wall. I regretted ever having mentioned that negotiation class to him. "But you would be better. And if not you, there has to be someone else," I pleaded.

"I can't. I'm off for the next few weeks, remember?" He paused a moment. "I guess there's always Jerry."

I paced the length of the lobby. "Anybody else?"

"Nope. It's you or him, and I think we'd all prefer you."

Jerry, the sports director, had all the backbone of cooked spaghetti, and he mostly thought all the center was good for was picking up girls. He'd screw this up royally.

"So what will it be?" Benjamin asked.

I sighed. "Okay. I'll do it."

"Good. I'll double your salary."

I laughed. "Wow." I was basically a volunteer, on the payroll for a dollar a year so I'd be covered by the liability insurance.

"You'll be great."

I heard Rachel say something in the background.

"I'll let you get back to it," he said. "Let me know what you work out."

"Thanks for nothing."

I hung up, and things immediately got worse.

Handsy Harry shuffled out of the ballroom, clearly drunk. He made his way to the coat check.

The last thing I wanted was an encounter with drunk Harry. He was bad enough sober. Checking my phone, I had a decision to make. It was cold as hell outside, and the rideshare app showed another three minutes before my driver would arrive.

Nonetheless, I pushed through the revolving door to the street and was assaulted by the frigid night air. But, I reasoned, three minutes of bone-numbing cold was better than a single minute with Harry. I clamped my legs together and rubbed my arms.

As I shivered, the next phone check showed two minutes.

"Heys there, Andy Pandy…" The slurred speech came from behind me.

I turned to confirm the bad news. *Double shit.* It was Harry.

"What's you doin' out here all alone?"

Now I was freezing and *hadn't* avoided the creep. "Waiting for my ride," I mumbled through chattering teeth.

"Yous look cold."

No shit, Sherlock. I ignored him and looked down the street. The app had said my car would be a white Prius. "Go away, Harry." I'd learned long ago to not be subtle with him.

He grabbed my wrist and pulled. "I'll give you a ride," he said laughing.

I pulled away and backed toward the curb. "Get lost, Harry."

"I could warm yous up." He moved closer. "We were good together. We could be again."

"No," I repeated. "Touch me again, and you'll regret it."

Suddenly, Harry was yanked back and spun around.

"The lady said no," Carlyle explained forcefully, backing Harry against the glass. "Now leave."

I hadn't noticed him come out of the hotel.

Harry straightened his coat. "I was just—"

"You were just leaving," Travis told him as he shoved Harry to the left.

Harry almost lost his balance. "Says who?"

"Travis Carlyle. And this lady is with me."

Everyone knew the Carlyle name. It had even more effect on Harry than if Travis had admitted he was Satan himself. "All right, all right," Harry said, backing away. "I didn't mean nuthin'."

I watched him weave his way down the street, several drinks past his limit. Then, I was surprised to feel a coat settle over my shoulders.

"You should have brought a coat," Travis lectured.

I wriggled my arms into the sleeves and pulled the coat tight around me, reveling in the protection from the elements. "I did, but the coat check idiots lost it." My teeth still chattered, and the numbing cold was my only excuse for why it took me another second to add, "Thank you."

"Anything for my date."

"I am not your date." I stomped my almost frostbitten foot in emphasis.

"You are until you're safely away from dickwad over there." He placed an arm around me. "Now act like it, or would you like me to leave you alone with him?"

Talk about bad and worse options. Reluctantly, I slid an arm around Travis and looked up. "Only until my ride arrives." Meeting his eyes was a mistake. His piercing blues made it hard to look away. When he took my frigid hand in his warm one, it became even harder.

I was saved by the ding of my phone, probably the one-minute warning to be ready.

"I'll take you home." His words sounded like a command instead of an offer.

Now I had two assholes demanding that I trust them to drive me home. I was over this shit. "No." I pulled away.

"No?" It seemed he wasn't used to having his commands questioned by common folk.

"The opposite of yes. You must have heard of it before."

He shook his head. "Is obstinate your middle name?"

Another couple exited the hotel, cutting off the snarky reply I was about to lay on my not-date. They nodded at us and turned down the street to our right.

That's when I realized I was not just a poor girl playing dress-up, but my responses made me rude and inconsiderate as well. "Sorry. It's been a long night. Thank you very much for the loan of the coat and for rescuing me from…" I nodded toward Harry. "…him, but no thank you on the ride. My Lyft is almost here." I looked down the road but didn't see a white Prius.

"I'll wait with you."

Instead of a small white car coming to my rescue, what I did see was Harry waiting partway down the block, watching us. Watching me. *Pervert.*

"How long?" Travis asked.

Pulling up my phone, I was aghast. The previous alert had been my fucking driver canceling on me. I was back to the screen where you selected the level of service, and the soonest one quoted seventeen minutes till pickup. "Uh…"

Travis shifted from foot to foot. His tux jacket was better than nothing, but not as good as this coat he'd let me use.

I'd brought my phone and a few dollars for drink tips with me this evening, but no wallet, which also meant no credit card. Cabbies didn't drive for free, and I was again forced to choose between horrible alternatives. I turned to face him. "Straight to my apartment, without a stop at your lair?"

He laughed. "Lair? You really don't like me, do you?"

"Not very quick on the uptake, are you?"

"I'm not a bad guy, Adriana."

"I'll be the judge of that," I insisted.

He took in a long breath. "If you're going to be insulting, perhaps you should ask your friend down the block for a ride." He cocked his head toward where Harry was pacing in a small circle to keep warm.

"I'd love to ride with you, kind sir." Anything was better than the Harry alternative.

He extracted his phone and typed a long message. "George will bring the car around in a minute.

"Of course you have a driver." My sarcasm got the better of me before I could stop it. "And I'm sure the articles about you aren't true."

"Don't believe anything you read about me."

"So, Carlyle, you don't drink the blood of small children?"

A black limo pulled to the curb. I walked to save bus fare, and this man traveled in a limo, with a dedicated driver. Life was not fair.

"How can I get you to reevaluate your opinion of me?" He pulled open the back door and gestured for me to enter.

I slid in. "You could get me home without speaking."

He followed me in and closed the door. "That's not happening." He leaned forward. "Thank you, George, for waiting. We'll be taking Miss Moreno home first. Which is…"

I rattled off my address.

"Certainly, sir." George tipped his hat toward the mirror. "Miss Moreno."

My God, he had a British accent.

"Love the accent, and it's Andy," I corrected.

George nodded. "Good to know, Miss Moreno." The doors locked as we pulled away from the curb.

"George," Travis asked, "have you ever seen me drink the blood of small children?"

"Why no, sir," George answered as if he was being questioned about the weather.

I looked out the window.

Asshole Harry glared at the limo as we rolled past.

Since I was pretending to fit in with the polished Manhattan crowd, I didn't roll down the window to flip him the bird.

When George turned south down Fifth Avenue and continued past East Fifty-Fifth Street, I got concerned. "George, the Queensboro Bridge is the easiest way there."

"Yes, Miss Moreno. I plan on it." He continued driving southbound.

The bridge entrance was off East Fifty-Ninth, and we were driving the opposite way.

"I think we should discuss the future of the community center," Carlyle said, stating his real purpose for offering me a ride.

"No." I was trapped with him until we made it over the river into Queens, but he was going to have to work harder than this to get me to talk. I had to make him feel it was more important to him than it was to me.

"No?" The king of the world still couldn't seem to comprehend anybody telling him *no* to his face. *Arrogant prick.*

I retrieved my phone and glared at him. "I'm dialing nine-one-one if you take me anywhere but home."

In a quick movement, he disarmed me of my phone. "Some amount of trust is a good quality." He hit a button by his seat, and the privacy glass rose between us and the driver.

Because the very stylish little secondhand clutch I had for the party was minuscule, I was without my pepper spray.

Now I was totally fucked, trapped in a car going somewhere that was not my apartment with Satan himself and no defense.

CHAPTER 12

Travis

Adriana was a snarling lioness. "I swear, if you—"

"Calm down, Adriana. George needs to stop for food. It's been a long night." He was following the instructions I'd texted him when I asked to be picked up with my guest.

Her sea-green eyes held mine for a quizzical moment. "We're making a food stop for your driver?"

"Yes, and his name is George." It wasn't a total lie. "Is that a problem?"

She folded her arms in front of her, making those tantalizing tits swell dangerously, but she didn't object.

"Is that a satisfactory explanation?"

She peered outside. "Is the penthouse on Central Park West your only lair in the city, or make that the tri-state area?"

"No other places in the city, lair-like or otherwise, but I do have a place in the Hamptons."

"Of course you do. Don't we all?" she scoffed. She rattled off the street my Hampton escape was on as if it were her summer home.

"Adriana, how do you happen to know where I live?"

"You've heard of research?"

I schooled my face. Perhaps her dismissive treatment of me wasn't what it seemed.

"May I have my phone back, please?" she asked. "I promise not to call the cops on you."

I offered the device. "Feel free to call them if we travel south of Forty-Fourth or north of Sixtieth."

She wedged it into her ridiculously small clutch. "I will."

"What bank did you meet with?" I asked. "Right after your meeting with me?"

She eyed me curiously. "First Atlantic, why?"

"Just wondering."

She looked out the window.

"Were they generous?"

She snort-laughed. "A bank? That'll be the day. They're so tight they squeak when they walk."

"Stranger things have happened."

She looked out the window. "Enough small talk already."

A half block later, we stopped in front of Junior's, and I heard the driver's door open and close.

Adriana peered out the window and pointed. "George has good taste. Their motto is *A taste of Brooklyn in Manhattan*."

"I know."

Her expression showed that I'd once again surprised her. "I figured you for a French food type," she said. "Le Cirque or Le Bernardin."

"What? I have to eat on white tablecloths? I'm not allowed to enjoy tacos, a hot dog, or a pretzel from a cart?"

She laughed. "I've seen the pictures of you out with your *dates*." She added air quotes. "It's one high-end hot spot after another, never a pizzeria, much less a hot dog cart."

The driver's door opened again.

I slid down the privacy glass.

"Here you go, sir." George handed over two to-go containers and plastic forks.

"Thank you, George," Adriana said. "What is it?"

"A surprise," I interjected.

"My pleasure, Miss Moreno," George said.

"Andy," she insisted.

"George," I said, saving him from an argument with Adriana. "Now, on to Miss Moreno's abode, if we could."

"Aren't you going to let him eat his dinner?" Adriana demanded.

"I'm saving mine to share with my wife," George answered.

I opened my container. The lid hid the contents. "Dig in."

She opened hers and screamed. "You got me cheesecake. George, I love you." She stuffed a bite in her mouth and hummed. "Junior's has the best cheesecake in the whole city."

"You're thanking the wrong person, Miss Moreno," George said as we pulled into traffic.

She glared at me. "You?"

I closed my container without eating a bite. "Cheesecake all around. Consider it a peace offering for our discussion on the future of your community center."

"Hmm…" she said before taking another bite. "It's not my community center. It's for all of Queens, you know, one of those little outlying boroughs across the river where your cooks and maids live." She gathered another mouthful of the dessert and sucked the confection off her fork.

For a moment, I fantasized about kissing those lips.

You cannot be thinking about her like that. Focus, man. You have a job to do here. My dick had its own opinion and jerked to attention.

"George, where do you call home?" she asked.

George hesitated and checked the rearview mirror.

I am the master of compartmentalization. I took in a deep breath, banished that image of Adriana from my mind, and nodded.

"Manhattan, ma'am."

"This is really good." She motioned to the closed container between us. "Aren't you going to eat yours? Or do you only drink blood this time of night?"

The attitude on this woman was infuriating. "You can have it if we can begin what I hope will be a civil discussion about the future of the community center."

She scooted the container next to her thigh. "Fine. Talk."

Finally, success. "As I said this afternoon, we would like to help with the transition to another location, and I'd like to know what you think would be the best way to accomplish that."

She swallowed another bite and looked over at me with a one-shoulder shrug. "Benjamin thinks we should talk to you. Me, I think we should burn your ass in the court of public opinion and the city council rather than give in. I have no idea what Isabel and Paula will think once they hear about your little scheme."

From the clippings I'd read, I knew those names as the agitators who had given us so much trouble on the Plaza project. But the way she glanced at me for a split second gave her away. She'd mentioned them as a power move.

"May I?" she asked, picking up my cheesecake.

"Certainly."

"I'm listening," she said after the first bite.

I was now exactly where I never let myself get in a negotiation. Dad had forced a deadline on me, and Adriana had made me chase her all night and put me in the position of making the first move. I had until we reached Queens to close this deal.

I straightened up and watched her for a reaction. "If you and Mr. Schwartzman support us on this, we will find you an alternate location that is just as good—"

"You mean as close as we now are to transit? Don't you see? That's the whole problem. Where we are now is perfect."

I kept my tone calm. "A suitable location with similar facilities for the center."

She swallowed another bite. "How are you going to find us a place like we have now? Did you know we have indoor basketball facilities and a pool? You can't just clear out some cubicle space in an office building and put together what we have."

"All of that can be accommodated."

"You'll personally find us a place?" she asked.

I hadn't planned on being personally involved, but I nodded anyway. "We can talk about the specifics tomorrow."

"I'm busy tomorrow."

"Too busy to save the community center? I thought we already had coffee on the calendar."

She shrugged. "I told you, I think we can stop you and save the center through community action." She went back to taking tiny bites of the cheese-cake. "Either way, thank you for this." She held up the container.

"My pleasure." I sighed. The winner in a negotiation was often the one willing to walk away. Or who at least appeared willing to walk away. And she had me cornered. The Queensboro Bridge appeared before us, and I didn't have much time. "I'll find you a place with almost-as-good access to

59

transit and with equal or greater square footage, number and size of rooms, and all the amenities you have now—all the way down to equivalent bathroom stalls." With the money we had on the line, all this was small potatoes.

"It sounds okay, until I think about how that might affect our rent payments."

That was a concern I'd expected. "We will subsidize the rent to be equivalent to your current payments for ten years." Going in small increments wasn't going to work tonight. I had almost no time to lock down this deal. If I didn't, we would either be waiting to build for years or out forty-five million. Actually, it would be much more than that if I figured in the loss of the income we expected to generate from the Towers project. Dad would be pissed as hell with either outcome.

She nodded, appearing impassive, but the little crinkle around her mouth gave her away. "Twelve years." Her phone dinged from inside her clutch.

"Do you need to get that?"

She shook her head. "Whoever it is can wait."

"Ten years," I repeated.

We soon transitioned to the surface streets in Queens proper.

"We need another dozen small study rooms and a theater room."

I sensed victory. She'd gone from rejection to adding minor conditions. "I'm sure that can be handled. Do we have a deal?"

"I don't know."

George turned us north, and her place was not far.

She waved her fork at me. "We'll need to be able to pay for extra staff during the move, to break down and set things up."

"A half a million to cover extra staff time," I suggested.

"And we'll need to approve the location, of course."

"Naturally." I added my own addendum. "You will personally need to approve the location." No way was I doing this with the short-timer, Schwartzman, only to have him leave and for her to still be in the picture and unhappy with the selection. "Plus, you'll need to convince your friends Paula and Isabel to go along and not cause a problem."

She visibly winced and then nodded. "Of course." She hadn't counted on that.

Checking the cross street, I knew we would be outside her apartment soon. "Do we have a deal?" I asked again.

She quietly looked out the window as the addresses went by, torturing me on purpose. A pair walking down the sidewalk caught her eye as we turned onto her street, and her gaze followed them.

Sweat had formed inside my jacket. I could apply the pressure of silence as well. It was a sweet deal for her; I was sure of it.

But only she knew if it was enough.

George stopped and put the car in park. "We're here." He exited to come around and open the door.

"Well?" I prodded.

She looked behind us. "Yeah, okay."

I relaxed. We had a deal.

She faced me again. "If you put it all in writing," she added. "And you pay us the five hundred K moving allowance plus another five hundred K to cover the rent subsidy, all up front so you can't back out." She extended her hand.

George opened the door on my side.

"Deal." I took her hand and shook, then I slid out onto the sidewalk.

She followed, accepting my hand out of the car. She looked down the street again toward the guys in the hoodies, her mouth hardening.

"I'll get you the money Monday, and we can issue a joint press release. We'll need to start looking at properties right away," I added to pull her focus back to the business at hand. Getting her invested in the process would make it harder for her to back out later.

"Right," she said, turning back to me and starting to take off the coat I'd loaned her.

I grabbed the lapels and held them shut. "Not until you're inside… George, I'll return as soon as I show Miss Moreno to her door."

She shook her head violently. "No need."

"A gentleman always accompanies a lady to her door," George said, supporting me.

"If he was a gentleman, that might apply," she shot back, showing her angry side again.

Fuck this. If Adriana wanted a fight, that's what she'd get. "I can walk with you or carry you. Your choice." This prickly pear of a woman needed a lesson in civility.

She huffed. "Do your high-society princesses go for that line?"

George smirked.

When I didn't answer, she mounted the steps. "You're impossible, Carlyle."

I followed her through the door. She might think me impossible. But she was irritating, and I could be determined.

She made a show of shrugging out of the jacket and handing it to me. "I'm inside. There's no mugger. You can go now."

"Do you really want to be carried?"

"Argh." She pulled the coat back on and started up the stairs. She turned and the coat opened to give me a glimpse of a hard nipple showing through her slinky gown. "You suck."

"When the situation calls for it." I knew how to suck, and I'd start with that nipple.

Now that we'd reached an agreement on the center, I felt free to admire her ass as I followed her up the stairs. And I did. *Body built for sin*—my own description came back to me in a rush.

"This isn't necessary," she said on the second-floor landing.

"Spencer and Chelsea are important to me. You're important to them, so I'm doing what I have to do." It was also what I always did, but she didn't deserve to know that. I enjoyed the view up another flight.

She grumbled something that ended with *caveman* as she walked down the dingy corridor, searching in her clutch. She took off my coat and handed it to me with a perfunctory, "Thanks." Inserting her key in the door, she added, "One more thing, Mr. Big Shot."

"What is that, gorgeous?" The hallway wasn't as cold as outside, but her nipples still taunted me through the thin fabric.

Her mouth quirked up at *gorgeous*, and she paused before turning the key. "Didn't I tell you to cut the cheesy pickup lines?"

"You are gorgeous, and I positively mean that in all seriousness." If it irritated her, I'd keep it up.

She smiled slowly, and her tongue darted out to moisten her lips before she opened the door. She passed inside and turned around with a genuine bedroom look in those inviting green eyes.

Was she going to ask me in? It was too soon. We hadn't concluded our business yet. That was a honey trap I wouldn't fall for. "I told George…" I stuttered. "I'd be right back down."

She blinked twice, and the seductive look was gone. "We also need a public apology for how the Plaza project was handled." I could tell she understood that she'd shoved the knife in deep with this last demand.

I gulped.

She twisted the knife. "In the *Times*." Smirking, Adriana waited in the doorway for my answer.

"I—"

"It's the only way we'll get Isabel and Paula to keep from rallying the troops against you." She held the cards in this battle, and she knew it.

"Of course."

I shuddered as the door closed behind her, and the lock clicked.

"I'll be by first thing," I said through the door.

Dad would rather give up an extra few million than agree to an apology, particularly in the *Times*. I was sure of it.

I'd thought I'd defused the situation, yet she'd turned it around on us, on me. She was a cunning vixen. Dad's meltdown was going to be nuclear, and he'd mention my incompetence again with reference to Leo. But this wouldn't harm our reputation, and those were my marching orders. He'd have to deal with it.

Back in the car, I dialed Mindy.

"I know it's Saturday, but I'll need you in the office early tomorrow, say six a.m."

CHAPTER 13

Adriana

Without Carlyle's coat, I started shivering in my icebox of an apartment. I locked the dead bolt and leaned against the door. The cold wasn't the only reason I shivered. Seeing Simon and his buddy Hugo hanging out on my corner had unnerved me. The last thing I needed was him knocking on my door.

Travis had said something I didn't hear clearly about *first things* through the door, but I didn't dare open it for fear that I'd blurt out an inappropriate invitation. I needed him out of my building before I reconsidered and did something stupid. I'd almost invited him in for a beer. Did billionaires drink beer, or only champagne and two-hundred-dollar bottles of wine?

Being called *gorgeous* by a certified billionaire? That was the stuff of my dog-eared romance novels, not the kind of thing that happened to an ordinary girl like me.

But I had to focus. I knew better. He was a Carlyle. He was the devil, and besides, he had to be from some other planet to say, *"I positively mean that in all seriousness."* Nobody talked like that—not even Mr. Evengood, Hightower's senior English teacher who was from freaking England.

At any rate, my final demand for a public apology had clearly taken him by surprise. After a terrible start, this had turned into a successful evening.

I'd faced down the Lion of Lower Manhattan and won. Making him pursue me for the negotiation, then making it clear I was the one willing to walk away, and finally adding that last demand had all worked. *Thank you, Professor Markowitz. Your course on negotiation has paid off at long last.*

I'd survived the evening with Carlyle and was proud of the deal I'd managed—a new space at a flat rent equal to our current payments, with Carlyle footing the cost to build it out to our specifications. Plus, I knew we could move for less than half a mill and pocket the difference.

Now I was done with Travis Carlyle, except of course, for Chelsea and Spencer's wedding. The rehearsal dinner, a walk down the aisle with him after the ceremony, and then the reception—I could handle that, and there would naturally be plenty of alcohol available to make it tolerable.

Then my phone signaled a message.

SIMON: We could get together next week

He could go fuck himself. Six months ago, I'd broken it off with him for the third and final time, as far as I was concerned, so I deleted the message. He was probably still on the street waiting to hear from me. He could freeze out there for all I cared. When he didn't respond, I knew I'd won another round.

I toed off the heels that had tortured me all night and wriggled out of the dress, trading it for sweats and a jacket.

Reading before bed was my routine, but before I could get settled with my book, I got another message.

It wasn't Simon. It was an old *Stop the Plaza* group text thread.

PAULA: I heard that now some Manhattan assholes want to
tear down OUR community center
ISABEL: What?

She would blow a gasket when she learned that the Manhattan assholes were the same ones as before. The next messages were more concerning.

ISABEL: Hearing that makes me want to rethink gun control
PAULA: We beat them last time without resorting to violence.
We can do it again

ISABEL: I still like the idea of showing them some justice
    Queens style - see ya there
PAULA: Let's meet at the Full Belly Deli on Sunday to plan
ME: I can't make it Sunday. How about later next week?

I waited with crossed fingers.

    ISABEL: Sunday doesn't work for me either
    PAULA: We shouldn't wait too long
    ME: Agreed

This was not going to be easy, but I had to get them to slow down. I had to have everything complete, including the new location, or Paula would find a way to blow it up on principle.

When nothing more showed up, I plopped down on my cozy reading sofa and opened my paperback to relax. So what if the title of my current book was *Secretary to the Bazillionaire*? It was fiction.

I knew regular girls didn't stand a chance with rich guys. Okay, there had been Anna Nicole Smith who married a Texas billionaire. On second thought, she didn't count because she'd been in *Playboy*. That hardly made her a regular girl, and it proved my point. You had to be high society, or an actress, or maybe a tennis star, to travel in that orbit.

What did I care? Rich dudes were mostly all assholes from my experience. The parents of Hightower students were prime examples—entitled snot buzzards. They cared enough about their brats to pay for a top-flight education, but that only involved writing a check. They were all too busy to look over homework with their kids.

I returned my focus to the story in front of me. I didn't have to believe these billionaire fairy tales could come true to enjoy reading them any more than I had to believe in warp drives to like a sci-fi movie.

I turned the page in my novel and then another. The hero had just kissed the heroine up against the wall, and things were getting heated when I set the book down to deal with another annoying message. I should have turned my phone off.

SATAN: Thank you for taking the time to talk with me this
    evening. I positively do look forward to working with you

on this project, and I'm certain we'll find a suitable location for you.

Why did the two-faced devil have to be so nice? I searched my memory for a moment. Had I been polite to him even once this evening? Nope.

ME: Thank you for the cheesecake

There. I could control myself. And it had been delicious and a thoughtful gesture even if he did probably get the idea from Chelsea, the traitor. But I could be high class when the situation called for it. And since I was from this side of the East River, I remembered to thank the help.

ME: Also thank George for driving me home

Carlyle probably thought my message was superfluous since it was George's job to drive wherever his highness commanded…
Then another message came in.

SATAN: Have a nice evening.

He had me trapped in this cycle of nice words tit for tat.

ME: You 2

One page later in my book, the kiss had gotten so heated that the heroine was dry-humping the hero's leg when another message lit up my phone screen.
He was the devil indeed for tearing me away from my story, just when things were heating up.

SATAN: It could only have been a nicer evening if I'd gotten another dance with you.

I would not admit that being pressed up against him had been titillating. *Hell no.* His superpheromones had been so strong that I didn't dare repeat the experience until the post-wedding rituals required it.

ME: Good night, Carlyle
SATAN: My friends call me Travis.
ME: Good night, Carlyle

I wasn't his friend. How could I be after what they had done to Daddy? Carlyles were the destroyers of neighborhoods.

I curled up with my book again, determined to banish Travis Carlyle from my thoughts. I made it through two more pages before the phone annoyed me again.

SATAN: See you tomorrow morning. Sleep well.
ME: No thanks. Monday
SATAN: We have to start looking at properties tomorrow.
Monday won't work.

What was this *we* shit?

ME: I'll be touring locations with Chelsea when she gets back
SATAN: No you won't. We'll be doing this together. You
agreed.

I'd had the upper hand the whole time, so I settled the argument with a two-letter reply.

ME: No
SATAN: Yes. We have to conclude this quickly and you have to
approve the property.

Shit. I had agreed to *personally* approve the location.

ME: I don't want to be that close to you
SATAN: Us together, or the deal is off.
ME: Is that you being nice?
SATAN: It's me being direct.

I let him stew for a minute before answering.

ME: OK You certainly know how to charm a girl

SATAN: You really don't like me, do you?
ME: Very perceptive of you

That seemed to shut him up, so I went back to my book, where the billionaire was not a destroyer of neighborhoods and a jerk I was stuck working with.

Damn Benjamin for putting me in this position.

CHAPTER 14

Adriana

The sound of someone pounding on my door woke me the next morning. I hid under my pillow for a few seconds until I remembered my brother had mentioned coming over.

I rubbed my eyes and squinted. Light peeked in through a gap in my curtains, but that still didn't give him the right to wake me up. This was too fucking early after what I'd been through.

The persistent knocking started again.

I rolled out of bed and found my robe. "Hold on," I yelled.

The pounding stopped.

Worrying about how I was going to keep Paula and Isabel from hating me had made sleep almost impossible. I almost ran into the dresser while cinching my robe around my waist. It was not a good sign that I couldn't walk straight and tie my robe at the same time this morning.

"Serg, I'm not in the mood today," I yelled as walked out of my bedroom.

My brother, Sergio, was already worried about what to get his girl for Valentine's Day. He meant well, but I should have insisted on lunch instead of breakfast to listen to his thoughts and give him feedback.

I crossed the room, yanked open my door, and gasped.

Instead of my brother, Travis Carlyle—Satan in a Suit—stood there. He held a coffee in one hand and had the other fist raised, ready to bang on my door again. "Good morning."

Who the hell wears a suit on a Saturday morning? I should have slammed the door in his face, but I had better manners than that. "What do you want?"

"I said I'd be over first thing." He held up the cup. "I brought you coffee."

I moved close to the door. I couldn't have him think I was inviting him in. "What for?"

"I thought you might drink a cup in the morning."

"I do." Often more than one. "I meant why are you freaking here?"

He checked his watch. "Because I said first thing in the morning, and it's now first thing."

I leaned against the doorjamb. "What time is it?" I rubbed my eyes, trying to avoid being obvious as I looked him over. He looked just as perfect this morning in a suit as he had in that tux last night. It was criminal the way the sight of him woke me up.

"Ten after eight."

I blinked a few times and put all thoughts of how gorgeous he looked out of my mind. Looking good didn't make up for being a jerk with a black hole where a heart should be. I blew out a breath. "I'll call you later."

Satan didn't budge. "No. You're coming with me." He was back in command mode. "We have properties to look at this morning. May I come in?"

"You're kidding. This morning?"

"Yes."

"You're mean. It didn't need to be this early."

"I'm efficient." He smiled. "Now, may I come in?"

On a school day, I would already be at Hightower, so this wasn't really early, but it was Saturday. I was groggy and pissed off, and he was to blame. "I have a better idea. Let's do this another day. I didn't sleep well. And my brother may be coming by." I poked a finger in his chest. "Now go the hell home, Carlyle. I'll call."

He grabbed my hand and moved closer. "I thought about you too," he whispered, as he brushed a kiss over my knuckles.

"Wha...?" Maybe it was those damned pheromones again, or maybe it was what he'd said, but my stomach buzzed for a second before I regained my sanity. He didn't mean he'd been thinking about me personally. He couldn't.

"We need to talk." When I didn't answer he added, "Now."

I'd kept my eyes locked with his, lest I give in to the temptation to check him out again. There was something very soothing about his mellow baritone.

My neighbor's door opened, and Mrs. Kozlowski peeked out. *Just my luck.*

Breaking free of the trance his voice had put me in, I moved out of the way and waved him inside, closing the door behind him. My neighbor had a big mouth and would be trumpeting the fact that I'd had this guy at my door this morning. A million questions would follow—questions I didn't need getting back to Simon.

"You and I have to select a property this weekend before any community opposition forms," Carlyle began. "We need to have a solution, a new location picked out so the project can be explained as relocating the community center to newer accommodations, not killing it."

We were supposed to be on opposite sides, but his concern mirrored my own. It was an odd twist of fate, if he was sincere.

"George is downstairs," he added, looking around my small apartment.

Naturally, it wasn't tidy, and I instantly felt self-conscious. He was probably used to spotless surroundings kept that way by whole crews of dusters, cleaners, and picker-uppers. I moved to the kitchen.

"We need to get started," he said.

Mama's words echoed in my head. *"Never ever fail to offer a guest something to eat or drink."* I couldn't help myself. "You want a muffin before you go? I can heat one up for you."

"No thanks." He followed me into the kitchen and set the coffee down.

Maybe it was the pheromones he'd transferred to me with that kiss on my knuckles, but I found I'd moved from angry to resigned. "I forgive you," I told him.

He lifted a brow. "For what?"

He could not be for real.

"You show up at my door without any notice and expect me to go somewhere with you at the drop of a hat? Is that normal in your world? Because it isn't in mine."

"I told you I'd be by first thing, and I am. Get dressed, and we can argue on the way." He said this as if it were a command.

But I wasn't a follow-commands woman. "Not today."

He crossed his arms over his chest. "I thought you wanted to save your community center."

"Fine," I snarled with a bit more venom than he deserved. Now fully awake, I threw up my hands and added frustration to my mood. I retreated to my bedroom and resisted the urge to slam the door. I wouldn't agree easily, but if I did go with him, what the hell was I supposed to wear? He was in a suit, so I settled on work attire, pulling a clean black skirt from a hanger and a pale-blue button-down shirt to go with it.

I had only just pulled on fresh underwear when I heard more loud knuckles rapping on my front door.

"Andy?" *Fuck.* It was my brother.

I threw the robe on again and flew out of the bedroom. "Hide," I whispered, shooing Carlyle toward the bathroom.

"You're kidding?"

"Hurry. It's my brother."

"So?"

"Time to get up, Andy," Serg called from the hallway, banging on the door again.

"Please," I begged Satan. I didn't have time for an argument.

"You said you'd help me," Serg yelled.

Carlyle shook his head. "I don't know what kind of men you're used to, but I don't hide."

I huffed. "It's your funeral." I went over and opened the door.

Serg walked in and stopped immediately when he noticed Carlyle. He looked between me and the suit with narrowed eyes. "Are you just getting out of bed?"

"Of course, I was in bed," I shot back. "Where do you sleep?"

"What's going on here?" Serg snarled, his eyes locked on Carlyle.

"Nothing, Serg." I moved between the two men and tied my robe tighter.

My hothead brother's fists had already balled up. "And who's the suit?" Serg disliked suited Manhattan assholes as much as I did, maybe even more.

"Travis," I said, leaving off his last name to avoid getting blood on my carpet.

Satan stepped forward, offering his hand. "Nice to meet you. A mutual friend, Chelsea Hobbs, asked me to escort Adriana to preview some properties." His voice was smooth and cultured, without the sharp edge of my brother's. "She's running late."

Serg recognized Chelsea's name, and that did the trick. His posture loosened, and he took Carlyle's hand. "Sergio, man. This one's brother." He nodded toward me.

"Adriana mentioned you might stop in." Carlyle kept up the handshake longer than I expected, pumping vigorously. The cords on his neck stood out.

Veins bulged on Serg's face as he took on a rosier hue. "Nice to, uh, meet ya," he grunted. "Any, uh, friend of Chelsea is a friend of ours."

I smirked when I noticed how Carlyle gritted his teeth.

Serg finally pulled his hand back and shook it out.

Men.

Carlyle smiled. He had won that testosterone challenge.

Serg showed his annoyance at losing by barking at me. "Shouldn't you be dressed?"

"Yeah, yeah. It's not like you never woke up late." I scurried back to my bedroom, now that it looked like Serg would mostly behave himself, and slipped into my clothes as quickly as possible. Makeup would have to wait.

"That your ride downstairs?" I heard Serg ask in the other room.

"Yes," Carlyle answered. "I brought it to make a positive impression with the rental agents. We want them to take Adriana seriously."

I fumbled with the buttons of my blouse. I'd gotten them off by one hole on the first try.

"Wow, man. It'll sure do that. What does that run an hour to rent?"

"Just helping out Adriana," Carlyle said. "And Chelsea."

I tucked in my blouse, surprised Carlyle hadn't taken credit for owning the limo. I totally would have.

"Cost is no object where Adriana is concerned," he added. "She's worth it."

I held back a laugh and checked myself in the mirror before opening the door.

"Yeah, she totally is," Serg answered, looking over at me.

I threw him a questioning glare. "I am what?"

"Always fucking late," my brother said. He never gave me any credit.

"You're the one who's always freaking late," I argued.

"You look nice," Serg said, uncharacteristically shifting into nice-brother mode.

"Thank you."

"Are we going?" Carlyle asked. "Or should we stay and spend some more time getting to know each other?"

"We don't want to be late, now do we?" I took my phone off the charger, adding it and my key to my purse. I pulled my down parka from the closet.

It had a stain on the front that didn't go with my polished attire, but it was better than freezing to death.

"That's dirty," Serg said, as if I didn't know how to dress myself. His nice-brother phase had lasted all of two seconds.

"Do you have another one?" Carlyle asked. "First impressions matter."

"No." I hated that now both men were ganging up on me. "The coat check last night gave my good one to someone else, remember?"

"We'll make do." Carlyle snatched the parka from my hands and held it open for me.

I suppressed the urge to tell him I wasn't the kind of China doll he was used to who couldn't handle her own coat. "You'd think they would have noticed the mismatched red belt," I explained as he helped me.

He straightened my collar. "What color was the coat?"

"Black. Serg, we can figure out a gift for Val later." I had to get these two separated before Serg learned Satan's last name. "Val's his girlfriend," I explained to Carlyle.

Serg's shoulders fell. "You said that yesterday."

"We have plenty of time before Valentine's Day."

"Anything but chocolate," Carlyle added.

Although I agreed with Satan, I refused to give him the satisfaction of hearing it from my lips.

We let Serg leave first.

"You really need a new parka," Serg whispered as he passed.

"Got a few hundred you want to give me for that?"

That shut him up, and we followed him out after I locked my door.

Downstairs, George held the limo door open and Carlyle offered his hand at the top of the steps.

"What are you doing?" I demanded.

"A gentleman offers a lady a hand."

Serg shook his head and walked off. "Suits," he grumbled.

I stayed rooted to the spot. "What? You think I'm going to trip?" I asked. "I'm weak. Is that it?"

"No." Carlyle's jaw took on a firm set. "I think you should be treated like a lady."

I'd been called a girl often, a woman sometimes, and a lady never. But I took his hand rather than argue. As soon as I did, that uncomfortable tingle attacked my senses again, and I knew it was a mistake. "Just this once."

"No promises."

There was something wrong with the water in Manhattan if he mistook me for a lady. I ducked into the limo first and slid to the far edge of the seat. Distance between me and this man was called for. When George closed the door for us, I finally relaxed. "I'm glad we left when we did."

"You used my first name, so I take it you didn't want him to know I was one of the dreaded Carlyles?"

"You're smarter than you look."

"And you don't swear as much as your brother," he noted.

"Comes with being a schoolteacher."

"Understandable." He nodded. "What size shoe do you wear?"

"You're weird." Looking down at my feet, I noticed a scuff on the right shoe I hadn't seen the last time I wore these. I ignored the question and crossed my legs to hide it. "How did you set up property viewings this quickly?"

"My assistant arranged them."

Of course, he had an assistant he could order around. Gods like him didn't do any actual work, they only commanded other people to do it.

"You made her work overnight?"

"She was happy to come in early this morning when I told her what we were doing and how important it was to you."

That was low. That made me sound like the bad guy. "Liar." I groaned and held out my hand. "Your card." When he looked perplexed, I repeated it. "Your business card, or do you use carrier pigeons to communicate?"

He produced a card. "Anybody ever tell you it's rude to call someone a liar?"

I slid the card into the pocket of my coat. "If the shoe fits. Now, what's her name?"

"Who?"

"Your tie is too tight if you don't know who—your slave."

"My assistant's name is Mindy. Why?" he asked, catching up. He fidgeted with the knot of his tie. "And she's not a slave. I pay her very well."

"That doesn't give you the right to treat her like one. And I need her name so I can call and thank her personally for the Saturday overtime... Unless you already did."

"We have five to look at," he answered, meaning he hadn't thanked Mindy. That would have required having a heart somewhere under the suit. "George, let's go."

CHAPTER 15

Travis

George pulled into the flow of traffic, and Adriana looked out the window rather than at me. Her attention elsewhere and her position as close to the door as possible were clear signals.

But signals I decided to ignore. "Don't get discouraged if the first properties don't tickle your fancy. We have many options."

"Many options. Got it. How long am I your captive?"

"You don't like me, do you?"

"Nope. I feel like we've covered that. I'd rather tour the prospects with Chelsea when she gets back."

"That's not an option. The timing won't work. And isn't it presumptuous of you to say that when we only just met?"

"I know your type, Carlyle, and that's good enough."

I was sick of everyone in the fucking city judging me, based on what they'd read or been told, all without a moment of interaction with me. I calmed my voice. "What type is that?"

"A rich asshole who thinks that just because he has money, his opinion matters more than anyone else's."

I sighed. We needed to work with each other if this transaction was going to go down without damaging the Carlyle name. "George, pull over, please."

She had no idea how good a deal she was going to get from us as opposed to any other developer.

George's stop was rather abrupt.

I waited until Adriana looked at me. "I get that you don't like me or the situation." I didn't add that I found her annoying as well. "We have to find a new property," I explained as dispassionately as possible. "That means we have to work together, regardless of what you think of me. Can you do that?"

"I guess." Her words said yes, but the shake of her head as she kept her gaze out the window said no. "I wish you'd never made an offer on the building."

"It's a parcel of land, which includes all the buildings on that side of the block, not just yours. And having us involved is your lucky break."

"Sure," she said sarcastically, with another shake of her head that said she didn't understand her situation. "I think if we fought you we'd win, and we'd keep our community center."

"Maybe," I admitted. "But it's a prime location, you know that. Even if we pulled out today, it would be somebody else tomorrow. And let me tell you, any of those other guys would have you and your community center out of there immediately, with absolutely no compensation."

"But—"

"Or we could buy the property, and you could fight our plans to develop the Towers. Then, with us as your new landlord, how many rent increases would the center be able to handle before it closed?"

She slumped over as the implication hit her.

"I'm going to be very generous with you. I've already committed to subsidizing your rent for ten years. Now you have to decide, do you want to find an alternative location or close the center? If you'd rather shut it down, tell me now, because there are a million better ways I could be spending my Saturday."

She sucked in a resigned breath. "Sure, I want to keep it open. I'm here, aren't I?"

"Good enough. That means you and I are a team on this. Remember, first impressions matter. These agents carry weight with the landlords."

"Gee, thanks." She looked down. "Sorry my good coat got lost last night."

"I meant your attitude."

"Oh."

"George, drive on, please."

She was quiet for the remainder of the short drive to our first property.

Being in the real estate business ourselves, we had a complete list of every commercial real estate broker in the city, all the way up to the home numbers of the presidents of the companies. Mindy had dialed this morning and put me on when they answered. All it took was her saying my name, and that I wanted to arrange a showing this morning. We had gotten positive responses from every one of the firms we contacted.

There was an advantage to being well known. Nobody wanted to miss an opportunity to do business with us, or refuse us and get on our bad side.

I glanced over and wondered if Adriana had thought about me last night. The admission that I'd thought about her had slipped out before I was able to stop it. It wasn't like me to admit something that would give another person leverage.

Thankfully, she hadn't said anything. Maybe she'd missed it. I glanced over, and her gaze was still fixed out the window.

George pulled to the curb in front of our first stop.

"We won't be long," I told him, opening the door and sliding out.

I got out of the car, and she wiggled out of her dirty parka before exiting —a good choice because of how it looked, and a poor choice given how cold it was this morning.

I offered her my hand.

She exited without accepting it.

Stubborn woman. But it wasn't worth the argument.

She wrapped her arms around herself for warmth. "This location isn't going to work."

I'd expected that reaction. I was following the time-honored real-estate selling principle of starting with a terrible property to make the others look good by comparison. "At least come in and take a look-see to have something to compare the others to."

"I don't need to go inside to understand that the access to transit isn't good enough," she complained.

"It would be rude not to at least meet the agent inside and take a look."

She nodded. "We can't have that now, can we? Lead the way."

So being called rude got to her…interesting.

WE FINISHED THE TOUR OF THE SECOND BUILDING ON MY LIST, AND IT HADN'T gone any better than the first.

I guided Adriana ahead of me to the door leading back to the lobby. I brushed against her back and her ass when she had trouble with the door.

It opened slowly.

I knew she was pretty, but the contact was a jolt of electricity to my system that I wasn't prepared for. When I didn't remove my hand quickly enough, she turned and looked up. I feared a complaint.

Instead she said, "Sorry. It's heavier than I thought."

I caught the lemon scent of her hair and nodded, unsure I could put together a coherent sentence in the moment. There was something dangerous about this obstinate woman.

She continued through the door, and I followed, moving my portfolio in front of me to cover the erection forming. This woman would be the death of me, if I wasn't careful. She'd been fascinating last night, and alluring this morning.

I'd have to keep my distance, not only to remain professional, but the Towers project was too important to let anything or anyone screw it up for me.

The listing agent followed us into the lobby. "What did you think?" Her smile was hopeful.

"Thank you for showing us around," Adriana said before turning for the door.

The listing agent touched my arm. "You have my card. Call me if you have any questions."

I turned and shook her hand before exiting the building. "She will."

The door had closed behind Adriana.

"Thank you for the opportunity, Mr. Carlyle." She'd missed what I said.

"I'm just helping Ms. Moreno learn the ropes. She's the decision-maker here."

The agent followed me out. "Thank you for your time, Ms. Moreno." She waved when Adriana turned.

Adriana pasted on a half smile. "Yeah, thank you."

George opened the car door for us.

I followed her in, clutching the folder of rental specifics that Adriana hadn't even bothered to look at.

The broody woman covered herself with her down jacket. Her attempt at a smile disappeared as soon as the door closed. "Well, that was a total waste of time."

"What was it you liked best about the place?" I asked.

"I hope it isn't the only space available and we have other alternatives."

"No, really. Name one thing about it that was acceptable."

"I didn't see mold. How's that?"

"That's better. A positive attitude always helps."

She shot me a glare. "You're an ass."

"I'm trying to help you."

"Help?" she screeched. "If you want to help, call off the purchase of the property so we can stay where we are."

"That's not an option."

She turned to face me. "Why the hell not?"

Instead of fighting fire with fire, I turned a hose on it with a cool voice. "Adriana, being belligerent doesn't change any of the facts."

"And changing the subject doesn't explain why we can't stay where we are."

I blew out a breath to hold my temper in check.

"Shall we move on to the next one?" George asked.

"No," Adriana answered. "He hasn't answered my question."

"Yes, George," I insisted.

George decided my opinion carried more weight than hers and started toward the next property.

"Look," I said. "It's not financially viable to change the plan." The additional reason Dad didn't want to upset the Fontana Group wasn't for me to discuss with her. "The purchase contract was written in such a way that we can't back out."

"That sounds like a failure of the finance one-oh-one level."

"We're getting off the topic," I insisted.

"Can't back out, or don't want to?"

"I already suggested it, and the answer is can't."

Her eyes narrowed, and she nodded slowly. When she didn't follow up, I took it as a sign that she accepted my answer.

But when we stopped at the next building, she surprised me. "I really don't want to be doing this with you."

I thought we'd gotten past this. "Why? Because you want to see the community center disappear?"

Her lovely green eyes darkened with anger. "No."

"Really?"

"Of course not." She sighed. "But it would be so much better if…" She didn't finish the sentence.

"If you weren't saddled with me?" I finished for her.

"Exactly. I don't need you along to babysit me while I look at a building."

Her words stung. I'd been completely professional through all of this, and I certainly had more experience with real estate than she did. But in the end, it was the results that mattered. If she wouldn't make a choice with me at her side, so be it. My job was to help them select a location they could live with and get it done soon.

I slid out of the car and offered my hand to her again.

One more time, she refused. This was getting old.

I closed the car door after her. "I'll introduce you and stay in the lobby until you're finished. Just consider me your transportation."

She nodded and marched coatless to the entrance, not giving me a chance to pull open the door for her.

I hurried to follow, watching her ass the whole way. Hell, she was the one who'd ditched the long coat, and I was human. She looked undeniably delectable in that skirt—nice legs, nice ass.

The agent waited just inside the lobby door. "Good morning, Mr. Carlyle. Emma Peterson." She extended her hand to shake. "I think you'll love this wonderful building."

After shaking, I stepped back. "Ms. Moreno is in charge of deciding whether the space is right. I'll wait here while you show her around."

"Certainly." She shook Adriana's hand and opened her arm in the direction of a doorway to the left. "This way, Ms. Moreno."

"Thank you," Adriana said as she passed me.

I nodded and once again watched her ass for longer than was appropriate while she strode—no sashayed—to the door. Just because I watched her didn't mean I fantasized about my hands on those hips, her naked in front of me as I…

Fuuuck. I clamped my eyelids shut and took a deep breath. It was time to focus.

I pulled out my phone and dialed. "This is Travis Carlyle. I'd like to arrange a delivery."

CHAPTER 16

ADRIANA

As I entered the next building, I could still feel where Carlyle had bumped into me earlier. It was like a brand on my skin that I couldn't ignore. It reminded me how it had felt to be in his arms on the dance floor at the party.

But it didn't change the fact that he was an asshole gentrifier and destroyer of communities.

I followed Emma through a door off the lobby into a large open space, glad to be out of Carlyle's presence. Every time he looked at me, I had to check to make sure that my clothes hadn't ignited from the heat of his gaze.

Why did such a wicked personality have to be graced with a body like his? And that voice?

Travis had said we needed to work together. He'd also said I could consider him nothing more than transportation, so that's what I'd do. I didn't need Satan's help. "How are you, Emma? Thank you for seeing me this morning."

"You know, busy. But don't get me wrong, I was thrilled to get the call from your office. Saturday morning is the perfect time to preview a building—no crowds to distract, if you know what I mean."

"Yeah."

"How did you find us?" she asked.

"Your building was recommended." It wasn't a total lie. Satan's slave assistant had compiled the list for us.

"Very nice. Who recommended us?"

"My, this is an open space," I said turning to gaze at the expanse.

She nodded and waved her arm around. "Yes, a blank canvas, as it were. Except for the restrooms, elevators, and stairs, you can lay it out however you like. The demising wall is that sky blue one."

"Okay..."

"I've always wanted to work with you guys," Emma continued. "How long have you worked for Mr. Carlyle?"

I'd come in his limo and dressed like a businesswoman in my pencil skirt and blouse so I would be taken for a woman working with Satan, so I should have prepared for the question. Instead, I blurted the truth, "I don't exactly work for him."

Her brow crooked. I'd made a mistake.

In an attempt to recover, I added honey to my words. "It's a joint-venture project. I mean, our situation is somewhat complicated."

"Oh, of course." She laughed. "The way he watched you, I figured it had to be more."

That caught me by surprise. I hadn't meant to imply we were involved.

"It's not what you think," I insisted.

"If you say so." She shrugged. "He's even more handsome in person than in the photographs."

Naturally, I thought. She didn't understand that the camera couldn't capture the wicked pile-of-shit personality.

She handed me a folder of papers. "I can be discreet. Now, what kind of TI were you looking for?"

I had no idea what that was, or for that matter, what the demising wall she'd pointed out was, so I went with, "It depends," while clutching an arm around myself and trying not to shiver. The lobby had been heated, but this empty space was not.

"Don't worry, the heat works fine," she said, noticing my discomfort. "It's just not turned on right now. You're awfully brave, not wearing a coat in this weather."

"I left it in the car."

"We can go back and get it," she offered.

"No, I'll be fine. We're on a tight schedule. Lots to see."

Alarm showed in Emma's face.

Her expression said I'd caught her by surprise. "You're looking at other buildings?"

Professor Markowitz's words came back to me. "*Let them know you have other options, even if you don't.*"

"Yes, so we mustn't dawdle."

"Right." She started off toward the far end. "We're very flexible. Very. Would you prefer triple-net or gross?"

"I wouldn't want to commit yet," I said, once again lost in the jargon.

"Very understandable. If you give me your card, I can shoot you the utility and tax numbers from the last tenant."

She thought I was a corporate type with business cards in my wallet. "That would be nice. But sorry, this came up last minute, and I didn't bring any cards with me." I rattled off my email address, and she typed it into her phone.

"And your phone?"

I gave her my cell number as well, and a test message dinged in my purse as soon as she typed it in.

We walked around the windows, but without any walls, it was hard to picture how it would look when finished.

She went on with mentions of escalation clauses, load factor, and pass-throughs, more terms I didn't understand. It was now obvious that I wasn't prepared for the complexity of this and needed Carlyle's help.

"What about a pool?" I asked when we got near the door that returned us to the lobby.

"Sorry. We should have gone over my handouts before we started. Yes, we have a pool on the eleventh floor, and for a fee, it's open to tenants, with a sliding scale based on occupancy."

I nodded along until she finished. "I mean a pool of our own."

"Uh…" Her eyebrows winged up. "We'd have to get the engineers involved, and then I'd have to check with the landlord. I'm not sure they would…" Her words trailed off, indicating she thought it would be a hard no.

Carlyle had said his company would cover the moving expenses, so I added, "We'd be open to negotiating a fee for that." *Fee* was probably the wrong term, but I went with it.

Her expression gave away the response even before her words came out. "That's the sort of tenant improvement that is very specific and makes the space hard to relet, so I think using the common building pool would make more sense." It sounded like a watered-down *no fucking way, sweetie.*

"Perhaps." She didn't know I represented the community center, so of course she didn't understand why that wouldn't work for us.

"What do you think? Will this fit your needs?"

I checked the time. "Thank you, Emma. I'm afraid we need to get going to our next appointment."

"Thank you for the opportunity, Ms. Moreno."

Satan paced in the lobby. He nicely didn't ask me anything until we were outside the building. "How did it go? Is this the one?"

"Thank you…" I turned. "Oomph." And ran straight into him, not expecting him to be so close. My hands landed on his chest—more specifically, the hot, thick planes of his pecs—lingering just long enough to make my mind go blank and my legs go weak.

He grabbed my shoulders to steady me. "Are you okay?"

"Sorry," I mumbled and pulled back, dropping my hands from his intoxicating warmth. This man wielded dangerous, dragon-strength pheromones.

He cleared his throat, his soft blue eyes asking the unspoken question— had he felt it too, the attraction? He stepped back. "You were saying?"

Did my blush show? After taking a few seconds to compose myself, I tried in vain to avoid admitting defeat, but there wasn't a way. "I think this is going to be harder than I expected." I swallowed my pride. What else could I do? "I am going to need your help." Saying that stabbed my heart. He represented both the death of the community center as we knew it, and our best and probably only hope of moving to a new location and keeping the services we treasured.

"How can I help?" he asked immediately. The man was a robot. There wasn't even a hint of gloating in his words. If I'd been in his shoes, I wouldn't have been able to help myself.

"Maybe you could come along on the next one to answer some of the financial questions, seeing as you said you'd…" I searched for his word from before. "…backstop us on the financial impact of the move."

He looked away. "If that's the way you'd like to handle it."

Once again, no gloating or looking down his nose at me the way I'd expected, so I chanced looking like an idiot with a question. "What is triple-net?"

"It delineates who is responsible for what payments related to the property." He said this as an education, not the lecture I'd expected. "Such as…"

His phone rang. The ringtone was the theme music from *Jaws*. He raised a finger and pulled it out. "I need to take this."

"Travis," he answered with clipped precision. He listened and didn't seem able to get in a word edgewise except for twice saying, "Can we make it later? I'm busy now."

It didn't sound like a pleasant conversation.

After a moment, Travis hung up the phone with an angry finger stab at the screen. "George, back to Adriana's apartment, please."

George accelerated swiftly. "Yes, sir."

"We're going to have to cut this short. I have to go back to work for a meeting."

"I don't understand." Somebody could ruffle this man, and I wondered who.

"Work," was his one-word answer.

"Tell them to stuff it. It's Saturday."

"I suppose that's how you would handle it if the headmaster of Hightower called and said he wanted to see you in his office right away?"

I shrugged. "I guess not."

"Are you available tomorrow to tour some more properties?"

"Sure." Delay would not work in my favor. I had to make enough progress before meeting Isabel and Paula that I could derail any plans they might be cooking up to cause a stir. That was my part of the bargain. "Your boss sucks. I still say tell him no."

"I can't."

I couldn't picture Travis staying quiet.

He blew out a breath. "He's my father." The statement hung in the air like stale smoke.

Looking out the window, I smiled. Travis's ringtone for his father played in my head. *Jaws*—how appropriate. I put a hand to my mouth to hide my giggle. Satan's master was the giant shark.

CHAPTER 17

Travis

I arrived at Dad's condo as he'd demanded and knocked.

When he opened the door, I stood tall. "What is so urgent?"

"I'm due downtown in a short while." That explained nothing. "Come in." He waved me by.

I entered, slipped off my coat, and turned.

"Nadia is off shopping," he said. "And there's something I thought we should discuss outside the office." Marrying the Bulgarian ex-model had proved to me that Dad could make serious mistakes at times. But she was a mistake he wouldn't admit to—another comment best kept to myself.

Anyway, the news that I didn't have to make nice with his wife was a relief. I hung up my coat and followed him as he walked toward the floor-to-ceiling windows in the living room. "I came as soon as I could."

He looked out over the city, clearly pondering something. Asking, or rather directing, that I come here was unusual for Dad. He preferred to summon me to his office, so something was off.

He pointed south. "You know we can see our new company building from here." That was, of course, the real reason he'd moved out of the Upper West Side penthouse I now called home. This condo didn't have the prestige of the top floor, but it had the right location and windows with the correct view.

I joined him at the window. "I know."

Moving into his current office on the fifty-fifth floor of the new company building had been an achievement he relished every day.

"It takes a lot of work," he said. "I'm sure that whichever of you succeeds me will put in the effort."

I nodded, still uncertain where he was taking this conversation—other than using it to remind me that he'd created a competition between Luca and me to determine who would take over the company. And that was yet another reminder of how I didn't measure up to my older brother, Leo.

"To attain what we have, it pays to always be on the lookout for new opportunities, but also to have a capable staff in place."

"Certainly." I nodded again, still without a clue what he was getting at.

"This Queens business could be a real headache for us," he mused.

An understatement if there ever was one. "I'm working on it."

"Nadia doesn't see the danger that I do, but I think it's best to not argue about it." He'd promised his wife that he'd bring their son, Luca, into the business, and the results had been terrible. This was only the latest evidence from my vantage point.

Message received. Don't tell Nadia what I was doing or how badly we thought Luca had screwed up.

My half brother spent minimal time in the office and was too busy working on his golf handicap and fucking his way through the city's female population to give real-estate development the attention it deserved. Luca's people skills were lacking on a good day, which was the kiss of death in the property business, because approvals were a political process in this town.

Rather than betray his promise to Nadia and fire Luca, Dad needed me to clean up the mess. In typical Dad fashion, he'd kept his hands clean and made it my job to implement the details. So far this was nothing new.

Dad went back to looking out the window. "We've come a long way, haven't we?"

"Yes, we have."

"We need to grow, which means recruiting more talent, so I want you to run out to Chicago tomorrow and interview a VP candidate for me."

"I'm busy tomorrow." What I wanted to say was a lot less diplomatic.

"His name is Alfonse Applebottom, and no, that's not a joke," Dad deadpanned.

"I'm busy tomorrow."

He bulldozed right over my repeated objection. "You'll meet him tomorrow. It's what his schedule allows. Deena will email you the details."

And what about my schedule? Simple answer, Dad didn't care. My time was his to waste. He'd screwed up today's planned property visits to *clean up this Queens mess* by demanding I come right over, and now he was hijacking my Sunday as well.

Dad left the window. "Let me know what you think of this guy, and I trust you're seeing that this Queens business doesn't drag our name through the mud. Any questions?"

I shook my head. This was typical Victor Carlyle. He'd just declared two projects as top priority and expected me to accomplish both simultaneously.

I followed him to the bar. Today was not the day to bring up Adriana's demand for an apology in the *Times*. I would hold off on that.

CHAPTER 18

Adriana

Back in my apartment after the depressing morning of viewing buildings, I pulled out my phone and dialed the number on Satan's card.

"Mr. Carlyle's office," the cheery voice answered.

"Is this Mindy?"

"Yes," she said tentatively.

"My name is Andy Moreno, and I have to apologize for your boss. I'm the reason he made you come in early on your weekend. I had no idea he'd do that."

She laughed. "No need to worry. When he explained your need I was happy to do it. When my son was growing up, he spent a lot of time at that community center getting help with his schoolwork. Without that center, he wouldn't have been able to go to LaGuardia."

LaGuardia was our nearby community college.

"Well," I said, lifting my jaw off the floor. "I'd like to thank you for your effort. I'm sure Travis appreciates it too, even if he doesn't say so."

"Well, thank you. He can be positively taciturn." Carlyle's odd use of language had apparently rubbed off on her. "Good luck on your search, and please call if there's anything I can do."

"I will," I assured her. "It was wonderful talking to you, Mindy."

After the call, I grabbed a soda from the fridge and took a few minutes to berate myself for assuming the worst about Carlyle. Then I changed gears and started on my least favorite part of being a teacher.

I was only halfway through grading the stack of papers when my phone rang. The process had gone slowly because every time I closed my eyes, I saw him—my personal Satan. He wouldn't leave me alone, repeating the embarrassing conversation over and over in my head.

"*She was happy to do it,*" imaginary Carlyle said on repeat.

"*Your slave,*" I repeated just as often.

I was the rude one for assuming he had to be lying.

My phone buzzed on the table. Chelsea's name was on the screen when I turned it over and answered the call. "Hey, girl. Getting nervous yet?" With the wedding about a week away, it was likely.

"No way," she screeched. "I've been waiting all my life for the chance to marry a man like Spencer. My whole life."

I could visualize her stabbing the air for emphasis with those last words. So much for me being able to predict her moods. "Have you been drinking?" That was the most likely explanation for her volume.

"No. I'm high on life."

"Then what's up?"

"You've made me wait all morning. Normally you call me first thing."

What had I made her wait all morning for? And why was everybody hung up on first thing in the freaking morning? "Thank you for inviting me to your party. It was fabulous," I ventured.

"I want all the details."

Maybe she hadn't been angling for a compliment on the party. "I thought you were beautiful. You and Spencer make a lovely couple."

"Did you think nobody would notice you left with that very eligible bachelor?" she asked.

I stood and walked around the table, trying to recall last night. I'd met a ton of people at the party, way more than I could remember. Also, the rich tended to take good care of themselves, and many of the men were objectively handsome. "I don't know who you're talking about. I met a lot of people, but I'm not very good with names."

"Does that mean you weren't actually holding hands and wearing Travis's coat like I heard?"

I closed my eyes. Shit was about to go down. "It's not what you think. The coat check idiots lost mine—obviously gave it to somebody else. He offered me his since I was freezing. He was being uncharacteristically gentlemanly, trying to prove he's human."

"Curious minds want to know. Is that why you slipped away in his limo?"

I sighed and reversed course around the table. "You're making something out of nothing. The rideshare was going to take too long, and he offered to drop me off. I don't even like the guy, remember? It was either accept the ride or freeze to death."

"Nice of him. Tell me, how gentlemanly was he between the sheets?" She giggled.

I started another loop of the table. "It was just a ride. I told you, I don't even like the guy. Less than zero interest."

"Don't get me wrong, I totally approve," she said, as if I hadn't spoken. "Travis is a great guy, quite the catch. And the smolder when he looked at you last night was off the charts."

Smolder? "Agree to disagree. He's a heartless suit, and your attraction radar needs recalibration. There's no interest on either side." I was on a roll now. "Zero. Nada. Zilch. As a matter of fact, you can count me as repulsed."

"Really? Then why did your brother catch him in your apartment this morning?"

"Shit." I was going to have to kill Serg. "He told you that?"

"Yup," she said triumphantly. "He asked why I had you two checking properties for me."

I kept lapping the table. "That was all Carlyle. He just up and—"

"Lied for you. I know. Serg also said you weren't dressed, something about a skimpy bathrobe. Don't worry. I played along. I get it that you don't want your brother to know who you're sleeping with. So stop beating around the bush. How was it?"

"Look, this wedding planning is scrambling your neurons. Nothing happened. I told you, I don't like him. He doesn't like me. He didn't stay the night. The guy just showed up at my door this morning and woke me up." I was babbling. "So what did you tell Serg?"

"I said I wanted to diversify away from Manhattan. You know Queens better than I do, and the Carlyles know the ins and outs of real estate."

I shivered. "You told Serg his last name?"

"Yeah. Oh, shit… I forgot his company messed up your dad's business. How bad did I screw up?"

I stopped and sat. It was suddenly cold in here. "Pretty bad."

"You're right. This wedding madness is making me forget everything else. I'm sorry."

A knock sounded at the door.

"Hold on, somebody's here. It's probably Serg again. He's freaking out over what to get his girl for Valentine's Day."

"Tell him diamonds always work."

I stood. "You would say that."

"I did it again, didn't I?"

"Yup. This is Serg we're talking about, not one of your yachting buddies. Hold on." I loved Chelsea, but sometimes she could be clueless about the realities of people like us, who lived in the outer boroughs.

I set the phone down and shuffled to the door, revving myself up to yell at my brother for not calling first, and also for tattling to Chelsea about Carlyle.

Only when I opened the door, it wasn't Serg.

"Sign here, please."

CHAPTER 19

Adriana

For a second, I stood at my door dumbfounded. "You must be on the wrong floor. I didn't buzz you up."

"It was blocked open downstairs," the delivery guy explained.

I was going to have a talk with Mrs. Herndon. Her kids were always doing that.

The tag on the kid's shirt, right below the ketchup stain, read *Hermes Messenger Service*. He looked barely old enough to drive. He held out an electronic pad. "Sign here, please, for the packages." Three large packages sat at his feet.

"There must be some mistake. I didn't order anything."

The messenger looked at the number on my door and checked his pad. "This is the right place."

Still unconvinced, I asked, "Who are they for?"

He shrugged. "They only gave me this address. No name."

I took the pad and signed. "Who are they from?"

He took the pad back and swiped it once. "Bergdorf Goodman."

"But I didn't order anything."

He shrugged and was already several steps down the hallway when I leaned over to bring the boxes inside.

"Who was it?" Chelsea asked when I picked up the phone again.

"A delivery guy. Somebody at Bergdorf Goodman screwed up big time because they sent me three boxes."

"I love that store," Chelsea squealed. "What did you get?"

"I told you, I didn't order anything." On my salary, I was more of a JCPenney's shopper. "Somebody got the address wrong."

"Open them up. Maybe there's a receipt inside or a packing slip that'll tell you who it's for."

"Hold on." I had to fetch a knife to cut the tape.

"Let's switch to FaceTime," she practically panted. "I want to see." She was more excited than I was to peek at what one of my neighbors had purchased. Who knows if they'd gotten the wrong building or just the wrong apartment.

I accepted the FaceTime request after slitting the tape on the biggest box.

"Oooh," Chelsea cooed as I opened the box to find a marvelously puffy navy down parka.

I laid it out on the couch so she could see it.

"What brand is it?"

I was busy checking the box for a receipt or packing slip. When I didn't find one, I checked the label on the coat. "Moncler. Is that French?"

"Italian." She sighed. "And to die for."

I didn't know squat about brands, but anything Italian at that store had to be expensive. I slipped my hand inside and instantly felt the warmth it promised, and it was lined with something softer than my old parka.

"Did they include a packing slip or an invoice to say who bought it?" Chelsea asked.

"Not in this box."

"Then put it away and check the others."

I lifted the parka to fold it back into the box, and an envelope slipped out.

"What's that?" Chelsea had seen it too.

"A card." When I opened it, my heart skipped a beat.

Impressions matter. First impressions matter most.

"What's it say? What's it say?" she implored.

Damn him. "It says *first impressions matter.*"

"That's odd. Nothing about who bought it?"

"It means that Satan bought it." The nickname spilled out again before I could catch myself.

"Who?"

I sighed and shook my head. "Your friend Carlyle. He sent this."

"I knew you two would hit it off." She whooped with joy. "He likes you," she singsonged.

"He does not," I argued.

"Hey, Spence, Travis is sweet on Andy. He got her a present—actually, presents."

"I told you," I heard Spencer say in the background.

"He totally did," Chelsea whispered. "So, you can tell me. What really happened last night?"

"Nothing. Nothing at all." She certainly didn't need to know about the tingles I was trying hard to forget. "This is because he thought my coat was too grungy for the property hunt this morning."

"He's right, you know. First impressions do matter."

Spencer's head popped up behind Chelsea's on the screen. "What did he get you?"

There was no avoiding it, so I turned the camera toward the parka again. "A coat."

"From Bergdorf Goodman," Chelsea added.

"Nice. Did Chelsea mention he asked about you?"

"Yeah, he totally did. He's into you," Chelsea agreed. "Hey, what's in the other boxes?"

I put the phone down to open the second box and showed them the contents. "Another coat."

Not just any coat, but according to the label, a Burberry coat. And when I felt the material, it was super soft. It had to be cashmere.

"Nice," Spencer said. "I like Burberry."

"Try it on. I want to see." Chelsea was giddy.

I pulled it up, slipped my arms in the sleeves, and flipped the phone for a selfie.

"That's so you," Chelsea said.

I ran my hands down the sides of the coat, and the softness—oh, that softness almost put me in a trance. I could die just petting this coat.

"Yup. Very nice," Spencer agreed.

I found another card and opened it. "A second card." I held it up to the camera. "Same as the first."

"True words," Spencer commented.

The third box contained three shoeboxes.

"Shoes," Chelsea squealed. "I'd know those boxes anywhere. And he got you three pairs. I'm jealous."

"What's so special about those?" Spencer asked. Either he couldn't read the writing on the boxes or the name Louboutin didn't mean anything to him.

She turned to her groom. "They're Louboutins, silly."

"Why three pairs?" Spencer asked, echoing my question.

A quick check of the box labels revealed three of the same style and the answer. "He got three different sizes of the same shoe because he didn't know my size." This explained that off-the-wall question this morning. Luckily the eight and a half pair was right.

"I'm jealous," Chelsea said, looking pointedly at Spencer.

"Holy shit," Spencer said. "I'm going to have a talk with Travis about showing me up."

"I love you anyway," Chelsea murmured, giving him a loud smooch on the cheek. "And you, you lucky girl, I'd say there's nothing wrong with my attraction radar. He likes you."

"I told you, didn't I?" Spencer repeated.

I didn't know what to say and kept the phone pointed anywhere but at my face, which burned red.

"We'll let you go so you can make your call," Chelsea said, waving goodbye on the screen just before the feed cut off.

Unfortunately, I knew exactly what call she meant, and the way I'd been raised didn't allow any way to avoid it.

After surfing the Bergdorf Goodman website and cringing at the prices of the coats and shoes he'd bought me, I selected the contact and hit the call button.

"Hi, Adriana. I was just thinking about you."

The timbre of Travis's voice, even over the phone, was deep and mellow, but it was the words that got to me.

"I was about to call," he added quickly. "I've got bad news for you. Well, you might think it's good news…"

I waited, looking for my opening and still digesting the *"thinking about you"* comment. It was the second time today he'd mentioned thinking about me. What was I supposed to do—admit to thinking about him as well? *Screw that.*

"I'm being sent to Chicago, so you'll have to preview the rest of the buildings tomorrow by yourself."

He'd said I might think that was good or bad, and surprising myself, I chose bad. "I'm not sure I'm ready for that." Bullshit, I didn't know nearly enough. What if I totally screwed this up and the community center paid the price?

"Of course you can. I have faith in you."

Somehow, that made me feel better than I had a right to. After all, he was Satan, and I was a nobody. He probably buttered up everyone with that charm.

"George will pick you up at eight," he continued.

"Give him the day off. I'd rather take Ubers anyway."

"Don't argue. George will drive you. Carlyle's don't Uber." His tone was stern. "Just look at the space," he continued. "And envision how you would lay it out to be the new community center. Is it large enough, does it have the space you need? Don't get into the details with them. Have them give you a term sheet instead. We can look at those later, but do ask about TI limitations."

"I'm out of my depth. What are TI limitations?" TI was a term Emma had mentioned that I hadn't asked about.

"TI is short for tenant improvements," he explained. "You want to make sure you can modify the space to fit your needs."

"How long will you be gone?" I didn't mean to sound desperate, but this was suddenly a big responsibility.

"Probably only a day."

"I'd feel better if I did them with you."

"It has to be tomorrow. You work Monday, don't you?"

"Yeah." A big snow was the only way Monday classes would get canceled, and none was in the forecast.

"You're a smart lady. You'll be fine. All you need is confidence."

My heart tripped for no reason when he rolled out the *lady* compliment again. I should have realized it was a gimmick slick, rich guys used to get their way. Regardless, I responded with, "Thanks."

"I'll talk to you when I get back about the location you chose, and we can go together for a second showing on Monday afternoon. How's that?"

I didn't seem to have a choice. "Sure." I was less than one-tenth as confident as I sounded. "Thank you for the coats and the shoes," I blurted. "But I can't accept them. I'll borrow something to wear."

"Didn't your parents teach you that it's rude to refuse a gift?"

"That applies to a T-shirt or a box of chocolates, not what you sent. Do you have any idea how much those coats cost or those shoes?"

"It doesn't matter."

Translation, he was rich enough that he didn't care.

My words tumbled out in a rapid stream. "Yes, it does. I looked it up, and the coats cost over four grand and the shoes another three. I can't accept them. I won't." Saying this was the right thing to do, even if letting go of them would physically hurt.

"You're upset about the shoes and coats? Is that all?"

"Didn't you hear me?"

For a few seconds, he was silent. "Calm down, Adriana. Consider them part of a uniform, work tools. We're negotiating a very large transaction when you consider ten years of lease payments. I need you—we need you—looking like you can afford this. We're a team, and you need to look like you belong working with me."

"And without an expensive coat and red-soled heels, I don't belong because I'm from the poor side of the East River, is that it?"

"Listen, I told you first impressions matter. The fact is, all the real estate representatives you'll be meeting tomorrow are women. They'll know from the shoes alone that you're worth their time. Or do you think they won't judge you?"

"I get it." Unfortunately, he was right about the shoes. Women could spot the red soles a mile away, and they would mark me as at least well-paid by the billionaire real estate mogul.

"You choose the coat that you think makes the best impression and wear nice clothes and the red-soled shoes. We need you looking your best, which is positively gorgeous, if I may say so— Sorry, I've got a call coming in that I need to take. Knock 'em dead, Adriana."

The line went silent, and I was left to ponder what he'd said.

Of course, he was right that the right clothes could make a good impression, and if I wanted to look like I could afford to make a high-dollar deal, Louboutin heels and a designer coat were a good start.

I straightened my back. Meeting the snobby parents of dozens upon dozens of Hightower students had taught me the way they carried themselves and talked.

I can do this.

Another knock sounded at my door.

When I checked the peephole for a change, my day got even weirder.

"Sign here, please," another delivery guy said when I opened the door. At least he only had one box.

This time I didn't argue, but signed and took it inside. When I unwrapped the plain white paper, my eyes got misty. The box was labeled Cabot Jewelers. I knew of the place, and my fingers trembled when I opened the large case inside. "Holy shit."

I closed my eyes, but when I opened them again, the box still contained a pair of sapphire earrings, a matching sapphire necklace, and a diamond tennis bracelet. It was all so beautiful that I had to force myself to start breathing again. No way was I calling Chelsea to tell her about this latest box.

When I caught my breath and was sure I could speak logically, I dialed his number one more time.

"Hi, gorgeous," he answered. "Before you yell at me, just listen."

I ignored his plea. "What is your game, Carlyle? I told you the coats and shoes were too much, and now you send me a million dollars worth of jewelry?"

"Hold on. First, it was all supposed to arrive together, and second, it's for the same reason."

That made it only slightly more tolerable. "My costume as your assistant?"

"My protégé, not my assistant. They're being told you have decision-making authority. I want you looking the part."

That surprised me. I was supposed to act like I was the big shot? "Oh, so no tank top and ripped jeans?"

"Get serious. We're on the same side here. We both want this search to be successful, and I know what I'm talking about. Dress yourself up. First impressions matter."

There was that line again. "And I'm supposed to look like a snotty Manhattan rich girl because appearance is more important than substance?"

"You think most wealthy people are snotty? Is that it?"

"Of course not." He'd hit the nail on the head, but admitting it would be insulting to him. I would have been fine with that yesterday, but today it didn't feel right.

"Do you teach for free?"

"Uh…" The change in subject caught me off guard. "Yes, I volunteer at the community center."

"I meant Hightower."

"They pay me," I answered tentatively. They paid very well, as a matter of fact.

"More than what the public schoolteachers earn, as I understand it."

"I do a good job." I also earned every penny by dealing with the entitled kids who attended the school.

"Before you fall off that high horse of yours, just remember it's those snotty Manhattan types paying the high tuition that makes your salary possible."

That put me in my place. "Fine. I'll dress the part. But I'd rather wait and do it with you." The appearance part I could pull off, but the substance part still scared me. What if I didn't ask the right questions? What if I couldn't answer a simple question they had?

"We don't have time."

"I don't see what difference a few days makes."

"There's a deadline I have to meet."

I should have realized he wasn't the one calling all the shots. "Your dad?"

He sighed. "I'll talk to you later tomorrow. I'm sure several of the buildings will work, and you can tell me which is your favorite."

His nonanswer about his father made it clear I'd hit a sore subject. I'd gone into this conversation mad, and now I felt shitty about it. "Thanks for your help."

"I'm sure you'll look positively gorgeous. You'll do fine."

Positively gorgeous? *Give it a break.* I thought we were past that, but he was still trying to butter me up.

An hour after hanging up, I'd planned my wardrobe for tomorrow.

If the snobs valued appearance over substance, I was just the person to pull this off. Tomorrow, I'd be playing the part of an important cog in the powerful Carlyle machine who could afford the nicer things in life.

I was ready to play in their world on their terms and find a new location for a revitalized Astoria Community Center. They would have no clue that I was actually the poor girl from Queens with maxed-out credit cards and a pile of student loan debt.

Then there were those stupid words he'd repeated, *positively gorgeous.* Was it possible that he'd meant them sincerely? That thought sent an unanticipated rush of heat through me.

Maybe, just maybe, I had to admit that I'd screwed up and been too quick in judging Satan in a Suit—just the teeniest bit too quick. But he still didn't get off the shit list for the Carlyle Plaza.

That heat chilled quickly when my phone rang with Daddy's face on the screen. I was going to have to make sure he never learned of the time I spent with Satan. Slipping up on that would lead to a match-to-gasoline moment.

"Hi, Daddy…"

CHAPTER 20

Adriana

Sunday morning, George rolled up outside exactly at eight.

According to my weather app, this morning was even colder than Saturday had been. I wanted to stand on principle, but I'd given in and was now wearing the pricey Moncler parka Travis had sent. It was puffy and decadently toasty.

Maybe people wouldn't notice the logo. Lying wasn't my style, and the last thing I needed was an, "Oh, I've always wanted one of those. Where did you get it?" Even if the coat was beautiful.

I'd paired it with a conservative top, a businesslike pencil skirt, better-than-workday makeup, and of course the red-soled shoes. Lucky for me, they weren't five-inch heels. The last thing I needed was to wobble when I walked.

I left the cold lobby for the even colder street, rushing to the car door and the warmth it promised. George rounded the car and beat me to it, holding the door open with a flourish.

"For Christ's sake, George, I can open my own car door."

"You look lovely this morning, Miss Adriana." He delivered the line with a genuine smile, ignoring my complaint.

"Thank you, but that doesn't change anything."

"Mr. Carlyle's instructions were very clear."

"George." I stared him down for a few seconds to no effect, then gave up the battle and slid onto the bench seat inside. "Thank you."

The door closed, and it felt positively lonely in the spacious rear of the limo. I shouldn't have missed sharing this with Travis. It had to be my apprehension about this task that had me wishing for his company today.

I'd been taught to hold all rich people at a distance. They weren't to be trusted, and the Carlyles were the worst of the worst. I was lucky to not have to spend the day with him, right?

"Are we ready?" George asked after buckling up.

"As ready as I'll ever be. And you can call me Andy. Everyone does."

"I have my instructions, Miss Adriana."

"I bet you do. Let's get started." Apparently, when a Carlyle said *jump*, you asked *how high*?

Having a driver instead of taking the bus or an Uber felt overly decadent, but Travis had insisted—something about impressions again. "*Carlyles don't Uber,*" he'd said.

I smoothed my skirt. The real-estate ladies would have no clue that I was actually a poor schoolteacher from Queens.

I WAS JUST ABOUT FINISHED AT THE THIRD PROPERTY ON THE LIST OF SEVEN TRAVIS had given George for me to look at. Once again, my question about putting in a pool had tanked the showing. This agent's answer was the same as the others' had been—that kind of modification would make it hard to lease the space to any follow-on tenant. And this latest rental agent's demeanor had gone completely sour after that.

"I can't believe Mr. Carlyle thinks a pool is a good idea. Maybe I should talk to him about that," the agent said, mirroring the attitude I'd gotten from the prior two.

"I'm the decision-maker on this project."

"Of course you are, dear," she said with syrupy sweetness.

They still couldn't accept anybody but Travis. Maybe that was the way the Carlyles did business, or maybe these agents saw me for who I was, just a girl playing dress-up, red-soled heels and all.

Dejected, I thanked her for her time.

Out on the street, I let George open the car door for me without argument.

He walked around and climbed in behind the wheel. "Are you ready?"

I wasn't approaching this issue properly. If I continued the way I was going, I'd blow the chance at getting any of these properties to accept our center as a tenant. "I'm not getting anywhere," I told him. "Let's call it a day, George."

It was a blow to my pride, but I had to pull up my big-girl panties and admit I was going to need Satan's help.

"I can't do that," George responded, catching my eye in the mirror.

"Pardon?"

"Mr. Carlyle instructed me to drive you to each location on the list. He also said you might balk."

"Mr. Carlyle was right about that but screw him. I'm done for the day." Even from a thousand miles away, Satan was trying to run my life. "Tell him you tried, but I ran away."

"That would get me in trouble."

Exasperated, I huffed. "We can't have that, now, can we? Drive on."

Last night, I'd been willing to give Travis Carlyle the benefit of the doubt, but today he was earning his nickname, Satan.

I was in the middle of touring the second-to-last property when my phone rang with a ringtone I couldn't ignore. "Could you excuse me for one moment please? I need to take this."

The agent nodded and walked off to a discreet distance.

"Hi, Daddy," I answered.

"Angel, we missed you at lunch." Disapproval laced his voice. "That's the second time in a month."

"Sorry, Daddy, it couldn't be helped. Something came up. Serg was supposed to let you know I couldn't make it."

"He did," Daddy said drawing out the words. "He also said you might have a new man in your life you're spending time with. Is that the reason? Because if so, you could have brought him along."

Damn Serg. "He's wrong about that. There isn't a new man in my life." The time I was spending with Travis Carlyle didn't count.

"Serg said he was a suit from Manhattan."

"He is, but it's just business."

"Don't ever trust one of those. They'll promise you one thing and deliver another. Be careful."

"I will, Daddy."

"Good. We look forward to seeing you next Sunday then."

"Daddy, I can't. I've got the wedding."

"Forgot about that. Then the week after. For your mother's sake, don't forget."

"I promise." How could I forget? I'd had Sunday lunch with my family forever. I heard Momma in the background.

"Great, Angel. Your mother's calling so I'll let you go."

"Bye, Daddy."

I hung up and got back to business with the agent.

CHAPTER 21

TRAVIS

I SAT BACK IN MY CHAIR AND PUSHED THE PLATE AWAY. THE FIRST-CLASS LOUNGE at O'Hare had nice-looking food, but my mood ruined the enjoyment of it. Today had been a total waste of time.

The résumé had described a strong candidate, but the man who met me was anything but. Alfonse wanted to be called Alfie, and after ten minutes with the guy, I decided a cartoon character's first name fit him perfectly.

Although everybody puts their best foot forward in their résumé, this guy had read too many books about how to embellish his accomplishments. Detailed questions about his work experience made it clear that "led a project to improve efficiency" had been him assisting the lady running the project, and his contribution had been scheduling meetings and writing reports.

I gave him the full ninety minutes and regretted it. It was as if Dad had sent me here as a punishment.

I opened my phone to see the two messages that had come in earlier, during the interview.

> DAD: Call me about the interview.
> ADRIANA: It didn't go well

I'd put them both off until now, hoping to catch an earlier flight back to New York. Our pilot had told me the company plane was in maintenance, so I'd had to fly commercial.

I decided to deal with Adriana first and dialed her. As soon as she answered, I asked, "What happened?"

"The first three were pretty terrible. They weren't taking me seriously. As soon as I brought up the pool, they wanted to explain the problem to you. It was like I didn't matter, even with the shoes."

"Let me guess, they thought it would hurt the value of the space for the next client?"

A girl walked by with safety pins pierced through her eyebrows. *What message did she want to convey with that?*

"Something like that," Adriana answered after a few seconds.

That was not what I wanted to hear. We were going to miss Dad's deadline if we didn't move quickly. "Then maybe we have to leave the pool off the list of requirements." It was a suggestion I'd considered earlier, but she needed to learn for herself how difficult it would be to include a pool.

"That is not an option. The pool is the most important part of the Astoria center. We are the only community center around that can offer that. The pool is nonnegotiable."

"There must be other ways to provide low-impact exercise." She'd mentioned she was proud of the aquacise classes they offered.

"But not the swim lessons. Anyway," she continued. "I wanted to stop and wait for you, but George told me you'd forbidden us from stopping until I'd toured all of them, so I did."

"And which one did you like the most?" I lifted a spoonful of soup to my lips. It had grown cold.

"None of them."

I'd given George the entire list, so I had a problem if she couldn't decide among them. "Which one was the closest to what you want?"

"You're not listening. None of them, because they all shot down the idea of a pool. We'll have to expand the list."

"And if I can change their mind about the pool, which one is the top of your list?"

"I guess Dunston Boulevard."

Now I was in deep shit. Changing anybody's mind about a pool would be a tall order. "Mindy and I will review the possibilities." The list had been complete, and I didn't know of any other property the right size. If I couldn't find a place to move the center, shit was going to hit the fan.

"When are you back?" she asked.

"Tonight. I'll call you when I have news."

When the call ended, I hoped for a miracle. It wouldn't be like her, but mentally I had to cross my fingers that Mindy had missed a great option.

After checking the airline app and learning that my flight was delayed even further, I dialed Dad.

"How did the Applebottom interview go?" Dad asked as soon as he picked up the call.

I worked to not laugh at Dad's mention of this guy's name. "He's not worth bringing back for a second interview. Why were you in such a rush to get me out here to talk to him?" I probably shouldn't have asked that second bit.

"Don't take that tone with me," Dad snapped. *Yup, the question was a bad idea.* "He came highly recommended by Tom."

"Tom should have his head examined, because the guy is not management material."

"Then it's unanimous. Luca interviewed him over the phone and had the same opinion."

I almost cursed Dad out when the test became clear, and I'd failed.

"I need to get to the gate for my flight. I'll catch you later, Dad."

We hung up, and I would have kicked myself if I could figure out how to swing my leg like that.

Luca had been smart enough to interview Alfie before committing to a trip out, and I'd fallen for Dad's instruction to waste a day here without thinking through the problem. *I am such a dumb shit to have missed this obvious test. This round goes to Luca.*

Going back to the Queens problem and locating a place for Adriana's beloved community center to land, my finger poised over Mindy's contact for a second. Then Adriana's words came back to me. She thought I asked too much of Mindy, and maybe she was right. This could wait until morning.

As I sat back in my chair, one building came to mind that we hadn't looked at, and I knew it wasn't at full occupancy. All I needed was for Mindy to verify what space was available. One more opportunity.

I got up and brought a glass of wine back to my seat. It wouldn't make the plane leave sooner, but it would soothe the wait. Today I was striking out all around. I drained the glass quickly and went for another.

CHAPTER 22

Adriana

Monday morning my phone vibrated in my purse more than once during my second-period class. I checked it at the break.

> SATAN: Call me.
> SATAN: I think I found the place.
> SATAN: Call me so we can look at it.

He was certainly persistent.

I walked down the hall until I found an empty classroom and closed the door. After yesterday's disappointment, my hand was jittery with excitement as I selected his contact and hit the call button.

It had only rung one time when he answered. "Thanks for calling, Adriana."

I started right away with the most important question. "Tell me this place will allow us a pool."

"They will."

I let out a long, audible breath. "You're sure?"

"Absolutely," he said with conviction.

"I'd almost given up. You told me the ones we looked at over the weekend were the only possibilities out there."

"This one got overlooked."

"What's wrong with it?" I asked, looking for the trap in this. "Is it a one-hundred-year-old dump of a building with no heat?"

"Very new construction actually and not far from the current location."

"And we can look at this evening?"

"That'll be too late," he insisted. "I'll have George pick you up after fourth period. Between the lunch period and the fifth period you have off, that should give us enough time to see it."

I almost asked how he'd gotten my schedule, but then remembered his father was a trustee of the school. His name carried weight.

"Where is it?"

"I'll pick you up in front of the school. Be on time, gorgeous." Then he was gone. The slippery bastard hadn't answered my question. *Which building could it be that's near our current location?*

As he'd promised, Carlyle's limo was outside at the curb when I walked out of school.

Travis emerged from the back seat as I trotted down the steps.

George held the door open for us. "Good morning, Miss Adriana."

"Good morning, and it's Andy."

"That coat looks positively magnificent on you," Travis commented as I slid onto the seat.

"Thank you. I called the hotel, and they still haven't found mine." It wasn't as cold today as it had been yesterday, so I'd chosen the decadently soft cashmere coat instead of the parka. A girl needed some protection from the cold. Two days after the party, my coat hadn't been returned and was unlikely to ever show up.

"Smith and Wollensky, George," Travis said after he closed the door.

"You said we were going to see the building," I complained. Smith and Wollensky was an upscale steak house here in Manhattan. I'd seen the menu. You couldn't get out of there for under a hundred a person.

"We are. As soon as we eat. I have lunch reservations."

"No."

"Yes."

"No." I had to put my foot down, and we'd only gotten a block from school. "George, let me out."

Travis shook his head and sighed. "Then we can sit in the car and starve while we wait until the time of the showing. Remember, I'm on your side. We both want to find a new location for your community center."

George swung the car to the curb.

"I see what you're doing, Carlyle," I said. He had the negotiating playbook open and was running straight through it—establish rapport with the opposing side and convince them, me in this case, that your goal aligns with theirs.

"What am I doing? I'm offering a woman who hasn't eaten lunch yet an opportunity to do so. Tell me you're not at least a little hungry."

"Okay," I relented. "But I'm picking the place."

George looked back at me in the mirror. "Where to, Miss Adriana?" His wink said he enjoyed seeing me take Carlyle down a peg. I got the sense it didn't happen often enough.

"George, do you know where Berkley's Deli is?"

He held up his phone. "I can find it, Miss Adriana."

"It's Andy."

He didn't respond.

"YOU SHOULD HAVE ASKED GEORGE TO JOIN US," I TOLD SATAN AS WE STOOD IN line to order.

"He brings his lunch from home," Carlyle said as if that excused being rude. He scanned the menu on the wall behind the register. "What's good here?"

"Almost everything. Just avoid the salt cod."

He nodded. "Got it."

After I ordered with Fran at the register, Travis made his selection. I slid down the counter to face an angry-looking Lou.

"I heard that," he said. "I should add a double helping of salt cod to your sandwich so you can learn to appreciate it. We can call it a surf and turf."

"Fine," I shot back. "As soon as you convince Fran to eat it."

Fran laughed. "That'll be the day."

Lou shook his head and worked on my sandwich. "Heathens."

"No onions and easy on the horseradish," I reminded him. I watched diligently to make sure he didn't carry out his salt-cod threat.

After Lou handed over our sandwiches, I followed Carlyle.

He selected a window table, and I took a chair across from him, rather than next to him. Yet when our knees brushed, I got that uncomfortable zing of excitement again. Pulling back, I reminded myself that this was a business lunch, nothing more. Plus, I hated him, or at least disliked him.

"Thank you for lunch," I said just before diving into my sandwich. I could be civil.

"My pleasure, and here you said you wanted to skip it," he commented, gesturing across the table to the two roast beef sandwiches in front of me.

I finished chewing Lou's masterpiece and swallowed. "You know, in some boroughs it's considered rude to comment on how much a woman is eating, and I've just started."

He opened his turkey club and sprinkled some additional pepper. "I've heard that, and I was only commenting on your original refusal to stop for lunch. So tell me how you ended up teaching."

I told him, and he listened.

"Are they all that entitled?" he asked.

I'd digressed to talking about dealing with the often angry parents when poor Johnnie didn't get an A in my class. "I've been offered all-expense-paid vacations, if you can believe that. They're used to being able to buy whatever they want, including their children's success."

"I've heard."

"But that's doing nobody any favors. Some of these kids are going to get into very good schools with very difficult courses and fail because they never learned to work hard, and now is when they should be learning those lessons. They've been given everything they wanted their entire lives. I never was. I worked for every single thing I've attained."

"And you teach them that? That they'll need to earn what they want rather than have it given to them?"

"Yeah. It's a life lesson they'll need. I mean, their parents aren't always going to be there to fix things for them."

"And in the process, you get to stick it to the upper-crust idiots because you have the power of the grading pen."

"It's not exactly like that," I protested. It was entertaining the see the parents grovel on occasion but not the whole reason I ran my class the way I did.

"I think your strategy is sound. I like it."

My chest swelled with pride. "Thank you."

"You seem to use the word *rich* in a derogatory manner a lot, though."

"I don't mean it that way. I'm merely making accurate observations."

"Is that why you chose Hightower?" he asked. "So you could stick it to the rich?"

"The school pays better." I kept my answer short. His observation may not have been the sole reason I chose Hightower, but I couldn't deny it was a benefit.

"And without any of those rich parents around, you wouldn't get paid well." He'd mentioned that before, and I couldn't poke a hole in that argument.

Instead, I switched subjects. "So what's your game, Carlyle?"

"Game? No game. I'm merely enjoying a meal with a positively—"

"If you say gorgeous one more time, I'm going to start a food fight and mess up that very nice suit of yours."

"We can't have that. I was going to say interesting woman. Is that allowed?"

I twisted my water glass, still on the defensive. "I suppose, but don't think for one moment that you're succeeding in bonding with me over a meal. I despise you, and I like it that way."

"See," he said laughing. "I say something nice about you, and you turn around and insult me. I'd be interested to know what has you so set on hating me when I've done nothing to you. We should be getting along for the sake of both the community center and your friend Chelsea."

My jaw clenched. He'd done nothing to me but *ruin my father's dream.* "Don't try to make it about me when you're the monster."

"Why is it that you jump so quickly to incorrect assumptions?"

"I'm not assuming anything about you. You're one of those developers busy gentrifying our neighborhoods into oblivion, and that's enough to know your character."

"You know nothing about me personally."

"And I'm happy to keep it that way."

"See?" He pointed. "Making assumptions again."

I pulled my napkin out of my lap. "I want to leave."

"Stay," he commanded. "We need to finish this. You need to tell me what's really going on with you."

I pushed back my chair and stood. "I don't need to do squat."

"You do if you want to save your community center."

I shook my head. "You're going to pull out of the agreement because I won't sit down with you over a couple of sandwiches?"

A few nearby customers turned their attention to the scene I'd created by standing and raising my voice.

"My ex," I explained, nodding at Carlyle. "You know how it is." I sat down again and whispered.

He leaned forward. "Ex?"

I kept my voice low. "Around here people are accustomed to domestic squabbles. It's better than accusing you of blackmailing me."

"I'm only stating the fact that I pride myself on being honest, and I won't work with someone who isn't honest in return."

His insult hit with the force of a punch. I'd never thought of myself as dishonest. I sat and bit off another chunk of the sandwich in front of me while I composed my thoughts. In the end, I went super short and super blunt. "You ruined my father's life."

He looked truly taken aback. "I don't even know your family."

Disclaiming responsibility for his actions was what I expected from the kids I taught, not a grown-up like him. "You bought land to build the Carlyle Plaza and demolished the building my father's business was in."

"I'm sorry your father was caught up in that. We paid relocation payments."

I shook my head. "That's a joke. What gives you the right to destroy neighborhoods? To shove working people aside, uprooting families and businesses to build shiny monuments to yourself and your family?"

His jaw ticked. I'd hit a nerve. "Do you live with your parents?"

"You saw my place. You know the answer to that, and changing the subject doesn't change what you are."

"You must hate children then," he growled.

"I teach kids, for God's sake," I shot back. "Why would you say that?"

"Do you plan on having any?"

I winced. His questions were getting worse by the second. "That's way too personal for me to be discussing with you."

"Do you?" he insisted. "Yes or no?"

"Do you, Carlyle?" Turnabout was fair play.

He stabbed the table with his finger. "Yes or no, Moreno?"

I couldn't afford a shouting match, not over a hypothetical. "When the time is right, yes."

He straightened, and a smirk grew on his face. "Children move out and start new families, having children of their own who also move out when they get old enough. They all need more places to live than existed when their parents first got married. We build those places, and I'm proud of it, *damned* proud."

He made it sound virtuous, but I couldn't let him confuse me about the destruction he'd wrought in my family. "Build somewhere else. Don't destroy my neighborhood."

He snorted. "Look around and tell me where you see vacant space in this city. There isn't any."

The truth in his assertion made me wiggle uncomfortably in my chair. "I still don't like it."

He was on a roll as he stared me down. "Obviously you'd rather have more fucking people living on the streets."

That hurt. "Not true, and you freaking know it."

"Without more buildings—large, taller ones—there'd be no place to house the expanding population, and I am sick and tired of this bullshit that we destroy homes. We fucking create way more homes for people than those we take away to make room for the newer, bigger buildings. Of course, we could always tell people they can't have kids, can't raise a family in this city. Maybe you'd like it if we had a one-child policy like China."

Somehow he'd gotten me on the defensive now. "I would never suggest that."

"Look, Adriana," he said, shifting to a conciliatory tone and lifting his water glass. "I understand that building new structures impacts people, and that's why you and I are here. Carlyle is determined to provide just compensation to people and organizations who are displaced." He sipped his water.

"Starting now, huh?"

He ignored my dig about the Plaza and checked his watch. "We should eat more and talk less so we can make the appointment."

I attacked my sandwich, and he did the same with his.

His words rattled around in my head, though, making me feel distinctly uncomfortable. He was right that progress had to happen, but his idea of just compensation was seriously fucked up.

A few bites later he said, "I hear you that Luca didn't treat the people affected by our Plaza project well. He isn't handling the compensation on this project." A bite later he added, "Or any others, if I can help it."

His words struck me as heartfelt, and I needed him more than he needed me. "I'm sorry I said those things about you. I do understand that progress and building are inevitable. I appreciate you taking the time to work with me on the center's situation."

He nodded but didn't add any words, signaling that our argument was over for now.

When I'd almost finished my sandwich, I asked, "You're not going to tell me where it is, are you?"

"The building?" He shook his head. "No. I'm going to show you."

He polished off his sandwich first. "This was good," he said, leaning back.

I decided he meant the food and not the talk. When I finished my sandwich, I asked for a bag for the second, which I'd ordered to take with me.

AS SOON AS WE EXITED THE DELI, GEORGE RUSHED AROUND TO OPEN THE DAMNED door again.

This time I didn't argue. I just handed him the wrapped sandwich. "I hope you like roast beef on sourdough."

George beamed the widest smile at me and accepted the sandwich with a gloved hand. A hint of mist showed in his eyes, if I wasn't mistaken.

Travis's phone buzzed, and he pulled it out.

I winked at George, "I had them hold the onions."

"Thank you, Miss Adriana."

It was going to take more than a sandwich to get him to call me Andy. But if we'd found a proper place to relocate the community center, I wouldn't be seeing much more of George anyway. Because I liked George, that thought unsettled me. "You're welcome, and call me Andy." It was worth a try.

The sun was bright, and I hoped it was an omen after a solid two weeks of overcast.

Travis scowled, looking up and down the street.

I held my arms up. "What can have you making a face like that on a day like this?"

"My brother," he muttered, urging me to get into the car. He entered the back seat after me, producing a silk scarf from his pocket and unfolding it. It was beautiful.

I held up a hand. "Don't you freaking dare try to give me something else."

He laughed.

Then I saw the wicked smile, the one that melted my armor just a bit each time he showed it.

"This is your blindfold," he announced, as if it was the most natural thing in the world to blindfold a woman after sharing a meal.

I scooted farther away, a sudden chill threatening to engulf me. "Blindfold? I'm not doing anything kinky. Not with you, of all people."

"Me of all people?" The question left another one unspoken in the air between us. *How far would I go into kinky with the right person?*

I tried levity. "Just no. I'm scared of the dark."

"Only until we reach the building," he insisted.

George's smile relieved me of the dread I felt. He was in on to whatever this was, and George seemed trustworthy. He might obey his boss's orders to use my full name, but I doubted he'd follow his orders to dispose of a body.

"Why?" I asked, sensing this was more of a game than a threat.

"Because I don't want you prejudging the space based on what the outside looks like."

Why hadn't my first guess been that it had to do with our real estate search? "It's that bad, huh?"

"It might be different than what you're expecting."

Relieved, I sighed and turned my head away from him. "Okay."

After the scarf was in place, I added, "George, don't let him take me to one of his lairs."

"Not to worry, Miss Adriana. You're safe with me."

CHAPTER 23

Adriana

We'd spent a good twenty minutes in the building, and so far it looked great.

Carlyle hadn't let me remove the blindfold until we were inside, and with the windows papered over, I had no idea what street we were on.

The carpeting was new, and the paint on the few walls was fresh. This was definitely not the dump I'd been afraid it might be. There was space enough, and an area near the far wall was two stories tall, so that would work for our basketball courts. The restrooms were new, clean, and spacious, which hadn't been the case in the other buildings I'd toured.

"And the pool?" I asked.

"This way," Carlyle said.

I followed him down a hallway and couldn't help but notice the width of his shoulder and the narrowness of his waist from this perspective. *Concentrate, girl. You are here to check out the building, not the man.*

He opened a set of double doors to an unfinished space. It didn't have any exterior windows, which was a relief. "We can dig an in-ground pool here."

"They'll allow that?"

"Certainly. It's just a matter of permits." He put his hands in his pockets. "So, what do you think?"

Hearing that confirmation gave me goose bumps. Even if this hadn't been the only building that would allow a pool, I would have placed it high up on the list. "I like it."

He extended a hand to shake. "We have a deal then."

Suddenly, fear struck me. "I'd like to run it by Benjamin to make sure I haven't forgotten anything important."

He kept his hand out. "Then we have a deal pending Benjamin's approval."

I nodded and shook with him. "We do."

"You've saved your community center."

With those words, a tremendous weight lifted off me. But it hadn't been me alone. *We* had saved it. I remembered my talk with Benjamin about alternative outcomes. If we stopped the Carlyles, there would be another bidder just around the corner, and I knew now there was zero chance anyone else would have put in this much effort to find us a space, much less help us afford it.

Travis checked his watch.

I'd checked the time a few minutes ago and spoke before he could. "We should leave. I need to get back."

"Right." He opened his arm toward the door. "We can write the press release on the way."

I stopped in my tracks. "Pardon?" This was moving too fast.

He rubbed the back of his neck. "The press release about the relocation. You announce that you've found a new, improved location, and that will forestall any community opposition to our project at your current location. We need to get it done right away."

"*You* need to have it done right away," I corrected. "Is this the deadline you're up against?"

He nodded. "It is."

"I can't do that. Benjamin would need to approve something like that."

"We can meet with him after your workday," Travis suggested. He seemed to have forgotten the caveat that we needed to check Benjamin's availability. Masters of the universe like him didn't bother with those trivialities.

"I'll see if he's available," I suggested.

"Shall we go?" Travis urged me toward the door we'd entered through.

There was a crowd of people moving through the lobby as we exited—more people than I'd sensed when we came in. But that had probably been the blindfold and my focus on not tripping. This had to be a big building.

When we reached the street, I gasped in horror. "Not here," I croaked. How could I possibly champion moving the community center to this building after having spent years vilifying the Plaza and the people who'd destroyed my family to build it? I spun on Carlyle. "How could you?"

He moved toward me.

I backed up with a hand out to stop him.

"How could I what?" he asked loud enough that the guys walking by on the sidewalk looked over. "Save your community center by getting you space in the only building where I have the leverage to put in a pool?"

I didn't care what the passersby thought was going on. "You're an asshole, Carlyle. This is exactly what Daddy warned me about. You promise one thing and deliver another." Our people would see it as the Carlyle monsters taking over our community center.

"What's wrong with this building?" he asked.

He didn't deserve an answer, and I couldn't stand to be near this building for another second. "I have to get back to class." I strode off toward the closest subway station and added, "Asshole," for good measure.

"Wait," Carlyle called after me.

Since we were in my borough, I responded in Queens fashion with a middle finger over my shoulder.

George pulled alongside and lowered his window. "Miss Adriana?"

I looked back, and Carlyle was still on the sidewalk outside the Plaza, so I stopped. "What? Did he send you to abduct me?"

George laughed. "No. I'm off duty now if you'd like a ride back to school." When I didn't respond, he added, "Please."

I pulled open my own door and got inside. "Thank you." The last thing I needed was to be late for my sixth-period class.

"My pleasure, Andy. And the sandwich was great."

I smiled. "You won't get in trouble for this, will you?"

He laughed. "No way. Mr. Carlyle has a rough exterior, but he's a great guy."

"We can agree to disagree on that." I was glad I hadn't changed his contact name from Satan.

The whole drive, I wondered if taking over our community center and absorbing it into the Plaza had been his plan all along. He'd mentioned raising our rent to unaffordable levels as one of the alternative scenarios.

The center had been the galvanizing force opposing his efforts to put up the Plaza, and this could be the long-term plan to shut us up so he could pillage more blocks of Queens.

Write the press release in the car? Right, and all before we had a signed lease in hand or had gotten a dime of the money he'd promised—bait and switch, just like Daddy had said to watch out for.

CHAPTER 24

Travis

I shook my head, still replaying the events in my mind. Nobody had ever walked away from me and flipped me off—not until Adriana Moreno.

Damn, that woman could be annoying.

I'd half expected her to flip off George as well, but when he'd pulled up, she'd looked my way once and then accepted the ride. Just had to be sure she wouldn't open the door to find me in the back, I guess.

Unfortunately, my trip back to the office yielded no breakthroughs or insights into what I should do next. But I had to keep moving forward.

"He's waiting," Deena said when I walked up to Dad's office. "He's not happy."

What else is new? If I knew what the hell *girding my loins* meant, I would've done it before I pulled open the door.

Dad checked his watch as I entered.

Xavier, our CFO, was there as well, and he mimicked Dad. Then he mouthed what Dad was no doubt thinking, *"Phone off?"*

Because Xavier was being an asshole for some reason, he didn't deserve a response, but I gave him one anyway. "I was touring a property." I took a seat in front of Dad's desk.

Dad swiveled in his chair and plucked a potato chip from the plate behind him. "Travis, where do we stand on the Towers issue? The short version." He popped the chip into his mouth.

Xavier grinned, as if me on the spot was his entertainment.

"I'm getting close. I think I've identified the right property for relocating the community center."

"How much longer?" Dad asked.

Xavier made a note.

I cleared my throat. "I'm not there yet. Originally I thought I'd have it wrapped up by tomorrow."

Xavier smirked. "That sounds ominous," he said with enthusiasm the situation didn't warrant.

"What's changed?" Dad asked.

"I don't have buy-in yet on placing them in the Plaza."

"The Plaza?" Dad said. "I'll have a word with Luca. He'll go along."

"He's not the issue," I admitted. "I haven't talked to him yet because the other side is balking."

"Who's their negotiator?" Dad asked. "Maybe we know somebody who can grease the skids, so to speak, get them motivated."

"Adriana Moreno," I answered. "She's their director of education. I've established a rapport with her, and I don't think getting someone else involved is a good idea."

"Today was your deadline," Dad reminded me.

Xavier smirked but wisely kept his trap shut.

Arguing with Dad that it had been an impossible deadline wouldn't get me anywhere. "I'm working on it."

Dad pushed away from his desk. "I think I've heard enough. You should finish this up immediately."

"Are the guidelines the same?" I asked.

Dad stood. "Whatever you need." He checked his watch. "I have things to get to."

Xavier left first, and when I went to the door, I closed it rather than leaving. I took up position behind the chair I'd occupied. "What's going on?"

Dad sat back down with a sigh. "Gordon heard about the Towers transaction and asked Xavier to brief him on it."

"Not you?"

He nodded. "Not me."

"Did you ask him about it?"

Dad sighed. "I talk to Gordon as little as I can, and he's off on some stupid safari in Africa right now. Xavier brought a note from him saying he wanted Xavier to sit in. And here we are."

When we'd gone public ten years ago, the lawyers had insisted Dad name a nonfamily member as chairman, even though family members owned the controlling interest in the company. It was some bullshit to appease the SEC, I was told. Therefore votes didn't count and experience in the industry didn't count, so long as the person wasn't related to us.

The transaction had brought in the capital we needed to grow, but it meant naming Gordon Neville chairman of the board, a decision Dad had since regretted.

"Is he the one worried about the PR blowback on this deal, or are you?"

Dad chortled. "I've got a thicker skin than that, but of course Gordon's terrified. He thinks the Plaza's bad press episode cost him a shot at joining the board of Glenside. Such a pity."

I nodded along, waiting for him to continue. We also belonged to Glenside Country Club, but Dad had never been interested in being on the club's board. *"Too political,"* he'd explained.

Dad's fist clenched on top of his desk as he spoke. "Little shit blames me, and not a year goes by that he doesn't bring it up."

I'd heard exasperation in his tone when discussing our chairman, but this was the first time Dad had let his mask drop to show his true feelings about Gordon Neville. It was a bad sign that our chairman didn't trust the CEO. With this new information, the sudden rush to head off any local opposition finally made sense.

"I'd hoped," Dad said. "Actually, I'd expected to have it all wrapped up without any drama before he heard about it, but somebody bent his ear."

"All the way to Africa? Who?" I asked, although I had my suspicions.

"Luca, most likely." Dad's suspicion mirrored my own. "He's been buttering the old man up for years, expecting to succeed me."

Luca had always been more interested in politics than results. This was as close as we'd ever gotten to discussing which of us Dad would promote to succeed him next year. But asking about my prospects wouldn't be appropriate with this Queens matter unresolved.

Dad pushed back from his desk. "What's your next step?"

Adriana's last words came back to me—*asshole.* "I think I need to switch the negotiations to the center's manager, Schwartzman. The Moreno woman is acting emotionally."

Yes, it was a stereotype to call a woman who disagreed emotional or irrational, but in this case it was true. The space at the Plaza met all her criteria. She'd even said so herself, until the mere name of the building unhinged her.

Dad stood. "Your call. I'll let you get on with it then. You know what's at stake."

I wasn't sure I did. I'd thought it was only the company's reputation, but now it seemed like more. Back at my desk, I contemplated how to get Adriana to remove herself from the negotiation so I could resume with Schwartzman.

CHAPTER 25

Adriana

I'd called Benjamin while George drove me back to school, and he'd agreed to stay late to talk to me. Now, in his office at the community center, I wasn't sure where to begin.

Benjamin seemed to sense I needed prodding. "What's the problem, Andy?"

"I think we might be screwed," I blurted. All afternoon, I'd worried that I'd fallen for Carlyle's sweet talk. "I thought I negotiated a good deal, and we looked at a zillion places to move, but…" I didn't know how to explain it, especially with how quickly things had moved and the fact that I'd forgotten to loop Benjamin in on what I'd agreed to. "If I didn't sign anything, we're not committed, right?"

"Calm down and start at the beginning," he said in a soothing voice.

So, I did, explaining that I'd been surprised to see Travis at the party, he'd given me a ride home, and I'd agreed to the terms he suggested while in the car.

"That's not so bad. And then?" he prodded.

I explained viewing all the properties, both with Carlyle and without, and how he'd sent me clothes to wear so I wouldn't look like the poor girl I was.

Benjamin laughed at the part about the women noticing the red-soled shoes first. "Do they really cost a thousand bucks?"

"About," I confirmed. "Anyway, Carlyle said a ten-year lease was a big deal financially, and I had to look like the kind of woman who could authorize a commitment like that."

Benjamin nodded. "I agree. That's a very astute observation on his part."

The way I felt right now, I hated to agree with him. "I guess." The shoes made me feel powerful, like I could take on the world. "But in the end, none of them would let us put in a pool."

Benjamin shook his head and sighed. "It is unusual." But I knew he understood my drive to make sure we didn't lose the water activities. "So where does that leave us?"

"Carlyle called this morning and said he'd found one more property that would allow a pool."

Benjamin leaned forward.

"I looked at it, and it's very nice—a fairly new building, lots of space, big clean bathrooms, room for an in-ground pool."

"But?" he prodded.

I cast my eyes down before I got the courage to say it. "But it was in the Carlyle Plaza."

"So?"

My mouth dropped open. How could Benjamin be so casual about it? "Don't you see the problem? That would put us under the Carlyle umbrella and make us subject to them raising the rent."

"Andy," he said, pressing a finger to the desk. "The one thing we know is that we aren't going to be able to stay at this location. If not to them, the building will be sold to another developer. It's inevitable."

I held my tongue until he finished. "But this makes it so he—they—can raise the rent enough to close us down. He even said if we didn't want to move, one of the alternatives was for them to buy this building and squeeze us out with rent increases. Now he's setting us up for that at the Plaza because he'd be the landlord."

Benjamin rubbed his chin for a moment. "Depending on the lease terms, I suppose. What does the lease say?"

That stopped my runaway train of anxiety. "I don't know. We didn't get that far."

Benjamin pointed an accusing finger at me. "Then you don't really know that he's setting us up for that, do you?"

"No," I admitted sheepishly. "But it's their style. My dad dealt with them and got screwed."

"Didn't your father deal with Luca, and not Travis? Do you want to be judged by whatever your brother says or does? I know I wouldn't. So is it possible that he's different and you're wrongly lumping them together?"

I bit my lower lip. "I guess." My answer felt like a betrayal of my family. Daddy would have been furious to hear those two words come out of my mouth. Daddy had insisted none of the Carlyles could be trusted. He was sure of it, as if it was genetic. But the argument that I shouldn't be judged by my brother's actions hit home.

"I don't see why you don't want to fight for the terms we want. What if he surprises you?"

I nodded, realizing I hadn't thought it all through thoroughly enough. "This is why I like talking to you. You see things I've missed."

He laughed. "Not according to my wife. Rachel constantly points out things I miss."

Maybe that's why the bankers always traveled in packs. Everybody needed a second or third pair of eyes to see all angles of a problem or opportunity.

I sighed, trying to center myself. This meant Benjamin thought there was still a chance we could save the community center, and I had more work to do—if I hadn't burned my bridges.

Time was not my friend if I wanted to patch things up with Travis, so I dialed as soon as I walked to my tiny office. I shut the door. The call went to voicemail.

Should I say I apologize, or I'm sorry? Apologize was the wording the parents of my students would most likely use, but it sounded too formal to my outer-borough ears.

I didn't have to decide when the call went to voicemail a second time.

He had my contact in his phone. So he knew it was me, and he didn't answer. Had I blown it by calling him an asshole? Twice?

I left my office and paced down the community center hallway and back again.

I tried a third time.

"Travis Carlyle," he answered coldly. He could have started with, "Hi, Adriana," like before. But that was prior to my name-calling.

I started right in. "I'm sorry for what I said. Can we talk?"

"Where are you?" he asked. It wasn't a no, but it also wasn't a yes, or a sure, or an of course.

"The community center."

"Dinner. Rosalini's at seven." His words were clipped again. No small talk or pleasantries. Just a command to meet him at seven. At least the restaurant was a short walk from my apartment instead of downtown.

"Yeah, okay."

"See you then." The call ended without another word.

I had screwed up things between us. Unlike before, he hadn't demanded, or even offered, to pick me up or have George drive me. His shift away from obnoxious chivalry shouldn't have bothered me, but it did.

As I left a little while later, I told Benjamin I'd set up a dinner meeting with Carlyle.

"Good luck," was his only comment.

CHAPTER 26

Adriana

At home, I contemplated my outfit choices. Travis would most likely still be in the suit he'd worn to perfection earlier today—red power tie and all. The red-soled heels and a business suit would put me on even footing with him, but I discarded the idea.

Yeah, the expensive shoes gave me confidence, but that was me molding myself to fit the snotty Manhattan businesswoman stereotype, not the badass-from-Queens me. Although tempted by its luxurious warmth, I also went with my ratty old parka instead of the expensive Moncler one over a turtleneck and jeans.

I'd accused Carlyle of using our stop at Berkley's Deli to try to bond with me in one of Markowitz's negotiating tactics, and now I had to try the same thing at this dinner. I needed him to bond with me if I was going to have a chance of saving the community center.

As I turned left out of my building, I saw them.

The two thugs at the corner were a part of the reason people considered this neighborhood a rough one. The Borodin brothers were the kind you were smart to steer clear of, even in the daytime.

Snow threatened, but it hadn't arrived yet. I continued toward the brothers, burying my hands in my coat's pockets. It wasn't something I'd do if I'd thought I might have to run.

Simon Brody had a reputation, and being one of his on-again, off-again girls gave me protection against the likes of the Borodins. They wouldn't want Simon coming for them again.

Two years ago, Vadim, being the slower of the two, had yelled, *"Chica, I think you like I show you good time,"* as I passed. He hadn't seen Simon waiting for me in his car.

Vadim limped less now, but I still saw it.

The brothers looked me up and down without a word as I continued past them to the restaurant.

As soon as I pushed through the door at Rosalini's, the aromas of fresh sauce and herbs reminded me of lasagna baking in Momma's kitchen. Good Italian restaurants like this one always smelled better to me than places that specialized in steaks or seafood. Italian was comfort food, enjoyable and filling, not pretentious.

Tension goose bumps prickled my skin as I scanned the room for Satan. I checked the time—I was five minutes early. A second look around the space brought an unforced smile. I located Travis in a booth at the back, still impeccable in his charcoal suit. And, yes, still with his tie all the way up like it was first thing in the morning instead of the end of the workday.

Is Satan such a robot that he doesn't know how to relax? That was an interesting thought, but not why I was here tonight. I had to salvage the relocation process I'd blown up at lunchtime.

Bucky, a longtime waiter here and a friend of Simon's, waved, and I nodded back.

Moving toward Carlyle, I knew that in the end, protesting the Carlyles' latest project wouldn't save our community center, only working with this man would, so it was my responsibility to repair the damage I'd caused. The table he'd picked would be perfect, quieter than the center of the room, less chaotic than a table near the door—almost an intimate location.

He stood when he noticed me approaching—a gentlemanly move that for once I didn't object to. "Adriana," was his simple greeting.

"Travis." I offered my hand. That zing occurred again as he shook my hand. It was as if he was coated in something intoxicating.

I released his hand after a longer-than-cordial shake and involuntarily licked my lips. His touch had sent a dangerous signal that I tried to ignore. Unfortunately, it was a signal his gaze mirrored.

No wonder the tabloid sites featured him with a constantly rotating cast of beautiful women on his arm. He had magnetism that would be worth a fortune if he could bottle it. We might dislike each other, but my body wasn't responding to the logic of the situation. And I sensed his wasn't either.

Averting my eyes, I slid into the booth across from him. Under the table, I wiped my palm on my jeans. The tingle from his touch didn't immediately go away.

He sat back down, eyeing the breadbasket already on the table. "You wanted to talk." Lack of sufficient eye contact was a bad way to start off. We were back to logical, and I'd screwed up our working relationship.

Water and menus appeared before I could begin. As luck would have it, Bucky was our waiter. "Can I get you started with something to drink? Perhaps an appetizer?" He looked first at me and then at Travis for an answer.

Travis opened his hand in my direction. "Red or white?"

"Chianti for me, please."

"That sounds good," Travis said. "How about a bottle?"

I nodded.

"And bruschetta?" Travis asked, mangling the pronunciation.

I nodded. "Sounds great." That would give us finger food while we talked and keep me from being drawn into those probing blue eyes that looked right into my soul.

"Be back with that right away," Bucky said before pivoting.

I held Travis's eyes and started my spiel before he could sidetrack me. "I'm sorry I got emotional today and called you names. It was uncalled for." Straightforward and to the point. I only hoped he was open to my peace offering.

He lifted a piece of bread from the basket, and I was afraid he might remain closed off. I didn't quickly forgive or forget people who called me an asshole.

He buttered the bread. "I understand." He drummed his fingers on the closed menu. "I think Mr. Schwartzman—"

"Please…" Before he could say any more and refuse to work with me, I extended my hand across the table to cover his. "Will you forgive me?" Would my touch communicate that I truly was sorry and wanted a do-over, a reset?

He didn't flinch. Instead, he looked down at our hands. He turned his over to grasp my fingers. It took a few seconds before he gave me the answer I needed. "Yes, of course."

Whatever pheromones he was coated with played with my emotions again. Nerve endings all the way down to my toes lit up like fireworks. Did he really forgive me? I didn't want to let go of the warmth of his touch and the energy that moved between us.

He thumb traced a circle on my hand.

I wished I could read his thoughts through our contact. Had he merely decided the easy way was to agree to anything the emotional woman wanted to get her to shut up? Some men were like that.

His thumb continued the motion. "I suppose we all get emotional at times."

Before he could say more, I took the initiative. "I propose that we have a nice dinner and get to know each other a bit better before we say anything about your project or my community center."

He nodded and released my hand, but he still hadn't given me a full smile. "Very well. Have you eaten here before?"

I took that as a yes. "I'm half Italian, so yes, of course." My phone dinged with an arriving message, but I ignored it.

After looking up, his eyes appraised me with a slight squint. "Half?"

"My mother's Greek," I explained. "But she makes a mean lasagna, and don't even get me started on her baked ziti Bolognese."

He smiled as his thumb traced a slow circle on my palm.

One smile, so I was making progress on the reset. "I also love tacos," I offered. "But you can't tell my mom that."

"Me, too—the tacos part. See? We have more things in common than you think."

"Right," I scoffed. "So, Travis, what do you do when you're not…" I almost blew it and said *gentrifying the outer boroughs*. "At work? I see pictures of you out and about, dinners and such." I carefully didn't mention that the gossip sites liked to focus on his very busy dating life. "Do you play polo, climb skyscrapers, or fly jet airplanes in your spare time?"

"Adriana, your mind works in the most fascinating ways."

I shrugged. Talk was a favorable sign. "I hope that's a good thing."

"I read." Already an activity we had in common. This was good. "I run when I can, and I dodge paparazzi. Sometimes that seems like a full-time sport."

I laughed.

"I never played polo because the game seems silly to me, climbing skyscrapers never occurred to me, and I like to leave the flying to others. It's probably safer that way."

Banter was good, but the jury was still out. Would he ask about me and make this a two-way conversation, or would he clam up?

Bucky returned with our wine and the plate of appetizers. "Are you ready to order?"

Travis nodded. Instead of opening the menu in front of him, he looked at me. "What do you recommend?"

I didn't need to open my menu. "It's all good here, but tonight I feel like chicken, so I'm going to have either the chicken marsala or chicken parm."

"We'll have two of whatever the lady wants to order," he said.

Why was the man who had been totally okay telling me what to do to at every turn suddenly refusing to make a choice? "You can pick a pasta if you want, or freaking anything."

He grinned across the table. "I'm not the one who's half Italian."

I sighed and mentally flipped a coin. "Chicken marsala tonight."

Bucky scribbled on his pad and nodded. "Anything else for either of you?"

I didn't say anything.

Travis shook his head, and Bucky left.

I picked up one of the small toasts. "Bruschetta," I said slowly, emphasizing the *skeh-tah* at the end of the word. "The C is hard."

His eyes narrowed.

Had I insulted him? "Sorry, the schoolteacher in me does a little too much correcting."

"The same schoolteacher who avoids the f-word and uses freaking instead?"

My cheeks warmed. I nodded and finished chewing. "That obvious, huh? Teachers are required to set an example and avoid the f-word."

"It's endearing." He lifted his glass. "To teaching better manners to the younger generation."

The heat in my cheeks went up a notch. I clinked my glass with his. "To better manners."

We both sipped, and I noticed golden specks in his irises for the first time.

I switched the conversation back to him. "Do you always work all weekend on your projects?"

He sipped his wine. "When it's called for."

"And why does my community center call for it?"

"Tell me, Adriana, why is the pool so important to you?"

"We're proud of being the only community center with a pool." That much was true.

"That may be, but you're clearly motivated by more than that." Another truth.

I swallowed hard. "We give swim lessons, and those are important to me." Not only had Travis moved the conversation away from himself, but he'd also hit the topic I least wanted to discuss.

"Who was Katarina Xenakis? I saw her name above the pool entrance." That detonated the atomic bomb. My uncle had requested the name, and Benjamin had granted it.

I wasn't prepared for this. I hadn't realized he'd noticed her name. An arctic chill ran down my spine as I recalled the day it had happened. I had to redirect. "I feel like helping me with this community center is more important to you than it should be."

"It is very important to me," he answered. "Just like it is you."

"Why?" I asked. I lifted my glass to my lips to fill the seconds.

Locked in this battle of wills, he sipped his wine. "Is this about her?"

"I can't talk about it."

"Why not?"

"I promised."

"Then," he said slowly, "we're at an impasse." He lifted his wineglass and after a sip, cast his gaze around the room. "I like this place."

I gave in. It was my responsibility to fix what I'd wrecked. "She was my cousin." It came out half as a sob.

True sympathy showed in his eyes. "I'm so sorry. What happened?"

If I meant getting us back on track, I needed to be completely candid, regardless of the hurt and regardless of my promise. I blinked back tears. "We were at the beach." Moisture slid down my cheek. "Katarina and my sister were playing in the water on an old air mattress."

He nodded, encouraging me wordlessly.

"They were having a splash war against two boys. The current started taking them out." Blinking wasn't working anymore, and more tears escaped. "Suddenly a seam split. The air starting coming out…" I sniffled and lifted my napkin to my eyes.

Before I realized it, Travis had joined me on my side of the booth and his arm was around my shoulder. "I'm so sorry you had to go through that." His comfort felt real, not condescending.

I scooted farther into the booth to give him room, and he moved with me, never breaking contact. "Thank you." I dabbed at tears.

He caressed my shoulder. "You don't have to say more, if you don't want to."

"You deserve to know." I sniffled again and straightened, determined to finish this. "Neither of them knew how to swim. I screamed and ran into the water, but I couldn't swim either."

This was the hardest part. "The lifeguard pulled me from the water, and I woke up spitting and coughing on the beach. He'd had to revive me. By the time he finished with me and went back out..." I sobbed and curled into his shoulder. "It was too late for Katarina."

Travis hadn't stopped holding me close and rubbing my shoulder. "I'm so sorry," he repeated.

I couldn't keep from shuddering under the guilt I'd carried for years. "It was all my fault." I sniffled and blinked furiously. "If I hadn't gone into the water, the lifeguard would have saved her. If I'd known how to swim, I could have saved her." I sobbed into my hands.

"It's not your fault. The girls shouldn't have gone out past where they could stand up."

"But it is. Mom had suggested I take swim lessons, but they weren't offered at the Queens YMCA. I could have gone to the Y in Brooklyn, but I thought it would take too long on the bus." I put my face in my hands, ashamed. "So it is my fault. I was lazy, and Katarina paid the price."

"And so," he said, rubbing my back, "now you're on a mission to teach as many people as possible how to swim."

I pulled my head up and nodded, but I couldn't look at him. "Did you know that over a hundred people a year drown in this state alone?"

"That's a huge number."

I wiped under my eyes again with the napkin. "Saving children from becoming statistics like Katarina is the goal. If I meet one parent whose child was saved, it'll all be worthwhile."

A warm hand cupped my chin and turned me to face him. "Andy, I want you to listen to me." Intense eyes bore into me until I nodded. "Katarina is not your fault. You're a positively amazing woman, and your dedication to bringing swim classes to Queens is the most admirable thing I can imagine."

Bucky returned with our entrées. "Careful, the plates are hot," he warned as he leaned in to set my meal in front of me.

I looked up. "Thank you." I saw worry in his eyes as he noticed my tears.

"Are you all right, Andy?"

"I'm fine," I assured him. "Just reminiscing."

Although Bucky nodded, he didn't look convinced. He put Travis's plate across the table and left.

Travis didn't return to his seat, but pulled the plate and silverware over to our side.

As I ate the first few bites of my dinner, I became acutely aware of the warmth of Travis's leg against mine. A minute ago it had been a soothing touch, and it still was, but it seemed more than that now that my tears had dried.

"And your sister?" he asked.

"She couldn't swim well, but somehow she made it to where she could stand." I'd ended up in the hospital for two days. "In deference to Katarina's family, Daddy forbid us to ever discuss that day again, and none of us have…"

"Until tonight," he offered.

I nodded sheepishly. "What about you, Carlyle? What are you passionate about? You didn't tell me why you're devoting so much time to my little community center problem." I missed his arm around me, and the gentleness of his fingers on my shoulder.

He took a bite of the chicken. Of course he stalled, but two could play this game, so I lifted a forkful to my mouth and waited.

"It's a company thing," he explained after finishing that bite. "A family thing." He jammed another bite in his mouth.

"Explain." I knew the tactic well—when faced with an uncomfortable question, stuff food into your face to find time to formulate an answer. I'd learned it well at my family's dinner table.

His face said he didn't like being put on the spot.

I waited. *I spilled my truth. Now it's your turn, tough guy.*

CHAPTER 27

TRAVIS

ADRIANA ASKED ME WHY THE TOWERS PROJECT WAS SO IMPORTANT, AND I HID behind chewing my food as I digested what I'd learned tonight about her plight.

I hated to hear of the guilt she'd been carrying around for years about her cousin. After that I couldn't very well tell her about one of the proudest moments of my life, when I'd pulled a girl from the surf. It would have only compounded Adriana's pain since she hadn't been able to do that for her cousin.

Unlike most schools in the city, the private schools I'd gone to all had pools, and swimming was mandatory. At Hightower, I'd even been on the swim team. The early-morning practices hadn't been my thing, so I'd only lasted two years.

Dad had thought me weak when I'd explained why I quit, so I'd decided to try again. Only the coach wouldn't take me back. "*Some things you only get one chance at,*" Dad had said. "*So don't do a half-assed job at anything you try.*" Since then, I'd done everything he'd asked of me with complete focus.

"What's wrong?" Adriana asked.

I hadn't realized my thoughts were visible on my face. "I just can't imagine going through that."

140

"I can't say it doesn't hurt, but all I can do now is move forward with my life."

"Adriana," I told her, looking deeply into her eyes, "I admire your strength."

"Stop it." She looked away and toyed with the food on her plate.

I'd managed to embarrass her—*interesting*.

"I opened up to you. Now it's your turn," she said after a moment. "Tell me why this is so important."

I swallowed. "This is really good." I tapped my fork on the chicken.

"Stalling won't get you anywhere."

I ran my fingers through my hair. This would be just as hard as listening to her grief, but I owed it to her. "Dad is retiring next year, and either me or Luca will be promoted into his job."

She nodded. "And you want the job?"

"Of course. It's expected. I'm the oldest. I've been preparing for it since… For a long time. But lately, nothing I do seems good enough to please him. I'm not measuring up. I keep getting reminded that I'm not as good as… I should be." This was one thing I couldn't fail at.

"Fathers can be like that," she agreed.

Looking into her eyes, I still saw the pain she'd just confessed about her cousin and decided to be honest as well. "We need to help each other. I need this win. Dad needs this community center situation not to blow up in our face," I told her.

"Then stop the purchase," she pleaded. "Let us stay where we are, and there won't be any damage to your stupid reputation."

I shook my head. "We're past that point now. Luca bought the property at a very good price, but he screwed up the contract, and Dad can't back out. I told you that before."

She nodded. "That sounds stupid."

She didn't understand Luca. Stupid was only the first of his faults. "Then there's this other problem," I continued. "The chairman of our board is super sensitive to negative press about the company."

"Your dad's not chairman?"

I shook my head. "He was, but now he's not." This was leverage she could use against us, but felt I could trust her to not abuse it. Why? I didn't know for sure. I just saw it in her eyes.

"So it became your job to keep us from putting up a fuss."

I took another sip of wine. "I told you from the beginning that I would be generous and my goal was to find a location you're happy with."

"Except that no place is going to be as good as where we are now," she clarified. She was fixated on the one solution she couldn't have.

"Unfortunately, you have to move. We can thank Luca for that."

"This brother of yours deserves a swift kick in the balls."

"Half brother, and be my guest. But I still need you and Mr. Schwartzman to be happy with the location we find, and I think the Plaza can be that for you. Dad wants a joint press release—"

"To head off any trouble and safeguard your precious company reputation," she guessed.

"That's about the size of it." In a normal situation, I would never have told the other side what I'd just confided in Adriana.

At the same time, she had to see that I was the only one who could get her a new community center location with the pool she desperately desired —even if it was in the hated Plaza.

"This sucks." She forked another bite of the delicious dinner that was cooling off.

"I think it's quite tasty," I teased.

"Not the food, the situation. The Plaza."

I probed. "What is wrong with the Plaza? It's a beautiful building."

"That's the one place it can't be. Not there."

With that proclamation, my hope disappeared. Neither of us could get the other what we needed.

CHAPTER 28

Adriana

"Why?" Travis asked. "Why can't the center relocate to the Plaza?"

"Because of what you said earlier," I explained. "You'd have control of our lease."

He grasped my hand and turned toward me. "What did I say that makes you think that is a bad outcome?"

I pulled my hand away. I couldn't fight for the center, fight against him like I needed to, while he was touching me.

His eyes widened with concern, but he didn't reach for me again.

"You told me that one option, which would take longer, but still get rid of us..." My voice trailed off to barely a whisper because the outcome was so bad. "...was to raise our rent to where we couldn't afford it."

He had the audacity to laugh. "Adriana, that is precisely why having us write the lease is perfect for you. I told you before that our company would subsidize your rent in a new location to keep it comparable, but if you're in a building we own, I can write the rent to be flat for ten years at a thousand a month. Would that satisfy you?"

My mouth dropped open, and my heart skipped an incredulous beat or three. A thousand a month was almost free. "You can do that?"

He took my hand again, and this time I didn't resist. As our eyes locked, I sensed I could finally trust this man.

"I can, and I will as soon as we can find a piece of paper. Can you sign off on the press release we need?"

The snow had started outside. I cast a quick glance at our plates. "If you throw in a ride home after we finish dinner."

He smiled and lifted my hand to his lips. "It's a pleasure doing business with you, Adriana Moreno."

With giddy pleasure, I began attacking my dinner, and Travis did the same.

"Maybe after the wedding, you'll let me take you to a nonbusiness dinner."

Warmth spread to my core almost as fast as my smile bloomed. "I don't like you well enough for that."

"Only because you don't know me well enough," he countered.

I hid my smile behind my wineglass. "Think so, huh?"

He nodded and then slid out of the booth. "I'll be right back."

I watched his fine ass as he strode to the restrooms—a very fine ass. Taking a breath to cool down, I realized this banter had to stay hypothetical.

Daddy would kill me if he knew I was even having a business meal with a Carlyle.

I plopped my face in my hands. This wickedly sexy guy was the very definition of off-limits. We would make quite the couple at Chelsea's wedding in the Bahamas. I'd be the off-limits maid of honor to his wicked best man.

I pulled my phone out to find the message I'd ignored before.

> BENJAMIN: The bank says a million was wired to us from Carlyle Heights Group. Great job!

I couldn't believe it. After blinking a few times, I reread it. Travis had sent the money he'd promised, and he didn't even have the press release he wanted so badly or any written agreement with us.

What a way to end a day. We'd secured a location where we could have a pool. Travis had said we could have a cheap lease for ten years, and he'd sent the money.

I finished my wine and closed my eyes, replaying last Friday night when he'd driven me home. He'd said he would get us the money Monday, and he had. That was today. If he wasn't the kind of man I could trust, I didn't know who was. Could this day get any better?

The booth seat jostled, and I snapped my eyes open, horrified to find my personal nightmare had slid in next to me.

"Hi there, Pussycat," Simon said. "You didn't call me back." He edged closer on the seat. He smelled of cigarette smoke.

I scooted away. I hated that nickname almost as much as I did him.

"I'm hurt." He picked up Travis's fork, spearing a piece of chicken and putting it in his mouth. Travis's fork, Travis's food—a power play I'd seen before. "It's time for this separation to end," he mumbled through his bite.

"Read my lips, Simon. It's over. There is no more me and you."

"You don't mean that. And you can make it up to me tonight," he said, his mouth still full. He put his hand on my shoulder.

"No," I said again.

CHAPTER 29

TRAVIS

I SAW THE GUY TOUCH HER JUST BEFORE SHE SAID *NO*.

It took me two strides to reach them. "Get your hands off her," I growled.

Adriana cowered against the wall.

The guy whipped around to me. "Get lost, fucker." He kept his hand on her. He was sitting, and I was standing—not good for him.

"I'm going to count to three," I said sternly, "and you're the one who's going to leave."

Adriana's eyes were wide with fear.

"One," I said, my adrenaline already hitting the red line.

"Or what?" the guy asked, laughing. "You going to whip me with your tie?"

People at neighboring tables snickered.

"Two."

He didn't move.

I grabbed his hair with my left hand and smashed his head down into the plate, holding him there with my weight while I grabbed the wrist that had been on Adriana with my other hand, twisted it, and yanked it up behind his back.

He yelped in pain.

"Three. What about now?"

"Fuck you."

The place went deathly quiet. No one snickered anymore.

"You don't touch a woman when she says no. Do you understand me?"

When he didn't say anything, I applied more pressure to his arm.

"I didn't mean anything by it," he pleaded.

"Are you ready to leave, or should we see if your arm breaks before your elbow?"

"I'm leavin'. I'm leavin'."

I released him and stepped back.

The chances were sixty percent that the guy would take a swing at me. His watch was on his left wrist, which made him a righty, and that's the arm I'd twisted. It wouldn't be any good for a punch just yet.

He jumped up out of the seat. "You're going to pay, fucker." Marsala sauce streaked the left side of his face, but it was the anger in his eyes that made him truly ugly.

I widened my stance as I'd been taught because his words raised the odds to ninety percent.

He lunged at me and swung with his right fist.

I dodged left and grabbed for his wrist as he extended. Then it was a matter of twisting and pulling until I had him spun around to face the door, with his arm bent up behind his back again. Grabbing a fistful of hair, I forced him forward. "Now you're leaving."

Ten seconds later, I'd walked him to the door and pushed him through.

He started swearing at me as soon as I shoved him out and let go, but after the door closed, I couldn't hear a thing.

There were a few claps at first and then applause as I walked back to our table. That guy must have been known around here as a bully.

I held up my hand to acknowledge them and sat down beside Adriana. "Are you all right?"

"I could have handled him," she complained.

"Sure, but are you all right?" I asked again.

She sighed like I was the dumbest shit. "That was not smart. Simon's a real mean one."

"Your Simon is a bully," I countered. "So what's his deal?"

"He's my ex, and tonight he didn't want to take no for an answer."

"That guy? Your taste sucks."

"You wouldn't understand. Anyway, like I said, ex."

"What's his last name?"

"Brody. Why?"

"Who's his boss?"

"What do you mean?"

"Who's the bigger fish in the fucker's little pond?"

By the speed of her reply, everybody knew the pecking order. "Zack Jankovic. Why?"

"I'll fix this for you. Simon will get a visit tomorrow reminding him to stay away from you."

"No," she pleaded. "You don't understand. Don't get involved. That'll only make things worse. I know how to handle Simon."

I'd seen the fear in her eyes with that fucker's hand on her, and I wouldn't allow her to be subjected to that again. "If you don't stand up to bullies, it only emboldens them. I know some guys who will make the message clear." Nobody messed with the guys I had in mind. "He won't dare cross them."

Adriana gave up the argument, but she crossed her arms, still looking pissed.

The server arrived. "I'm sorry, Andy. I didn't know he'd show up."

"Bucky, why the hell did you call him?" Adriana demanded.

"I didn't have a choice," Bucky said. "He said I had to call the next time you came in."

Adriana shook her head in disgust.

That explained a lot. This Simon shithead was the bully around this neighborhood and had everybody convinced he was the wolf to obey. Tomorrow, this wolf's boss would meet the dragon and learn the true meaning of fear. Then, sure as shit traveled downhill, this shithead would hear from his boss.

"Would you like any dessert?" Bucky asked. "On the house?"

I made an executive decision and shook my head. "Just the check."

Adriana looked up. "We should talk about the press release you want to issue."

"I'll send over my suggested wording in the morning," I said as I took care of the check.

"Send it to Benjamin. I'll be in class."

I nodded. "Sure thing." I texted George that we were ready to be picked up and stood to help Adriana into her coat.

148

She waved at Bucky on the way out, for what reason I had no idea. The guy had ratted her out to her shitty ex.

Outside, I turned up my collar against the ball-freezing cold. "I could sure use a dose of that Bahamas warmth about now."

"Me too."

I took her hand in mine.

She didn't object, but interlaced our fingers. She even served up a smile in response. "Thank you for tonight. I enjoyed dinner."

That was a success sweeter than any in recent memory. "As did I."

She hip-bumped me. "I told you you'd like the food."

"It wasn't as good as tacos, but it was good," I joked.

"Just good? This is almost as good as it gets."

"Fine. It was very good, but it was the company I enjoyed most."

Her cheeks flamed red. "I'm going to have to change my opinion of you if you start acting all nice for a change."

I winced. "Oh, that hurts."

"I'm sure you've heard worse."

I had. When I felt her shiver, I let go of her hand and snaked my arm around her to pull her close—close enough that my cock woke up. It hadn't been easy, but I'd remained completely businesslike this entire time, because the job demanded it. The job was paramount.

"How long will he be?"

"He's normally very quick." Holding her, although it was only against my side, was good enough that I willed George to stay away another minute.

My telepathy skills sucked, though, because George turned onto our street a block away and stopped in front of us.

Before opening the door for Adriana, I surveyed the street in both directions. That's when I saw him.

Simon the Weasel hadn't retreated to his den. He was up the street waiting and watching, maybe hoping to catch Adriana alone.

I spun her to me and brought my mouth to hers.

Caught off guard for only a second, she quickly pulled herself flush against me, and my cock sprang to attention. I had one hell of an imagination, but the feel of her was even better than I'd thought it would be.

CHAPTER 30

A<small>DRIANA</small>

T<small>HE KISS TOOK ME BY SURPRISE</small>. H<small>IS TONGUE SLID ALONG THE CREASE OF MY LIPS</small>, and I opened for him. He tasted like wine. What began lazily intensified quickly.

In an instant, I had only one thought—*more*. I wrapped a hand behind his neck and another around his waist, pulling myself to him. No, welding myself to him, my soft against his hard, my nipples trying to cut their way through the layers of fabric to reach him.

The sound of the traffic driving by was replaced by the thunder of my pulse in my ears. His hands caged my face as he took the kiss deeper. He kissed me like his life depended on it.

And in that moment, despite my efforts to hate him, my body knew our moments together had been building to this. I kissed him back with equal intensity, our tongues battling for control. The world stopped turning. Nothing else existed but the two of us, clinging together trading breath, sensations, and emotions.

Every velvety stroke of his tongue drove me insane with a need for more. It was like the kiss had awakened me to what kissing could be, what kissing should be. I could read his desire in his touch, in his ragged breaths, in his actions, and in the rigid cock pressed against me.

He wanted me, and I wanted him. It was elemental, the primitive need of two bodies to couple and become one. Only the cold of the wind on the street kept me from ripping his shirt off and demanding he rip mine off as well.

Then he pulled back, taking my bottom lip between his teeth and tugging before releasing it. "Are you okay?" he asked, cupping my face in his hands.

Dazed, I nodded, still feeling the ridge of his cock between us, the pressure of my breasts against the hardness of his chest, the longing in his eyes and the warmth in my core. Yes, I was a hell of a lot better than okay.

"Tell me," he demanded.

The noise of the traffic a few feet away came back into focus. "Yeah, I'm good." My brain shifted from animal to intelligent human and I added, "We should probably continue this in the car."

He released his lock on my face, and I reluctantly untangled myself from him.

He opened the door for me and looked up the street for a moment after I climbed in, before joining me. "Let's go, George."

I hadn't retreated away from him on the seat the way I had in the past, but he didn't take advantage of the invitation to sit next to me. I didn't know what happening between us. Maybe he didn't know either.

Okay, he was next to me, but we didn't have any contact. He could have let his leg loll to the side and we would have touched, but he didn't. He didn't take my hand.

I wasn't in a skirt, so I could have as well, but didn't. It was as if we were awkward teenagers not sure what came next. I'd never been kissed like that before and maybe never would be again. I replayed the moments in my mind. "What—"

"I'm sorry," he blurted.

I straightened up. "For what?" The man had given me a graduate-level course in kissing and he was sorry?

"I shouldn't have done that, but I saw your ex up the street, and I had to make sure he knew you weren't his any longer."

"You're kidding, right?"

"I know it was inappropriate because we're conducting business, but it was the best way to keep you safe."

I tried to process the words and fit them with the way he'd acted, how the kiss had felt, and I knew they didn't fit. He'd felt what I'd felt. I was sure of it. I could tell real from acting, and he might have meant it as a show for Simon, but it hadn't ended up as an act.

"I'm sorry," he repeated.

I reached for his hand, and when we touched, the zing was back. The attraction was real. "You're sorry because we crossed a line while you're working with me to relocate the community center?"

He squeezed my hand and nodded. "Exactly, but Simon needed—"

"To get the message," I finished for him.

"Yes."

I asked the logical next question. "It would be okay to kiss if we weren't working together?"

He looked straight ahead. "Yes."

"Like, after we've tied up the loose ends with the place?"

He nodded. "Yes." Still only a single syllable, but I found it was the answer I'd hoped for. "If we wanted to."

I ran my tongue over my swollen bottom lip, relishing the memory before switching subjects. "How did you learn to do that—what you did in the restaurant?" I'd never seen anybody take down a guy like Simon that fast or so easily.

"Do what?"

"The way you put the hurt on Simon. Are you ex-military or something?"

"Not exactly. But being rich can paint a target on your back."

"You mean like getting mugged?" I laughed. "One look at me and they know I don't have enough to make it worth their while."

"More like kidnapping."

I gulped. That was a scarier answer than I was prepared for.

"Dad thought we should be prepared for anything, so we had training from ex-military instructors—a lot of it."

"Wow."

"You use books, words, and tests to teach your kids. I gave your buddy the only kind of lesson he understands."

"I could have handled it," I insisted. Embarrassing Simon in public was likely to backfire.

"He needed to learn a lesson. The next girl he intimidates like that might not be able to handle him as well as you can. Then what?"

I didn't have an answer to that, and before I knew it, we were in front of my building.

When the car stopped, Travis offered his hand to help me out, and this time, I accepted it. I knew enough not to argue with him when he walked me to my door.

After inserting my key, I turned. "Thank you again for dinner. I had a very nice time." I looked up at him, focused on his mouth.

He stepped back. "As did I." The same formal words he'd used before. "Good night, Adriana." He waited for me to turn the key and open my door.

As I closed it, he turned and left, the gentleman with the rules—no good-night kiss. And I had gotten the supposed *fake* kiss to send a message to Simon. In Carlyle's mind, that made it okay.

I turned the dead bolt and leaned against the door. He was weird. A champion kisser, but weird the way he applied his rules.

Then reality swept in to ruin my mood. It was for the best that he'd left the way he had. Yes, he was appealing, but cutting class had been, too. Both were bad choices with worse consequences.

For me, the idea of Carlyle was exciting, but about as wise as a convicted felon. Daddy would have a fit, a heart attack, or both. But what Daddy didn't know wouldn't hurt him for the business aspect of this.

It was unfair how much importance could be attached to a family name, but once our working together was done, I would have to face it. We were as different as any two people could be. That was the truth.

I went to the window and looked out at the street. Travis was on his phone outside the car. I lifted the window a crack to hear.

His voice floated up to me. "Simon Brody needs to stay away from Adriana Moreno. He'll know who that is. The number one's name is Zack Jankovic… That's right. The mild form of the message is fine." Then he got into the car and the door closed.

Oh, Travis, what are you doing? You do not want to go anywhere near Simon.

A text arrived a few minutes later.

SATAN: Sleep tight.

Arguing about leaving Simon alone wouldn't do any good. Travis's demeanor when I'd asked him to drop it had been clear. He'd gone into boss mode, and nothing I could say would change his mind.

It was another signpost that he was from a different world. The fucking rich were clueless about how things worked around here and arrogant enough to think they didn't need to know.

ME: You 2

Two hours later, I lay awake, still thinking about the man who felt trapped by his family's expectations, the same man who needed to stay completely off-limits to me.

CHAPTER 31

Travis

Tuesday morning, I was in Dad's office, summoned again after calling to tell him I'd wrapped up the Towers issue that Luca had created.

"It's done," I said. "The situation is diffused, and the article will be on the website of the *Times* this evening."

Xavier was here too, and annoyingly, he wrote a note like a lawyer keeping track of items for cross-examination.

I didn't understand why Dad tolerated it.

"You worked this out with that Moreno girl?" Xavier asked.

I acknowledged him with a look. "She's who they assigned. As I said, we have a deal."

Dad drummed his fingers on his desk. "Let's have it. What is this going to cost us? The details."

Dad's expression was impassive as I went through everything from the moving subsidy to the rent subsidy and the improvements we'd make to the Plaza space.

Xavier's expression was dismissive and got worse as I went along, and he continued making those stupid notes of his.

"A pool?" Xavier scoffed. This was the first thing he'd said about this project Dad had given me. "That sounds like a red herring. Wave the pool in front of you forever and get you to buy your way around it with a set of ever-bigger concessions."

"You gave me a deadline," I reminded Dad. "I brought the deal home within the time frame and in a manner that eliminates a community uprising against us."

Xavier gave the slightest shake of his head, but kept his mouth shut.

Xavier is irrelevant, I reminded myself. *A note-taker.* What mattered was how my resolution of the mess Luca had created was scored by Dad. I'd made the decision that speed and zero community pushback were more important than the bottom-line additional cost.

"Thanks. And how soon do they sign on to the press release?"

"They already have, and it goes live on the *Times* website shortly. It states clearly that this is a voluntary move on the part of the community center and allows them to expand their services. It'll short-circuit any complaints."

Dad nodded. "That's good."

I'd gotten the important factors right. This round went to me and made Luca the loser.

I stood. "It's done, so if you'll excuse me." I left without another word.

Xavier could fuck off with his insinuations regarding Adriana. I'd kept my fly zipped and my hands to myself while doing business with her, just like I was supposed to—with the exception of that kiss, but that didn't count. It was meant as a warning to that fuckhead Simon and had nothing to do with our deal.

I'd met the impossibly tight deadline Dad had set. Luca, Xavier, Dad— they could *all* go fuck themselves. This was a win for the company and didn't give the chairman a PR problem he could blame on Dad.

CHAPTER 32

ADRIANA

TUESDAY AFTER WORK, I HURRIED TO THE TRAIN THAT WOULD TAKE ME TO THE community center. I was lucky enough to snag a seat and opened my phone to reread the messages that had come in while I'd been in classes.

> BENJAMIN: Good news. First Atlantic Bank called. They want to up their donation to 50K.

That was completely unexpected. I thought they'd been uninterested.

> BENJAMIN: I toured the space you found with Mr. Carlyle, and I agree with you that it's perfect. He's sending over a planning team tomorrow to work on a layout. Unbelievably quick.

Travis personally taking Benjamin to see the Plaza was not something I'd expected, nor that he'd be working on the new layout already.

> BENJAMIN: I signed off on the press release with one alter-

ation. I added your name to it because you did all the hard work.

Also something I hadn't expected.

> BENJAMIN: First a million dollars up front, and now an unbelievable rate for our new lease? The center won't have to worry about money for some time to come.
> BENJAMIN: I'll have to have you negotiate the lease for our apartment when it comes up.

Everything about these messages was jaw-dropping. It was like we'd been caught up in some time warp the way Travis was expediting everything.

For a moment, I felt eyes on me, but when I looked around the car, I didn't see anyone I recognized and went back to my phone.

> BENJAMIN: Come to the center when you get off. We'll set a date for a community meeting after you get back from your trip.

The thought made my stomach churn. I wasn't the get-in-front-of-a-crowd type.

∾

BY THE END OF THE AFTERNOON, BENJAMIN AND I HAD SETTLED ON THE FRIDAY after I returned from the wedding for the community meeting. It would give people sufficient notice to plan.

As I was preparing to leave, Serg came up to me, anger simmering in his face. He hadn't come to visit me at the community center in months. "I heard you had dinner yesterday with the suit." His voice was a snarl.

His accusation could only be about Travis. "So? We're working—"

"Don't give me that shit," he accused. "Dinner is not business."

"It was. Check with Benjamin. I concluded a deal with him to relocate this community center over dinner last night. What did you accomplish last night?"

He turned and stormed off. I gathered my things and spent a few minutes double-checking that I'd rearranged my tutoring sessions around the wedding this weekend.

As I was finishing, Serg reappeared, seeming calmer. "Sorry about before. We're a family, and family sticks together. I don't think you should see him again."

"No plans to."

"Can I borrow your phone? Mine is giving me problems?" Serg looked down and scuffed his shoe on the carpet. "Please."

"Problems?" Last time I'd *loaned* my phone to Serg, it had taken a week to get it back.

"Val sort of broke it," he admitted.

"What is sort of?"

"I called it off with her, and...it didn't go well." He pulled his phone from his back pocket. The screen was trashed, which explained his anger earlier. My brother came by his passion honestly. He was a hothead, as quick to love as to loath. This was how his breakups went—messy and most often angry.

With a sigh, I handed my phone over. "I want it right back."

He nodded. "I promise." After meandering over to the corner, he started tapping on the screen.

This time I didn't have to wait long to get my phone back, and I even got a *thank you* from my brother.

CHAPTER 33

Travis

On Tuesday afternoon, I was cooling off in my office after the meeting with Dad and Xavier. Having to tolerate Xavier's criticisms had grated on me. I'd shifted to contemplating my next move when the door burst open and Luca charged in, with Mindy on his heels.

"You asshole," he yelled with a pointed finger.

"He wouldn't wait," Mindy explained.

"It's fine," I assured her.

She backed out and closed the door behind her.

"Good afternoon to you too," I said.

"You're intentionally trying to tank my profitability numbers on the Plaza with your deal to move that stupid community center into *my* building. Well, I won't allow it. You don't have the authority to write a lease of any kind for *my* building."

"I do, and I did. Check with Dad if you don't like it."

"Bullshit."

I stood and pointed. "You see that patio?" I had a rare office with an outdoor patio more than fifty floors up. "The next time you ignore what my assistant tells you, I'll personally throw you over that railing. Now get your ass out of *my* office and make an appointment next time you want to yell at me for fixing your fuckup."

He sputtered something incoherent and left.

The only part I'd caught sounded like, "You'll pay."

I leaned back in my chair and remembered that kiss with Adriana—the kiss that had been meant to warn off her turd ex-boyfriend, but had rocked my world.

Now that our business was concluded, the rules had changed. She was fair game.

I typed out the message to her that I'd planned.

ME: I'd like to ask you on a date.

It was direct and to the point.

A simple *okay* would suffice. An *I'd love to* or a *that would be great* would be even better.

I waited for a reply.

A half hour later, I still had zilch on my phone. How could I have misread that kiss? The chemistry had been there, on both sides, I was sure of it.

I sent a follow-up message.

ME: Dinner, a play, breakfast, your choice.

After another hour of waiting, I sent a third message.

ME: Even tacos, if you like.

A reply never came.

Women didn't ghost me. I had the opposite problem. They all wanted to become Mrs. Carlyle. It came with being wealthy. So I broke up with my *dates* before they became too clingy or expected too much. Being treated this way by Adriana was new territory for me.

But she was appealing exactly because she was unlike the women I normally dated. They all looked the same, acted the same, and had the same priorities in life. God forbid a bad picture of them got posted online. Their end games were all the same, a ring and a yacht. None of their goals in life involved anything as honorable as preventing drownings.

CHAPTER 34

Adriana

That evening, I still hadn't heard from Travis, so I decided to call my sister. Jules needed to hear about the community center, and she was the only one I trusted enough to confide in about Travis.

"Hey, Andy. What's up?" she asked when she answered.

And so, I told her.

She listened to me ramble forever about dancing with him, touring buildings, how he handled Simon, the kiss, all of it. It had been a whirlwind five days.

"Should I call him?" I finally asked.

"It's up to you, but that's not the way I would handle it. You're special. If you don't matter enough for him to be the first to call, he's not right for you. You deserve better than to have to chase him down."

"Oh." That hadn't been the answer I wanted.

After Jules's advice, I'd waited patiently for a call or a text—any communication from Travis since the community center relocation had been announced on Tuesday. Maybe two days, or two and a half, shouldn't be a big deal, but he'd been the one to kiss me on a public street. He'd been the one who said being involved with me would have to wait until after he'd gotten the relocation press release he needed for his dad.

Thursday evening, my phone rang with Jules's face on the screen. I answered my sister's call with the same answer as yesterday, "No, I haven't heard from him."

"That sucks," she said.

"Yeah, but it is what it is. It's no big deal." She'd been the one to say if he didn't care enough to call, it wasn't meant to be.

"That's not what I hear in your voice," she said.

My current ghost status did not equate to him being interested in anybody's book. "I guess he doesn't care about me, never did. I'm irrelevant now that the deal is done."

"I'm sorry. From what you said, it sounded like he was into you."

"Clearly, I got it wrong." I wasn't worth the effort, since he no longer needed me to get his precious press release. Typical rich Manhattan snob— I'd served my purpose, and now I was out of sight, out of mind. I was the same to him as his housekeeper. Once I'd served my purpose, I should retreat to my side of the East River.

"Maybe he just got busy."

"Yeah, too busy to call or text?" Hell, I knew how to multitask well enough to text while sitting on the toilet if my day was that hectic.

"That's a problem," she agreed. "But you'll see him down there for the wedding and find out one way or the other."

I supposed I could handle one weekend of awkward. "Look, Jules, I have to pack." It wasn't a total lie, and I needed to be done here. She'd come back to the issue of Travis, trying to figure out how to fix it, because that was who she was, a fixer.

"Right. God, am I jealous. You're going to have to tell me in excruciating detail how wonderful it is so I can dream about being able to go when I fill the jar."

She had a gallon pickle jar left over from one of her more off-the-wall diets. She put a few dollars in it every once in a while to save up for her dream trip. Unfortunately, the jar wasn't filling up very fast.

"I will. Why don't you put a buck in right now?"

"Let me check." I heard her rustling around. "I've only got five singles in my wallet, and Mom says I need to eat more protein." Mom was always lecturing Jules about her eating. I ignored Mom, but Jules didn't find it that easy.

"Forget what Mom says. Put the dollar in if it's the right thing for you and your happiness."

"How'd you get to be so smart? I guess I won't go hungry if I downgrade to a salad tomorrow and put one in the jar."

"See? There's always a solution," I told her. She just had to get out of her own way.

"Or I can find some guy to blow and get a little extra protein that way."

I couldn't contain my laugh. "Sure. Tell Mom that's your solution and see what she says."

"Scientifically, though…"

I waited for one of the sex factoids she was always showering me with.

"Semen contains this compound called spermidine that is—"

"Stop," I cut her off with a laugh. "So your solution is cock-sucking with a little gargle action at the end?"

"Actually, spermidine is very healthy for you," she said. "For the whole body."

"Glad to know that. Now, I gotta pack." I wasn't going down this rabbit hole with her.

"Love you," we said simultaneously before hanging up.

At least I'd avoided an extended brainstorming session that would end up with her suggesting I do something awkward about Travis—like offering to sample his protein.

I'D JUST FINISHED PACKING WHEN MY PHONE RANG.

"Andy, I need to come over," Serg said when I answered.

I rolled my eyes, not that he could see. "Now is not a good time."

"I need to talk. It's about Val."

"You just broke up with her, so what is there to talk about?" I did *not* want to discuss the merits of him getting back together with her. Once he started, it would be hours.

"Please," he pleaded.

It was hard for me to resist him when he sounded like this, but I'd had too much drama in the last few days to add his to my plate. "Is she pregnant?"

He went from pleading to outraged in an instant. "Shit, no."

"Then it's not important enough to come over tonight."

"I just need your perspective." He was back to pleading like an award-winning actor.

"Listen carefully. Not tonight. I'm busy… And anyway, I'm going to see you tomorrow," I couldn't help but add. But then I ended the call with a satisfying punch of the big red button.

CHAPTER 35

Travis

George drove me home from work Thursday evening.

I opened my phone, and once again I had no message or missed call from Adriana. The most recent message, however, was one that normally I would have enjoyed.

> MAREN: I'm in town for a quick layover, if you're free.

She was a flight attendant for Scandinavian Airlines I'd met a few years ago, and a fun diversion if she happened to stop in town at the right time.

> ME: Sorry, I'm busy. Maybe next time.

I turned over the phone and looked out the window at the people bundled up against the blowing snow and cold. It wasn't the kind of storm that would shut the city down, but it would certainly inconvenience us.

Two fucking days since I'd reached out to Adriana—two days and still no response. It drove me nuts to think I'd been played that way, that I'd read her responses wrong.

That she could beguile me like that was just another of the qualities that made her different from most of the women I dated—hell, any and all of the women I dated. Caring that she'd blown me off was my fault and a problem time would heal. The wedding wouldn't be fun, but I could manage.

My phone rang, and I almost ignored it, given my attitude, but the screen showed Spencer's name.

I cradled the phone to my ear. "Hey, Spencer. Don't tell me you're getting cold feet."

"No way, man. But I do need a favor."

"Of course."

"Our flight to Nassau got canceled, and—"

"Say no more," I interrupted. "You can join me tomorrow, if you're not allergic to flying private." This was one of those times I was glad we had two company planes.

He sighed audibly. "Thanks a million. Can you get us there early in the morning? We need to meet with the officiant and the wedding coordinator at ten."

"No problem." I didn't know that for sure, given the storm, but I would do everything in my power to help them. "I'll let the crew know. We'll be flying out of Teterboro, and I'll have them coordinate directly with you on timing."

"You're a lifesaver, man… There's one other thing."

I waited, sensing hesitation in his voice.

"That message you wanted delivered? It hasn't been received yet, so she might want to be careful."

Fucking hell. "Thanks. See you tomorrow." I hung up. "George, we need to get to Adriana's place right fucking now."

George took the next right. "Yes, sir. Is there a problem?"

"She's in danger," I explained. "Big danger." And I had caused it.

George pressed on the gas and ignored the yellow light, hurtling through the intersection.

"Careful," I cautioned as I searched for the seat belts back here, which I never used.

"I care about her as well," was his answer.

As well? George's answer clarified something for me. I wasn't just thinking about getting a slice of pizza with Adriana, I cared about her. *I cared.*

I dialed her number again. It went to voicemail, as it had each time I'd called.

My stomach churned. Why hadn't I considered that Simon could have gotten to her and that could be why I hadn't heard from her?

Spencer's ex-military buddies were supposed to have already made it clear to Simon's boss that continued use of his extremities depended on him reeling Simon in.

While George jetted through traffic on the slippery streets, I called our aviation department to discuss tomorrow's flight schedule and give them Spencer's contact info. For a few minutes it kept me from obsessing about the danger I'd put Adriana in.

Dread knotted my insides as we crossed the river into Queens. This was new territory for me. I didn't consider myself a robot, but I also didn't get emotionally involved with my dates—not until now. I'd known Adriana was different, hadn't I? But I couldn't have known how she would affect me.

CHAPTER 36

ADRIANA

WHY DID MY STUPID BROTHER HAVE TO POUND ON MY DOOR SO HARD, AND WHEN I was on the toilet?

I ignored him, hoping he would go away. It didn't always work, but I'd told him how I felt about him coming over tonight, so it might.

I washed up slowly, with the water only dribbling, hoping that if he didn't hear any sounds, he'd leave.

He didn't. The knocking started again and graduated to the kind of pounding that would make my neighbors angry at me.

Walking to the door, I took in a full breath to yell my head off and wrenched it open. The breath left my lungs without a sound.

"Thank God you're okay," Travis said, out of breath.

I narrowed my eyes, both confused and excited to see him. "Why wouldn't I be?" I didn't get his full meaning, as my mind was instead concentrating on the fact that I was wearing sweats with a hole in the knee and a tank top, not the outfit I would have chosen if I'd known he was coming over.

"Simon. He hasn't gotten the message to stay away from you yet."

If he hadn't come to apologize for ghosting me, I didn't want to hear anymore. "You came all the way from your Manhattan lair just to tell me that?"

"May I come in?"

Just then, Mrs. Kozlowski's door down the hall opened, and she craned her head out. "What's all the commotion?"

"Sorry," I said in my most sheepish voice. "I wasn't dressed to open the door quickly enough for Mr. Carlyle's taste."

"My apologies," Carlyle said. "It was my fault for being excited to see Adriana."

"Okay then." She closed her door, and I slid to the side, ushering Satan in.

The tingles as he brushed by me were just like before and ate away at my anger. I looked down to confirm the obvious. My hardened nipples poked at the fabric of my tank, making it clear that the impulsive part of me would forgive him for anything.

I closed and locked the door behind us and folded my arms high over my chest. "You could have called me instead of just showing up."

"I did," he insisted as he pulled out his phone and pointed the screen at me. I could see a string of text messages from him with nothing back from me.

I snatched the phone. It didn't make sense. "I didn't get any of these." I put his phone down and extracted mine from my purse. Opening the messaging app confirmed what I already knew—I had no messages from him. I pointed my phone at him. "See? You must have been texting some other girl."

"There is no other girl." His face scrunched up. "I thought you were ignoring me."

He couldn't honestly mean there was no other girl. He was the billionaire Lion of Lower Manhattan who every woman on that island wanted to land. "*Ghosting* is the term, and no, I wasn't," I informed him.

"You didn't delete them?"

With a sneaking suspicion, I checked his contact page on my phone. "I'm going to freaking kill him."

"Who?"

I tapped the button on my phone. "That should fix it. My stupid brother blocked your number."

His face lost the tension it'd had when he'd arrived. "I'll be happy to kill him for you."

"Be my guest." I sighed. "I thought you'd ghosted me and were being a jerk now that the press release was out." I picked up his phone again and scrolled. "What did you say anyway?" I couldn't believe it when I got to the message. My eyes practically bugged out of my head. "You want to date me?"

He took the phone back. "I thought I'd made that obvious at our dinner. Once the project had finished, I mean. And I was hoping to get an answer from you."

"An answer?" I croaked as I thought back to that kiss on the street.

He moved a step closer. "Yes, Adriana, is that too much to ask? Tell me what you want."

If two days of silence had driven Manhattan's Casanova to my doorstep, what I wanted was to be that woman he wanted to date, even if it was only for a week or two, given his history.

His jaw ticked as he waited for my answer.

I wanted to override my normal self-control and do something reckless, something daring. My current romance novel lay on the table next to him, and I knew what that heroine would do now. She'd say the hell with propriety, and the hell with slow.

I grabbed his lapels and pulled myself up to him, lips to lips.

He was clearly surprised, expecting words, not actions. For a heartbeat, he was still as my mouth took his. Then, he opened for me, and our tongues dueled. The beast was out of his cage, and he pulled me close with a hand on my back and another grabbing my ass.

I wanted this. I wanted all of it. The feel of my breasts pressed against his chest, the taste of his desire on my tongue, the woodsy scent of his hair in my nostrils.

When he curled his fingers in my hair and angled me for better access, I opened wider, letting him win the battle of our tongues. He surged in, exploring and teasing with velvety strength.

Our kiss on the street had been a slow, hot lesson in how good a kiss could be, but this one quickly eclipsed it. This was an explosion of dynamite powered by passion and amplified by the two days neither of us had known what the other was thinking.

I relished how quickly his cock hardened against my stomach and groaned when his hand at my ass pulled me closer against the impressive length. "Trav," I groaned into his mouth.

He turned and pinned me against the door. There was nothing soft or gentle about this man now. He was all hard muscle, heat, and animal instinct. He was a man driven by desire, and I had done that to him.

I loved that I could have this effect on him. Giving in to the craving, I wrapped my legs around him, grinding against the ridge of his erection to get friction where I desired it—no, needed it.

His body was hot and hard and oh so right. Fighting for a bit of space between us, I fumbled to undo the buttons of his shirt. Clothing was only in the way now.

Ever since our first encounter, my body had been lusting for skin-to-skin contact with him, and it was a yearning I needed to sate. I had to touch him, to be touched by him. Just like in the book on my table, nothing else mattered. I broke the kiss and ground against him. "Does this answer your question?"

A knock.

The door behind me shuddered with another knock. "Andy?"

Fucking Serg. I pushed at Travis's chest.

"Fuck," Travis breathed in my ear, not letting me go. "Be quiet and he'll go away."

"No, he won't," I breathed back.

"Andy," Serg said louder with another two knocks.

CHAPTER 37

Travis

Fucking Sergio.

I pulled Adriana away from the door, hating her brother right now.

She unwrapped her legs from my waist, and I quietly settled her to the floor.

She gave me one more kiss with those soft lips before stepping back.

When the time came, I'd relish that mouth on me.

She pointed to the bedroom door, silently mouthing *"Go."*

I hadn't hidden from Sergio last time, because as a rule, I didn't hide from anything. But the stormy look of terror in her eyes said this time deserved to be the exception to that rule. So, for her, I quietly shuffled to the bedroom.

Adriana straightened her clothes and yelled at the door, "Dammit, Serg, I said not tonight." She turned to shoo me away.

I closed the door behind me and looked down at my cock, still straining to be let loose. Yes, having her brother see me like this would end with some blood on the floor. I put my ear against the door while I willed my steel arousal to go down.

"Let me in. I have to talk to you," Sergio said.

"Serg, no means no."

"Let me in or I'll camp out here all night long."

I heard Adriana huff, followed by the click of the dead bolt.

The "Thanks," from Sergio was followed by footsteps and the door closing again.

"What is so freaking urgent?" Adriana demanded.

From her tone, I could picture her face, red with anger.

"It's Val," he said.

"Go ahead," she said with a resigned tone.

"I think I want to get back together with her."

Adriana sighed loudly. "Who broke up with who?"

"Duh, I broke up with her," he said as if it was inconceivable that it could be the other way around.

"And has she said she wants to get back with you?"

"No."

"Then you want to go crawling back to her and say you made a mistake?" Adriana asked. "Beg her to take you back? Is that it?"

The way she'd phrased it, I could guess Sergio's answer before he spoke.

"Fuck no," he said. "Why would you put it like that? I don't crawl or beg."

"Because it's a pussy move," she insisted.

Right on, Adriana.

"Freaking man up, Serg, and live with your decision. If she wants a second chance, make her ask for it. If she doesn't want you bad enough to ask, she's not right for you."

"Yeah, you're fucking right."

"Damned straight I'm right," Adriana agreed. "You may be uglier than a dog and stupider than a rock—"

"Easy there, Sis."

I clamped my hand over my mouth to contain the laugh.

"But," she continued, "you're still a Moreno, and we have pride. It's the one thing nobody can take from you."

"Fuck yeah, we do," he agreed.

"What about—"

"Get outta here," she interrupted. "That's all the advice you're getting tonight. If you want to hang out, you can help by getting me another box of tampons down at—"

"Maybe another time," he said as fast as he could get the words out.

Good move, Adriana.

"Can you loan me some money?"

"You're unbelievable, ya know? What happened to the money I loaned you last week?"

"It's gone. I need a little more."

"*It's gone, and I'm a baby,*" I mouthed silently to myself. *What a loser.*

She mumbled something, but didn't tell him to get lost like she should have.

"Thanks, Sis. See ya." Sergio was a leech.

I heard the door open.

"Don't come by again when I say not to, Serg." The door closed.

I moved away from the bedroom door before Adriana pulled it open.

She backed up a step when I moved closer. "That was close." She sighed. "He almost caught us."

"It doesn't matter."

Her gaze snapped to mine, poky nipples signaling the desire that I hoped still burned within her.

It wasn't easy, but I avoided staring at her chest. "What's wrong?"

"I'm not sure… Serg would kill you, or me, or both of us if he knew we were…"

"Were what?" I challenged. "Dating? You never did answer my question, verbally at least. It's a simple yes or no. I want to date you, Adriana Moreno. What do you want? Your stupid brother doesn't get a say. Nobody does except you."

She rolled her bottom lip between her teeth and sighed. "It's just…"

CHAPTER 38

Adriana

Travis's jaw ticked as he listened to me hem and haw. "You're a grown woman. Now make up your mind," he demanded. "And I don't give a fuck what your brother thinks, and neither should you. It's your life to live."

It was my life, but it affected others as well.

I took in a long breath. "My family can't know, but for this weekend away —yes." I'd told him he had a terrible reputation, but I don't think it sank in.

His brow furrowed. "Secret dating?"

"And just this weekend," I emphasized. We'd be out of town, but we'd still have to avoid Serg. That was as much as I could risk.

His head bobbed tentatively, eyes cast down, his frown turning scowl-like. He clearly didn't like what I'd said, but I was scared. Secrets like this didn't keep well, and I was lighting the fuse on a problem that could explode at any moment.

He captured my face in his strong hands and moved to only a breath away. His blue eyes were magnets, snapping mine to his. The passion I read in them both excited and terrified me. "All that matters tonight is you and me."

I nodded. We'd gone from zero to a hundred kissing against the door, and now we had to figure out how to start again.

"But I'll leave, if that's what you want," he added.

I shook my head. "No."

"Be positively certain, gorgeous." There was that compliment again. "Because I only make one offer to be a gentleman."

"I'm positive," I said, pushing up to close the final millimeters between our lips. I threaded my fingers through his hair and enjoyed the taste of him.

A hand came around behind my neck, and his lips crushed mine so heavily I thought I might bruise. But this time, our tongues didn't battle for control. They danced a tango of passion, velvet against velvet—so different from the kiss against the door. It promised a night to remember.

I breathed in the spicy, manly scent of him as his other hand slid under my tank to cup my breast. When he tweaked my nipple between his thumb and forefinger, it sent a zing to my core. I let out a whimper I couldn't control. "Oh, Trav."

He kissed his way from my ear down to my clavicle. "Knowing you're braless drives me crazy." My breathing became ragged as I cataloged that for later—braless was his weak spot.

He pulled up the hem of my top a few inches. "We should lose this."

Nodding, I lifted my arms.

He snatched it over my head, throwing it to the side. His eyes feasted on me. "You're positively gorgeous, Adriana."

The heat of a blush burned in my cheeks as goose bumps pebbled my skin—the sudden chill of losing my top? The top was thin anyway, so more likely it was my excitement. I was even getting used to his *positively gorgeous* comments.

He kissed his way across my collarbone to my shoulder. Both his hands went to my breasts, but he didn't squeeze like they were stress balls, or pull like they were handholds the way all my previous boyfriends had. His touch was almost reverent, except for the nipple-pulling, which sent little jolts through me.

Moving away from his mouth, I started where I'd left off on his shirt buttons. "We should lose this too, I think."

He nodded but didn't stop worshiping my breasts. I finally got the buttons undone and had access to his skin, to his chest and sculpted abs. I ran my fingers over the ridges and valleys of hard muscle. He let go of my breasts as I pushed the shirt off his shoulders. I immediately missed the contact.

He pulled his hands between us to undo the buttons at his wrists. *Oops.*

When he'd freed himself of the shirt and shucked it off, I got the whole picture—broad shoulders, impressive pecs, an eight-pack to make any Hollywood hunk jealous, and those arms…my, those muscled arms. I went for his belt.

But he pulled my hands away and lifted me off my feet. "So impatient."

"Yup."

Good thing I'd made my bed this morning because a second later, he deposited me there. He straddled my thighs and looked down hungrily.

"We can turn off the lights," I suggested.

"I want to see all of you. I'm going to enjoy watching you."

His desire mirrored what my book boyfriends said. I ached for him. "Less looking and more doing," I groaned, arching my back.

"Do you eat a five-star meal with the lights off?"

I shivered. Did he mean he was going to eat me out on our first time? I'd read about it in books, but I'd only had the experience twice. And Gerry hadn't come close to what the books described.

His tongue darted out to moisten his lips. When I tried for his belt a second time, he pulled my hands away and held them captive over my head with one of his.

"You're no fun," I challenged. I knew how to please a guy, and it started with stroking before sucking him.

He lowered himself to kiss my nose. "Slower, gorgeous."

A kiss on the nose, being called gorgeous, and a guy who wanted to go slower? I'd been transported to an alternate universe.

Simon had been pretty typical of the guys I'd been with—not that there were a lot—always rushing to the finish line, *his* finish line to be exact.

Still holding my hands over my head, Travis kissed his way from the shell of my ear down my neck to my throat and continued down my chest.

I squirmed until he reached my breasts. Then I arched my back to meet his mouth and whimpered as he circled the breast with his kisses and finally took the taut bud of my nipple into his mouth.

He sucked on me hungrily, teasing, taking, releasing, and repeating.

Every touch, every suck, only increased the ache in my core. With his strength, there wasn't anything I could do to change the tempo. All I could do was revel in the pleasure he delivered.

He took his time before he moved to the other breast, driving me crazy with his mouth, with his teasing cool breaths on my wet skin, and with the gentle tugs on my nipples.

I writhed under him. "Please let me touch you."

"No lower than my shoulders," he whispered, looking up from my chest and releasing my wrists.

"That's not fair," I objected.

"Those are the rules for now."

Keeping to the rules for once in my life, I threaded my fingers through his hair and massaged his scalp. *For now* meant I'd get my turn.

He shifted off me to the side. One hand moved to my breast to continue the torture while he kissed his way down my stomach. His other hand traced light circles on my inner thigh over my leggings, moving ever higher.

I pulled at his hair to get him to meet me, but it didn't work. His fingers traced over my sex with just the right pressure. I gasped. Even through the fabric of my leggings, it was so excruciatingly good I was sure my panties had just melted from the heat. "More," I moaned as I bucked my hips into his touch.

"Easy there," he said, giving me another stroke.

Easy for him. It drove me insane that he wouldn't let me touch him more than this. I wanted skin. I wanted to feel the heat of him, his hard muscles, his hard everything. I wanted to drive him to the edge the way he was torturing me.

The joke was always about the teenage boy who couldn't control himself with the girl and came in his pants before he could whip it out. But if he kept this up, tonight I was going to be the one who came before he got his equipment out, before I got to feel him inside me.

He stroked me a few more agonizing times. All I could do was tug at his hair. "This isn't fair."

He stopped and moved up the bed to kiss me. The feel of his chest on mine, skin to skin, was a good start, and the taste of him as our tongues danced again made me forget the stupid rules and snake a hand down his back.

He replaced my hand on his shoulder as he deepened the kiss. I arched my back as his hand finally slid inside my leggings and down to travel the length of my soaked slit.

"You're so wet for me," he breathed into my neck.

I nodded wordlessly, taking a sharp inhale as he circled my clit. "Oh yeah." The trembles he gave me were even better than those from the vibrator in my upper drawer. Wanting much less between his hand and my aching sex, I lifted my ass and pushed the waistband of my leggings down. It wasn't a technical violation of his rules because I was touching myself and not him.

He helped me and pulled the clothing all the way off, including my panties. Sitting up, he parted my legs. "You're gorgeous all over."

Feeling incredibly exposed, I pulled my knees back together. I'd done it in the dark, with moonlight coming in, or in the day with the sheets over us. With lights on, I was too self-conscious to stay spread-eagled like this.

He got up and turned on the side table lamp before flipping off the overhead light. "Better?"

I wouldn't have pegged him for a considerate lover—not that I'd had one before. Nodding, I eyed the gigantic bulge in his pants. "Except when do I get to see you?"

"If I don't go slow, gorgeous, you won't be able to walk tomorrow."

"Promises, promises," I teased.

The look in his eyes cautioned me to be careful about challenging him. I yelped as he pulled me down to the edge of the bed and knelt between my legs. "Is this okay?"

I trembled, but still got out, "Green light." I writhed under his mouth as his lips traced up my inner thigh. "That tickles."

"Tough." He stopped just short of my apex and switched to the other leg. Every kiss ratcheted up the anticipation for when he would reach where I wanted him.

Seconds later, I got my wish as two fingers traced through my wet folds, finding my entrance waiting for him. He didn't warm me up with a single digit, but slid both in. His tongue caressed the length of me, finding my sensitive bud, circling and flicking.

I bucked my hips up into him, grinding into his face and fingers, clawing for purchase in his hair. "Oh my God, Travis. Holy fuck." I might have yelled the words, but I could hardly hear them over the pounding of my pulse in my ears. "Holy shit."

"You okay?" he asked. His scruff scratched against my thighs as he lifted his head.

I nodded. "So much better than okay."

"I could do this all night long. You taste so sweet."

I used my grip on his hair to bring his mouth back to my little bundle of nerves because I couldn't take it all night long, and I couldn't wait either. I sobbed out his name as he tongued me and worked those fingers against that secret spot inside. Each movement sent me higher, toward that cliff of pleasure I wanted him to fling me over.

He flattened his tongue against me on a slow stroke, crooked those fingers inside me, and the tremors came quickly, building to clenching contractions. "Travis," I cried out I don't know how many times. His magic tongue rode out my never-ending climax with me.

When the waves receded, I lay there boneless, panting, pleasure wringing all the strength from my muscles. He got up, and I managed to scoot up the bed and held out my arm. "Your turn," I panted, laying my head against the pillow and closing my eyes.

I heard the sound of shoes hitting the floor, of his zipper, and then of foil tearing. When I opened my eyes, I locked on the sight of him fisting his cock, stroking a few times. A drop of precum glistened at his tip.

I crooked my finger. "I want to taste you." It was something I'd never said to a guy before.

Stroking with one hand, Travis used the other to wipe the drop from the head and brought his finger to my lips. With any other guy, my request would have gotten me a mouthful of dick. Yes, this man was different.

I sucked the salty drop, but only when he stepped back and released himself to roll on the condom was I able to gauge his girth. *Hung like a horse* was the phrase that came to mind, but maybe *hung like a rhino* was closer. He was wielding the kind of weapon that could destroy a woman.

It was probably a good thing I'd stretched myself a few times in the shower with my jumbo dildo, even if the toy didn't match Travis's equipment.

Finishing with the condom, his hungry eyes raked over me.

This time, I didn't close my legs.

CHAPTER 39

Travis

I settled between her legs and leaned over to kiss her with my tip notched at her entrance. "Are you sure?"

She nodded, but her real answer was to wrap her heels behind my thighs and pull me closer.

I tried to go slowly, letting her acclimate to my size, but she kept using her legs to leverage me in farther and faster.

Her voice broke on my name when I pushed in to the hilt, buried completely in her slick warmth. She was so tight, so warm, so fucking perfect. I began to move, to thrust, to relish the feel of her.

The animal in each of us took over. I pounded in, and she bucked up to meet me stroke for stroke, all the time keeping our gazes locked.

She clawed at me like a wild animal and grew both wetter and tighter around me. Her breaths were ragged, as were mine. We were scrambling up the hill of building pressure to find the release we both craved.

I thrust in deeper, harder, grinding against her clit as she bucked and tensed. Then I felt it—the explosion, the release of all that tension as her eyes clamped shut and she screamed my name again. The contractions of her climax around me wrung out my own ecstasy as I pushed in to the hilt and went rigid. White dots appeared in my vision as I exploded into her, pulse after pulse. I couldn't stop.

As I locked my elbows to keep from crushing her, she held my eyes captive and something passed between us. It was like she could see inside me, past the defenses I kept up, into the darkness that was my empty heart.

She shook her head. "That was…"

"Great," I finished for her. That was too mild a word to describe it, but it would do for tonight. Panting heavily, I settled onto her, nuzzling her neck and breathing in her scent.

"Better than great," she wheezed, bringing me to my senses. I angled my chest to the side so she could breathe.

I kissed her long and slow, but didn't slide out just yet. I wanted to savor this. For the longest time, we didn't change position, didn't talk. I massaged her breast, and she stroked my back. Once again, our eyes communicated everything that needed to be said.

I knew this was right, she was right, and I could tell she felt the same way. This was not going to be one-and-done. I'd known she was different, but hadn't guessed how different.

Eventually, I withdrew to take care of the condom and brought back a warm washcloth for her.

She traced the tattoo on my forearm. "Who is Leo?"

I took in a quick breath. With any other girl, I would have and lied and explained it was the sign I was born under. "Leo's my older brother—was… He died."

"I'm so sorry." Her eyes said she truly was.

I blinked back the threat of tears. I'd trained myself to not cry. "*Grown men don't cry,*" Dad had always insisted. "Leo was the oldest, and he was supposed to take over the company. I was the spare, so to speak."

She snuggled against me and rubbed my arm. "There's nothing spare about you, Trav. You're the real deal."

"Maybe now. When he died, all his responsibilities fell to me."

"Like taking over the company?"

"Yes." Her hand flattened on my chest, and it soothed me, loosening my lips on a topic I never discussed. "If I can measure up," I added. More than ever, that was the question.

"It's important to you?" she asked.

"There's nothing more important in my life. Nothing."

She rested her head on my shoulder. "I wouldn't worry, Trav. You'll do fine. I can feel it." A minute later she added, "I've decided you're a pretty nice guy after all, Carlyle."

I laughed.

She lifted her head. "What's so funny?"

"You're the first person to ever call me *nice*." It was the kindest compliment I'd had in a very long time. "Probably because you haven't tried one of my omelets yet."

She thrummed her fingers on my sternum. "That bad, eh?"

"You'll see." I pulled her tighter against me. "When you come to my place."

"Not happening. Weekend only, remember?"

I pulled the blankets up around us and gave her a squeeze. "My place is warmer than this icebox."

An hour later, we warmed up the room with round two.

CHAPTER 40

Adriana

When I woke Friday, my bed was empty—and cold enough that it had been that way for a while. Turning over, I felt it again, the internal glow that came from phenomenal sex. Travis hadn't woken me, probably a good thing with as tired as I felt.

In one of my romance novels, the hero would have gone out to get the heroine her favorite breakfast, or at least her favorite coffee. Only Travis didn't know what mine was.

I turned on my phone. My finger hovered over the Satan contact, but I didn't press it. Being the clingy, needy girl wasn't a good look on me, so I put the phone away and hoped he brought me something sweet, like a donut.

An hour later, I was showered and ready to head to the airport for my flight to the wedding. Hanging out with the rich kids would be a pain, but Chelsea was worth it. My heart felt a little different now, as Travis still hadn't returned, or called, or texted, or probably even given me a second thought.

Great. I had to face the truth. I wasn't the heroine in one of my novels, and he wasn't the dashing billionaire swept off his feet by me. I was only another notch on his bedpost, and I'd been dumped, like those *other* women I'd read about.

Me putting a weekend time limit on us had probably done it. Then his words came back to me. *"All that matters tonight is you and me."* Yeah, he'd pretty much spelled it out. One night was all that mattered to him

Pacing through my tiny apartment, I kicked at the pile of clothes on the floor and decided it was just as well—good, actually, because we existed in different worlds, the proverbial two ships passing in the night. Now I wouldn't have to consider sneaking around or how I would explain him to Serg if he caught us.

All good. We'd gotten some insta-lust out of our systems, and that was enough. He would stay on his side of the river, and I'd stay here, only crossing to his side for work. I was happy with that. I *would be* happy with that.

The tingle between my thighs and the pleasant ache of all my well-worn muscles argued the opposite. My traitorous body didn't know what was good for me, but my brain did. I could do mind over matter when it mattered. In his arms, it hadn't felt like a one night lustathon, but his absence only proved that my radar was faulty.

Nervously, I checked that my phone wasn't on silent—nope, I'd just been dumped like a wad of chewing gum, spit out and forgotten, to be replaced by another. It didn't matter. I'd see him at the wedding and then never again.

I kicked the pile of clothes again. At least nobody had seen us, so there was no real shame. Only I knew I'd been added to his one-night-stand list.

～

Two hours later, my knee bounced nervously in the airport waiting area. Would I bump into Travis here or not until later at the wedding?

Regardless, a few days in the warmth of the Caribbean would be a welcome luxury. I'd never been to the Bahamas. Hell, I'd never been south of Atlantic City.

My phone buzzed in my purse, but when I checked, it wasn't Satan.

"Did your hot billionaire ever get back in touch?" my sister, Jules, asked when I answered the phone.

Last she knew, Travis hadn't called. "Uh...yeah." I wiggled in my chair, still feeling the aftershocks of our night together. He'd definitely gotten in touch—lots of scorching-hot touches.

"What came up? What did he say?" she asked, probably sensing my change in mood. Ever the optimist, she'd been sure something had come up at work for him, while I'd thought he was done with me.

"He'd been trying to reach me, but Serg screwed with my phone and blocked him."

"Serg can be an ass. So what did he say—Travis, not Serg?"

"He came over last night," I said innocently, although there was nothing innocent about what we'd done.

"Details. I need details."

The agent at the gate announced that preboarding was starting.

"We're about to board. It'll take too long to explain." And there were too many people around for me to relate to what she wanted to hear. "I'll just say we got to know each other a little better."

Jules squealed. "I can't wait to hear."

But I finished with, "Then he dumped me."

"That sucks." Her voice changed, now filled with pity I didn't want. "What did he say?"

"Nothing. He just left before I woke up. It's his standard routine it seems."

"Hmm…"

"That's what I've read at least."

"You're doing it again," she pointed out. "You're prejudging."

I wasn't, but it wasn't worth the argument. Twisting my boarding pass in my hand, I tried to remember the name of her latest out-of-town hookup. She was a consultant being sent here and there on assignments. Her current one in Seattle hadn't been her favorite, yet she still seemed to find a man every place she went. "What's going on with you and Pete?"

"It's Pedro, and he's been fun, but I called it off. I'm leaving in two weeks, and he says he likes the rain in Seattle. Can you imagine? That's even worse than not liking tacos."

"Sorry to hear that." It was sad, but not unexpected, given my sister's history.

"I bet you're totally going to bang Travis's brains out this weekend."

"You forgot. He dumped me."

"Eh, if not him, then another hot, rich guy. There should be plenty of them at the wedding."

"Doubtful." I looked around the departure area. Besides Serg, I could see Wendy Breton, Ed Thorpe, and Ginny. When I spotted Harry, I looked away quickly.

Travis was nowhere to be found. With his wealth, he probably never flew commercial.

"It's exactly what you do at weddings," Jules continued. "You hook up with someone for the night or the weekend to add a little spice to your life before returning to your boring reality. Aren't they almost all from Manhattan?"

"Yeah. I'm the lone black sheep."

"Then it sounds like a perfect wedding-hookup situation. Weddings are meant for trying out alternatives that you wouldn't at home. Be bold. Take a risk."

"Maybe." With all the one-percenters coming, it wasn't like I'd bump into them later at the bodega on the poor side of the river where I lived.

"You have to."

The agent announced, "Boarding group A, first-class passengers."

"I gotta go. We're boarding." As a maid-of-honor perk, Chelsea had provided me with first-class tickets and a suite at the resort.

"Have fun, and don't do anything I wouldn't do," Jules said cheerfully. That eliminated almost nothing. "Call me tomorrow with a hookup update."

"Can't. I didn't add the international plan to my phone."

"Monday then, as soon as you're back."

I agreed and hung up. Hoisting my backpack and purse, I followed Serg to have our boarding passes scanned.

He turned around. "You look different this morning."

That was not a good line coming from him. "I'm excited to get out of the freaking cold." That part was true.

"If that's what you want to go with," he said dismissively.

I stayed quiet because the last time he'd said that, I'd just gotten back with Simon. Admitting that to him hadn't led to a good conversation.

CHAPTER 41

Travis

Spencer whispered something in his bride-to-be's ear.

I looked away, out over the pool area of the resort, and thought about Adriana. I imagined her sunning herself on one of the loungers, maybe reading a book. Enjoying the Bahamian sun away from the New York City winter.

What color would Adriana's bikini be? More importantly, how skimpy would it be?

Based on her shyness last night, maybe she'd be a full-hipster-bottoms kind of girl, instead of choosing a thong that would drive me crazy. But I could hope.

She'd looked so peaceful this morning when I left, and even now, I couldn't get the feisty woman out of my mind. Then I turned my phone over to find the continued bad news.

I'd left her a note to call me when she woke, and so far, complete radio silence. It bothered me.

"Hey, thanks for the ride," Spencer said, sipping his orange juice as he looked out over the beach.

"Yeah, you're the best," Chelsea cooed as she stroked her groom's arm. She couldn't seem to keep her hands off of him.

"What else is a best man supposed to do when the bride and groom can't get to their own wedding on time?"

"This sure beats New York weather," Spencer said, patting her hand.

I looked away, feeling like I might be intruding with all the PDA going on.

Chelsea stroked his leg. "Yeah. It's not bad."

Spencer toyed with a ringlet of her hair.

Shifting away, I searched the beach for someone to watch—anything to take my mind off the public fondling going on next to me. The *oohs* and *ahhs* that came from Spencer's bride were embarrassing.

I forked the last of the fruit off my plate and pushed back from the table. "I'm going to get some work done while you two…whatever." I'd bet anything returning to their room was on the agenda.

"Okay," Chelsea said between moans of pleasure. "But don't forget you're picking up the maid of honor and her plus-one. They're arriving on the noon flight."

I almost puked up my fruit when she said *plus-one*. Last night, Adriana had started talking about us being a very temporary couple, but she certainly had never mentioned bringing a date to the wedding.

Now her not calling me made sense—it sucked bilge water, but it made sense. I'd been dumped. I stood, putting aside my glass of juice without drinking it. "I'll have the resort arrange a ride for them."

Chelsea swiveled on me. "Absolutely not. That's no way to treat my best friend and maid of honor. You're the best man, so it's only appropriate that you pick them up."

"Yeah, man," Spencer agreed. "It's your duty. No excuses."

I nodded and rose to leave. "You two be good now." It might be my duty, but I didn't need to like the idea of picking up and driving Adriana with her fucking date. I'd never been tossed over by a woman, and having it happen like this sucked. I didn't like this feeling one bit.

CHAPTER 42

Adriana

After immigration, I slid my passport back into my purse and looked across the lines for my brother.

With no Serg in sight, I turned on my phone, but it showed no service. That's when I remembered I hadn't bought the international-calling option.

Turning the device off, I rolled my bag toward the doors to ground transportation and the cab line. Serg was a big boy. He could make his own way to the resort, or maybe to wherever the blond bimbo he'd sat next to on the plane was going.

Since Carlyle hadn't been on our flight, I could probably avoid him until the rehearsal dinner tomorrow. My first order of business would be to find a bar by the pool, where there had to be a daiquiri with my name on it. I exited the building and breathed in the warm Bahamian air outside. Closing my eyes and tilting my head up toward the sun made everything perfect after leaving frigid New York behind.

Then I lowered my head and learned it was not such a perfect day after all. Fucking Travis Carlyle leaned against a car. The asshole looked as delectable as always. "Adriana," he called with zero enthusiasm.

Yup, cold and calculating, just as the article had described him.

Carlyle had discarded me like a used tea bag, so why was he here? He could have at least had the decency to avoid me and not rub it in that we hadn't even lasted twenty-four hours.

Lust tingled my skin at the sight of him, while anger had me clenching my teeth to keep from screaming. But it was too late to run away, so I pulled up my big-girl panties and strode over, putting my opinion of seeing him on full display—zero smile. I could do ice queen as well as any girl. "What are you doing here?" I snapped with all the venom I could muster. I didn't know whether to slap him, kick him in the balls, or both.

"I was sent by Chelsea. She thought it would be the right thing to do," he said coldly, surveying the crowd, probably so he didn't have to look at me. His tone made it clear that picking me up hadn't been his idea, and his disappearing act this morning had been planned. Yup, I'd been one more pathetic notch on his bedpost.

To be fair to Chelsea, she didn't know what had happened between us. Nobody did. Or ever would.

My traitorous body erupted in goose bumps being this close to the man who'd redefined the word *orgasm* for me last night but was a total douchebag for leaving me without a word. "I can get my own cab, Carlyle." See? Unlike him, I could be polite and a normal human.

"Good morning to you too, Moreno," he said, pointedly switching to my last name.

I caught a whiff of him and had to remind my lady bits that we were not heading to playtime with this schmuck. My body and my brain were on two very different tracks, and it was time to prove the brain was more powerful. "I'll get a cab." I dug my fingernails into my palms to keep from screaming the words.

"No, you won't." His fists balled and relaxed twice. "Spencer told me it's my responsibility to transport you and your *plus-one* to the resort." That explained why he was here looking like he'd swallowed a lemon. He didn't want to be around me any more than I did him.

"Tell the groom that I ran and you couldn't catch me."

He snorted like that wasn't possible. "Where's your plus-one?"

"Probably chasing the blonde with big tits he met on the airplane."

That stopped the great and powerful Carlyle for a full three seconds while his mouth fell open. He shook his head. "How can you associate with a dick like that?"

"I don't have a choice. He's my brother."

CHAPTER 43

Travis

"Serg is your plus-one?"

Adriana nodded. "Yeah. What did you think?"

Fuck if I knew what it was about her, but the thought of her with somebody else as her date had short-circuited my logic and self-control. I'd just been mean to the object of my desire.

God, why did this woman turn me into a jealous jerk? I never acted this way. There were always other women to be had. They were everywhere, and letting a woman know I was jealous gave her power I shouldn't relinquish.

Yes, last night had been mind-blowing, but somehow it had been more than tremendous sex with Adriana. We'd shared a connection, or at least I'd thought we had. She was real.

"I left you a note, and when you didn't call…"

Her mouth dropped open. "I didn't see a note, and when you left in the middle of the night and didn't call, I thought you'd pulled a dick and ditch on me."

"No way. I had to leave early to get to the airport." I took hold of her shoulders. "Spencer called. They needed a way down here because their flight got canceled. You looked so peaceful. I didn't want to wake you."

She looked down at her feet. "I'm sorry I thought you were... Never mind. I'm starved, and I could really use something alcoholic."

"They have burgers and tacos by the pool," I suggested as I hefted her bag into the trunk and shut it.

She nodded. "Sounds great, so long as I can also have a daiquiri."

"Anything for you, Adriana." I took her hand and led her to the car door. Her acceptance of my touch was a welcome relief. "I guess we both jumped to the wrong conclusions."

She nodded.

"Are we good?"

She moved close and wrapped her arms around me. "We're good."

The heat of her soft tits against me was exactly what I needed. Things were back where they should have been all along, and in spite of the public setting, my blood surged south. I could already imagine some after-lunch delight.

"Shit." She quickly broke the hug and backed away, checking the crowd. "We can't have anyone suspect, especially not my brother."

I opened the door for her, the gentlemanly move. "Then I'd better get you to the hotel. The rooms have curtains."

That earned me a wicked smile that went straight to my groin.

AT THE RESORT, I WAITED WITH HER AT THE FRONT DESK AS SHE CHECKED IN.

"Andy," the voice boomed from the entrance behind us. It was her idiot brother.

Adriana took a discreet step away from me—not a good sign.

Sergio strode up, and recognition flashed a second after he got close enough. He pointed a finger. "You're the guy—"

"Chelsea's friend," I finished for him. "Yeah. I'm in the wedding. Spencer's best man."

Sergio scratched his nose. "Cool. I'm just here as a wedding guest, the price of a free trip to paradise, thanks to my awesome sis." He tapped Adriana on the shoulder.

"What happened to the blonde you were all cozy with?" she asked.

I listened intently. Maybe Sergio would be out of our hair and off to meet this new girl. Then I could get my hands on this minx of a woman I couldn't get out of my head. Just the thought made my cock twitch.

"Oh, Iris is awesome. I'm starved. Let's get lunch." He took Adriana's elbow and nodded toward the exit to the pool area. "Hey, good seein' ya again, Travis."

Behind his back, I caught Adriana giving me a slight warning headshake. Our lunch was off.

"You too, Sergio." I turned for the elevators. *Her fucking brother, of all people.*

Five minutes later, up in my suite, the room phone rang.

"Trav," Adriana said when I answered. "I told Serg I had to use the bathroom. Sorry about lunch, but we can't. I can't have Serg see us together."

"What's the problem?"

"I gotta go."

As the call ended, I sat on the bed. If avoiding Sergio was going to be the rule, this was shaping up to be a very complicated weekend.

CHAPTER 44

ADRIANA

I PUSHED AWAY WHAT WAS LEFT OF MY BURGER AND SIPPED ON MY DAIQUIRI AT A table overlooking one of the pools, remembering the way Travis had made me feel last night. It was a set of memories I'd carry forever. And right now they made me salivate at the thought of getting rid of my brother and finding Travis's room.

Travis was right that I'd jumped to a conclusion I shouldn't have, and it bugged me. Normally I was deliberate and didn't make hasty judgments. Then I heard my sister in my head. It was time to follow her advice—be bold and take a risk this weekend. Travis would be that risk. Normal me would have avoided this feeling, but then normal me hated rich snobs from Manhattan, and here I was itching to bang one.

Normal me would have stopped to search for clarity this morning. When we'd finally fallen asleep last night, I hadn't gotten any of the vibe that he was done with me. Normal me would have taken that feeling and given him the benefit of the doubt. Normal me would have leaped into his arms as soon as I'd seen him at the airport.

I could have mentioned that Serg was coming to the wedding as my plus-one, or I could have said out loud that I wanted to spend time with Travis this weekend. Either way, we wouldn't have ended up upset with each other.

New rule—no assumptions.

Serg checked his watch. "Why the hell do we have to wait to get into the room? I need my suitcase."

I ignored his complaint and took a minute to remember the name of this latest girl. "Where is Iris staying?"

"Just down the beach, about a half mile or so."

"So, an easy walk then?" I hoped he'd get the clue that he could head over there, and soon.

"Yeah." He checked his watch again.

"What do you need your suitcase for?" He'd better not say condoms.

"Nuthin'."

"Not drugs, I hope?"

"How stupid do you think I am? Never mind. Don't answer that... I want to shave."

His scruff looked like he hadn't shaved today or yesterday. "Are you sure you want to go that direction? A lot of girls like a light scruff more than a clean shave."

He rubbed at his jaw. "What do you think I should do?"

"She's your date, not mine. Ask her."

He rubbed his jaw, then pulled his phone out and smiled at what he saw.

"What?" I asked.

"She's already missing me, so the scruff stays." He didn't get up.

"Why are you sitting here with your boring sister when you could be getting cozy with her?" It was no mystery what my horny brother wanted to be doing.

He turned the phone over. "I'll hang out with you for a while. Let her miss me some more."

"Or she could find somebody better, a guy who doesn't make her wait."

He thought about that for a moment and puffed out his chest. "Nah, not likely." Serg wasn't short on ego.

I sipped from my drink, stuck with him for now.

"Let's call Jules and make her jealous," he suggested, grabbing my phone off the table. He looked at the screen and then me. "Why don't you have service?"

"I didn't buy the international plan."

"Are you nuts? What if I have to get a hold of you?"

I hadn't thought about that, and of course he'd made it about himself. "It's just a few days." I shrugged.

He fiddled with my phone for a minute. "What's your pin for the phone company?"

More interested in my drink than the stupid phone, I gave it to him.

He handed it back to me. "Now you're all set."

Miraculously, I now had service. And probably a huge bill waiting. I stuffed the phone in my purse.

Serg ate a fry from his plate and pointed the next one at me. "There's something different about you today."

I stretched. "I'm enjoying the warmth."

"Aren't you going to call Jules? It'll be fun."

"Later." Calling Jules now could be a disaster. She might go nuts asking me about Travis, and I couldn't have that with Serg here.

His gaze locked on an attractive redhead with big boobs and the tiniest yellow bikini I'd ever seen walking by the pool. "Yeah, we can wait. I'd rather hang with you for a while anyway."

Several men's eyes skated to the redhead—lucky girl. "Like the scenery?" I prodded, jerking my head toward Miss Teeny-Weenie Bikini.

He smirked. "It's not bad." When the girl laid down on a lounger, he scooted his chair back. "I've gotta hit the head. Be right back."

When he was gone, I retrieved my phone to text Travis.

> ME: I'm stuck with my brother—I'll text you if I can get free for a while

Travis's reply only took a minute.

> SATAN: That's not going to work.

I stared at the message, trying to decode it. Did he not want to see me? Maybe he had work and couldn't be interrupted.

Serg returned, walking slowly. His head swiveled to Miss Teeny-Weenie Bikini.

"You just went to the bathroom as an excuse to ogle her, didn't you?"

He shrugged. "She has a nice ass, and that thong is something else. I mean the way it—"

"I don't want to hear it." *Do all men think like that?*

"Hey, can you loan me a hundred of spending money to take Iris out?"

"No." *Loan* in Serg-speak didn't ever imply repaying me. Also, he had

198

just been drooling over Miss Teeny-Weenie Bikini's butt crack, and in seconds he was back to focusing on the blonde from the plane. He was unreal.

Suddenly, the chair next to me screeched against the concrete. Travis pulled it out and sat. "Hi, Sergio." He scooted the chair in and closer to me.

My brother shot him a quizzical look. "Hey, man."

"What—?" I started, not sure how to finish the sentence. This was not the place for Travis to be.

Travis gave me a broad smile. There was a twinkle in his blues. "Sorry that took so long, gorgeous. Now that my work is done, we have the rest of the day together. To go over our toasts." The heat in his eyes was unmistakable. Even my idiot brother would see it sooner or later.

This could go to shit fast. Knowing exactly how to handle Serg, I whipped out my wallet. "Serg, how much did you say you needed to take out Iris?" I hated saying *needed* instead of *wanted*, but this had to be sugarcoated for my stupid sibling.

The wheels turned slowly in Serg's brain as he looked over at Miss Teeny-Weenie Bikini. "Three hundred."

I counted out the twenties for Serg's blackmail. It was a good thing I'd gone to the ATM before leaving. Still, this left me with almost no cash and credit cards that were very nearly maxed out.

Serg snatched the bills when I offered them. "See ya." He waved and headed in the direction of Miss Teeny-Weenie Bikini. Yes, he checked her out before changing direction for the lobby. Would he ever change?

I turned to the man who'd almost declared himself my date in front of Serg. "That was stupid. He was going to leave soon, and we could have just avoided him."

"I told you before. I don't hide, and neither should you. We're dating." He said that last part like it was a fact carved in stone. He pulled what was left of Serg's meal toward him.

"For the weekend only." Jules had urged me to be bold, and this was my version of that.

"I'm hungry." He took two fries from the plate and gobbled them down without acknowledging what I'd said.

I took another bite of my burger. "We shouldn't be out in public together like this. Serg is many things, but he's not stupid."

Travis lifted a brow and ate another fry.

"Okay, so he's not the sharpest tool in the shed," I admitted. "But I don't want to take a chance on my parents finding out."

He lifted another fry and pointed it at me. "Worried about what your father will think?"

I sucked in a breath. "Terrified is more like it. I don't think you understand how badly you—I mean, your family hurt him."

He nodded. "I think I have an idea, but it wasn't me, and I am not my half brother."

"That won't matter to him." I couldn't believe how nonchalant Travis was being about something I knew was playing with live dynamite.

"These are good." He plucked another fry from the plate. "Trust me. I'll deal with your dad."

"How?"

"That's where the trust comes in. I would never do anything to hurt you or your family." He dipped another fry. "Have I given you any reason not to trust me?"

Travis was delusional, but with repetition, I could probably get through to him about how serious this was. I sucked in a slow breath. "No. But we're still keeping it under wraps here and limiting this…" I waved a hand between us. "To the weekend."

"And when we return to the city?"

"I won't want to continue this. It's risky here, but idiotic there."

"Then maybe eating by ourselves isn't the smartest thing." He motioned to my plate. "Are you done yet?"

I nodded and plucked one of the fries, dipped the end in ketchup, and sucked seductively. "I'm still hungry, just for something else."

His eyes went wide. "Are you trying to kill me, girl? I'm going to need a minute."

I slid to the side and looked down at the bulge in his shorts, proud that I could cause that reaction so quickly. "Hands in your pockets might work."

He pushed the plate away. Looking into my eyes, he licked his lips. "I think I'd like to eat in my suite." His smile broadened. "And something that's not on the room service menu."

Liquid heat drenched my core as I pressed my thighs together. Yes, two could play this game.

He closed his eyes, taking several deep breaths.

"What are you doing?"

"Thinking about baseball."

I laughed. "Does that work?"

"Usually."

A minute or two later, Travis opened his eyes and scarfed down another two fries. "Ready?"

"First I want you to stroll over that way." I nodded to the right.

"Why?" He was clearly surprised that I would turn down his proposal for some naked fun.

I was almost as surprised myself after the night we'd shared, but I had to know something. "I want you to tell me everything you notice about the redhead in the yellow bikini." I left out the word *thong*.

He shrugged, then stood. Snaking both hands into his pockets did a reasonable job of obscuring his arousal. I watched him walk over and back, glancing at the girl and then returning his eyes to me—intense eyes, hungry eyes.

He retook his seat. "Her roots say she's really a brunette, and she has two moles on her back. Is that what you wanted to know?"

"And?" I fished.

The corners of his mouth turned up and amusement danced in his eyes. "You're jealous," he accused.

"No," I objected. "Well, maybe a little. You didn't notice her—"

"Dental-floss thong?" he finished for me.

I nodded.

"She's trying awfully hard, but to answer your rather obvious question, I couldn't care less." He placed his hand on mine.

The heat scorched my skin as desire skittered through me.

"Because even though she objects to the characterization, my woman is positively gorgeous."

I gulped. His words warmed me from the inside out. For the weekend, I was his woman.

"If you're feeling insecure," he said with a lifted brow, "I could buy you a suit like that."

"No way." Wearing something that daring was the real recipe for making me insecure. I opened the vinyl portfolio with the tab for the meal.

"I've got this." Travis took it and wrote down his room number, dropping a twenty inside for an additional tip.

After he stood, I grabbed the holder back. "No way, Mr. Big Shot. I ordered for me and my brother, so I pay." I scratched out his room number and substituted mine.

"What's the big deal?"

"I don't want your money. I pay my own way." That had always been a point of pride with me. "It's the way I was raised."

He shrugged at my explanation. "Sunshine, you are…"

"Aggravating," I finished for him.

"I was going to say *different*."

From the tabloid pictures of the jewelry and clothes the women he'd dated wore, their expensive tastes had been pretty obvious. I imagined he'd probably been used by those women as a meal ticket to indulge their tastes more often than not.

A minute later, he was holding my hand and towing me into the elevator. "I don't think we need to mingle for a while, do you?"

"Do you have a better idea?" I teased as he punched the button for the top floor.

My answer came in the form of a kiss that started as soon as the elevator doors closed.

I'd misjudged him, and he me. Now it was time to go bold or go home. Threading my fingers through his hair, I pulled him close. Monday would come soon enough, and I planned on making the most of this weekend.

CHAPTER 45

Travis

On Saturday, to avoid being seen together, Adriana and I went to lunch at a hole-in-the-wall restaurant on the other side of the island. That had been followed by some time at a beach as far away from the wedding venue as we could find. And now we'd just finished the walk-through of tomorrow's ceremony.

"Thank you, Trav," Adriana said as she pulled her arm from mine at the end of the aisle and walked ahead across the lawn where the ceremony would take place.

The guests were arriving this afternoon, and this evening would require mingling with the wedding party while ignoring each other, according to Adriana's rules.

I hung back a few paces from the woman of my desires as we returned to the resort. Adriana wanted to avoid PDA, but that was not going to keep me from admiring the way her ass swayed and how nice her legs looked—legs I could still remember wrapped around me.

"This is just like when we were here," Chelsea's mother mused, pulling me back to the present. "The ceremony is going to be lovely."

"Positively lovely," I agreed only half paying attention. As much as I tried to avoid it, my eyes drifted back to Adriana again and again.

Chelsea's mother decided I wasn't a worthy conversation partner and targeted Spencer's dad. The retired admiral gave her a one-word answer, even shorter than my two words.

The rehearsal dinner was next, and my self-control would be tested. Chelsea had assigned us seats, and as best man, mine was right next to Adriana's.

"Do we all get to call you Trav now?" Ed Thorpe asked as I slowed, gesturing toward Adriana.

"She does it to annoy me. I gave up correcting her."

"Should I call you Trav too?" he joked.

I scowled at him. "Try it."

"Yeah, maybe not," he said before slinking off.

Trav. Adriana had shortened my name several times today, and from her lips, I kinda liked it. Before her, only one person in my adult life had used anything but my full name. It came with keeping people at a distance and being powerful in the city.

Okay, maybe it was also because of the article that had been written about that poor schmuck, Orrie Varr. He'd called me Trav. And the article had detailed the fact that I'd purchased the company he worked for and subsequently fired him for that offense.

It wasn't exactly true, but I didn't object because it gave me leverage in negotiations. I was that scary fucker you didn't cross. What nobody else knew was that I'd fired him because he tried to blackmail me over a picture he'd taken of me and a partially undressed girlfriend in the park. Vanessa, the girl in question, was an aide to the mayor, and she could have lost her job if I hadn't dealt with the weasel.

As we reached the dining area, hunger got the crowd seated quickly.

Every few seconds, I caught a whiff of the lemony scent in Adriana's hair and wished I could pull her closer and bury my hands in it, my nose in it.

Suddenly, the annoying clicking of shutters came from behind us, and I turned—fucking paparazzi. It took me a second to locate the two maggots and shoot them the finger.

Chelsea saw them too. "Can't we do anything about them? This is a private party."

I shook my head. Having dealt with generous doses of this in the city, I knew the answer to that.

"Just ignore them," Spencer said. "Since we're outdoors, there's nothing we can do."

"I'm not giving in to them. No one is robbing us of this splendid weather and view," Chelsea added. "They're not chasing us away."

Adriana just sighed.

"Pretty nice island, huh?" Harry leaned around me to ask Adriana.

"Very nice. I definitely don't miss the snow and the slush," she answered sweetly. "Too bad it's only a few days."

"It's nice," I agreed. "But I think I'd miss the bustle of the city after a while."

"You mean, your office?" Ed laughed. "Cuz you're a workaholic. I bet you spent the day in your room working."

I picked up my glass. "The work doesn't do itself."

He laughed. "See? That's what I'm talking about. You need to loosen up, Carlyle, and have a little fun. This is a party."

"I agree," Wendy said from across the table. "The best man should have some fun." She added a wink. "He might even find someone to have fun with."

Adriana leaned ever so slightly into me and coughed. "You, a workaholic?" she asked with mock horror. "I can't imagine that." This from the same woman who'd already accused me of being too work-focused.

Wendy batted her eyelashes. "It sounds like you need a fun coach."

"Yeah, Trav," Adriana chimed in. "You should try a fun coach. I can't think of anything better."

"I'll help," Wendy offered.

I ignored her, rolling my eyes until she looked away.

The dinner went by with agonizing slowness. I was next to my girl, but couldn't act like it. I caught her scent, listened to her interact with the others, and enjoyed her laughter, but I couldn't touch her or drag her away to some-place dark. It was torture, so close and yet so far.

A fork clinked against a glass several times.

I followed Adriana's gaze to Spencer as he lifted his drink and announced, "To a new life together."

The table joined him in the salute to Chelsea.

After the sip, I kept my glass high. "To making new friendships." I meant it for Adriana, but Wendy shot me a devious grin as the group repeated the toast.

A few other toasts followed before the conversations broke off into small groups, the lively chatter lubricated by champagne.

I kept quiet and focused on my thigh against Adriana's as she chatted with Chelsea.

"What do you say, Travis?" Wendy asked, drawing my eyes away from Chelsea and Adriana.

"Pardon?" I had no idea what she'd asked.

"Dancing tonight?" Wendy clarified. "Harry says there's a rocking club just down the street."

"Um… Maybe not. I have to check back with the office."

Ed pointed his fork at me. "See? Workaholic."

"Andy, what about you?" Harry asked.

"I have to hang out with my brother," she answered.

Harry looked less than pleased. He hadn't planned on a protective brother being a part of the equation. He also didn't know I wasn't letting him anywhere near my girl.

Moments later, the horde of waiters returned to swap our dinner plates for desserts, which were announced as rum cake with chocolate syrup.

Before I could start on it, my phone rang with the *Jaws* music.

Adriana's eyes snapped to mine. "Let it go to voicemail."

"I can't." That was the awful truth of the matter. I was trapped.

"Yes, you can, and you should," Adriana said as I rose to take the call.

"Yes, Dad. What is it?" I answered.

"See?" Ed remarked as I stepped away from the table. "His father has him on a short leash."

"I've emailed you some material," Dad said. "We need to talk about it. Call me back just as soon as you've gotten it."

As I headed for my room, I noticed Sergio at the bar, watching the table I'd just left.

He lifted his beer bottle in salute.

I waved, and curiosity got the better of me. I had to find out why he was here. "What happened to you and Iris?"

He put down the bottle and checked his watch. "Meeting her at the casino." He focused on the watch and scrunched up his face. "In twenty minutes."

I grinned. "Good luck tonight."

"Yeah. Her parents' flight got canceled on account of the storm, so her room is all ours tonight."

"Cool." I slapped him on the shoulder. "Enjoy."

He slid off the stool. "That Wendy chick has the hots for ya. I can see it." He nodded toward the dinner table. He had been watching us.

I looked back toward the table, but at Adriana, not Wendy. "You think so?"

"Oh yeah. She's a sure thing." He laid a hand on my shoulder. "You get this for me?"

I nodded, but only because he was Adriana's brother. Luca sucked too, but at least he had an excuse. He wasn't my full brother.

"Tap that tonight, man," Sergio said, looking again at Wendy. Then he was gone. Instead of heading for the lobby door, he turned down toward the rehearsal dinner.

I watched him have a few words with Adriana. She pulled her purse off the floor. He was shaking down his sister for more money—a total sleazeball.

It took the bartender all of about ten seconds to realize she'd been stiffed. "Where'd he go?"

"I got it." I pulled out a twenty and laid it down. "Keep the change." Then I headed up to my suite to deal with Dad.

CHAPTER 46

Adriana

As soon as Serg said he'd be spending the night at Iris's hotel, I gladly handed over my last two hundred to keep him away. "That's all of it. Seriously, I don't have any more."

"I won't be back tonight, so you have this place…" He nodded toward the building. "To yourself, if you wanna, ya know…"

I nodded. "Thanks."

"Yeah." He grinned. "Don't stay up worrying about me."

I'd long ago stopped worrying about where my brother might be when he didn't come home, and he knew it.

After Serg left, Harry had a glint in his eyes that I definitely didn't want to see. He'd heard the entire conversation.

Until my Harry repellent, Travis, returned, I'd have to be on guard.

After the dinner, the group was standing around talking. Most, like me, had a glass of champagne in their hand.

"What happened to Travis?" Chelsea asked. Spencer stood close with his arm around her waist.

"Work, I guess." I shrugged and looked around. I wasn't faking it. I didn't know.

Spencer nodded. "His dad is one hell of a taskmaster."

I took that in and looked out over the beach. I felt sorry for Travis. He shouldn't have to put up with his father interrupting the weekend. We were here in paradise, on a scheduled wedding trip, with Travis as an integral member of the wedding party. His father should have been able to wait until Monday, and Travis should have been able to demand it as well.

I wandered away from the group to visit the bathroom.

"Hey there, Andy Pandy. We need to talk."

God, I hated that name. "Get lost, Harry." I shifted to the left.

He blocked me. "I can help with your money troubles. How about a thousand?"

I knew I should've taken the conversation with my brother away from the table. Gritting my teeth, I forced myself to stay civil for Chelsea's sake. "No thanks. I have a job. I earn my own money."

"A job like the Sugar Palace?"

I froze in place. Somehow he knew. "What do you want, Harry?"

The Sugar Palace was a gentleman's club. I'd worked there for a while to afford college. It was a seedy joint where none of the customers could be called gentlemen. I'd long ago put that period of my life in a box and locked it away.

Since it was in the Bronx, I'd never run into anyone who knew—until now.

A smug smile lit up his face. "Like I said, we should talk."

A couple approached, and I didn't speak until they had passed. "Not here."

He opened his arm toward the beach, and I strode off, looking for someplace private.

Chelsea waved as we passed them.

I waved back to her and continued toward the koi pond area, which appeared deserted. Reaching it, I spun. "You wanted to talk, so talk." I backed up a step when he got too close for comfort.

"We were good together. I think we were good together, don't you?"

If this was going to end up with him asking for a date, I was going to puke. "No, we weren't. That's why we broke up."

"That was a big misunderstanding," he insisted. He was delusional.

209

"I caught you with your tongue down Tammy Westinfield's throat and your hand up her skirt. That is not a misunderstanding."

"I agree that was a mistake."

"The mistake was going out with you in the first place," I gritted out, trying to keep my voice from rising to a yell.

He grabbed my wrist. "We're going dancing tonight. And then later…"

I pulled free. "No freaking way."

He grabbed me again.

"Let go." I tried to wrench free, but couldn't.

"After that, we'll see where things lead," he said, clearly not getting the message. "Make it two thousand."

I kicked at his shin but only grazed his leg. "Let go of me."

Travis appeared, running up behind Harry.

Harry didn't see him, his grip only tightening. "We're leaving together."

"Fuck you," I yelled, no longer worried about people hearing us.

"Let go of her," Travis bellowed.

Harry turned just in time for his face to meet Travis's fist. With the satisfying sound of a crunch, followed by a yelp, Harry let go of me and staggered backward. His hands went to the blood spurting from his nose. "You fucking broke my nose," he whimpered.

"That's just a start," Travis said, towering over Harry. "You come anywhere near her again, and it'll be much worse."

"Fuck you and the horse you rode in on," Harry said stupidly.

Travis wasn't amused. He punched Harry in the gut—hard.

The man doubled over, the breath leaving him on a whoosh. Stumbling backward, Harry fell into the koi pond. He surfaced, sputtering. "I'll tell them," he warned me.

Travis pointed a menacing finger at Harry. "No you won't, Hornblatt." Travis spit the name out like it was rotten fish. He put an arm around me. "She's mine, and I protect what's mine. You say anything, you do anything, and you'll be attacking me. You are never going to come near her again, or even utter her name. Try it, Hornblatt, and it'll be the last thing you do." The frost in his voice sent a chill through me. He meant it.

Harry went pale. "But she's just a…" No more words came out.

Travis turned to leave and pulled me with him, his arm around my waist. This was the second time he'd gone crazy when another man put his hands on me, and the second time I'd felt safe with him.

Halfway up the path, a man held a camera with a gigantic lens. I hadn't noticed him earlier.

"I got a super shot, who's the girl?" Camera Guy asked.

Just great. I'd never had an opinion on paparazzi until today. Now I hated them. There were going to be freaking pictures of this splattered across the internet. Momma would be horrified.

"None of your business," Travis said, towing me past the man.

"Got a quote for me?" Camera Guy asked, following us.

Travis ignored him.

"Why'd you do it? Did he threaten to out you?" Camera Guy asked Travis, without realizing how close to the truth he was, just about me. "Did he make a move on your girl? Did he insult your doll collection? I hear you have a nice one." Camera Guy followed us. "He must have deserved it."

I felt Travis stiffen.

Travis stopped us and turned slowly. "He threatened and criminally assaulted my date," he growled. The tone of his voice scared even me.

Camera Guy stopped.

Travis had just told a paparazzo I was his date, and there was no way to put that genie back in the bottle.

Daddy would shit a brick if he saw that comment in the press. Lucky for me my father had no time for *"that kind of crap."* But there was no guarantee someone wouldn't tell him or show him.

"I neutralized the threat." Travis scowled. "If you have any more questions for us, I can arrange for you to join him in the pond."

"Totally justified," Camera Guy squeaked as he backed away. He probably regretted angering Travis with that doll collection bullshit.

"I'll get you," Harry yelled after us as he climbed out of the fishpond.

His anger hit me like a punch to the gut, because he could hurt me with what he knew.

"Ignore him," Travis said, leading me away.

Travis's words didn't help, but clinging to his arm gave me strength. I did my best to compose myself for questions from the other guests, questions I didn't want to answer.

"I've had enough of tonight's party," Travis announced.

"Me, too," I agreed. Avoiding the other guests was one way of avoiding their inevitable questions.

"Our room?" he suggested. Of course, he meant his suite, as if after last night it was our room for the length of our stay here.

"Perfect, if I can order a chocolate sundae from room service." Tonight's shitstorm deserved some ice cream therapy, and I wanted to be behind a door, far away from Harry.

"Sure can." He turned us away from the dinner crowd and toward the building.

As we rounded shrubbery and were finally shielded from the dinner area, I snuggled against Travis. My blood sizzled with the excitement of being alone with him again behind closed doors. "That's not all I want..." I added a taste of sultry to my voice.

He nuzzled my hair as we walked. "Gorgeous, if you want more, you only have to ask for it. There's just one rule."

"Rules are no fun," I joked.

"You have to get past your schoolteacher's vocabulary and learn some dirty talk so you can tell me exactly what you need."

I shivered against him at the thought. Prudish me didn't talk during sex.

"Cold?" he asked.

"No." I tried on my new persona as his dirty-talking date. "I'm horny and thinking of all the ways you can fuck me."

He walked us faster. "Now that's my girl."

CHAPTER 47

Travis

Seeing Hornblatt's hands on my Adriana had made my blood boil. Sure, I'd broken his nose, but that had been me holding back from what I really wanted to do to him. She was mine. Should I have said it out loud? No. But that couldn't be undone now.

I towed my woman along the hallway toward the suite. It had been sheer torture to be next to her this evening and not be able to touch her, dance with her, or kiss her. She insisted on this hiding shit, but it sure sucked.

If I didn't have her in the next three minutes, I was going to lose my goddamn mind. At the suite, I searched my pocket and finally found the key card.

With a beep, the door unlocked, and Adriana eagerly pushed inside. I kicked the door closed behind us, and she became a wildcat, attacking the buttons of my shirt and then starting on hers.

For my part, I fumbled with my wallet and finally found the condom. In a quick minute, we had each other's clothes off, and I tossed her onto the bed.

She bounced with a giggle. She licked her lips and eyed my erection as I stroked myself. "I haven't been able to think of anything all night except this."

"Me either."

With parted lips and hungry eyes, she watched as I rolled the latex down.

"You want this, don't you, gorgeous?"

"Fuck yes, Trav. I need you."

"Tell me more, gorgeous. Tell me what you want."

She spread her legs. "I want you to fuck me senseless with that dragon cock of yours."

"Dragon cock?" I liked the sound of that.

"I like it better than elephant dick."

"Me too." Climbing up, I dragged the head of the *dragon cock* through her wetness. My breath caught with the anticipation of entering her.

"Give it to me, Trav," she pleaded, hooking her ankles behind me and pulling me close.

I slid inside. Glorious hot, tight wetness enveloped me as I pushed in deep.

"You fit me so well," she panted as she arched into me.

"Yeah." It was true. We connected as one. It was a feeling I hadn't had with a woman before. I savored the connection of being in her, caught up in the rhythm, our gazes locked. In the past I'd avoided long eye contact with my partners.

She held me tight and whimpered with each thrust. "More." She clawed my back. "Harder, Trav, harder."

As I followed her instructions, I felt myself losing control. I went deeper, meeting her with each piston of my hips. It was primal, grunting and moaning as flesh slid through flesh, both of us sating a primitive need to connect.

She raked her nails down my back, urging me on.

I was getting close, too close. I slid a hand between us to finger her clit. "Come for me, gorgeous. Come for me."

She trembled under me as I worked her sensitive nub. "I'm almost…" Before she could finish the words, her inner muscles clenched around my cock and she let out a cry. She shuddered under me, her legs spreading wider as she held on for dear life.

Her orgasm broke my last thread of control as my balls drew up and my climax let loose. I pushed in deep and held as I spilled my load inside her.

This woman was just right for me and too much all at the same time. She'd taken over my thoughts, and it wouldn't be easy to give her what she said she wanted and walk away after this short wedding trip.

I'd have to start a new negotiation with my little temptress, one that involved us being a couple when we returned to the city.

CHAPTER 48

*A*DRIANA

W*HEN THE CONTRACTIONS OF MY CLIMAX PASSED AND THE TELLTALE PULSES OF* Travis's cock inside me subsided, he rolled off to the side.

We panted as he stroked lazy circles around my nipple. His eyes locked with mine, sending a nonverbal message I understood all too well. I would miss this too when we got back home and couldn't be together.

A minute later, he rose. Yes, I'd miss this, and I had to brand every minute with him into my memory to savor later. I watched him in the dim light as he walked to the bathroom to dispose of the condom. God, the man had a magnificent ass. When he returned, I lifted up on one elbow to watch again and giggled. His still semi-erect cock swung side to side with his steps. It was a legit big, swinging dick, the real deal.

"What's so funny?" he asked from the side of the bed.

"Nothing. I just like looking at you…" I made a little back-and-forth motion with my finger.

He grinned. "You mean this?" He swiveled his hips, making his cock strike one hip bone and then the other.

I couldn't help but laugh. "Yeah."

"Get used to it, gorgeous. If you like it, I'll be doing it a lot."

"I'll try." He was such a sight to behold. I doubted I'd have time to get used to it, at least in the little time we had. That wasn't a cheery thought.

He slid back into bed, and I snuggled close, laid my head on his shoulder, and swung a leg over his thigh, basking in the feel of my skin against his. We'd been physically coupled, and now, in my postorgasmic glow, I felt equally emotionally connected to him.

He lifted the clunky phone from the nightstand and dialed. "Hi, do you have ice cream sundaes? That's good. I'd like two chocolate sundaes... Room eight-oh-four." He listened, then looked at me. "Nuts?"

I nodded vigorously.

"Yes. The works on both... Thank you." After hanging up, he said, "Ten minutes. You'd better get dressed."

"Why?" I complained. "I like it right here." I pulled myself harder against him.

"Because," he insisted. "We are not eating ice cream in bed." He wrapped his arm around me. "You get five minutes of snuggle time."

"Snuggling not manly enough for you?" I teased.

"I'll have you know, I'm a champion snuggler when the time is right, but we are still not eating ice cream in the damned bed."

I accepted my five minutes as a win and closed my eyes. As I breathed him in, I concentrated on the way our bodies felt against each other. I was tempted to grab his cock, but decided against it since I didn't need him giving room service a show when he answered the door.

When the knock came, I stayed in the bedroom.

Travis turned on the lights in the other room and allowed the desserts in.

I waited until I heard the door to the hallway close.

His eyes bugged out when I joined him in the main room in my birthday suit. "I said dressed."

"I think you're overdressed." The sundaes sat on a tray on the glass table, so I took one of the chairs and lifted a spoon. "Well?"

He stepped out of his pants, and I got another swinging-dick display as he strode past me to close the curtains. I'd seen a couple eating naked at a glass table in a movie and always thought it would be hot to do it in real life.

When he returned, he took his seat on the other side of the table. "You're a naughty girl, and I like it."

I started by spooning some of the chocolate syrup from the side of my dish. "That's a good thing, right?" I had to work up to the questions that had been gnawing at me since the incident with Harry.

A broad smile grew across his face. "A very good thing."

Yes, sir, eating ice cream across a glass table with the lights full on did qualify as naughty.

I licked the chocolate and waded into the subject. "You threatened Harry."

"Damned straight. He threatened you. I couldn't let that stand."

I swallowed before continuing. "But you said you'd kill him."

He lifted a spoonful of ice cream. "Your point?"

"Did you mean it?"

He put the spoon into his mouth and licked it clean, making me wait for the answer. "I don't mess around, and half-hearted threats don't get results."

I looked down at my suddenly restless leg under the table, unsure what to do with the unease I felt at his dangerous answer. "For me?" In one week, he'd threatened both Simon and Harry to keep me safe. Nobody had ever come to my defense like that, and I hadn't thought a man like him existed— dangerous and protective of someone like me.

"Look at me," he commanded as he held his hand out across the table.

I rested my hand in his and raised my eyes to meet his cold ones. "Nobody gets away with putting a hand on you. Nobody, not a dirty, low-life scuzzball like your ex, or a rich, entitled scuzzball like Harry."

How was I worth that kind of defense? "But—"

"No buts. Firm rule. Nobody lays a hand on you, period." The possessiveness in his tone was both chilling and sexy hot.

"I was going to say I can handle myself."

He ate another spoonful. "Of course you can, but that doesn't mean I'll stand idly by if some moron steps out of line with my girl."

There it was again, that possessiveness in his answer. "Thank you. I appreciate it." I dug into my sundae to keep from talking. I wasn't going to rehash our argument about how long I'd keep that title.

He raised his spoon after swallowing. "My turn with a question."

I nodded.

"What was Harry threatening to tell people?"

I should have expected the question. Knowing him, I wasn't going to be able to avoid it, so it was time to face this music, even if it got me booted out of here. It was part of my past, and something I'd had to do. I couldn't change that now.

I twisted my bowl around, nervous about how he would react. "I don't come from a rich family, and NYU is expensive. I took out loans, but even that didn't cover everything, so I had a job to make ends meet."

Travis nodded. "With his family money, I can see that Harry wouldn't understand working for a living, but it's not something to be ashamed of."

I twisted the bowl again. "I worked at the Sugar Palace."

He shrugged. "I don't know the place."

Swallowing hard, I explained. "The polite term for it is a gentleman's club. Otherwise known as a strip club."

He didn't say anything.

I had to get it all out and learn my fate. "I was a dancer, and our customers weren't gentlemen."

"That must have been hard." His eyes filled with concern.

I nodded. "Hard doesn't begin to describe it. Every dance was demeaning. Some of the girls enjoyed the power it gave them over the men, and some had become numb. I guess because they figured it was the life they'd been born into. For me, it was the only way to pay rent."

He nodded. "You don't have to say any more."

Would I lose him over this? If I hadn't been across the table from him, I would have melted against him and accepted the out. But to be honest with him, I had to continue. "I hated every minute of it." I shook from the memories. "Guys would assume that they could get a blow job for an extra fifty. It was that kind of place." I lowered my head and wished I had some mouthwash to rinse away the vile taste that covered my tongue. "Sometimes that fifty would have solved my empty fridge problem." I took a breath. "Now you know what I am."

He reached across the table to lift my chin. "But you didn't take the fifty."

"No." I gave the slightest shake of my head. "My daddy didn't raise that kind of girl." The other girls had made it seem like the simple solution to money problems. I closed my eyes, remembering how hard those days had been. "But once a stripper, always a stripper, and that's something my parents can never find out."

"Look at me. That experience doesn't define who you are. It only proves that you're a survivor."

I could see he didn't get it. "If it gets out, I could lose my job—not to mention that it would kill my parents."

"It won't get out," he assured me.

"And how would you like Monday's headline to be *Billionaire Caught with Stripper?*"

"Ex-stripper," he corrected with a laugh.

"It's not funny. If I don't go to dinner with Harry, he'll yell it from the rooftops. That's a label I can't ever lose. It can't be undone."

"He won't."

"You don't know Harry. He'll take it to the school himself to get back at me if I refuse."

"I know him well enough to know that I have the upper hand. His dad wants an investment from our company. I'll make it clear again that messing with you is messing with me, and I can pull that investment if I want to. And I'll tell his dad why. His father would cut him off quicker than a hangnail if he screwed up the deal, and Harry knows that."

I shook my head. I couldn't be sure that was enough leverage. "I have to agree to the dinner."

"And when he wants more? What then? You didn't prostitute yourself to put food on the table, and you sure shouldn't now. The only way to deal with a blackmailer is to put a loaded gun to his head."

That was another reference to killing Harry, and Travis delivered it with a stone-cold voice. "You wouldn't."

"I'll do anything to protect you."

That was both the scariest and hottest thing anyone had ever said to me. I stood.

"You haven't finished," he pointed out before scooping another spoonful into his mouth.

"I thought it was what I needed, but I was wrong." I rounded the table to him.

"If not this," he said, putting his spoon down, "then what do you need?"

I took his hand and pulled. "You."

CHAPTER 49

Travis

Sunday morning had dawned bright with a clear, blue sky that promised perfect weather for the wedding. Adriana had gushed about how this setting was the perfect place to celebrate Spencer and Chelsea finding each other.

But while the officiant spoke, I zoned out, my eyes fixed on the woman who had occupied my thoughts continuously since that damned engagement party. Hours of hot sex with her all weekend long had done nothing to dull my attraction.

Adriana was cute, the way she glanced over and mouthed for me to *cut it out*. It was just like her to want this ceremony to be perfect for her best friend.

Of course that only made me focus more intently on her as the officiant droned on. If I ever had a wedding, I'd make sure to have an officiant with less to say.

As the couple exchanged their vows, Adriana shed tears of joy for her best friend. The rings were placed, and applause broke out after Spencer dipped Chelsea extremely low for the requisite you-may-kiss-the-bride moment.

The photographers darted around taking pictures as the new Mr. and Mrs. MacMillan walked slowly back up the aisle. A moment later, it was our turn to follow, and I held out my arm for the maid of honor.

Adriana played her part well. She reluctantly placed her arm in mine, as we'd rehearsed, but kept her smile wide and bright. She still wanted to look the part of being the not-date, and I obliged—for now.

We had one more night together, and in my book, the sooner we could get back to the room, the better.

One of the photographers split off from the wedding couple and clicked away, focused on us as we walked the length of the aisle. When we reached the end, the photographer left us and moved to Wendy and Ed behind us.

Adriana pulled away and rushed to embrace Chelsea. She was quickly swept away in the crowd of well-wishers as I stood back. After that, I could only admire her from afar.

At the reception, I mingled, not too close and not too far from her. The conversations were boring, but I played my part.

When it was time for dinner, we sat at the separate tables we'd been assigned, and all I could do was choose a seat that faced hers. She did the same, and we exchanged glances when we thought nobody would notice.

Every time I got a coy smile from her, it went straight to my groin. I'd been cataloging her smiles this weekend, to savor after I had to give her up. As I cut through the chicken on my plate, I wondered if there was another parcel the Carlyle Heights Group could buy in Queens that would mean we could work together again. I couldn't come up with one.

As I gave my speech, I stepped to the side so my view of the newlyweds also had me looking directly toward Adriana. It was all I could do, and clearly not enough for the woman who had bewitched me for the last several days.

One thing was clear. We had to talk about continuing this past the weekend. I was not done with her yet.

CHAPTER 50

Adriana

When the toasts began, I was so captivated by Travis's voice that everything around me disappeared into mist. It wasn't just that he was eloquent; it was the smooth baritone of his voice that caressed me like a warm shower.

I was going to seem like a klutz by comparison. We all raised our glasses when he finished, and I got lost in his eyes as he tipped his champagne flute in my direction. After a sip, I checked my notecards. I was going to have to up my game. My turn wasn't until after the father of the bride.

But that came soon enough.

Before I could begin, Travis stood and introduced me as the positively gorgeous maid of honor and longtime friend of the couple.

His words froze me in place. Well, that and his eyes glued on me. With butterflies in my stomach, I pulled out my index cards and got down to business. "I met Chelsea…"

Travis's encouraging smile every time I looked in his direction helped me get through my speech without stumbling, but not without crying. I was truly happy for Spencer and Chelsea.

Chelsea looked back at me with equally teary eyes and nodded.

I wrapped up with, "I only wish that when it comes to be our turn, each of us gets as lucky in love as you two." As the crowd clapped, I couldn't stop my eyes from drifting toward Travis.

His eyes were fixed on me, but there was something in his expression I couldn't read. Did he want me as badly as I wanted him, or was the playboy in him put off by my gushy proclamation?

Then I admonished myself silently. Those were thoughts and questions I shouldn't have ventured anywhere near. We were a weekend fling, nothing more. I picked up my champagne. "May you always show us how wonderful love can be." I raised the glass high. "By having five children."

Chelsea's eyes went superwide as the crowd laughed and everyone tossed back their bubbly.

Later, when the dancing started, I searched for Travis and spied him across the room, talking with a group of men. I recognized a few of them—a state senator, an actor, and several important businessmen who had children at my school. It was a powerful group, all of them wanting a minute of Travis's time. He'd been mobbed like this during the cocktail hour before dinner as well. It was then that I'd realized my weekend fling was probably the most powerful man at this gathering.

When Travis glanced my way, I tugged my chin toward the dance floor as inconspicuously as I could. He nodded, held up a finger, and smiled. The most powerful man here wanted me. It was a giddy feeling.

Then Wendy sauntered up, brushing her breast against his arm and whispering into his ear. My mood shifted instantly. I took a step forward, but then thought better of it. I'd been the one to insist on secrecy.

Travis shook his head at her and went back to talking to the man on his left. Yet Wendy was undeterred, not moving away. Resisting the insane urge to march over there and claim my man, I looked away. It was the only way to keep from getting an aneurysm. God, I hated that woman.

I fidgeted during my wait for Travis to extricate himself from the group. I desperately wanted his hands on me again, and a dance was the only way to pull it off in public.

Then Ed's voice startled me from behind. "Would you honor me with a dance?"

I turned. "I think tradition says I'm supposed to dance with the best man. My feet are killing me, and I don't think I can manage two dances."

"Then ditch the shoes," Ed suggested.

A quick check showed a lot of the women were already dancing barefoot. Out of polite options, I slipped out of my heels. "Okay, if we make it quick."

"In my experience, girls like it long and slow," Ed said with a wink. "At least with me."

I laughed and let him lead me onto the dance floor. At least without my heels I didn't tower over him.

I only wanted Travis touching me, but I tolerated Ed's respectful hand on my hip. He wasn't trying to pull me close and paw me like Harry was with his dance partner.

As we turned, Travis materialized behind Ed. "I believe this is my dance."

Ed must not have seen the determination on Travis's face. "You can have the next one."

Travis put a hand on Ed's shoulder, towering over him. "I said, I believe this is my dance." The words may have been polite, but his tone told a different story.

When Ed looked up to see the warning scowl on Travis's face, he got the message. "Sure thing."

"You didn't have to be mean about it," I said as I settled into Travis's arms.

"I wasn't mean," he argued.

"What would you call it?"

"Direct. I hated seeing another man's hands on you, and I wanted to be clear."

I found I actually liked his show of jealousy from the leader of the pack. "I only have eyes for you," I whispered, snuggling close. "Now that you've got me, what are you going to do with me?"

The music changed to a sensual slow song, and the dance floor became more crowded.

Travis maneuvered us into the middle of the crowd and pulled me closer. As we swayed to the music, all I could think of was how quickly we could remove the fabric between us. "How much longer do you think we need to stay to be polite?"

"Another hour maybe," he answered. "We best cut this short for now." When the song ended, we went in opposite directions.

I sought out Chelsea and Spencer to congratulate them again. On the way, I had to steer around a group that included Harry. As I passed, he left the group to follow me. I changed direction to find the restrooms.

Half an hour later, the slimy bastard's voice assaulted me from behind. "Three thousand."

I spun, preparing to kick him in the balls. "I told you, I have a job, and I'm not interested in any money for anything for any reason from you."

"Are you sure you'll have a job when you get back?"

My mouth dropped open at his audacity. "If you say anything, so help me God, I will hunt you down and cut off your tiny balls," I threatened. Travis had said threats needed to be dramatic.

"Call me if you change your mind after you get back."

I lifted my middle finger. Nothing could possibly make me change my mind about him. "Watch your back, Harry."

He laughed. "You don't scare me, little girl."

Travis suddenly appeared behind Harry. "If not her, what about me, asshole?"

Harry spun and backed up quickly. He tripped over my outstretched foot, landing on his ass. "You're going to hear from my lawyers," he whimpered as he scampered away.

As I followed the sound of the continuing shutter clicks, I found Camera Guy once again nearby.

"Are you okay?" Travis asked, pulling me away.

I nodded. "Ignore him. He's just an insecure little prick."

Travis breathed into my ear. "Who cares about polite? I've had enough of this party."

"Me too."

Without giving me the kiss I craved, Travis left.

Our agreement was for me to wait five minutes before going up to the room—the longest five minutes of my life.

CHAPTER 51

Travis

Adriana's sweet ass wiggling against my morning wood woke me. Sunlight beaming in through the crack in the curtains we hadn't quite closed reminded me our time together was over. "Good morning, gorgeous." I slid my hand up her midsection to cup her breast.

"And it was a good night too." She purred as I circled a nipple and tweaked it. She turned toward me. "I have to get up so I can get to the airport on time."

I looked over at the clock. "You have plenty of time."

"No, but I have just enough." A moment later, she scooted down under the sheets, grasping my cock.

"You're insatiable." I'd been lucky enough to find a woman whose appetite matched mine.

She pumped her fist on me a few times and licked the head of my cock. "Are you complaining?"

I sucked in a breath. "Not one little bit." I shifted to the side so I could reach her breast.

"I want to remember what you taste like," she said from under the sheets. "Maybe you want to watch?" She pulled the sheets off and wrapped her lips around my cock, looking up at me.

Hell yeah, I wanted to watch. Every guy's fantasy was to watch his woman taking him in her mouth.

She sucked me deep. Fuck, this was something else. Her hand joined the action as she sucked and licked and hummed. The vibrations... Damn, it was as if she was worshiping my cock. She took me deeper, and I felt the back of her throat as she kept sucking and pumping me with her fist. She swirled her tongue over my tip every time she pulled away.

I groaned. "I'm not going to last."

She pulled her mouth away and pumped me harder and faster. "Come for me, Trav. I want to watch."

CHAPTER 52

ADRIANA

I PUMPED HIM HARDER, WATCHING THE STRAIN ON HIS FACE, THE WAY HIS ENTIRE body tensed.

Without warning, he jerked me away and pinned me down on the bed. "That's not the way we're going to end our time together, gorgeous. I'll come, but it'll be with you screaming my name and wishing we had another week here."

I wasn't going to get to watch him, but I had gotten a taste of him to remember. "I already wish we had more time."

He moved down and sucked my nipple into his mouth, releasing with a pop. "You know, we could stay longer."

"Maybe a master of the universe like you can make your own schedule, but I have to teach." This was the way the world worked. There were the bosses who made their own rules, and then the rest of us who had to live by a million rules.

"You'd have plenty of time if you flew with me."

"No thanks. Chelsea has finely tuned radar. We wouldn't last half the flight without her figuring out what we've been doing in our spare time." I pulled his head up and took him in a kiss. "Find a condom and get busy. We really don't have any time."

He turned over to pull a condom from the nightstand and started rolling it on.

"I want you to fuck me with that big dragon dick of yours." I'd learned that dirty talk really got him revved up.

He rolled it on faster.

I spread my legs, and he positioned himself over me. "Now fuck me hard with that dragon dick. Like you mean it."

He teased me by running the head of that magnificent cock along my slit.

"Give it to me hard and fast, Mr. Bossman." He was still moving too slowly.

I moaned when he pushed in swiftly, all the way. This is what I needed, what I craved, and what I wished I could continue getting from him.

He began to thrust. "You're so wet for me, gorgeous. So fucking tight. So fucking wonderful."

I urged him on with more dirty talk, telling him to not hold back, to go faster, to go harder, to give me all of the dragon cock. I locked my ankles behind him and rocked up, angling just right to meet his heavy thrusts and get that delicious friction on my clit. The pressure built quickly toward an orgasm that was likely to rip me apart.

"You like it hard, don't you, gorgeous?"

With all the intense sensations, I couldn't manage a response longer than, *more*.

"I can feel you getting close," he growled. The way the cords of his neck stood out and all his muscles were tensed, he had to be close too.

A nod between panted breaths was all I could manage as my blood sang and my core tightened around him.

He took one of my nipples in a hard suck as he moved his hand between us to find my swollen clit.

I was on a hair trigger, and two strokes were all it took to throw me over the edge. The orgasm ripped his name from my lips as I gripped his ass to pull him deeper. I was still convulsing around him, my legs shaking, when he thrust one last time, hard and deep. He stilled inside me, his whole body tense, and the throbs of his release began.

Eventually he collapsed onto me, sweaty and panting. I didn't care about the weight. At that moment, connected the way we were, I only had one care —that once I left for the airport, it would be over.

"My God, that was—"

"Incredible," I finished.

"Super incredible," he corrected as he shifted off my chest so I could breathe, or so he could cup my breast, or both.

"Can we stay here for just a minute?" I asked.

"As long as you want."

"You know something?"

His finger circled my nipple. "What?"

"When we first met, I thought you were so wicked that I listed you as Satan in my contacts."

"I know. You showed me your phone, remember?"

I'd forgotten about that. "I'm going to change it."

"To what? Voldemort?"

I giggled. "No, silly. Trav. Because I think you're actually a very nice guy."

"Please don't tell anyone. The mean rep helps me in my work."

CHAPTER 53

Adriana

On the flight back, I had the window seat. The morning sunshine above the clouds was bright and the air smooth, just like the weekend had been, a few days of fairy-tale opulence.

At the wedding, I got to pretend I could fit in with the upper crust. They tolerated me, probably because I was maid of honor to Chelsea and anything less would have affected the wedding. None of them dared get on the wrong side of Chelsea or her parents.

Serg wasn't on the flight with me this time, as he'd decided to stay another week so he could hang out with Blondie. A cheap motel away from the beach had been all he could afford, and he'd probably paid for it with money I'd given him and he'd squirreled away.

The smoothness of the flight ended when we began our descent through bumpy cloud cover. And beneath the clouds, the view was just as dingy and cold as it had been when we left New York. The plane shook as we touched down back at JFK. When the brakes threw me forward, it was a clear jolt back to reality.

My weekend fairy tale had ended. I'd boarded this flight, admittedly in first class, but still with the common folk. Travis had taken the newlyweds home on his father's corporate jet. Back at home, Carlyle would go his way and I'd go mine. End of story. Fairy tales were always short.

Even silently in my head, I couldn't say those words without tears threatening, but that too would pass.

When I turned my phone on after landing, I was bombarded with a half dozen missed calls and voicemails from my sister. I'd get to her later. First I needed my bag.

Once on the subway, a quick look around showed zero of the high-society crowd I'd spent the weekend with—not a single one-percenter in sight. I was back in my element. These were my people. The only thing keeping me from completely blending in was the suitcase I lugged with me. Nabbing a seat, I pulled out my phone for the unavoidable inquisition from my sister.

"Tell me about it," she demanded right off. "I'll bet it was perfect."

"Pretty much. Beautiful weather, beautiful beach, wonderful ceremony." And pretty spectacular indoor activities with Travis, but I wasn't offering that up.

"And banging the billionaire? How was that?"

"Uh, what are you talking about?" I tried.

"I saw the pictures. Hell, half of New York saw the pictures of your hot billionaire shoving an asshole in the water. The caption said you were his date."

I was busted. "For the weekend only. You told me to be daring. I just hope Momma didn't see it."

"She was visiting Aunt Louise, and I think I would have heard if she had. Don't worry. I won't bring it up. And the caption didn't give his name."

I blew out a long, relieved breath. "Thanks." The gossip rags were certainly already on to more current fare, and if at some point in the future it came up, I could honestly say I was not Travis Carlyle's anything, because I no longer was.

"Now, tell me. How was it banging a billionaire?"

"Jules, I'm on the train home. How about we not talk about this now?"

"I'm not letting you off the hook forever," she warned.

"Love you too. Bye."

On the walk from the train to my building, I turned the corner and saw Simon's friend Hugo pacing on the opposite side of the street.

He stomped in the cold and changed direction. That's when he spotted me and quickly looked away.

I continued down the street. His behavior was odd, but he was harmless, wasn't he? I'd never had a problem with him.

Out of breath from lugging my suitcase up the stairs, I inserted my key, but it didn't click the way it should have. The dead bolt was unlocked.

A grapefruit-sized lump lodged in my throat. I knew I'd locked it before I left.

CHAPTER 54

Travis

I LOOKED OUT MY WINDOW AS THE PLANE DESCENDED TOWARD TETERBORO. THE flight back with the Spencer and Chelsea, as well as the McAllisters, Evan and Alexa, had been long. Not that I normally considered a three-hour flight long, but because I was alone. I was the black sheep here, the oddball.

What the hell was happening to me? I wasn't ever allowed to feel sorry for myself. But in the pit of my stomach, I knew exactly what had come over me—Adriana Moreno was her name.

Without an internet connection, I'd been forced to watch the couples hold hands and whisper things to each other. The experience had scrambled my brain. I should have been looking forward to getting back to work, but a certain annoying woman kept hijacking my thoughts.

Rubbing my temples didn't help, at least not yet. A long run when I got home, plus a stiff drink followed by a check to see when Maren was getting back into town would probably work. That flight attendant could get into the most interesting positions.

I closed my eyes to remember our last time together. Two seconds later, I pictured a naked Adriana spread across my bed. I refocused, but no. Even trying to conjure up an image of Maren wasn't working. I could only wonder how long this spell of Adriana's would last.

Evan kissed the top of his wife's head. "Hey, Travis, when are you going to settle down?" he asked, as if he could read my preoccupation.

"The tenth of never." My standard response came out automatically. It was the one I'd used a few hundred times, but my delivery sounded off, even to me.

"Wendy Breton seemed pretty into you," Alexa teased.

I rolled my eyes. "Not my type."

A month ago, she probably would have been—good-looking, eager to get in bed. Unfortunately she was also the type to have a one-track mind. Make that a three-track mind—either shopping, vacationing, or looking at engagement rings.

Alexa's lips quirked up. "Maybe you need somebody more down to earth. Would a Queens girl be more your type?"

Internally I froze. Adriana wouldn't have said anything, so I must have been more transparent than I thought. I shrugged. "I've always stuck to Manhattan." It was historically true, and I'd agreed with Adriana's request to keep what we'd had together private.

"Manhattan women are all too plastic, if ya know what I mean." Alexa winked.

"Hey there," Chelsea complained.

"Present company excluded," Alexa corrected.

"The other four boroughs have a lot of…" Evan added air quotes. "Not-plastic women."

I didn't respond.

Evan patted his wife's knee. "You know Alex here is from Brooklyn."

I nodded. "I remember. The paps were all over that." I also remembered how cruel the tabloids were to her when they'd started dating.

"Want to know one of the benefits?" Evan asked.

"Good home cooking?" Alexa ventured, seeming unsure where Evan was taking this.

"That too," he said smiling back at her. "Any time I want to get rid of the paparazzi, I start toward the bridge, and they turn around and leave."

Alexa giggled. "The first time they followed us to my parents' house, the neighbors came out and gave them a taste of a Brooklyn welcome." She bent over laughing.

"Chased them down the street," Evan explained. "With baseball bats."

Alexa collected herself enough to add, "They scattered like the cockroaches they are."

I laughed along with them. "I'll have to try that sometime."

I was in the company of two obviously loving couples, and both of the men had once been like me—determined single playboys with a constantly rotating cast of beautiful bedmates.

They'd thought at the time they were happy, and I'd thought the same of them. Now they had both settled down, and to my eye, they were objectively happier than I'd ever seen them.

There was nothing wrong with that, I'd told myself in the past. It just wasn't for me. I hadn't been wrong any more than they'd been unhappy with a stable full of women—until they met the right one. But, since experiencing the difference one right woman could make in their lives, a switch had flipped and made them happier men. At least that was how Spencer had explained it to me.

By the time we touched down, I'd decided yet again that Adriana and I needed to revisit her insistence that we couldn't continue to see each other. It was time to have a talk.

CHAPTER 55

Adriana

I pushed inside my apartment, and my stomach bottomed out at what I saw.

The window by the fire escape was broken, and the room was as cold as out on the street.

"Shit," I yelled as I slammed the door shut behind me.

The rug near the window was covered in glass and wet from the snow or rain that had come in. This had never happened to me before, probably because all my neighbors knew I didn't have anything of value anyway.

I locked the dead bolt and went to turn up the heat, but the thermostat had been knocked off the wall.

Just great. The box had been ripped from the wires, and I had no idea how to reconnect them, or if it would work. So, even if I didn't have a broken window, I still had no heat.

I wheeled my suitcase into the bedroom and found more shitty news. Someone had taken a knife to my bed and slashed all the way down into the mattress. My small jewelry case was gone.

I'd given Chelsea back the large diamond studs she'd loaned me for the wedding, and now I was screwed. I had work tomorrow, and stud earrings were part of the dress code for female teachers. Another idiotic school rule—

they had to be studs. Hoops and chandeliers, I'd been told, weren't understated enough.

Slamming my fist on the dresser didn't help. I was up a creek, and I'd have to call Momma to borrow some. That would mean a lecture about the dangers of living alone in this city. My call would only give her more ammunition for the argument. I didn't need this shit.

When I turned, I stood tall and decided I could deal with this. I'd turn over the mattress until I could afford another. Then I opened my closet, and my stomach dropped again. All my skirts and work blouses were gone.

What kind of sick idiot would take all my work clothes? Now I had a DEFCON-three work problem.

Today was Monday, and the stores were open, but my cash advances for the trip had maxed out my credit card, and helping Serg had emptied my wallet. I was due at Hightower first thing tomorrow and wouldn't get my paycheck until the end of the week.

I braced myself and got ready to call Momma.

But the phone in my hand started ringing first. It wasn't good. Simon's name was on the screen.

"Why are you calling?" I answered. "I told you not to."

"Because, Pussycat, you don't answer my texts."

"Get the hint, Simon. That's because I don't want to have anything to do with you." Simon never had been a good listener.

"I just wanted to check in on you, like a friend."

Damned Hugo hadn't been out in the cold for his health. Simon had stationed him there to watch for me.

"I'm fine. Now don't call again. Ever."

"I could help," he said quickly. "I saw from the street that your window looked broken."

Breaking in through the window didn't seem like his style, but he could have had someone do it.

"Because you broke it," I challenged.

"Pussycat, I wouldn't do that to you, and besides, I know you don't keep any money in the place." He'd been over enough to know that for sure. "Did they take anything?"

"Don't know for sure yet. I just got in."

"You check, and I'll stop by to see if there's anything I can help you with."

"Don't," I ended up saying to a dead line. "Asshole," I added for good measure.

I bundled up in an extra sweater, my tallest boots, and added the puffy down Moncler parka while considering how to word things with Momma. Before I got up the nerve to call her, loud raps on the door interrupted me.

Marching to the door, I prepared for a fight with Simon. I didn't need or want his help.

CHAPTER 56

Travis

When she swung open the door, she gasped—not quite the greeting I'd hoped for. "What are you doing here?"

I pulled my hands from my pockets. "Gorgeous, we need to talk." She was just as beautiful as when I'd last seen her this morning, but something was off.

She moved through the door, backing me into the hallway, and shut it behind her. "I told you, it's over. There's nothing to talk about."

I sighed. "We are not done, and you know it. You're just too chicken to deal with it. Now let's go inside and discuss this like adults."

"You call me a chicken," she shot back, close to a yell. "And I'm the one who's not an adult?"

I pointed a finger at her. "See? I make you passionate."

"Try angry."

We'd been too loud again, and her neighbor's door creaked open. "Can you two keep it down?" she yelled.

"Sorry," Adriana squeaked.

I reached around her, turned the knob, and pushed the door open. I turned her toward the door. "She's right. Get inside."

The door had just closed behind us when I stopped and turned on her.

"What the hell, Adriana? Why didn't you call me?" The window was broken, and there was glass on the carpet. The storm had blown in as well.

"Stop right there." She jabbed a finger in my chest. "We agreed that we couldn't continue this."

"There was no we," I said, taking the hand she'd touched me with. Just having her hand in mine felt right. I lifted it and kissed her knuckles. "I'm not willing to give up that easily, so we're going to talk about it." She needed to learn that I wasn't a man to be dismissed, regardless of what her family thought of my family.

"You don't understand. I can't."

She tried to look away, but I cupped her jaw. "You're the one who doesn't understand, gorgeous. I will solve your problem. It's what I do, and I'm damned good at it."

I didn't understand all that her father had gone through, but I would find a way to make it up to him. I was good at win-win outcomes.

I let go of her and walked to the window. "Do you have some plastic I can put up to keep the weather out until I can get this fixed?" I pulled out my phone and started taking pictures. "And turn up the heat too."

"I can't."

When I turned, she pointed at the box on the floor. "They broke the thermostat."

"Who the hell does something like that?" I shook my head. It didn't make any sense. "Okay, we have to get you out of here. You're coming to my place."

"No way." She put her hands on her hips in a sexy, defiant pose. "This is my home. You said you don't hide. Well, I don't run."

It wasn't the same. "This isn't habitable or safe. Or are you going to argue that it is?"

"It's not that bad. The super will fix it, and I'll be fine."

Bullshit. "I'm taking care of you, which means you're coming with me. Under your own power, or over my shoulder, those are your choices."

CHAPTER 57

Adriana

I huffed out a breath. "Don't I get a say in this?"

Travis shook his head. "Not when your safety is at stake. I'm taking care of you. Stop arguing and pack up what you need."

"Okay, but only until the window is fixed." I hated being bossed around, but had to admit that my insides melted just a little upon hearing he wanted to take care of me.

"Until I find out who did this to you and fix it so he doesn't ever come near you again," he growled. "And this is not up for negotiation."

Just when I thought Travis couldn't get any sexier, the intense protectiveness in his tone ratcheted him up another notch. Nobody had ever vowed to protect me like this. "Fine." Simon had roughed up Vadim, because Vadim's comment to me had been an affront to Simon's manhood, not because he wanted to protect me.

Travis shook his head. "It's freezing in here. You should pack up what you'll need so we can get going."

Trash bags in hand, I gathered up some casual clothes and shoes—which had oddly been left behind—and a few things from the bathroom to add to what I had in the suitcase I hadn't unpacked. It was not the time for folding or neatly packing things.

Travis's commanding voice carried into the bedroom. He was on the phone telling somebody that the window had to be fixed *now*. With that tone, he probably didn't get a lot of pushback.

The next surprise came when I opened my dresser drawers. They'd taken all my panties. "Shit," I said too loudly.

Travis was in my bedroom in a flash. "What's wrong?" Then, he noticed the empty drawer. "What was in there?"

"My underwear."

He shook his head. "He's a pervert."

The image I got of some guy I didn't even know stalking me and jerking off on my panties was too sick to dwell on. "What makes you sure it's a he?"

He snorted. "He stole your panties. He's a sick fuck."

"Maybe she's my size and needed more."

"Right." His smirk said he didn't believe that explanation any more than I did. "Trust me, I'm going to find him."

"And how do you intend to do that?" I asked. This dude from Manhattan who wore suits every day had the right intentions, but no clue what things were really like on the streets out here in Queens.

"Money loosens lips," Travis explained. "Then whoever did this will learn about my concept of justice." A smirk followed.

Dangerously protective Travis had shown himself again. I'd seen flashes of this side of him when he'd sent Simon packing at the deli, and then again with Harry. Travis certainly had the resources to loosen lips as he'd mentioned. Then I sensed he'd mete out some Queens-style justice without bothering with the cops.

We'd have to talk about this later. I was both honored—shit, now I was even thinking in Manhattanese, and I had to stop that. It both turned me on that he'd go to such lengths for me and worried me that he might go too far. Nobody had gotten hurt. I'd only lost things, and those could be replaced.

"Let me finish up." I'd been naked with him, yet I still felt self-conscious packing my bras in front of him.

He shrugged. "I'll be getting some pictures."

After grabbing bras and some more odds and ends, I emerged with three full bags to find Travis snapping pictures of the damage.

He took the bags from me. "Can you handle the suitcase, gorgeous?"

I nodded, and after locking up, I took my suitcase's handle and wheeled it down the hall behind him. *How surreal.* I hadn't expected to see him again after the wedding. It was supposed to be our little secret that we'd hooked up. Now, here I was getting turned on watching his fine ass in front of me and agreeing to go to his lair, or palace, or whatever it was, for a night until my apartment got fixed.

He looked back and shot me a smile. "You'll be safe at my place."

I had to remain strong. I'd walked away from him once. I could do it again tomorrow.

Out on the street, I laughed. "An Uber? What happened to George and your car?"

"The newlyweds took priority. I had George drive them home."

That was thoughtful of him. I slid my hand over to his as the car started the journey to Manhattan. "You wanted to talk."

"I told you, we're not done, you and I."

"For the time being," I countered.

"What is that supposed to mean?"

I *tsk*ed. "We've been over this. Your relationships don't last."

He squeezed my hand, and his eyes bore into mine. "And have you only dated people you thought you would end up in a long-term relationship with?"

"Not exactly," I hedged. "But I was often hopeful, you could say."

"And did that apply to that Simon creep? Are you going to honestly tell me you were looking for and expecting a lasting relationship with him?"

Simon was a subject I refused to touch. "Let's not argue about this. I'm just going in with my eyes open about your history."

"Adriana, the past is not always prologue."

"So, let's say I agree to date you. How is this going to work?" He'd once said he had a guest room for me, but we hadn't set any ground rules about staying with him or being with him.

"Very simple. I'm dating you, which means I'll invite you to accompany me to events."

"I've seen pictures of the kind of events you go to. Let's skip those. I'm not your high-society type with a closet full of designer gowns. Sweats and greasy takeout while watching TV is more my speed."

"I'll provide the appropriate wardrobe."

I gasped and pulled my hand back. "You can't buy me with a bunch of clothes."

"If it bothers you so much," he said calmly. "Consider them on loan. Any you don't want to keep, I can donate. And I'll also take you to dinner, all the normal things."

The mere thought of trying on some of the gowns I'd seen in the pictures of him with his dates gave me a giddy tingle. "These are invitations we're talking about?"

"You can say no, but I'd rather you didn't. You're gorgeous, and I'd like to show you off. Having you by my side is what I want—no, it's what I need."

There was the word, *gorgeous*, again. It made my insides do a little flip. Worse than that, being wanted by this man made my insides clench. He could have anyone in the damned city, and he'd chosen me.

After a second's pause to clear my head, I nodded, rather liking the idea of a few nights of playing dress-up. "Okay, but to be clear, I'm not keeping anything you give me." I would not prostitute myself again. Not to him or anyone else. I had to have this clear in my head. "The currency doesn't matter. You're not buying me."

"Don't put yourself down like that. Allow me to pamper you, and what you do with any of the clothes is totally up to you. Give them to Serg, if you want."

I laughed. "That's not happening."

"Lady, if you don't want any dresses," our driver piped up. "My wife would love some."

I'd forgotten we weren't alone, and shame at having our intimate conversation overheard kept me from saying anything.

Travis silently shook his head. Then his attention came back to me. "Good. It's settled."

I didn't need to answer. I'd known it even before he uttered the words. He was right for me. During the building hunt, Travis had asked what was important to me and why, and then he'd given me the pool I needed for the community center. He could have gone another route—raised the rent to something we couldn't afford—but he'd wanted to give me a gift, the perfect gift.

I looked out the window as we crossed over the bridge to Manhattan, his world, wondering how I'd fare in it. "I'm going to need to shop for a work outfit or two."

"After we get you settled."

I didn't argue. We were in an Uber with no space in the trunk anyway.

Travis texted someone on his phone.

When he finished, I offered my hand and intertwined my fingers with my very determined, very hot, very not-Simon boyfriend's—at least for a few days.

⟆

"Don't forget to rate me five stars," our driver said as he pulled the car to a stop in front of an impressive building on Central Park West.

The brass of the doors made them look like they were made of gold. In this part of town, maybe they were. Of course Travis lived in a building bordering the park. I bet he had a killer view too.

Travis didn't say anything, so I did. "Thanks for the ride."

A uniformed doorman opened the door for me. I almost tripped getting out, stunned to see George come out of the building, wheeling a luggage trolley.

"Good afternoon, Miss Adriana," he intoned.

"Hi, George. Have you already forgotten that it's just Andy?"

"I haven't forgotten, Miss Adriana."

The driver opened the trunk and started hefting my jumble of stuff onto the trolley. He didn't think to put the suitcase on the bottom, and it slid right back off the top of the garbage bags. Definitely not five stars.

George picked up the suitcase and rearranged things on the trolley.

"Finn," Travis said to the doorman, "Miss Moreno will be staying with me. Please show her every courtesy."

"Certainly, Mr. Carlyle," the man responded.

I'd been to Chelsea's building, but its entrance was nothing like the lobby behind these doors. The marble floors were probably normal for this part of town. But a two-story waterfall that fell into a giant aquarium had to be unique.

Travis greeted the lady behind the desk. "Yasmin, Miss Moreno will be staying with me. She gets anything she desires."

"Certainly. Very nice to meet you, Miss Moreno."

"It's Andy," I called back as Travis hauled me to the elevators.

"Yes, Miss Moreno," she replied.

Was there a damned law here that forbid using casual names?

The elevator door was open, and Travis ushered me inside.

"I'll follow in the next one," George said.

Travis nodded.

"Thanks, George," I got out just before the doors closed.

"Where are your manners?" I chided my boyfriend.

"I thank him with a very hefty bonus check at Christmastime."

"Money is no substitute for good manners. You should do better."

A bit of a giggle escaped him. "Are you already trying to train me?"

Was I? That was a not-so-nice girlfriend move. "Sorry. It was just a suggestion."

The floor number display changed to P as the elevator doors opened. Of course he lived in a penthouse. Didn't all Manhattan's insanely wealthy bachelors?

My building had sixteen apartments on each floor. This one only had two doors on the short hallway, which telegraphed in advance how spacious his penthouse was going to be. He steered me to the left with a hand at the small of my back. The door opened just before we arrived.

"George called to say you were on the way up," said the short woman with a British accent similar to George's. She stepped to the side as we entered.

"Katherine, Miss Moreno," Travis said in greeting. "Adriana will be staying with us." His hand didn't leave my back.

I noticed he didn't put a time qualifier on it, like for a week or for a short time.

"A pleasure to meet you, Miss Adriana."

I thought I'd try at least one more time. "You too, and I prefer Andy."

"I understand," she said.

At long last, I'd made some headway. I glanced around. This entry foyer was the size of my entire apartment. The flowers on the center table were real, not plastic.

"Miss Adriana," Katherine said, pulling my attention back to her. "Do you have any food allergies I should be aware of?"

She caught me by surprise. "Uh, no." And maybe I'd been too quick to declare a victory in the casual-name arena.

There was a ding from the elevators, and George appeared with the luggage trolley.

"What's on the menu this evening?" Travis asked.

"Chilean sea bass with lemon-herb pilaf and roasted asparagus. If that's acceptable?"

Travis looked to me to approve it.

I nodded. "Sounds delicious."

George wheeled in my things.

Travis broke contact with me to shut the door behind him. "Katherine, I have to go to work for a bit, and Adriana needs someone to accompany her shopping this afternoon."

Her response was immediate. "Yes, sir."

"Will Saks be acceptable?" Travis asked me, fishing in his pocket for something.

My money situation was clearly beyond his understanding. "No way. Target is all that's in my price range." I'd drooled over the window displays of Saks Fifth Avenue the one time I'd walked by, but I'd never ventured in.

He glared at me and pulled a credit card from his wallet. He offered it to me. "Now Saks is also in your price range."

I didn't take it. "I can't. It's not right."

He glared at me. "You can and you will. We talked about this."

To avoid an argument in front of these two, I accepted it when he shoved it at me again.

Travis turned to his driver. "George, pull the car around, please, for the ladies. I'll take a taxi to work and call when I'm done."

"Certainly, sir."

"What's my limit?" I teased, waving the black card.

"Let's say a hundred grand for today," Travis countered.

My mouth fell open. He couldn't possibly be serious.

Before I could gather my senses, he was out the door.

"Let me get my bag," Katherine said. "This will be fun."

CHAPTER 58

TRAVIS

I was finishing a call with our Boston office when my office door was flung open, hitting the wall loudly.

"What the hell?" Luca yelled.

I swiveled my chair away from my office window to face my angry-looking half brother and held up a finger.

Luca huffed, put out by being made to wait.

"I've got a visitor," I explained into the phone. "Talk to you later."

Luca paced back and forth like an angry bull. I ended the call and turned to face him. *Half brother*, I reminded myself. "Sure, feel free to barge into my office anytime and interrupt my calls."

If Mindy had been outside, at least I would have gotten a warning before Luca barged in.

"A fucking pool?" Spittle flew out of his mouth. "You're not putting a fucking pool in my building without running it by me first. You know how that'll make it almost impossible to re-let the space later."

"Pools," I corrected him. "Two." I held up two fingers. Maybe I shouldn't have tried to rile him some more, but I didn't give one shit about what he thought. The one thorn in my relationship with Adriana was what her father thought of us as a result of how Luca had treated him.

Luca seethed. His face couldn't possibly get redder. "No fucking way."

"Control yourself, Luca." I pulled a tissue and wiped a drop from the far edge of my desk. "Go ask Dad if he wants the Queens Towers acquisition to blow up in our faces."

"We'll see about this." He huffed and marched out with a middle finger salute over his shoulder.

I got up to get the door that he didn't bother closing.

Dad's call came not five minutes later. "You should have coordinated with Luca."

I remembered our conversation well. "You told me specifically that you'd handle him, so I didn't interfere."

Silence followed, a clear signal that he recalled his words as well.

"The pools are a requirement," I said, "of avoiding a messy community confrontation that will no doubt hit the papers." Because of our chairman's intolerance for bad press, it was my get-out-of-jail-free card in this fight.

"You're sure about that?"

"Absolutely. If you want to test it, send Luca to talk to them and then watch the papers the next day. Just don't blame me when he fucks it up, just as he did the Plaza."

More silence, then, "You two should learn to work together better."

"You're right." It was my go-to answer to avoid turning a fight between me and Luca into one between me and Dad.

I'd seen Luca work his chameleon act in front of Dad, so I understood why my father didn't see the Luca I saw.

Chapter 59

Adriana

Downstairs outside Travis's building, I recognized the car when George came around the corner.

"Does he always joke about large amounts of money?" I asked Katherine. The 100K comment had bothered me.

"He never jokes about money."

Finn, the doorman, opened the car door for us.

"Thanks, Finn." Katherine urged me to slide in first. "After you, Andy."

"Yeah, thanks," I added, surprised.

She smiled. "Sorry about upstairs, but we're not allowed to shorten your name at work."

"I'd prefer it if you did," I told her.

George started into traffic. "Did what?"

"Call her Andy," she explained.

"Proper names only is part of the training," George explained. "And the service we provide. Right, Katie love?"

"Right, love." Katherine, or rather Katie, smiled. "George and I are married."

"Oh." That caught me by surprise.

On the drive to the store, I learned that the pair had worked for Travis for three years now, and they considered him a wonderful boss. They'd been trained at a British butler school and prided themselves on following all of the traditional customs. Katie cooked and cleaned, while George was the butler and driver.

Katie's phone buzzed, and she checked the message. "Ah, this will be delicious. It seems Mr. Carlyle is joining us at four to select evening gowns."

I blew out a breath. "A command from His Majesty?"

"I'd consider it a strong request. Should I message him back that you refuse?" she asked, laughing. "That would get to him."

George laughed.

It surprised me how refreshingly normal these two were outside of His Majesty's presence. "I don't get the impression he's used to people refusing him."

"Nope," George said. "Not until you."

"No," I said. "Not this time. I don't want to mess with him." He'd gone out of his way to help me, and although I hated the idea of him spending money on me, I did owe it to him to tame my normal argumentativeness. At least today.

Katie shrugged and put away the phone.

"Is this normal? I mean, shopping with a woman he brings home?" I'd never known a guy who wanted to go clothes shopping.

"First time," George said with a laugh.

That surprised me.

"For either," Katie added. "He's brought a woman to dinner, but before you, dear, he's never moved one in."

The scary words *moved in* rattled around in my head for a moment. Travis was acting out of character, and doing it for me.

"What was originally on your shopping list?" Katie asked.

That brought me back to the task at hand. I explained my need for work-appropriate clothes for Hightower, and that a few skirts and shirts should do me for now.

Katie frowned as I explained the burglary. "Don't worry, dear. We'll get you set to rights."

~

George made another trip to the register to hang up more tops I'd been forced by Katie to buy.

"Trust me on this," she kept saying when I thought I had enough, and she disagreed. "A well-put-together professional lady does not repeat her work wardrobe within a month."

I tried the I-can't-afford-that-much defense. It didn't work. I tried the I'm-not-a-lady defense. That didn't work either. At that point, I gave up trying to fight her.

In the end, George had to make three trips to the car to carry all the garment bags of clothing that Katie had helped me pick out, insisting on way more mix-and-match outfits and suits than I'd thought necessary.

We'd finished work clothes shopping early, and now I'd already selected two gowns I thought would work. They were elegant enough to not scream *I'm an impostor from Queens.*

George had decided the ladies' formal wear section wasn't his cup of tea and said he'd browse the men's section.

"I can ring these up, if there isn't anything else," suggested Ursula, the saleslady helping me. She had called them a three and a four on the ten-point sexiness scale, which sounded appropriate for any event Travis was likely to take me to.

"I'm waiting for..." I looked for the right word. A week ago *wicked nemesis* would have fit, and while I might have liked to say *boyfriend*, I didn't dare utter that word aloud to a stranger. "My friend said he'd meet me here at four." He was helping me because of the burglary, and we hadn't talked about anything beyond that.

She checked her elegant watch. "Very well."

Precisely on time, Travis joined us a few minutes later. Striding up in his suit, he looked delectable. He was the only man in this section, but Ursula eyed him like he was the only man on the planet.

I tamped down the ugly snarl I felt coming on. He was mine. I'd been wrong to want to cut it off with him in Nassau. *Boyfriend* was what I wanted to call him for as long as I could. "All right. I've got two to show you," I said to Travis.

He nodded and checked his watch.

In the dressing area, Ursula's hands were jittery. "That's Travis Carlyle, isn't it?"

"Yup." She didn't wear a wedding ring, and there weren't a lot of single women in this city who wouldn't recognize the most eligible bachelor in Manhattan.

"You're friends with him?" she asked in a giddy tone. "Maybe you could—"

"He's my boyfriend," I said firmly, and damn, if that didn't feel good.

"Oh." Her bubble deflated as she handed me the blue, patterned gown.

Still feeling uncomfortable with the whole black credit card thing, I'd limited myself to three-digit price tags. One was a scoop neck in a blue pattern, and the second a floral with an open back.

The first gown got a thumbs down from Travis as soon as I walked out. Katie, standing behind him, had shrugged.

When I emerged wearing the second, Katie stood behind Travis with a more hopeful look.

I turned for Travis, and my stomach sank at his expression. "What's wrong?" I asked, crossing my arms and staring him down.

"You're not eighty. How about a solid color? And you need more..." He didn't finish.

"Where are we going?"

"Out."

I frowned. "You're not being very helpful."

Ursula didn't speak until we rounded the corner. "He's a man. He means more skin."

I nodded, understanding the direction he wanted to go, but not sure what was appropriate. The only formal dresses I'd ever worn had been my engagement party dress, which had been elegant, not daring, and my dress for the wedding, which didn't show any more skin than these two.

"What do you have that's, let's say, an eight?" I asked as I shimmied out of the gown.

"Let me show you some to choose from," she said. She hurried off while I hung up the pretty floral dress. She returned with two.

I chose the forest-green backless one with a deep V-neck. Ursula had deemed it an eight. After ditching the strapless bra, I held up the long hem and shuffled out to get Travis's read on this one.

Katie gave me a thumbs-up from behind him. But his broody majesty was less convinced. "Much better. That'll have to do if we can't find a better one. Or we can try another store."

"I'm sure we have several suitable choices to show you," Ursula said, likely trying to save the sale.

Back in the changing rooms again, I pulled the green silk off and slipped into a pale-blue number. It was similar, but had a high slit up one leg and a deeper neckline with sheer nude mesh down halfway to my navel. This one rated a nine on Ursula's scale.

Travis's eyes zeroed in on the way my leg peeked out of the high slit as I walked out. "That's a nice one." He added a half-hearted smile when I did my turn.

I returned to the dressing area after the underwhelming response. At least it wasn't negative.

"This one seemed to please him," Ursula said as she unzipped me.

I'd arrived looking for an elegant gown and now decided on daring. "Nice isn't good enough. I want mouthwatering. Let's go for a ten, if you have one that's not see-through."

She returned with a bright-red number. "If this doesn't blow his mind, you need to find a new boyfriend."

I slipped into it, and she zipped me up. Turning in front of the mirror, I understood what she meant. It wouldn't allow a bra—none of them would— but that wasn't the problem. "I don't see what style of panties go with this."

The gown had a daring diagonal cutout over the chest that put not just cleavage, but also serious underboob on display. An additional long, oval cutout on the hip ran from my rib cage down to my thigh, with a simple gold chain keeping it from opening too wide.

"That's what's most alluring about this one. You can't hide anything. You can choose a sexy contrasting color, and he'll dream about pulling them off. Or…" she drew the word out. "You can be naughty, and he'll know you're going commando. Trust me, that'll drive him crazy." She added a Cheshire cat grin.

I nodded and slipped off my panties. Sexy might have been the safe choice, but he was going to get naughty.

Katherine's eyes went wide as her head bobbed up and down when I came out and turned around.

Travis's mouth fell open, and his eyes raked over me with unmistakable lust. "Maybe we should go back to the blue one." *Yes, this dress was killer.* The beast looked ready to burst from his cage and eat me alive. "I'm not sure I want anyone else seeing you in that."

I turned again. "Really? Because I think this is the one. You said you wanted to show me off. Or don't you like how I look in it?" I added a pouty face.

He visibly gulped and checked his watch. "We have to go. The green and the blue will do nicely," he announced to Ursula.

Katherine pulled out her phone to summon George.

Back in the dressing room, I countermanded his order. "I'll take all three, the red one as well." I pulled the black card from my purse and handed it over. "Just hide it inside one of the other garment bags, please."

Ursula smiled knowingly. "I understand."

At the car, George asked, "Where should I deposit these when we return?"

Travis didn't hesitate. "In the master."

Katherine sent a smile my way.

Yes, *boyfriend* was the right term.

A text announced itself on the ride back to my temporary boyfriend's place.

> JULIA: The fight is all over the internet. Why didn't you
> tell me?

"My sister," I assured Katie, while I scrolled through the gossip sites. In the last one, the headline read *'Drunken New York bar fight moves to paradise.'* There they were for all to see, shots of me yelling at Harry, Travis hitting Harry, and Harry in the pond yelling at us. I was labeled a teacher from Hightower Prep, no name, and luckily, I didn't see the word *girlfriend* or *date* in any of them. I closed the phone.

"Everything okay?" Katie asked.

My expression must have worried her. "She's mad I haven't caught up yet."

"Sisters can be demanding," she agreed.

A half hour later, another message came in.

> GLEASON: I want to see you first thing in the morning.

Liam Gleason was the headmaster at Hightower, and shit was about to hit the fan.

CHAPTER 60

Adriana

The next morning, George drove me to Hightower early.

Mr. Gleason, our headmaster, was on the phone when he motioned me into his office. "Yes, we do have higher standards than that, and I'm dealing with it. I expect a resolution before the day is out."

A stack of paper sat on Gleason's desk. The first sheet was a printout from one of the gossip blogs, and guessing by the number of pages, he'd printed more of them than even I'd found.

He listened for another minute and hung up with a quick, "I'll get back to you shortly." Then his glower focused firmly on me as he tapped the stack of papers. "Close the door and have a seat, Moreno." His words were sharp, his face red.

I pulled the door closed, without slamming it, although that was how I already felt about the inquisition that would come next.

"Why would you get involved in a public brawl and drag this school's fine name through the mud like this?" Before I could say anything, he ramped up again, his face turning even redder. "I must've gotten a dozen calls already about this."

"And why do you start by assuming it's my fault? Is it because I'm a woman?"

That set Gleason back on his heels for a second. "I did not assume," he insisted. "That's what these…" He tapped the pile again. "…say. And the man who got hit is an alumnus. He and his family are big donors."

It became clear now. Harry, and maybe his family, had gotten involved and brought this to Gleason. The fact that I was a teacher at Hightower had never come up in the short discussion with Camera Guy. Outside of Chelsea and Spencer, I doubted any of the people at the wedding knew where I worked, so it had to have come from Harry.

I straightened. "Would you have preferred the headlines said Hightower teacher gets assaulted and molested by an alumnus at the weekend wedding? Because that's what it would've been if I hadn't been saved from your precious alumnus."

Gleason fumbled for an answer to that.

I noticed my personnel file on his desk and pointed. "Were you planning on firing me over this?"

"We're merely having a fact-finding discussion here," he hedged.

"Good, because the truth of the matter is I was saved from exactly that fate, by this hero." I leaned forward and tapped the picture of Travis. "Shall we call Victor Carlyle and tell him you think his son shouldn't have stepped in to stop your precious alumnus when he assaulted me, because it caused a public spectacle?" I knew I had him when Gleason's jaw hung slack.

"I had no idea," he mumbled. Of course he wouldn't want to call Travis's dad, because Victor Carlyle was a trustee of the school. That outranked a big donor's family every day of the week.

"Are we done?" I asked, standing.

"I think so. Thank you for clearing this up."

I walked to the door, holding back my smirk for later.

"Ms. Moreno," he said.

I turned. "Yes?"

"I'm glad to have gotten your version of events, because if you had been the cause of bad press for our school, I would have had to take action."

"Of course." I left his office and no longer felt like smirking.

This round went to me, but Harry was playing dirty and could have more tricks up his sleeve.

CHAPTER 61

Travis

(Four days later)

I woke up nestled against Adriana's warm back. I'd always enjoyed my hands on a woman, but now I'd become a champion spooner. She'd been under my roof for four glorious days now, and no, it wasn't becoming old. Next to Adriana was the perfect way to start the morning. Especially with a hand on her breast.

She shifted under my arm and gyrated her ass against my morning wood. "You finally awake, Trav?"

"Yeah, for about an hour now. I thought you were sleeping."

"Bullshit." She turned over to face me. "I didn't want to move because you were snoring so peacefully."

"I don't snore." I pinched her nipple.

"Ouch. Okay, okay, not snoring, just breathing heavily." She palmed my length. "Anyway, I wanted to let you sleep in."

I'd apparently needed it. "Thanks. How did you sleep?"

"Pretty well, except for getting jabbed..." She pulled on my dick. "By the wooden arrow here. How do you keep it up all night?"

"It's you, gorgeous. That's the effect you have on me. And it's not all night long."

"Damn near all night."

I fondled her breast. "You love it. Admit it."

She stroked me. "I do. Now get your ass up and make me one of those omelets you promised."

I rolled out of bed. "Neither of us is allowed in the kitchen until Sunday. Don't you like Katherine's cooking?"

"Of course. But I don't want to wait until Sunday to see if you can cook. I'm worried it was just a boast."

"It's not."

She slid out on her side of the bed and put her feet on the floor.

That thought struck me. She'd only been here a few days, and in my mind, she already had a side of the bed—my side, her side, our bed. I smiled when repeating it in my head didn't seem out of place. I'd never had that thought before. I'd sensed Adriana would be different, and I'd been right, *so* right.

She sighed heavily before standing. "What are we going to do about my parents?" She circled her hand between us. "This is going to kill them." She'd taken the step of asking what *we* were going to do instead of what *she* was going to do, which is what she'd agonized over for several days.

Plus, I had a plan that I expected to make things better.

I rounded the bed and took her in my arms. "It'll be okay. You'll see. They love you. They'll want you to be happy. Are you happy?"

"I'll be a lot happier when you find out who broke into my apartment."

It wasn't a straight answer, but it also wasn't a denial. I knew I was happy. We were okay, I decided, because if she asked me the same question, I might have answered that I'd be happier if Dad would make the CEO succession plan clear.

Midmorning, I was at my desk when my cell rang with Adriana's contact on the screen. "Hey, gorgeous," I answered.

"I wanted to remind you I'll be back late tonight," Adriana said. "I've got that meeting at the community center."

"Do you want me to come along to explain anything?"

She gasped loudly. "God, no. No billionaire sightings. That would be the worst."

"Fine." I hated not being able to help her through this. I excelled at selling, but she knew the audience best. "See you at home."

"The next period is about to start. TTFN." The abbreviated ta-ta for now was a saying she'd picked up from Katherine. It had become her new sign-off.

"Likewise," I said as I ended the call.

Adriana's mention of the community center reminded me that I needed to call Xavier's brother, Yannick, to make sure the permits for the pool construction would go smoothly. Having a contact on the inside certainly helped.

"I don't know that I can help yet on this particular one," Yannick said after we got through the initial pleasantries. That was a letdown. "At least not by myself."

"Which means?" I asked.

"It would help if you sent flowers to Janice Barnes. Then I can follow up. She might be open to having lunch."

"I'll take care of it."

I ended that call with a good feeling. Things were coming together.

An hour later, Mindy buzzed me. "A Mr. Webber is on line one from the city. Something about an application?"

"Thanks. I got it," I answered.

I picked up the phone and punched the button, mentally crossing my fingers for the right answer. "Mr. Webber, thank you for calling. What do we know?"

"I can't make any assurances about acceptance, but we do plan to add one or two vendors to our approved list, and I can get you an application."

My contact at city hall had come through with the right person to talk to. "Thank you very much, Mr. Webber. I understand you must follow your procedures. The ability to apply is all I'm requesting. Would it be possible for me to send a courier over to fetch it?"

"I suppose, but you understand the application deadline is over a month away."

After the call, I had Mindy arrange for the courier. The delivery of the thank-you gift to my friend in city hall was something I'd handle myself.

CHAPTER 62

Adriana

I left Hightower for the day and boarded the train, on the way back to Queens for the first time this week. Travis had wanted to have George drive me, but I couldn't risk someone seeing me traveling like that. In Queens, we rode the bus, the train, and occasionally a taxi or rideshare.

All this week, I'd been pampered, driven to and from work, living at the top of the world with a view out over Central Park, sleeping on a bed that had fresh million-thread-count sheets every day, eating meals prepared by an in-house chef—thank you very much, Katie—and having my laundry done for me, including ironing.

It didn't get any better, but tonight I had to fit in and couldn't have anyone see me as the girl living the high life across the river in Manhattan.

Nope, I was plain old me, the same Queens girl they knew last week with a dreary view out dingy windows, who slept on two-year-old ratty sheets that hadn't been washed in over a week, ate ramen for dinner half the nights of the week, and had the pleasure of reading on a folding chair in her dirty basement while waiting for the antique, coin-operated washer my landlord refused to replace to finish.

Was I spoiled rotten by George and Katie, not to mention Travis? Yup, and loving it.

～

AT THE CENTER, I COMPOSED MYSELF AS WE WAITED FOR THE START TIME THAT Benjamin had announced. Paula and Isabel were already in the crowd, and I prepared myself for their sellout accusations. I could appreciate that they didn't want anything to change, but it couldn't be helped.

We had no idea how many people would show up to the meeting explaining our move. But it turned out there were a lot of concerned users of the center and their families. Benjamin ended up moving us to the largest room we had, and there was still overflow.

The minutes ticked slowly by.

Eventually, Benjamin got everybody's attention. "Let's get started." After a brief explanation from him that the building was being sold and we had to move the center, he handed things over to me.

Talk about public speaking nerves, I was a complete mess for the first few minutes. Then I settled down to just a moderate mess. I fielded questions as best I could.

I spotted my parents near the back.

Momma waved.

I smiled and discreetly waved back.

Yes, we were moving to the new Plaza building.

No, I didn't have a firm schedule yet, but I'd post it as soon as I knew.

Then as I expected, Paula stood up. "Don't you consider moving into the very building we fought against a few years ago to be giving in to the gentrification crowd?"

The room buzzed with side conversations.

"Show of hands," I said. "Who would like us to provide fewer services and have less space than we currently do at this center?"

Predictably, nobody raised their hands.

"That sucks," came from the side, along with a few other comments.

"Who would like us to provide more services and have more space than we do now at this center?"

After a stunned silence, while people looked for the trick in the question, hands started rising.

"That's what we get by moving to the Plaza building. More space, and the funds to provide more community services."

The grumbling turned happy chatter.

"Will they make us use the back entrance?" Isabel shouted.

"The front entrance," I answered. "Remember, the people who moved into that building are your new neighbors. They may have come from across the river, or Long Island, but they're now fellow Astorians."

The meeting continued with a series of questions for me.

No, we were not adding a Starbucks inside the new location, but there was one only a block away.

No, we wouldn't be cutting down the study rooms or the classrooms. We'd be increasing the number of each.

The crowd became more mellow as we went on.

Lastly, I mentioned that we would still have a pool and indoor courts.

"You did great," Benjamin said as the last of the attendees filed out.

"Thanks, but don't set me up to do anything like this again. I can't take it. I felt like I was going to puke." What I was actually most afraid of was peeing myself.

He slapped my shoulder. "That goes away with practice."

I shook my head and backed away. "You said the same thing about getting a colonoscopy."

We both laughed. That comment had been directed at his wife last year when she was dreading her visit to the gastroenterologist.

Daddy approached with his arms wide open. "Angel, I've missed you." Benjamin wandered off.

"I've missed you too, Daddy," I admitted as he hugged me.

Momma followed right behind and gave me a hug as well. "We stopped by your apartment, but you weren't there."

I nodded. "I came straight here from work."

"It was yesterday," Dad said.

"Oh, yesterday." I hid my gulp of fear. "I went to the library to grade papers. It's warmer than my apartment." I didn't like the idea of lying to my parents, but I wasn't yet ready to tell them about Travis. There had to be a way to sugarcoat it. I just hadn't thought of it yet.

"I think you did a good job up there," Daddy said.

I relaxed. "Thanks. It was nerve-wracking. Public speaking is not my thing."

"We couldn't tell. You looked like a natural," Momma said, touching my shoulder. "Now, you're coming to lunch on Sunday, right? You've missed too many recently."

I looked down and shrugged. "I don't know. Because of the wedding, I'm really behind in my grading."

"No excuses, Angel. Hey, have you seen Serg? He hasn't called me back."

I shook my head. "Not since the wedding." They didn't need to know he'd stayed in the Bahamas because of a girl.

"If you see him, tell him to give his old pops a call. I heard of a job opportunity for him."

"Sure. I'll tell him." Although Serg was the last person I wanted to run into. My wallet couldn't take it.

Paula was waiting a few feet away, ready to pounce as soon as my parents left. She wasn't red-faced, but she didn't look calm either. "Do you really believe that shit you're spouting?" she demanded.

It was going to be a long night.

CHAPTER 63

ADRIANA

SUNDAY MORNING, I WOKE AND LAZILY SLID MY ARM TO THE SIDE TO FIND MY man. I sat up quickly when I found Travis's side of the bed cold and empty.

Then, my nostrils filled in the blanks. The aromas of coffee and bacon were faint but noticeable. Travis was cooking. Which is what he'd promised to do, and Katie didn't start her cooking until she knew we were up, so the food would be fresh off the stove.

Travis had promised to cook for me this morning. He'd also told me it was the day we got to make our own bed, as George and Katie had Sunday off. I hadn't known that two weeks ago, when George had patiently spent his Sunday driving me around to look at properties.

I got up, and after using the bathroom, I wrapped myself in one of the luxurious bathrobes to wander out to the kitchen. My man was humming to himself and swaying in front of the stove in nothing but an apron, with that fine ass of his on display.

I sidled up next to him for a peek at his preparations. "You should have woken me." I slid my hand down to his firm ass and squeezed.

He flinched. "Morning, gorgeous. Careful there. This is hot." Bacon sizzled in one pan, odd pinkish brown mushrooms in a second, and onions in a third.

What I assumed was eggs filled a bowl on the counter with two more frying pans to the side and a plate with a paper towel on it next to that. "I thought an omelet was easier than this. Wouldn't it be easier in one pan?"

With tongs, he plucked the bacon and placed the pieces on the paper towel. "Done right, each of the ingredients has its own flavor. That's why I keep them separate."

"It's a good thing you have eight burners."

"Doesn't everybody?" he deadpanned as he took the bacon pan to the sink.

I didn't dignify that with a response. "The mushrooms look off."

"Burgundy sautéed mushrooms. Don't knock 'em till to you try them."

I nodded. That explained the odd color.

A minute later he oiled the two remaining pans and placed them on burners. While the pans warmed, he chopped the bacon and grated cheese into a bowl.

I watched as he tested the two pans and decided they were hot enough, then poured half the egg mixture into each.

"Now we wait," he said, shifting the chopped bacon bits into a waiting bowl and turning the heat off on the onions and mushrooms. "If you want to make yourself useful, you can pour us some OJ. It's in the fridge."

I did as he asked to keep myself from snatching a handful of the delicious-smelling bacon. Then I sat at the table and gazed back at him in the kitchen.

He looked over his shoulder. "Like the view?"

"Very much," I said with a giggle. He'd caught me staring, but I didn't care.

He turned back to the stove, and I continued what I'd been doing as well, admiring this man and wondering how my life had come to this—living in a penthouse with a man who cooked for me.

In no time, he poured the ingredients in, flipped the omelets closed, and slid them onto plates.

"What do you think?" he asked when I was about a third of the way through my delicious meal.

I nodded and gave him a thumbs-up gesture as I chewed. "Delectable," I added after swallowing. "How do you get the eggs so fluffy?"

He sipped his juice before answering. "A little trick I learned from IHOP. I added a touch of pancake batter to the eggs before beating them."

My mouth dropped open. "You, with your personal chef and bazillion dollars, go to the International House of Pancakes like the rest of us?"

"What's wrong that?" he asked.

"I don't think they serve people in tuxes or three-piece suits there. Did you go in disguise?"

He shook his head. "How did you get such a distorted view of me?"

I shrugged. "All the pictures of you are out and about in fancy clothes, eating at fancy places, and with—"

"Fancy women on my arm," he finished for me. "And you fall for that shit?"

I lifted a shoulder. "Guilty as charged." I forked more delicious goodness to my mouth, something to keep me from talking.

"I told you not to believe anything you read about me. The stories and the pictures are all engineered to be clickbait. I'm just a guy. I fart, burp, and jerk off just like every other guy. Well...I used to."

I finished chewing. "Used to?" I raised a brow.

He smiled devilishly. "With you in my bed, jerking off is pretty pointless."

The pleasure he'd given me had been mind-altering, but it felt good to hear that he appreciated me too.

He tapped his fork on the omelet and his searing blue eyes held me captive. "What's the verdict?"

I kissed my fingertips. "Squisito."

His eyes lit up. "Thank you."

As much as I'd enjoyed the decadence of having a personal chef to do all the cooking, having a boyfriend who could cook was even better. I was going to miss this when it was over. "Do you have any other kitchen skills to show off?"

"I do." He rose and tapped the tabletop. "I thought we'd start off with—"

I jumped up and away. "No way. We don't have enough time. We have to meet that reporter about the community center move." Benjamin had set up a few interviews for me so the press could help sell the move. Paula was still stirring people up to oppose it.

Roberta from the *Ledger* had been particularly eager, so I'd scheduled with her this morning before the family lunch I could no longer avoid.

Travis chased me around the table, and in the end I made the time for my handsome billionaire boyfriend and the sturdy surface. Sunday was the only day it was available, after all.

CHAPTER 64

Travis

We were just finishing up an interview about the new community center with Roberta from the *Ledger* at a Manhattan restaurant she'd suggested. I'd insisted it was Adriana's interview and had refused to answer any questions.

The photographer who'd come along with Roberta had already gotten whatever shots of Adriana he wanted and now shifted back and forth behind Roberta. If they were going to include a photograph, it meant this would be a bigger deal in the paper than the one or two column-inches Adriana had thought.

"You should drive by and get a shot of the building," I suggested. "It photographs well."

The photographer shrugged.

I'd pointedly declined to have any shots of me. Maybe *declined* wasn't the right word. I'd threatened the guy with the wrath of God was more like it, and that had done the trick. The photographer now seemed to be getting me back by ignoring my suggestion.

Then Adriana's eyes widened, and she immediately looked away, a sour expression on her face. I turned to find Harry at the entrance to the restaurant. Adriana scooted her chair closer to me.

"Andy?" Roberta prompted.

"I'm sorry. What was that?" she asked.

Roberta looked down at her notepad. "How long before construction starts?"

Adriana looked to me.

I nodded. It was a question I'd prepped her for.

"I'm hoping it won't be long, but we need to secure permits first."

"And who are you going to screw to get that done?" an angry Harry yelled.

I stood quickly, my chair skittering away behind me. "Hornblatt, you watch your mouth."

Harry swayed as he approached, obviously drunk, even at this hour of the morning. "She's obviously screwing you to get the space. It's a fair question."

Roberta looked at me, not seeming the least bit surprised. "Tell us, Mr. Carlyle, is that true?"

"This is over." I pulled Adriana to her feet.

The photographer's camera was clicking away now.

"Of course it's true," Harry yelled, loud enough to stop all other conversation in the restaurant.

I pulled Adriana with me as we skirted around Harry. Roberta tried asking more questions that I didn't pay attention to.

"Running like the coward you are, huh, Carlyle?" Harry jeered.

I kept us moving and didn't respond. *Great.* At least two other guests had their phones up now to record the commotion.

"Your dad's a thief, and you're a coward. All you Carlyles are scum."

I kept my cool. "Go home, Harry. You're drunk."

Adriana yanked her hand away and launched toward Harry. "You leave Travis alone. He's a better man than you could ever dream of being."

I went after her, but got tripped by a chair the photographer had moved.

"You're the criminal in this room," Adriana yelled. "Preying on underage girls. How many has it been?"

While I untangled myself from the chair, Harry yelled back. "Shut up, you Carlyle whore."

The camera kept clicking in the background.

Then Harry hauled off and hit her. My heart stopped. She went down before I could reach them.

I saw red, and a second later, my fist collided with Harry's face. The asswipe fell back against a chair and then to the floor. Blood dripped from his mouth as guests scurried out of the way.

Adriana held the side of her face.

Harry cried out in pain. "I'll sue," he sputtered at me.

I had a good eight inches on him, and the weasel cowered as I threatened another punch. "Hornblatt, if you come near my girl again, I'll end you." I kept my face angry, my arm cocked, and let him decide whether we continued or not.

Harry scurried to his feet and ran.

I knelt beside Adriana and turned her chin to check. "Are you okay?"

She struggled to her feet. "I guess. It hurts like hell."

"I'm sorry. I should have been between you two."

"It's not your fault he's an asshole." She looked around at the other patrons still staring at us. "Take me home, please."

"Sure thing, Wildcat."

She gave a half-hearted laugh. "You're not going to be able to call me gorgeous anymore."

"Wildcat will have to do. If you'd hit him back, I could call you slugger."

"Very funny, big guy."

A camera's click made me realize the photographer and Roberta were still here. She was recording us with her phone, and she had an odd smile on her face. The old newspaper saying still seemed to apply, *if it bleeds it leads*. Our misfortune was her bread and butter. I could only wonder how this would affect her treatment of the piece about the community center.

I held Adriana close as I snaked us between the tables to reach the door. "He didn't break the skin, but that's going to bruise." Harry had left a trail of blood on the floor that we avoided stepping on.

Outside, Harry had moved down the street, but oddly, he was still hanging around. I moved us in the other direction on the sidewalk and hailed a taxi.

Roberta and her photographer emerged behind us, and when they noticed Harry, they walked down to where he stood.

The three of them were talking when our taxi drove off. Had this all been a ruse? Was there even going to be an article about the community center?

CHAPTER 65

Adriana

When we got back to his penthouse, Travis had given me a package of frozen blueberries wrapped in a towel. But after a little while, the cold hurt, so I lifted it off my face.

Travis checked his watch and shook his head. "Another two minutes, then off for twenty before it goes back on."

"Why do you have to be so bossy?"

"Why do you have to argue? Do you want the bruising to be bad?"

"Duh. No."

"Then ten minutes on and twenty minutes off. Now finish the ten."

I stuck my tongue out and put the blueberries back in place.

"You make a pretty poor patient."

"And your bedside manner sucks. You make a shitty nurse."

"Probably true, and not high on my priority list. I only care about one patient."

I had to admit…although I didn't like the cold pack, I very much did like that he cared enough to force me to behave. And I hated the sight of blood, but the memory of how he'd flattened Harry gave me a warm, tingly feeling. "Did I say thank you yet?"

"Not necessary. You're mine, and anybody who wants to attack you, even verbally, is going to have to go through me. Harry was just too stupid to understand that the first time."

"Still, thank you."

He came over and kissed my forehead. "Next time, you should duck." A minute later, he checked his watch again. "You're done with the cold for this cycle."

My phone rang. It was my brother.

"Hi, Serg. How was your week with Iris?"

"I knew there was something fishy going on at the wedding. You're dating that Carlyle creep, aren't you?"

Today was not my day. "None of your business." It wouldn't do any good to deny it at this point.

"I want a thousand bucks, or I'm going to Pops."

Bile rose in my throat. "You can't tell Daddy."

Travis looked over, concerned, mouthing a silent "*what?*"

"Watch me," Serg spat. "I want a thousand. And I want it today."

I couldn't believe he was my brother. I took in the long, slow breath that normally quelled my anger. It didn't work. Instead, I snapped. "No fucking way." I punched the end call button with force.

Travis cocked his head. "You swore. What's up?"

"My stupid brother wants money to not tell Daddy about us."

"And here I thought my brother was the worst," Travis scoffed. "What are you going to do?"

"You heard me. I'm done being his personal piggy bank."

Travis came and stood over me, scratching the top of my head. "You think he'll do it?" He shifted to kneading my shoulders.

My blood boiled. My brother had never made me so mad. "He always needs more money. He'll call again and lower his blackmail number, but I don't care. After dating Simon, I'm done. I'm not doing this anymore. I'm done bailing him out of jams."

Travis's hands stilled. "What did you say?"

Fuck a duck, my temper had screwed me over once again and I'd run my mouth. I'd never admitted this to anyone, not even my sister, but unfortunately I'd already said enough that a guy like Travis could put it together.

"Tell me Serg didn't force you to…" Travis wasn't going to let this go.

Damned temper. I swallowed and began. "Serg was into Simon for a lot of money. I mean a lot. Serg got beat up pretty bad one day. Then Simon paid me a visit and proposed a deal."

Travis's hands started massaging again. "You don't have to say any more."

But I had to get all out. "I'd turned Simon down before, and he said if I changed my mind..." I choked back a sob, remembering his words. "He'd let my brother live." I sniffled. "I couldn't let him die. He's my brother, for God's sake."

"He can't do that," Travis bit out, his hands leaving my shoulders.

I shook my head. "You don't get it. That's the difference between your reality and mine. You guys make death threats, and they're just scary. Where I live, with people like Simon, they're the real deal."

Travis came around and knelt in front of me. He took my hands in his. I couldn't make out from his eyes what he saw in me, but I was afraid it was the prostitute I'd become. Regardless of the reason, I'd whored myself out. I tried to stand but he held me down.

I looked away. "I'll go, now that you know what I've done and what I am." Tears pricked at my eyes. Because of my stupid brother I was going to lose the one man I'd ever really cared about.

Travis squeezed my hands. "What you are is my Wildcat, a very determined, very brave woman. You stand up for your family and friends, and I can't think of anything more admirable."

My tears started full force. "But—"

"No buts about it. When your brother was in trouble, you saved him from himself. Today, when Harry attacked me, you went after him. Nobody's ever had my back like that. Never." He stood, pulling me up, and wrapped me in a tight embrace. "I can't imagine what you went through, and I'm in awe of your strength."

I snuggled into my man's chest, my tears wetting his shirt, and held on for dear life. "You're pretty special yourself, Trav. As I recall, you're the one who's flattened Harry, twice now—for me."

"I told you, I protect what's mine."

"Am I really yours?"

"Of course you are."

His assurance filled me with hope. What I didn't ask was how long I would be his. Given his track record, the answer wouldn't be one I liked.

Travis rubbed my back. "If you're worried—" His words were cut off by my phone ringing again. As predicted, it was Serg.

"I'll give you the money to pay him," Travis said before I could answer the call. "Let me deal with your dad when the time comes. I've got something in the works."

"What?" I asked as I picked up the phone again.

"Later." Travis twirled his finger, urging me to get on with it.

"What is it, Serg?" I answered.

"How about three hundred?" My brother was as predictable as ever.

"I don't know. Three hundred is a lot." I hesitated, making him sweat for a moment.

Travis pulled bills out of his wallet and silently mouthed, "*Say yes.*"

"Okay."

"You're the best."

I didn't echo the sentiment, just hung up.

Travis shoved the bills at me. "Take it."

"I don't like this." I took the money anyway.

"It's just temporary."

CHAPTER 66

Travis

A half hour later, there was a knock at my door.

Adriana looked over from where she had her foot up, painting her toenails.

I shrugged, wordlessly answering her question. I had no idea who it was. Almost nobody was cleared up to this floor, and the lobby hadn't called up about a visitor.

I went to the foyer, and when I pulled open the door, it was Dad.

He walked in past me. "What the hell were you thinking? I need a word with you." His tone was as prickly as ever. He held a picture of this morning's fight with Hornblatt in his hand, so I knew what this was about.

I closed the door behind him. "Dad, this is a surprise."

"Yeah, we need to get a quick handle on this," he said as he continued into the great room. He pulled up short when he saw Adriana.

I broke the silence with introductions. "Dad, this is Adriana Moreno. Adriana, my father, Victor Carlyle."

"What is she doing here?" he asked me.

With cotton stuck between her toes, Adriana walked on her heels toward us and extended her hand. "Nice to meet you, Mr. Carlyle," she said in a much more pleasant tone than my father deserved.

Shamed into it by Adriana's politeness, Dad shook hands with her. "Ms. Moreno." He turned to me. "We should speak in private."

Guessing the subject, I had no intention of belittling Adriana. "Anything you have to say to me, you can say in front of her."

Dad's brows winged up for a moment before he re-composed himself. He shook the paper in his hand. "This is the second time now. I can't have officers of the company acting like this. What were you thinking, instigating a public brawl over a girl?" He said the last word with derision.

"Woman," I corrected. "And she's my woman." I caught a smile forming on Adriana's lips.

Dad shook the paper again. He was on a roll. "I expect you to act like a gentleman at all times in public and never to bring disrespect upon the company."

"He didn't instigate anything. I was physically attacked," Adriana said loudly.

Dad whirled and scowled at her. "This is family business, and you'll stay out of it."

My fists clenched. "You'll not talk to her like that."

Adriana wasn't done with him. "Trav protected me after I'd been knocked down. That's exactly what a gentleman would do."

I smiled, watching my woman put my father in his place.

"Your woman, huh? Is that why we gave up so much money for this deal, so you could get some extra on the side?"

"You take that back," Adriana said sternly. "You're insulting your own son."

"Shut up," Dad hissed. "This is a family matter."

I stepped forward. "And you apologize for insulting her."

Dad shifted his attention to me. "I will not."

Adriana took her volume up a notch. "You gave him an impossible task. You told him to finalize a deal with me in three days after your other son got you into a pickle." She got in Dad's personal space and pointed at him. "My father lost his business because of you."

Dad backed up a step.

Adriana matched him with a step forward. "The last thing I wanted to do was trust anybody named Carlyle. Your son is the one who proved to me that I shouldn't judge somebody by the jerk his father is."

Dad blanched. He definitely didn't like her implication. "I will not be talked to like that." He turned to me. "Nadia and I are going down to St.

Barth's for two weeks. When I get back, you better have decided what's more important—your position at the company or this girl." He turned and stomped out.

"Woman," my fiery Adriana called after him just as the door slammed shut.

CHAPTER 67

Adriana

I felt instantly sick as soon as the door slammed closed after Travis's dad. My lack of control had just put his relationship with his father in jeopardy.

I faced Travis, ready to be thrashed. "I'm sorry. I got carried away when he assumed this morning was your fault."

Instead of growling at me, Travis smiled and started to laugh. "You have nothing to be sorry about. He's not used to having somebody stand up to his bullying is all."

"Why do you work for him if he's like that?"

"I told you. It's my duty as the eldest. I have to."

I nodded. Travis might be smiling now, but I could do the math pretty simply. Whether it was today or next week, it was game, set, match. "I'll pack up my things and go."

"Hell no. What are you talking about?"

"It's pretty simple. Your father just gave you a choice between me and your job, and you have to keep your job to fulfill your family duty. Or did I miss something?"

Travis held out his hand to me.

I came over and took it. Even if he wanted me to stay the entire two weeks his father was gone, it wouldn't change anything except possibly to infuriate his dad more. Travis pulled my chin up, and I met those pale-blue eyes as they looked straight into my soul.

I gulped.

He seemed to always want to be touching me when he had something important to say. "I explained to you why I have been working for my father," he said slowly. "You're right, he gave me a choice going forward. So I choose you, and not for two weeks. I'll do anything for you."

My heart fluttered as I took in the words. "Are you kidding? You've known me less than a month, and he said he'd cut you out of the company."

"I'll straighten him out about you and me. When he calms down, he'll listen to reason."

I tried to blink back the tears that were starting again. "But he said—"

"You should be listening to me, not him."

Travis was making this really hard, but I couldn't allow him to torpedo his whole career over me, especially when I knew the odds of us lasting more than a month or two were essentially zero, given his history. Then, when it ended and he was sick of me *and* didn't have his job anymore, it would be more damage than I wanted to inflict on anybody.

"Do you honestly think he'll change his mind?" I asked. "Be honest now."

He nodded after a moment's hesitation. "Negotiations are what I do. When I get him to understand how important you are to me, I don't think he'll really want to hurt me."

If it weren't for his father's threat, I wouldn't want to give Travis up any more than he wanted me to leave. "And you don't think his decision is final?"

"He said it wasn't, so it's not. You heard him—two weeks. You have to stay for these two weeks and give me a chance to change his mind. If you leave now, he'll have won." Travis squeezed my hand.

I squeezed back.

"These have been the best weeks of my life." The emotion in his eyes matched his words. "Maybe you haven't figured it out yet, gorgeous, but I'm addicted to you. I've already fallen head over heels for you."

Those were words I never dared hope to hear. "Likewise, big guy."

"Is that a yes to staying two weeks and then seeing where we stand?"

What I wouldn't agree to was staying any longer if he hadn't persuaded his father by then. But that was a discussion for later, if that's where we ended up. I jumped up into his arms and wrapped my legs around him. "Yes to two weeks." Then started another of our shattering kisses.

I broke the kiss, and he let me down. "I need to make a call. I can't go over to my parents' house like this." I pointed at my face. The bruise would make my parents go ballistic regardless of how I explained it.

I dialed the phone and waited a moment. "Daddy," I said, sniffling when he answered. "I think I've come down with something, and I can't make it today."

With a huge sigh, he gave in. "Okay, Angel. Whatever is best for you. And we're skipping next week because we're visiting your aunt and uncle."

"Okay. I'll see you two weeks from now, I promise. Love you both."

After ending the call, I jumped up into my boyfriend's arms. My clothes were off before we made it back to the bedroom.

CHAPTER 68

Adriana
(Nine days later)

Thursday night, a week and a half after the showdown with Travis's dad, we were in the limo on the way to Travis's country club. Traffic was ridiculous, but we'd made the best of it.

I pulled my panties up and adjusted my dress as Travis wrapped the condom in some tissues and got his trousers back in place. Limo sex could now be scratched off the wish list.

A half hour later, I remembered something Jules had said when I told her about this outing. "Will any of the food be wrapped in gold foil?" I asked.

Travis laughed. "You have the oddest questions. No, I doubt it. Why?"

"My sister wants a report after, and she insists that's the latest craze."

"Feel free to tell Julia that the country club crowd is stodgy and not into the latest crazes."

I nodded and went back to watching the scenery go by.

Travis had been having daily calls with his father, but so far he didn't have any progress to report on his father's demand that he choose between the company and me. But, Travis had been quick to point out that most negotiations didn't make any progress until the very end.

If that was supposed to make me feel better, it didn't.

Travis was still confident that he could sway his father, and I hoped he was right, because things had been going so well. We hadn't encountered Harry again, and things on the Queens side of the river were good. Despite the fight at the interview, the resulting article about the move had been long and thorough and surprisingly positive. I'd been told it had been well received.

I now had four more days with Travis before it was time to make the hard decision it seemed he wouldn't, if his father wouldn't compromise.

Tonight we had a party to go to, and Travis had said our attendance was mandatory, so I'd done the obligatory decking myself out. George now stopped the limo at a guard shack, and the gate opened for us to enter.

We'd dined out a few times at off-the-beaten-path kinds of places where we wouldn't be photographed by paparazzi. Travis had taken me on a carriage ride around the park. With blankets galore to keep us warm, it had been magical, and Travis had turned out to be every little girl's dream of a prince.

The only fly in the ointment had been that so far he hadn't figured out who'd trashed my apartment. However, after acclimating to life at the penthouse, I wasn't in a hurry to move back to Queens.

But I still had to face my family next Sunday at lunch, which I couldn't put off again. Over the phone, I hadn't been asked any questions or accused of anything, so that was good.

We turned up a small hill toward our destination.

"It better be warm in there," I said as I checked my makeup again in my compact. The bruise had mostly healed and only needed a slight bit of concealer.

"Oh, they'll have the heat turned up," he assured me.

"Are you sure I'm dressed appropriately?" Under the warm parka I treasured, all I had on was a barely there scrap of pale-blue fabric.

Travis had insisted I wear this dress, one we'd bought at Saks Fifth Avenue that first day. Ursula had labeled it a nine on the sexiness scale.

"An elegant lady attending an elegant party," he said. "Every man in there is going to be jealous of me."

I nodded. It was hard, but I was learning to not argue when he called me a lady.

Luckily, I still had the sexier ten-point dress hidden from Travis. I was saving it for the dinner we had planned for Saturday night. I crooked my finger. "Come here."

He turned toward me.

I straightened his bow tie. "And every woman there is going to be jealous that I have you on my arm."

"You mean you're on my arm," he corrected.

"Or that I hooked you," I countered.

"Since I was the one to chase you, doesn't that mean I reeled you in?"

A minute later, George pulled into the circular drive at the entrance of the Glenside Country Club and rushed around to open the door.

"Are you sure you want to be seen here with me?" I asked, still nervous about attending this event. I'd enjoyed our time together, but it had reinforced how far I was from proper Manhattan material, much less country-club material.

"You'll do fine. They're just people, after all."

I'd tried to talk about my fears that I didn't fit in. But he still didn't get it.

At the entrance to the massive building, Travis held open the door for me. The gargantuan, fifteen-foot wooden door looked like it had come from some medieval castle.

Inside, it was as warm as he'd promised, and we were checking in our coats when the *Jaws* music started.

Travis fished his phone out of his pocket. "I'd better get this."

I nodded, although it made me nervous every time his father called to check in. It seemed the big CEO bossman had a little trouble understanding the concept of a vacation.

"Hi, Dad."

I waited.

"Uh-huh… Uh-huh… I understand… Yeah, tomorrow."

This end of the conversation wasn't telling me much, but Travis's face was. He didn't like it.

Travis hung up. And took a deep breath. "He's cutting his vacation short, and he wants to meet tomorrow morning."

My shoulders slumped. This was bad news. "Like a decide-between-the-girlfriend-and-the-company meeting tomorrow?"

He nodded and shuffled us over to the corner, away from the coat check. With one hand on my shoulder, he pulled my chin up with the other. This was serious. "I am not giving you up, and I plan to make that clear."

The sentiment had me teary-eyed, but I couldn't leave it at that. "But he said—"

"He says a lot of things. You remember when I told you that half-hearted threats don't get results?"

I nodded. I'd thought we still had lots of time to talk about his father's threat, but that option was gone now.

"*He* taught me that. I don't think he'll go through with it."

"And what if you're wrong?" I asked in a whisper.

"I choose you, gorgeous. I told you that, and I mean it. Chin up, and let's do this."

I nodded, pasted on a smile, and took his arm when he offered it to me, just as he had at the wedding. Then I braced myself.

We passed display cases full of huge trophies and a long row of portraits of stern-looking old men in suits—previous presidents of the club. The gigantic room we entered at the end was filled with couples even more elegantly dressed than at Chelsea's engagement party. The men all wore tuxes, and the women wore evening gowns of various lengths, some floor length and a few incredibly short.

Several men tried to hide their second glances in my direction as this dress did the thing it was intended to. I straightened my back and decided to make Travis proud of me. I could handle this crowd for an hour or two. How hard could it be? *Just smile pleasantly, don't say much, and keep your shoulders straight so the dress doesn't open more in the front than it already is. Oh, and don't trip on the sexy ice picks on your feet.*

Travis stopped as a man with a Russian accent caught his elbow. He introduced me as his girlfriend to Vasily something.

I smiled and kept my mouth shut while they talked about finance rates. Then, I spotted Chelsea, someone I could actually talk to. "I'll be saying hi to the newlyweds," I told Travis as I left his side.

He nodded. "I'll follow in a minute."

I left him behind and hurried over to Chelsea and Spencer. At least there was somebody I could relate to in this crowd.

Chelsea threw open her arms and squealed when she saw me.

After hugging them both, Chelsea pointed at my man. "I knew it. I just knew you and Travis would hit it off." She turned to her husband. "Didn't I say so?"

He lifted his glass of something amber and nodded. "That you did, my dear. That you did. Of course, I helped a little by singing Andy's praises to him at the engagement party."

Chelsea touched my elbow and leaned closer. "And how long has this been going on?" she asked.

"After we got back," I lied. I couldn't have them adding more fuel to the fire in case they repeated what I said to the wrong person. No one needed to get the idea that Travis and I had been doing the horizontal mamba while the community center deal was underway.

"Well, good for you," she said.

"I agree. When you get past all the bad press," Spencer said, "he's really a good guy."

I accepted a flute of champagne from a passing server. "I'm learning that."

A hand touched my hip, and I turned.

Travis had arrived at my side. "And how is wedded life?"

The couple looked at each other and giggled.

Chelsea was the first to speak. "It's been great. You really have to go down to Barbados and St. Barth's. They're a lot less crowded than Nassau."

Spencer lifted his glass like he was toasting her words. "Yup. We hit both of them on the honeymoon. Why don't you take Andy down there and get out of this goddamn cold?"

"I can't," I explained. "I have work."

"You do have a spring break," Travis corrected. "And I think it sounds like a positively splendid idea."

Only that was a month away. I didn't know if I'd survive as his girlfriend that long. His father was due back tomorrow, and if Victor hadn't softened his opinion of me, it would be over. I wouldn't let Travis sacrifice his career.

While Travis inquired about the details of their honeymoon, I looked the room over. I spotted Chelsea's parents, but that was it for familiar faces—until I noticed the gaudy bow tie and the uneven bald spot.

Xavier Breton was talking with a man whose back was to me.

I hoped it didn't mean evil Wendy was here somewhere. When his wife joined them and they shifted, I got even worse news than that. The other man was freaking Harry Hornblatt.

"Our chairman thinks everything revolves around the club, so I have to find him and a few other people and make excuses for Dad missing this," Travis said. "Will you be okay without me?"

I waved him away. "Go do your thing." I intended to stay glued to the MacMillan newlyweds to avoid any Harry encounters.

"At least I don't have to lick any boots," Spencer commented. When I gave him a curious look he continued. "His company's chairman is Gordon Neville. The guy demands constant ass-kissing. My dad won't even talk to him after doing business with him once. *A snake* is how he describes him. I bet Travis's dad wishes he'd never brought him into the company."

I nodded and watched to see who Travis approached. "Point him out when you see him."

Spencer pulled a confused face.

"So I know who to spill a drink on, if I get the chance," I explained.

"I like your attitude," Chelsea said with a giggle.

A few minutes later, Spencer pointed out Gordon Neville—balding, beady eyes, and the kind of nose that would get him cast as the bad guy by Hollywood.

~

TWO HOURS AND FOUR FLUTES OF CHAMPAGNE LATER, I WAS TOLERATING THE party and had avoided any encounters with either Neville or Harry. Chelsea and I were chilling near the shrimp cocktail while the guys were off in a group chatting about golf.

"I didn't want to ask in front of anyone else," she started. "But are you pressing charges?"

"What?"

"I saw the video of Harry hitting you last week."

"Honestly, I hadn't thought about it," I lied. I put my empty glass down. "Which way to the ladies' room?" The last thing I wanted to discuss was that episode, and I certainly wasn't pressing charges that would lead to more negative press for Travis.

She pointed. "Down that hallway. First left where it says Ladies Locker Room."

I thanked her and trotted off after checking that Harry wasn't in my path.

On the way back, I ducked behind a ficus tree in the hallway when I saw Harry walking with Xavier. They stopped right by the entrance to the hallway, not ten feet from me. A second later, a third man joined them—Gordon Neville, the Carlyle company's chairman.

"I can't wait to get rid of all of them," Xavier said.

"I'm working on my part," Harry chimed in.

What the hell was he working on?

"Yeah, I talked with the older son tonight," another voice said. It had to be Neville. "He has no idea."

"I gave the old man the evidence a few weeks ago, and he hasn't done a thing. You can definitely use that against him with the board."

"Are you sure it'll hold up to scrutiny?" Neville asked.

"Well enough for the board to toss Luca and the old man at the next meeting," Xavier said.

My blood froze. They were talking about Travis, Luca, and their father. Neville was planning to get rid of them all, and they had no clue. Spencer's father had been right to call this Neville butthead a snake.

"That leaves the older brother," Neville said. "I thought you said you could get the old man to fire him?"

"I'm working on it," Harry said.

"Then why hasn't it happened yet?" Neville asked.

"Hold on, Gordon," Xavier said. "My nephew said he'd get it done, so he'll get it done."

Harry was related to Xavier? I'd had no clue that was the case, and I doubted Travis did either.

"He's got it bad for his new girlfriend," Harry explained. "And she's got a hair-trigger temper. I figure I poke at them one or two more times, and there'll be fallout. I'll make sure it gets coverage, just like the last time."

Now the encounter at the interview made sense. Harry had set it up with that reporter lady. No wonder they'd been ready to get video and pictures. The photographer had only been there for the drama, which explained why that article had run without a photo.

My stomach twisted into a giant knot as the first tear scorched its way down my cheek. I'd reacted just exactly as Harry had wanted me to, and it was going to cost Travis and his family their jobs, their company, everything.

"I read the old man the riot act yesterday," Neville said, laughing. "I told him I was done being Mr. Nice Guy, and I'd have his balls for breakfast if he didn't cut Travis loose if he caused another PR problem for us. I told him Kwan, Parker, and Jenson will back me on that. He nearly shit his pants. Now it's up to you to get the kid in the press."

"I can do that," Harry said.

"This only works if the older son is the first domino," Neville said. "The old man has to fire him before the board meeting. I'll take care of the other two in the meeting itself. That gives you two weeks. I don't want to have to wait another three or six months to get rid of the older one."

"I'll get it done," Harry replied.

"Good," Neville said. "Then we'll be rid of the Carlyles. Xavier, you'll get operations, and finance goes to you, Harry."

A woman passed them, coming my way.

"We'll handle it for you, Gordon," Xavier said before stepping away, leaving Harry with Neville.

The woman stopped when she noticed me against the wall. "Honey, are you okay?"

I shook my head and didn't dare say a word, because Harry would certainly recognize my voice.

"Two weeks, Hornblatt," Neville said sternly.

Out of the corner of my eye, I saw the two leave.

"My brother said the meanest thing to me," I mumbled to the woman when I thought the men were far enough away.

"Come with me, dear, and let's get you cleaned up," the woman suggested, urging me toward the locker room.

Going with her, I ran the last few feet to the stalls and knelt. All the champagne I'd drunk came up.

"Dear, is there any way I can help?"

"It's just morning sickness," I assured her. The truth was too terrible to admit.

After a minute she left, and I kept dry heaving. I couldn't see a way out of this mess.

If I stuck around, Travis could get pushed out of the company tomorrow. If that didn't happen, and I was still in the picture, Harry would ambush us again and again until one of us reacted.

If I told Travis about the plot, his instinct would be to attack Harry, and that would create the very incident that had to be avoided. And, Harry was devious enough to force a confrontation in front of cameras and witnesses as he already had.

If Travis went to his father, it would be my word against Xavier's. The twenty-year company veteran would be the one his father believed, not me. I'd be the meddlesome outsider trying to create drama to ingratiate myself with his son or to cause trouble for the company to get back at them after the Plaza project.

Any way his father looked at, believing me and stopping the plot was the least likely outcome.

The only way to prevent Travis from losing everything he'd worked for and his goal in life was to take myself out of the equation tonight. Travis had to give in to his father and choose the company. And without me around, Harry lost his leverage to make Travis lose his cool.

After five minutes of composing myself and assuring the other ladies who came in that I was going to be all right, I finished fixing my makeup. Stoic face in place, I went back to the party, determined to do the right thing.

The fairy tale was over. What I had to do now was ruin my future with the one man I cared about.

It was the only way to save him.

CHAPTER 69

Travis

"I really, really think this is a great investment opportunity for you guys," Jamison somebody said again after cornering me for the second time tonight.

Bored to tears, I looked around for my Adriana so I could motion her over for a polite exit from this drone.

"The potential is just hugely tremendous, and the artificial intelligence possibilities are mind-bogglingly enormous."

I took in a slow breath. When these guys piled superlatives on top of superlatives, it always meant they didn't have anything substantive to say about their pet project. "Thanks for this, but I don't think—"

"And in the China market. Think about it."

Right now, I had zero interest in thinking about anything this bozo said. The sweet smell of jasmine hit me just before a hand stroked down my left arm.

"Oh, here you are, Travis," Wendy Breton cooed seductively. "Isn't it too bad there's no dancing tonight?"

"I was just thinking that," Jamison said, trying unsuccessfully to get Wendy's attention, although staring at her cleavage might not have been the brightest move.

I shifted a few inches away. "Wendy, have you met Jamison..." I twirled my finger.

"Harrison," the man filled in for me.

"He's got the most amazing things to say about his new project."

Wendy rubbed her tit against my arm as Jamison rewound to the beginning of his spiel.

I stepped to the right just as another hand yanked at my elbow. "You need to go," Adriana said with a glare at Wendy.

On my other side, Wendy argued, "That's a shame. The night is so young."

The anger on Adriana's face telegraphed that she was about to lose it. I took her hand. "You can stay, Wendy. Adriana and I are leaving—together."

Leaving Wendy stuck with Jamison, I happily slid an arm around Adriana's waist. She was mine and needed to receive that message. "I swear she just showed up."

"Sure. I really need to go home. We need to go now. *Now*."

I could see the wetness in her eyes. The Wendy thing had upset her. "Of course. Anything you want, gorgeous."

She walked with me through the crowded room before announcing, "Don't call me that." She was much more upset than I'd guessed.

"But you are positively gorgeous."

Her normal smile didn't appear. "Don't call me that. It just makes it harder."

Harder? What the hell? I stopped us. "What's going on?"

She chewed her lip for a second. "Not in front of these people." She left me and marched on toward the exit. Those words didn't bode well.

I followed her and texted George that we were ready to be picked up, then helped Adriana into her parka at the coat check. Her gaze kept shifting around like a scared rabbit.

With some other couples at the door waiting for their rides, I held her hand and stayed silent.

"Brought your whore with you, I see." The voice carried down the hall from behind us.

I turned to find that fucking Harry Hornblatt hadn't learned his lesson about insulting my woman. But before I could give Harry the beating he deserved, Adriana pulled me toward the door with both hands.

"Outside, now."

George pulled up as we exited into the cold.

I wasn't happy that Harry had gotten the last word tonight, in front of others, no less. "He needs to be taught a lesson."

Adriana opened the rear door before George could round the car and shoved me. "Get in. Now." She followed, leaving a perplexed George to circle back to the driver's door.

Once George climbed in, I told him to take us home and raised the privacy glass. I held my hand out for Adriana, but she didn't take it. "Now do you want to tell me what has you all bothered?"

CHAPTER 70

Adriana

"I can't do this anymore," I said. Even puking my guts out, I hadn't understood how difficult this was going to be.

"Do what anymore?"

I motioned between us. "Us." A single word had never been so hard to utter. I only wanted the best for this man, and breaking up with him was the only way to ensure that.

"You can't be serious. Sure, it's been a whirlwind since we were thrown together by Luca's mistake, but it's been wonderful—the best time of my life, and I thought you felt the same way."

It had been, but I couldn't let him see even a hint of that. I took in a breath and started the explanation I'd concocted. "I don't fit in your world. Your people aren't my people." It was partly true, but the full lie had to follow. "This isn't going to work between us. We can't work. I can't keep doing that." I motioned back the way we'd come.

He took my hand in his. When I tried to pull back, he placed his other hand on top. "We don't have to go to any more parties like this, if you don't want to."

I shook my head. "It's not just that."

"Tell me what the problem is, Adriana. Whatever it is, I can fix it. That's what I do—I fix things."

He was the fixer all right, and that was part of the problem. I'd allowed the issues with Harry to get out of control. Travis's efforts to save me and fix them for me were going to make his father fire him if I didn't leave soon enough.

Harry's attack on our way out had made that clear. Harry would keep at Travis, at us, and the mess would make it into the press.

"You can't shove a square peg into a round hole."

His hands squeezed mine. "You can't mean that. We fit together perfectly, and you know it."

"You accept me for who I am, but they don't, and they never will. They look down on me, and in the end, they will end up looking down on you exactly because you accept me for who I am."

"Fuck them," he spat.

"I went into the bathroom. They didn't know I was there, and the things they said were just plain mean," I lied. "They wonder how could you hook up with a girl like me. And when Harry tells them I was a stripper, it's only gonna get worse."

He shook his head. "I'll make sure that doesn't happen."

"You can't know that. Secrets like mine get out eventually. In my neighborhood, most people wouldn't give a damn, but the people you work with do, and they'll always hold it against me, against you. There's no changing that aspect of human nature." I had to look away as his eyes bore into me. If I hadn't already emptied my stomach, I'd be making a mess of the back of this limo right now.

"Please, gorg—"

"I told you to stop calling me that. I'm serious."

"So you want me to start lying to you now?"

Instead of laughing at his attempt at a joke, I took a long breath. "You said you'd do anything for me."

"Anything." His eyes pleaded. "Let me fix this."

That was the opening I needed. "There are a few things I need from you."

"Anything."

This hurt me as much as it did him, but I was determined to not let my emotions show through. "To start with, I want a month apart to reconsider."

The tic in his jaw indicated I might be pushing him too far.

I hoped what I said would give him the incentive to follow through on

296

the important parts, even though I knew I wouldn't be able to come back to him. Even if Neville and Harry didn't come after us again, his father's opinion of me wouldn't allow that without jeopardizing Travis's career. God, I hated his father right now. He'd destroyed my father's life and now ours.

Travis blew out a breath. "Okay. And?"

So far, so good. "I want you to go in to see your father tomorrow and tell him you choose the company and you've dumped me."

His eyes widened, and his jaw clenched. "I'm not dumping you. So you want me to lie to him?"

"I don't care how you explain it," I relented. "But saying it's over between us won't be a lie, and he needs to know that helping him run the company is what's important to you."

His thumb rubbed a circle over my wrist. "I'm done letting him dictate my life. I don't need to explain that we're taking some time off." He had trouble saying that last part. "And I told you, he won't be a problem. I can handle him."

"You said you'd do anything for me, and this is what I want. I have to know I'm not the source of tension between you and your father. Tell him it's over."

The hint of a tear appeared in his eyes. "A month?"

I nodded. "And you tell your father you're not dating me. It won't be a lie."

"Right." He blinked a few times and inhaled slowly. "Going to be the roughest month of my life."

It was going to be rough for me as well, especially knowing I wasn't going to be able to get back with him, no matter how much time passed. It was over now and needed to stay that way. But in the meantime, I needed him to have enough hope in us to save himself and not create a rupture with his father.

CHAPTER 71

TRAVIS

It was the longest fucking limo ride of my life. The silence was smothering, and my stomach tried to digest itself.

The first time I thought Adriana had dumped me was bad enough. I'd been angry and jealous. But this was the real thing, and much worse. I had no one to be jealous of, and no one to be angry at except myself.

She looked out the window, avoiding me. My only consolation was the wetness in her eyes. There was a part of her that didn't want to do this either.

That was the hope I had to cling to. As much as it sucked, instinct told me there would be no more arguing with her tonight. This would be a month-long wait and then a battle to win her back.

When George brought us to a stop outside my building, she sniffled. "I'd like George to drive me home, if that would be okay."

"Sure." It hurt that she even thought she had to ask. I wouldn't subject her to a late-night subway ride home. "You want to come up and change?"

She shook her head with another sniffle as a tear escaped. When I reached out to brush it away, she flinched.

That hurt like hell. I lowered the privacy glass. "George, please drive Adriana to Queens."

"Yes, sir." His eyes searched hers in the rearview mirror.

I took the plunge. "Can I call you tomorrow?"

She nodded. "Tomorrow night. I've got tutoring after school."

That was another reminder of how different she was from any other woman I'd dated. She volunteered to help children not even related to her prosper in school.

"Tomorrow night," I confirmed as I opened the door and let myself out of the car. "TTFN." I don't know why I used the expression. Perhaps because she liked it, and it implied another meeting shortly.

She nodded. "Talk to you tomorrow."

Even in the dim light, I caught sight of the tear that tracked down her cheek as I closed the door.

George drove off, taking with him all that was right in my world. My chest ached from the giant hole that had just been torn in it.

Like an asshole, I marched past our concierge, Yasmin, without acknowledging her. Somehow, I'd ruined this, and all that mattered was how quickly I could get to a bottle of scotch and make the hurt go away.

Upstairs, I slammed the door behind me, the only thing I could take my frustration out on. It didn't help. She'd left me and the safety of this place before I could find out who had broken into her apartment. That was unacceptable. I would add to the reward.

Loosening my tie, I poured double my normal allotment of Macallan. Bottle in hand, I settled on the couch and knocked back the glass as quickly as I could.

The burn as it went down and settled in my stomach was an indication that I needed more. It would only be enough when I couldn't feel the burn any longer. After the third quick glass, my screwup was coming into better focus.

She hadn't wanted to come to the party tonight. *"It's not my kind of thing,"* she'd said.

I should've listened, but like a dick, I'd thought of myself first, and my desire to show her off. I thought she'd get acclimated and end up enjoying herself. With my glass empty, I poured another large one as the room started to tilt. After kicking off my shoes, I lay on the couch. *Big mistake.* My cock hardened as the location and the smell of the leather brought back memories of Adriana riding me here last night. My brain knew she wasn't here and she wouldn't be arriving, but my dick hadn't gotten the message. It was just another reminder of how screwed up my life was now.

Looking around the room, there weren't a lot of places that didn't also conjure up memories of her, until my eyes settled on the wingback chair. Only a little unsteady, I made my way to it and plopped my ass down.

Somebody had made her feel inferior tonight at the club, and I had to find out who so I could take my revenge. Since she'd heard the slander in the restroom, it was obviously somebody's wife or girlfriend, which narrowed it down to half the guest list.

I poured another glass. This one I didn't chug, but sipped it. I needed a list of things to do better, that's what I needed—things to do better to keep a woman who was not after me for my wallet or my name.

Not take her to fancy events with stuck-up snobs like tonight, not take her to fancy dinners where the paparazzi would be outside the restaurant. She'd protested the shopping trip on her first day here, so not buying her expensive clothes had to go on the list.

But all the list did was confirm that she was unlike any of the women I'd dated before. She was special, and now she was gone.

I'd lost her because I hadn't listened when she'd said she didn't want to go to the party. *Who's the dumbass now, Carlyle?* I finished the glass and poured another. As I remembered what we had done this last week, my eyelids got heavier. It had been a good week—no, a great week—merely because she'd been a part of my life.

CHAPTER 72

Adriana

As we pulled away from Travis's building on Central Park West, my tears started for real. I hadn't had something good ripped away from me. No, I'd pushed away the best thing that had ever happened to me. That's what Travis was, the absolute best I would ever know.

"Are you okay, Andy?" George asked, checking on me in the mirror.

My lie was a nod. A few seconds later, I felt bad enough to admit the truth. "No, I'm not, but I will be."

"Is there anything Katie or I can do for you?" the kind man asked.

I shook my head. "I just need to get home." I raised the privacy glass and watched the city go by.

I used to feel good every time I took the train home from work and we crossed from Manhattan into Queens. It was coming home from the plastic world of Manhattan to the real world. Tonight, when George drove us over the bridge, I didn't have that feeling. Instead, I was leaving the island I'd just recently come to think of as where I belonged.

Travis had done that to me—made me see things from a different perspective and made me understand that some of the things I'd thought were true were not. He'd also made me think of him as the man I should be with for a hell of a lot longer than a few weeks. And he'd done it all in the short time I'd known him, through his honesty, his kindness, and his protectiveness.

I'd fallen for him, and too quickly to tell him I loved him.

After pulling up in front of my building, George shifted the car into park and turned. "What time may I pick you up in the morning?"

His question made me lose it all over again. I sniffled. "I won't be going back."

"I'm sorry to hear that. Katie and I will miss you."

"I'll miss you guys too."

Then he came around the car and opened my door for the last time.

I slid out and wrapped him in a hug. "Thank you for everything."

It took the stiff Brit a few seconds to return the embrace. "It's been my honor."

I let go of him. "Give my best to Katie, please."

"Certainly." He opened his arm toward the building door. "After you."

"I can walk myself up," I protested.

"Mr. Carlyle would have my head if I didn't see you to your door." Even here, I couldn't avoid Travis's commandments.

I relented and mounted the steps. Entering my hallway upstairs, I stopped when I spotted Hugo outside my door.

"What's wrong?" George asked.

"That's my door," I whispered.

George marched ahead. "You will leave," he commanded loudly.

That surprised Hugo. "What?"

George continued forward. "Leave now. If I get to three, you will most certainly regret it." His voice had changed completely. "One… Two…"

Hugo raised his hands and backed up a step. "Hey, man, I don't want no trouble. I'm just deliverin' a message."

George kept going. "Three."

"Andy, tell this guy you know me," Hugo pleaded as he pulled out a knife. "I said I don't want no trouble."

I hurried down the hallway, my heart racing. I couldn't let George get hurt. "George, it's okay. Hugo, what's the message?"

"Simon wants to talk. Maybe you can call him," Hugo said.

"Not interested," I told him.

Hugo stepped forward.

That turned out to be a mistake. In a blur of movement, George slammed Hugo against the wall and wrenched his arm up behind his back with his knife hand pinned against the wall. It looked almost the same as what Travis had done to Simon.

"Drop the knife and leave," George growled.

Down the hall, a door opened and quickly closed.

"Sure, man," Hugo squeaked as his knife clattered to the floor.

George shoved him down the hall toward the stairwell.

When the door to the stairs finally closed behind Hugo, I could breathe again. "Where did you learn that?"

"Four-two Commando of his Majesty's Royal Marines." He leaned down and picked up the knife. "I'll dispose of this."

As my racing heart slowed, I sucked in a breath. "I have a request."

George's brows rose. "Yes?"

I pulled out my phone and scrolled through my photo album. "I'm going to send you a picture. If you can, I'd like you to make sure that this man, Harry Hornblatt, doesn't come anywhere near Travis, and by the same token, don't let Travis approach him. This guy wants to instigate a fight with Travis, and we can't let that happen. It's very important." I located the picture and forwarded it.

George's phone dinged in his pocket. "Consider it done."

I couldn't resist the urge and gave George another quick hug. "I'm gonna miss you guys."

George backed away. "Stay safe now."

I nodded, slipped my key into the door, and unlocked it. Turning on the lights, I didn't hear George's footsteps leave until I'd safely locked the door behind me. Leaning back against the door, my tears started again. I was going to miss all three of them.

My window and thermostat had been fixed. Everything was clean and tidy, better than it had been, all thanks to Katie. I'd complained, but she'd insisted on coming over to clean up while I was at work last week.

After stripping out of the dress, I slipped into sweatpants, thick fuzzy socks, and two layers of sweatshirts. You couldn't be too careful in my drafty space.

I couldn't help sniffling as I hung up the dress carefully, certainly never to wear it again. It was only a reminder of what had been a short, enjoyable interlude in my life.

I wanted to curl up and go to sleep for a week, forgetting my troubles and the trouble I'd caused Travis, but I had work tomorrow and bills to pay. Hibernating wouldn't solve anything.

There was only one appropriate way to deal with how I felt, so I opened the freezer and pulled out my Moose Tracks ice cream. I filled a bowl with the frozen goodness—and I mean really filled it—then plunked down on my lumpy couch with a blanket. It took four spoonfuls to get the brain freeze started. Between the yummy goodness and the pain, it was a surefire way to take my mind off my troubles for at least a few minutes.

A little while later, when my phone rang, I ignored it. It was all the way across the room, after all. It rang again. I ignored it again. When it rang a third time, I mentally cursed Travis for wanting to keep talking, because it would only make things worse. The name on the phone wasn't his, though. It was my sister.

"Hi, Jules," I answered as I settled back on the couch with my bowl.

"Tell me about the party," she demanded breathlessly. "Did they have any of those gold-foil-wrapped strawberries I've heard about? Or anything else with gold foil, like on top of the cheesecake maybe?"

I scooped another spoonful of my ice cream. "Naw." I remembered what Travis had said. "The country-club crowd is too stodgy for that sort of thing."

"Anything else exciting? Like, did they have caviar and stuff?"

I scooped another spoonful. At least if we kept talking about the food I could avoid the horrible pain in my chest. "It might've been there, but I don't even know what the stuff looks like. And fish eggs…really?"

"So tell me about the party. What was it like?"

"Just people talking and stuff." My stomach turned over as I remembered listening to the worst conversation of my life, the one that had put me here tonight, alone. I spooned some more ice cream into my mouth, hoping for the brain freeze to take my mind off the trio of Neville, Harry, and Xavier.

"What is that?" she asked.

"What is what?" I asked, scraping up another spoonful, this one heavy with chocolate fudge.

"My God. You're eating ice cream, aren't you?"

I stopped the spoonful halfway to my mouth. "Uh, yeah."

"So what's wrong?" She knew me too well. "I've heard that spoon clink like a half dozen times. You only binge on ice cream when something bad has happened. So spill."

I debated how to put the horrible truth, and there wasn't an easy way. "We broke up."

"Oh, Andy, I'm so sorry."

"It was inevitable, you know. Me Queens, him Manhattan, me poor, him rich, it just wasn't gonna work. We are not alike at all."

"I don't get it. From what you've been saying, things were going well."

Jules and I had been talking almost every day, and I had been saying that because I'd thought things were going great with Travis and me. "Yeah, but everything comes to an end."

"So what happened? Did he want something kinky and you said no?"

"No. Nothing like that." We fit together better in bed than I wanted to say out loud.

"I still don't understand. Why would he take you to this fancy party just to dump you?"

"He didn't. I called it off," I admitted, trying to make it sound like a noth-ingburger. Now would come the hard part, because it meant lying to my sister.

"You crazy?" she shrieked. "Tell me you fell and hit your head, because I don't see any other reason you would do something so stupid."

Nope, this was not going to be easy. "The party opened my eyes, I guess you'd say. We are from completely different worlds, and with the shit some of the people were talking about me, I knew it wasn't gonna work. It was going to hurt his business. They were looking at him differently, because he chose me and I'm not one of them."

Jules was quiet for a beat. "I don't get it. I've never seen you back down from a challenge. Hell, you seek them out. You stripped to afford your degree. You fought the Plaza project, even though it was nearly impossible. You went and got the teaching job at that rich people's school when you knew you didn't fit the profile they were looking for. You don't ever settle for the easy thing, so what's different here?"

She had a point, not that I would admit it. "Those weren't that hard."

"You went out with Simon to save our worthless brother."

For a moment, I couldn't breathe. "You knew about that?"

"Everybody knew he owed Simon a ton. You think I'm stupid enough to think you would suddenly go for Simon if you didn't have to? Now that's what I call hard with a capital H. I don't know how you managed. I couldn't have done that."

I felt sick thinking about those days. "It wasn't easy."

"Back to you and Satan, who became your Prince Charming. What's really going on?"

Right now, I seriously regretted having told her my nickname for him. I doubled down on the lie. "Based on what I overheard in the ladies' room, they'll never accept me. Not ever."

"Who gives a shit what a bunch of rich bitches think about you?" She wasn't giving up.

"Travis does, or he will in time, because it reflects on him. Anyway, I don't want to talk about this anymore. I made my decision, and now I have to live with it."

"And it makes you feel so fucking good, you have to scarf down a ton of ice cream tonight."

"No. I feel pretty shitty about it because I… I don't know how to put it, I—"

"You love him," Jules suggested.

I'd danced around the idea by telling myself I was infatuated with him, telling myself I was falling for him, telling myself I liked him, a lot. I'd never considered using the L-word. But Jules was right. "Yeah, I think so."

"Which makes you stupid."

I admitted it. "That's me. Your stupid, dumber-than-shit sister, I guess."

We ended the call without any more arguing.

I'd been through the alternatives, and the only way to save the Carlyles, Travis most of all, was to take myself out of the equation. There was nothing else I could do about it. The rich guys from Manhattan were playing Monopoly for keeps, and it would determine the fate of the Carlyle company. If I stayed in the game, they would win and Travis would lose—and not just play money.

Now I was alone in my drafty apartment. Just me, the stupid girl with tears running down her face and half a bowl of ice cream still in front of her, who had work tomorrow.

My only consolation prize was that my move would keep Travis's father from firing him tomorrow and playing into their hand.

Later, I lay pathetically awake in my bed. All I could do was cry about what could have been. How many months would it be before I could lie down at night without my imagination running right back to the one man I couldn't have, the man I'd left, the man I'd hurt?

CHAPTER 73

TRAVIS

"Sir? Sir."

I pried my eyes open the next morning to find George prodding me. "What?" I closed my eyes again against the painful light. "Turn off the lights." Then I added, "Please," the way Adriana had been teaching me. The headache was a dull roar in my head.

The lights went off. "Sir. You shouldn't be sleeping out here."

Rubbing my eyes, I opened them again to find I was slumped to the side in the wingback chair. As soon as I moved, I knew why I didn't like this chair. It was a worthless, pain-inducing device.

"Sir," George repeated. "You need to get ready for work. Your father is expecting you in the office."

I struggled to my feet, and it wasn't just my head that ached anymore. I took two steps and pointed at the devil's chair. "Get rid of that thing. I want it out of here by tonight."

George picked up and examined my almost-empty bottle of scotch. "Yes, sir."

In a desperate need to pee a few gallons, I ambled toward the bedroom. "And I need coffee."

"Katherine is already making your hangover breakfast."

I nodded. "Good." I hadn't needed a hangover breakfast in at least two years, but today I would be breaking that streak.

"Sir, you should know that there was a man named Hugo waiting outside Miss Adriana's door last night with a message from a man named Simon."

I turned and hung on to the wall for support. "What was the message?"

"That Simon wanted to talk."

I rolled my eyes. I thought that guy had gotten the message, but apparently it hadn't been clear enough.

"She said she wasn't interested, and I made him leave," George continued.

I shook my head in disgust. "Fucking Simon again."

"One other thing, sir. I relieved him of a knife."

Fuck. That was bad. "Do you think she's safe?" *Safe* probably wasn't the right word for her neighborhood.

"In my estimation, he was only sent to deliver the message."

I relaxed. "George, I want you to drive her to and from work. We have to keep her safe."

"Yes, sir. I'm also to keep you safe from a Mr. Harry Hornblatt."

I nodded. "Good idea." Of course she was worried about me instead of herself.

"The DOW is up forty-one points, and the NASDAQ is off one-tenth of a percent," he said, giving me my usual morning update. "I best leave now if I'm going to take her into the school this morning."

I waved him off. "Go. I'll get a taxi to the office."

Once under the warm water of the shower, I hated that the other side of this two-person shower was empty. Waking up and showering with my gorgeous Adriana had been a pleasure.

Now life sucked. And what sucked worse was that there was nothing I could fucking do about it.

I CHECKED THE TIME AND DECIDED I DIDN'T HAVE TIME TO STOP AT MY OFFICE before going up to Dad's, so I pressed the button for the top floor. As the elevator climbed, disgorging passengers every few floors, I psyched myself up for this meeting.

By the time the elevator reached his floor, I was the only one left.

Walking up to the office, I decided it should be renamed the throne room.

I waved when his assistant saw me. "Good morning, Deena. I see he's back early."

"Yeah," she said less than enthusiastically.

I remembered that she'd scheduled her Hawaiian vacation to overlap with Dad's time away, down to the day and hour. That was the source of her mood. "Sorry about cutting your vacation short."

She lifted a shoulder. "I should have known." Then she nodded toward the door. "He's alone."

Although I would have much preferred to talk about Hawaii with Deena, I stepped inside Dad's office and shut the door behind me. "Good morning, Dad. Welcome back."

He grunted and pulled a potato chip from a bag. "I was disappointed to hear that you attended the party at the club last night with that girl."

So, that's how it was going to be? Not even a *good morning, son*? I intended to keep the promise I'd made to Adriana. "I sent her packing last night after the party. You asked me to choose, and I have." I kept my voice steady, although I felt anything but.

His eyes narrowed. "And you don't intend to start up with her again?"

"Of course not," I scoffed with what I hoped was sufficient acting ability to convince him. "She was very, very fun, but not a good match long term."

He nodded. "I agree. You need to find a woman of both breeding and substance, someone to help you carry on the family line. You're not getting any younger, you know."

This was a new line of attack for him. He'd never before insinuated I should settle down.

I smiled and nodded along, though I was disgusted by the way he approached my life like I was a stud and it was time to be mated with the right mare to produce a Derby winner. *Somebody give me a bucket to puke in.*

"Very good. Then where do we stand on that Vanquish project?" he asked. A few sentences of capitulation from me, and he was off to new business.

"Their counteroffer wasn't up to snuff, and I don't intend to respond this week," I told him. "I'll let them stew for a few days."

"Sounds good."

Ten minutes later, I was glad to be out of there, and because of how he'd acted, I wasn't the least bit sorry that I hadn't been completely honest with him. All I wanted was to call my Adriana and talk to her, but she was in class, and she'd planned that we talk tonight.

309

Leaving the elevator on my floor, I paused before I reached my office and settled for a text instead of a call.

ME: I miss you. Talk to you tonight.

"Good morning," Mindy said in her annoyingly cheerful tone.

I nodded. "Yeah."

"Who kicked your dog this morning?"

"No interruptions." I closed my office door behind me.

Taking my chair, I turned to the window. The scene didn't interest me the way it normally did. Where I used to imagine skyscraper possibilities, now I only saw gray, dingy buildings.

After minutes of waiting, I checked my phone again. No response had come. It was going to be a long fucking wait until tonight.

CHAPTER 74

Adriana

In the morning, George surprised me by exiting Travis's car outside my building. "Good morning, Andy."

At least the casual greeting meant Travis wasn't in the back looking to ambush me. He rounded the car and opened the door to the back.

"No thanks. I'll take the train." I had to get back to my pre-Travis routine.

He held the door open. "My instructions are to transport you to and from your work."

"Tell His Majesty, no thank you."

George's grimace said what I was afraid of. "He'll have my head if I don't."

I huffed out a long breath and climbed in. "Thank you."

"He misses you terribly," George said after a minute on the road.

"He'll survive. And I'd rather not talk about it."

"As you wish." George honored my request by not saying another word until he wished me a good day when he dropped me off.

THAT EVENING, I LOOKED LONGINGLY AT THE BOTTLE OF WINE IN MY FRIDGE AND was proud of myself when I closed the door without grabbing it. It had been less than twenty-four hours since I'd cut myself out of Travis's life, but it was a school night, and that meant drinking my troubles away was off the table, especially after my meeting with Gleason.

If I showed up for work tomorrow smelling like a distillery—or too hungover to function at the top of my game—he'd happily show me the door. Then he'd head straight to Harry and his family, claiming success with his hand out for another donation.

I settled onto my couch and opened my phone to read the message again.

SATAN: I miss you. Talk to you tonight.

I hadn't responded, and I couldn't without risking my sanity. I'd text him, he'd text back, and I'd end up crying again over the man I couldn't have.

I navigated to his contact and didn't even hesitate before changing the name to HERO. That's what I'd called him in Gleason's office this morning, and it was the truest description of him.

He'd been my hero more than once, truly saving my community center and our pool, as well as dealing with Simon and Harry. He wasn't the wicked public persona the press painted. He was the best man I knew.

Checking the time, I decided it was late enough that he'd probably be home. *Crap.* Just the word *home* made me tear up, because a few days ago I'd considered his penthouse my home as well.

Be strong, be strong. I repeated the mantra in my head. I needed to talk to him and find out how his meeting with his father went. My finger hovered over his contact for a few seconds before I pressed it.

Be strong.

"Hi, gorgeous."

This was exactly what I'd feared. My insides fluttered at the compliment, and it was a reaction I could allow. I let out a long exhale. "Hi." I held back the argument about him calling me gorgeous.

"How was your day, Adriana?" he asked.

"Fine." It was a total lie, but I couldn't possibly tell him how I felt.

"I'm calling bullshit. Because mine totally sucked, and I don't believe you had a good day either."

I cringed at the *totally sucked* comment and hoped he wasn't talking about his meeting with his father. "You're right. Some guy sent his driver for me when I'm perfectly capable of getting myself to work, and the kids were real brats today in second period. But I want to hear about how your meeting with your father went."

"What I'm hearing is you want me to be honest with you, but you don't want to return the favor and be honest with me. That's not going to cut it, gorgeous. So let's start again. How was your day, Adriana?"

His comment was spot-on and sucked the breath out of me. I didn't dare be honest with him about how I couldn't sleep and how much I missed him. *Be strong.* "I didn't sleep well last night."

"Me neither. I heard you had a visitor last night with a message from Simon."

Naturally, George would have mentioned that. "I told Hugo to tell him I wasn't interested in talking." *Was Travis jealous?* "You know how I feel about him."

"Until I find out who broke into your apartment, George will be driving you to and from work." His tone implied that wasn't going to change no matter how much I complained.

"I'll accept that for the time being, if you'll tell me about your meeting with your father."

"Did you miss me? Because I miss you." There it was, the demand to talk about my leaving.

"I got your message. It was sweet, and you know I miss you too. How could I not?"

"Then why are you doing this to us?"

This was exactly why I hadn't replied to the text. "I had to, and you said you'd give me a month." I had to get him back to focused on waiting.

"You're right. But I'm not sorry for pushing you to see reason."

He couldn't see me shake my head. "Thank you for sending George," I offered as a compromise.

It did the trick. "Dad had heard that I took you to the club last night. He wasn't happy about that."

I held my breath for the next part.

"He accepted it when I lied and told him I'd broken it off with you. I told him I was totally committed to the company, and he had the gall to suggest that I should find quote-unquote *'someone with breeding and substance to carry on the family line'*."

I could breathe again, now that his father wasn't firing him. I felt like laughing at his father's expectation that Travis start popping out babies as soon as he found some socialite *with substance*, but I kept that to myself. "Good luck with that."

"I know. You're the one for me."

And again we were back where I didn't want to be, on the subject of us. "He said breeding, and I'm an Italian Greek mutt from Queens, so that leaves me out. But otherwise, I take it you're in good with your father again?"

"As good as before it seems. He switched seamlessly to projects and projections, just like the robot he is."

Relief spread through me. I needed to hear that we'd cleared the first hurdle and he hadn't been fired, and he sounded confident he wouldn't be. "Thanks. I was worried. Hey, I've got papers to grade and some sleep to catch up on."

"Can I call you tomorrow?"

I heard the hope in his voice, and it hurt to squash it. "We shouldn't. A month, remember?"

"How about dinner on Saturday, like we had planned?"

"You certainly are persistent."

"You say that like it's a bad thing."

He was employing another tactic from Professor Markowitz's class: to make progress, and keep them talking and engaged. I resisted the trap of continuing the conversation. "Good night, Travis, and don't call me."

"That's not a fair rule."

"Good night, Travis."

"Good night, gorgeous." I also didn't fall into arguing the gorgeous comment like I would have before. I ended the call before he did.

Rising from the couch, I went to the kitchen and poured myself a glass of wine. One wouldn't hurt, and it would be my reward for not giving in to him.

Stay strong, I reminded myself.

Even with the wine, sleep did not come quickly, as every time I closed my eyes, all I saw was Travis, and all I could think about was how wonderful it had been in his arms and his bed.

I soaked my pillow in tears for the second night in a row.

CHAPTER 75

Travis

The next morning, I was only two bites into the eggs Benedict Katherine had prepared when the question came.

"What did you do to upset that poor girl so?" she asked in that British accent that made me feel like a chastised schoolboy.

"You tell me. Until the party at the club, I thought things were going pretty well."

"And you didn't do anything to upset her?" She brought over another plate, loaded with two strips of bacon and hashbrowns.

It was the same question I'd asked myself a million times in the last two days. "Why do you assume I did?"

"George said she looked like death warmed over when he drove her in this morning, and I judged her to be made of sterner stuff."

"The eggs Benedict is very good this morning."

She didn't acknowledge the compliment. "Whatever it was you did, wasn't a minor infraction."

"That's the problem. I didn't do anything—not that I can put a finger on. She said we didn't fit together. We were from two different worlds."

She topped off my orange juice. "Do you believe that explanation?"

I finished chewing and swallowing. "There has to be more to it than that."

She had a pensive look. "And she didn't say anything else?"

Since Katherine and George had become more like family to me than my actual one, I continued. "Just that she overheard women in the restroom talking shit about her, as she put it."

"Really?"

I began on a piece of the bacon, wishing the discussion with Katherine would make things clearer for me.

It hadn't.

AFTER GEORGE BEGAN OUR SHORT TRIP TO THE OFFICE, I ASKED, "HOW DID Adriana look this morning? Did she have anything to say that would be helpful? Did she ask about me?"

"Which of those do you want to start with?" he asked.

"Any. I'm having real trouble with this woman."

"Women can be an enigma at times. To answer your question, she didn't look like she'd slept well. But sir, you have that same look. Neither of you is dealing with this situation well. And she didn't have to ask about you. I may have mentioned that you weren't in the best of spirits."

"That's an understatement," I admitted.

"I'm British, sir. Understatement comes naturally."

"Go on."

"She has been quiet in the car, and hasn't confided anything to me, sir, if that's what you're asking."

It was. When we pulled up to the building, I debated not going in, but duty demanded my presence. Allowing my mood to give Dad a chance to question my devotion to the company was a loser's choice.

George opened the door, and I climbed out, buttoning my coat against the wind.

"Your girl sure can suck dick."

I whirled. It was Harry fucking Hornblatt.

"She can damn near suck-start a jet engine," he yelled loud enough to turn the heads of people on the street.

Strong viselike hands grabbed and turned me. "Get in the building," George insisted. He hauled me along. "He's trying to bait you."

Nobody got away with talking about Adriana like that. "I'm going to teach that fucking asshole a lesson."

"She doesn't want you to fight him," George grunted, shoving me toward the building's entrance.

"I should know," Harry yelled. "She got me off in record time."

"You don't want to disappoint her," George added.

I strode the rest of the way into the building, not even stopping to flip Harry off. George was right. I needed to cool off.

"Let me deal with him," George said.

Looking through the glass, I could still see him. "No. Not you either." I pointed at the photographer on the other side of the street. "It's a setup."

George flexed his fists at his side. "Sneaky little bugger." He turned to me. "If that is all, sir. I'll await your call."

"For now. And yes, I'll stay inside instead of giving the asshole the beat-down he deserves."

"That would be best."

Upstairs, Mindy greeted me with her usual upbeat "Good morning." But that was before I got close enough for her to get a look at me, it seemed. Her face twisted. "You look terrible."

"Thanks. That's maybe a little too much honesty for me today. No interruptions, please."

"Luca would like to talk to you."

I shook my head. "I don't give a single shit what he wants." That was maybe too strong to be appropriate at work, but today I didn't care. Maybe I was letting that fuckwit Harry get to me. "Sorry. I didn't mean to snap," I said as I entered my office.

She followed me and closed the door after us. "Katherine told me what's going on with Adriana. What can I do to help?"

"Just handle the phones and keep people out," I said. "I need some alone time." I needed a ton of alone time.

"Sure thing. Would you like me to reach out to her?"

"You've talked with her? Adriana?"

She smirked. "Twice. I could check in on her."

Why hadn't I expected this? Mindy kept in touch with Katherine, so why not with my Adriana as well, trying to keep my life coordinated?

"She doesn't want me to call, so I think not. Thanks anyway."

Mindy left, and I was alone with my thoughts. It was not the best decision because there was only one person who could make the hurt go away and keep my thoughts from turning dark. That person didn't want to talk.

Then I had an idea. I just had to figure out which one, which day, because all at once would be over the top in anyone's book. "I'm going to need some deliveries," I said after dialing.

~

I summoned George at the end of the afternoon and asked him to bring my present upstairs before we left.

Shortly after that, I heard the commotion outside my door.

"He's not taking visitors right now. You can't go in," Mindy said. She'd said that same line a few times this afternoon, but always softer.

"Fuck you. I need to talk with him." It was stupid Luca.

I raced to my door to protect Mindy. She didn't deserve to be treated like that. I flung the door open. "You apologize this second, and get the hell off my floor," I bellowed.

Heads popped up around the floor.

The elevator dinged, and George stepped out with the roses I'd asked him to get for Mindy.

Luca raised an angry fist in my direction. "You sold out my building for a piece of ass. You should be fired for that."

I was done with him. I stomped forward. "You apologize to Mindy, or I'll throw you off this damn building."

He braced for a fight. "Try it."

George got between us before I could deck the asshole and grabbed one of Luca's wrists. "He said the lady is due an apology. I suggest you make it now."

Luca turned white. He knew George's background and capabilities. Luca probably considered me a blowhard because I'd yelled at him, but never hit him. On the other hand, he knew George had killed in his prior occupation.

"I'm going to count to three," George said coldly. "One."

"Mindy, I'm sorry I swore at you. I meant no disrespect."

Mindy nodded. "Thank you, Luca." She was also on George's dial-it-back bandwagon.

Reluctantly, I joined, too. "Luca, you've been given incorrect information, and Mindy will pencil you in tomorrow for us to discuss it." The employees around us didn't need any more gossip fodder.

Luca took the out and nodded. "Tomorrow works."

George released him and retrieved the flowers. "These are for you," he said, presenting them to Mindy.

"Why thank you, George." She sniffed them. "They're lovely." She set the vase on her desk.

"Mr. Carlyle asked me to get them for you," George clarified.

Mindy smirked at me. "Did he now?"

CHAPTER 76

Adriana
(Six days later)

"I can't. Not yet. I'm not ready," I told Jules over the phone on Wednesday morning.

It had been a week since our breakup—technically eight days, and yes, I was counting. My sister had called me every day, trying to convince me to do what was right—in her mind at least—and give it another try with Travis. She held out hope because I couldn't trust her with the truth about what I'd overheard and the danger it posed to Travis.

She was being a good sister, and I was the bad one here. I had another week or so to go. I didn't know exactly how long before the board meeting where Neville, their chairman, planned to get rid of all the Carlyles from the company they had built.

I would never forget Neville's words. *"This only works if the older son is the first domino. The old man has to fire him before the board meeting. I'll take care of the other two in the meeting itself."*

"I still don't think you're going at this the right way," Jules said. "You didn't give it enough time. You might fit in better than you think."

"Speaking of time," I said. "I need to get going. My ride will be here soon."

"Just know I love you, even if you are stubborn and wrong."

"Love you too," I said, hanging up.

Bundling against the cold, I grabbed my bag and went downstairs to wait for George. The bad news was standing on the sidewalk across the street.

"You really should have agreed to go out with me," Harry yelled. At least he didn't make a move to cross to my side of the street. He had shown up yesterday morning as well, and George had coldly told him that if he found him on my side of the street, very bad things would happen.

"My answer hasn't changed." I lifted a middle finger to him as George drove up. It was stupid, but I waited for George to round the car to open my door for me. *"Proper etiquette,"* I'd been reminded.

After pulling the door open, George noticed Harry across the street. "Would you like me to take care of him?"

"Don't bother. Let him freeze his ass off."

"Pity."

∼

It was just before fourth period when Mr. Luce, our HR manager, caught me on the way into the classroom. "Mr. Gleason would like to see you in his office at the end of the period."

"Sure," I answered.

All during class, I wondered if it was the skirt. This was my first time wearing it, but it wasn't more than three inches above the knee. I knew because we'd measured before buying it.

Being called to the headmaster's office was never good, especially if Mr. Luce delivered the invitation. Plus, my lunch break was directly after this, and Gleason never finished quickly, so he was going to screw up my chance for a relaxing break. I'd been looking forward to a nice hot dog from a cart several blocks away, something I could indulge in and pretend I was feeling normal. Cutting into my lunchtime put the cart out of reach, and I'd have to settle for a prepared sandwich from the closer bodega.

When the bell rang at the end of the period, I gathered my things and trudged upstairs to Gleason's office. Happy about missing my hot dog indulgence, I was not.

The two previous times I'd been called to Gleason's office with Luce in attendance had not been happy days. I did commit the infraction of wearing hoop earrings very early on and had to listen to a twenty-minute lecture about the teachers' dress code. My single question about the men's dress code had taught me to nod instead of talk in front of the pair.

The second time it had been a stain on my blouse, courtesy of a science experiment gone wrong and a lab coat not buttoned up high enough. Standardized uniforms made it easy for the students by comparison—so long as their shirts were tucked in and their hair wasn't too long, all was well.

I reached the headmaster's doorway, and the pair were already seated, with the folder on the desk. I swallowed the lump in my throat and entered, wondering what my infraction had been this time. This whole scene would've been comical if it wasn't so serious. I couldn't afford to get in trouble after the way I'd dealt with Gleason last time.

The headmaster motioned to the chair opposite the desk. "Have a seat, Moreno."

I could read upside down as well as the next person. The folder had my name on it.

"It has come to our attention…" Luce began.

I braced, because those words were never followed by good news.

Gleason had the audacity to smirk. Whatever this was, it was his revenge for our previous encounter where I'd embarrassed him and threatened him with the Carlyle name.

Luce opened the folder and pulled out a piece of paper. "That you were dishonest on your employment application with us." He laid the paper on the desk and turned it to face me.

"We can't overlook this kind of behavior," Gleason added. "It's despicable."

I was at a loss, not understanding the problem, and I worked hard to school my face and remain passive. "What do you think the error is?"

"If this got out, it would be a very black mark on the school's reputation," Luce said.

"I still don't understand." Unwilling to give Gleason the satisfaction of watching me flinch, I held my posture straight.

"You didn't disclose the fact," Gleason explained, "that you were a stripper." The paper that had been underneath my application, which I could now see, was a printed copy of an email.

My blood threatened to boil with anger. This was Harry's doing, no doubt about it. "If you check my application, you will see that it includes my employment at the Sugar Palace. And I disclosed that I was a dancer."

"Stripper," Luce mumbled.

"*Dancer* was my job title," I said. "I put myself through college, and not only is it in my past, but it's a perfectly legal profession in this state."

Gleason closed the folder. "We're going to have to let you go," he said, as if letting me go wasn't the same as firing me.

I'd had enough. "For what offense? Filling out my application honestly?"

"Uh...for bringing disrespect to the school," Gleason sputtered. "You'll need to leave the premises at once."

I'd prepared for this after our last encounter and stared him down. "You can't do that."

"Watch me," he responded.

It might not save me, but I wasn't going down without a public fight. "If you'll check page thirty-nine of the employee handbook—" I started.

Luce's mouth dropped open, probably anticipating what was coming next.

"—After the school has conducted a thorough investigation, an employee facing discipline has a right to a disciplinary hearing, including the right to present evidence and witnesses," I noted, recounting the exact words from the employee handbook. I shifted my anger to Luce. "I am correct, am I not?"

"You are," he admitted.

I smiled at Gleason. *Take that, you ass.* I hoped he wouldn't want to take this public.

"Please wait outside for a minute," Gleason growled.

As I rose, I held back my smile, but I knew I had him. Rats like him preferred to hide in the shadows. I closed the door and waited while they figured out a face-saving way to retreat.

Then the door opened. "You may join us again," Luce said.

I retook my seat and crossed my legs.

Gleason's lips turned up slightly—not a good sign.

I crossed my arms.

Luce sat and tapped the folder several times. "Due to the seriousness of the charge, you are suspended until the hearing, which I will schedule for Friday next week. In the meantime, you are to have no contact with other employees of the school, students, or their parents."

I gritted my teeth as my stomach churned. Luce apparently had more backbone than Gleason, but there wasn't anything else I could do about it now. They'd made up their minds to get rid of me before I'd even walked in the room, and my demand to take it public had made them hesitate, but in the end, it hadn't been enough to tip things in my favor.

Fighting was the right thing to do, and I'd at least gotten an extra week's pay out of my refusal to go quietly. I would also get to drag Harry's connection to Gleason into the light at the hearing.

I made it into the stall of the downstairs bathroom just in time. At least in here, nobody could see my despair.

I was proud I'd fought them, but Harry had won, or at least he would after the hearing next week. He was such an asshole. The deck was stacked against me, and there wouldn't be any way for me to change the outcome now. I had no job and no savings, which would very quickly translate into no apartment.

Harry's words from this morning took on a new meaning. He'd created the buzz-saw that destroyed my livelihood, and he'd scheduled it for today when he could publicly taunt me.

If he was physically in front of me right now, I would kick him in the balls. Otherwise, I had no way to get back at him. He was insulated by wealth and privilege, and I was a nobody, an ex-stripper.

After cleaning up, I walked to the entrance and called George.

"Are you done early?" he asked.

"Yes, and I won't be needing any more rides to the school."

"I'm afraid Mr. Carlyle won't allow that."

"It doesn't matter what *Mr. Carlyle* wants. I won't be working here any longer. They've suspended me."

After a pause, he said, "I'm sorry to hear that."

I knew the sympathy in his voice was genuine. "Please don't tell Travis. I'd like to handle that." I had to keep it from him until after their board meeting so he wouldn't go ballistic.

"As you wish. I'll leave now to pick you up."

During the wait, I made a plan to be proactive against Harry instead of just ignoring him. Back in school, we'd all heard the whispers about cash payments from his family to keep Harry out of legal trouble with girls, some of whom I'd heard were underage, and where there was smoke, there was bound to be fire.

Since I could bring witnesses to the hearing, I would spend the time between now and then finding somebody willing to talk about their ordeal at Harry's hands. Then we'd see who had the dirtier background, me or him.

I also needed another piece of information, so I dialed the person who could tell me and hoped she'd keep her mouth shut about it.

"Mindy speaking," she answered.

"Hi, Mindy. It's Andy again."

"Good to hear your voice. How are you?"

"I've had better days, but I'm muddling through. I have a question, and I hope you can keep it between us."

"Sure. What do you need?"

"I know the company has a board meeting coming up. Can you tell me when that is?"

"That's an easy one. Thursday next week. A big day for Travis, I hope."

"Me, too," I admitted.

Travis had said he expected his father to announce the succession plans at this board meeting.

"He's really not coping very well," Mindy said. "I know he'd love to hear from you."

Tears pricked my eyes. "In time, I promise." I swallowed to force the lump in my throat down. "Thanks for the information. Please don't tell Travis we talked."

"You take care of yourself now."

I blinked back my tears. "Thanks, I will."

CHAPTER 77

Travis

On Friday morning, George was here in the kitchen eating a leisurely breakfast of strawberries on waffles, the same as I had in front of me.

I stared at the food, but all I could see was Adriana's face. I hadn't slept much, and this was only the second week of the month she wanted away. It was killing me. I'd whacked off in the shower again thinking about my sweet Adriana, my fierce Adriana, my sexy Adriana. It hadn't solved the ache in my chest.

Picking up my phone, I read the message that had come in last night. The newlyweds were back.

> SPENCER: We should catch up. I'm married, but it's not contagious. Beer tomorrow night before my trip?

I'd debated avoiding it until he got back, but this morning, that struck me as a wuss move.

> ME: Sure thing. 7 tonight work for you?

I watched the screen say delivered and the three bubbles appear.

SPENCER: Copy that.

Noting the time, George's presence concerned me. "Shouldn't you be on your way to pick up Adriana?"

"She doesn't need me anymore," he said casually, plopping another forkful into his mouth.

"I hope she doesn't, but she doesn't get a say in this. You drive her both to and from work until we find out who it was that broke into her apartment, and not a day sooner."

A crease formed in his brow. "She didn't tell you?"

Now, I was getting irritated. "Tell me what?"

He swallowed slowly. "Sir, she wanted to tell you herself. She's not working there anymore."

"Why the hell not?" I demanded.

"I don't know, sir. She said she wished to tell you herself."

I threw down my napkin and stood so fast that my chair fell over behind me. "This is not fucking acceptable."

Looking at George and Katherine's faces, I rephrased it, "Not you, George. I mean her not telling me is not acceptable."

Storming into my home office, I slammed the door and dialed. It went to voicemail. "Adriana, I just heard from George that you're not working at the school anymore. We need to talk. Now. You either pick up the phone and call me, or I'm coming to you. And I will find you. I'll tear every building in Queens apart brick by brick if I need to."

I paced for a few minutes, wondering what could've happened, before the phone rang showing her name. "George said you're not working at the school anymore. Why am I hearing this from him?" I blurted as soon as I answered.

After a silence, she said, "Good morning to you too."

Of course she knew how to put me in my place like a schoolboy. She taught high school brats for a living.

Appropriately chastised, I restated, "Good morning, Adriana. It's good to hear your voice. How are you?"

"Why, thank you for asking, Travis. I would be better if I didn't have some entitled, rich brat from Manhattan calling me first thing in the morning to yell at me."

"I apologize for that. It was uncalled for. The question still stands: what happened?"

"I didn't feel like inconveniencing George any longer. I figured it was the quickest way to get him to stop driving me back and forth."

"So you still work there?" I asked, needing to be clear that she had lied to George.

"Don't worry. I'm still on the payroll. But I don't want George driving me. It's a waste of his time."

I clenched and unclenched my fists to gain control of my temper. "We've been over this. He will drive you to and from your work until we find out who broke into your apartment and I know you're safe."

"No thank you."

"Yes," I insisted. "Either he drives you so I know you're safe, or I accompany you myself. Which will it be?"

She sighed loudly. "Arrogance doesn't become you, Mr. Carlyle."

"It's not arrogance you hear, Miss Moreno. It's merely a determination to keep you safe."

"Okay," she relented. "We'll do it your way for another week. Please don't call again, and give my regards to George and Katherine." She ended the call before I could say anything else.

Damn, that woman could be aggravating.

I returned to the breakfast table and George's questioning gaze. "She was trying to get out of having you drive her back and forth."

"Ingenious," he said. "What are my instructions?"

"Pick her up this afternoon and continue driving her until I say otherwise."

"Yes, sir. There's one other thing you should be aware of."

The pancake I'd forked stopped halfway to my mouth.

"That Harry Hornblatt chap heckled her from across the street yesterday morning. What would you like me to do next time he shows up?"

I was done ignoring the fucker. "Nothing. I'll take care of him." It was time to go nuclear.

LATER THAT MORNING, I FOUND XAVIER IN HIS OFFICE. "GOT A MINUTE?"

He motioned me inside. "Sure, what's up?"

I entered and closed the door behind me. "I'm having some trouble with the Hornblatts on a project."

Xavier leaned back in his chair. "And what can I do to help?"

"Cancel funding on the next tranche of their Hoboken project."

"Let me understand. You want me to threaten to cancel that funding to get their attention?"

"Not threaten," I clarified. "Inform them that we won't be participating. If they have any questions, they can contact me."

Xavier shook his head. "I can't do that."

"Yes, you can and you will," I insisted.

"*Your father*—" He emphasized the words. "—does not want to upset them. Some secret side project he's working on, but you know how that can be."

Yes, I knew all too well how Dad could be about those projects. Now my magic bullet against Harry had turned into a dud. I couldn't very well go to Dad and ask to pull the Hornblatt investment because Harry was bothering the woman I'd told him didn't matter to me.

CHAPTER 78

Adriana
(Three days later)

George drove me into Manhattan again on Monday morning.

In the back of the car, the smell of the leather reminded me of sitting with Travis. That made my insides hurt.

Even though I'd texted him to stop, Travis was still sending daily gifts. They had started last Friday morning with a cooler at my door containing a gallon of my favorite ice cream. It was followed Saturday by a stack of romance novels by my favorite author, then a pair of warm Uggs yesterday.

This morning, it had been a fuzzy throw blanket and a carton of hot chocolate mix outside my door with a note that read, *To keep you warm when I'm not there.* The sweet gestures reminded me of how far Travis actually was from the wicked man I'd thought him to be that first day.

I asked George to drop me off a block from the school, telling him I didn't want people looking at me funny for being driven to work by him.

He obliged, and when he'd disappeared around the corner, I turned around and walked in the other direction to the library since I wasn't welcome at Hightower. I hated that I was now lying to George about still having my teaching job, but it had to be done, at least until we got past the board meeting.

Once I located a quiet corner of the library to do my work, I inserted my earbuds and pulled out my laptop. It had taken me dozens of phone calls over the weekend, but I'd finally located two girls who were willing to talk to me about Harry, and I had recorded my conversations with them. This morning, I would type them up and look them over.

I hadn't convinced either girl to come forward and speak at the hearing—at least not yet—but I did have hope. If I wasn't able to convince either one or both to speak, I'd summarize their statements based on our conversation, and that would have to do.

I was just finishing up the second transcript when my phone vibrated. Turning it over, I saw the message I'd been dreading.

> Chelsea: I know why you've been avoiding me. Please call me, or do I have to come down to Hightower and yank you out of there? I know today is the day you have a long lunch break.
> Spencer and Travis must have connected, and now she wanted to complete the circle with me.

I'd dodged her intentionally, ignoring her messages or sending back excuses about being swamped with grading, because I was afraid—afraid that she'd tell Spencer and things would get back to Travis. Then everything would blow up in my face.

But now it sounded like the breakup news was out of the bag, and agreeing to lunch was a risk I had to take. She was just crazy enough to come down to the school, and I couldn't have that lie exposed.

Ducking into the stacks, I made the call. "Hi, girlfriend, how are things?"

"In a word, fantabulous," Chelsea said. "Except that I already miss my husband. He just left on this yacht-racing idiocy, and I worry about how dangerous it is." She took a breath. "Now that we have that out of the way, why didn't you tell me? I mean, I understand why it took a while for Travis to tell Spencer. *Guys.*" She said the word like it explained everything, which of course it did. "But you should have called me, or come to cry on my shoulder, or told me to beat the shit out of him for whatever the hell it is he did to you."

"I'm sorry. You're right. I've been too wrapped up in this shit to talk. I should've called." It was time to be honest with her. If I couldn't trust Chelsea, who could I trust?

"I caught you between third and fourth periods, right?"

"I don't have much time." It was mostly a lie, but the truth of my status at Hightower was dangerous.

Her tone turned serious. "I remember you have a long lunch break on Mondays, so I'm buying. Ruby's at noon, and I'm not taking no for an answer. Holding in the hurt is the wrong way to go, and you know it."

I didn't dare offer an argument. She was the best friend a girl could wish for, trying to do what best friends did, and I was being a shitty friend by avoiding her. I couldn't keep that up.

"You're not saying anything," she prodded.

"Right. See you there."

CHELSEA STARTED IN ON ME AS SOON AS I SAT DOWN ACROSS FROM HER AT Ruby's. "So tell me what he did."

"He didn't do anything," I said slumping into my seat, weighted down by my own guilt.

She appraised me warily. "Then what's this bullshit about you not being good enough for him and not fitting in? You're stronger than that. What are you hiding?"

Since we'd spoken on the phone earlier, I'd decided I needed to tell Chelsea the truth or risk losing her as a friend. It had been crappy of me to ignore her, but it would be much worse to mislead her when she'd finally found out the truth.

I straightened. "That's just what I told him."

"And what's really going on?" Her face showed honest concern.

Our server, Gus, arrived, giving me a moment's reprieve. We had Gus every time we ate here since Chelsea always picked a table in the corner. "Hello again. What can I get you ladies today?"

Chelsea went first. "Gus, the chicken lasagna for me, with the side salad."

I smiled at his. Smiling felt hard, being something I'd done precious little of in the last week. "Sounds good. I'll have the same."

Chelsea pointed at me when Gus left. "You were saying?"

"I can't be with him right now. It's not safe."

"I always thought you were the smart one, but right now you're making absolutely no sense. What does that mean, you can't be with him?"

"If I tell you, can you not tell Spencer?"

She shook her head. "He's my husband. I can't keep things from him."

"For a week or so?" I pleaded.

"That I can do. He's incommunicado anyway for the ten days or so he's on this stupid yacht race. I can only go to the website to see where they are, and the captain only posts stuff about the boat, the wind, and the waves. It's crazy. I mean, what if something happened? But he just *had* to do it." She shivered. "Sorry. Here I am babbling about my fears when we should be talking about you."

With Spencer out of town, I could breathe easier. "There's a plot against the Carlyle family, and they want to use me against Travis."

"You're going to have to give me more than that."

Gus arrived with our salads.

"We were at his country club for a party last week, and I overheard something I wasn't supposed to." I went on to explain the conversation and what they were planning against Travis and his family.

Chelsea pushed her salad away. "That's scary. But I don't get why you left Travis's place. Was it his idea to deal with it this way?"

Gus arrived with our lunch plates. I shook my head and sipped water until he left.

Chelsea cut into her lasagna and looked over at me expectantly.

"No, I just took myself out of the equation," I explained. "Harry was poking at me and Travis just to get a reaction they could photograph or record to get on the gossip sites and stir up shit for the company. Without me around, he can't provoke Travis. And Travis doesn't know anything about this."

Chelsea's jaw dropped open at that last sentence. She set her fork down. "So basically you're lying your ass off to him about this not-fitting-in bullshit."

I cringed at her tone. "I have to. I can't tell him."

"Why the hell not? You have to tell him."

I finished chewing my first bite of the lasagna and shivered at the thought of what would happen if I told Travis. "That would be a disaster. He'd run straight at Harry and punch his lights out, which is exactly what Harry and those other toads want." I shook my head. "You have no idea. You didn't see him. The two times Harry touched me, Travis was like an enraged bull and there was no way to calm him down or control him." I took another bite.

Chelsea gave me a knowing nod. "I guess I get that. Spencer is like that, a thousand percent protective." She smiled. "It's one of the things I love about him."

"I like it too," I admitted. "It's over-the-top caveman, and I'm not supposed to like it—feminism and all—but it's kinda hot."

She tipped her water glass at me. "You know what this proves, don't you?"

I lifted a shoulder. "What?"

"He's in love with you."

My cheeks flamed. "Get outta here. We were just having fun. You know his history. I was the flavor of the month." I'd hoped to maybe be the flavor of the quarter. Right about now, I wished I hadn't read all those articles about him.

She wagged her finger. "I see that look," she singsonged. "He's a rich guy, from Manhattan, no less, so he's screwing with your view of the world. But you're totally in love with him too. "

"I am not," I protested, crossing my arms for good measure.

"Now you're lying to me *and* yourself."

An odd feeling ran up my spine. *Guilt?* Had I been avoiding the L-word on purpose? "Besides, we don't fit together. I'm a complete fish out of water in his world. Even his father can see it."

"Cut that out. His father doesn't matter. I'll bet you can't stop thinking about him and haven't been sleeping well."

I sucked in a slow breath to avoid admitting that she was right.

"And now you've sacrificed the relationship to protect him. If that isn't love, what is?" She went back to her lasagna.

"I admit it. I like the guy…a lot. But…" But *what* was the question.

"Still lying," she said through a mouthful of food. After she swallowed, she added, "How did you feel when you left him to go back to your apartment? Shitty, right?"

I gave in and sighed. "You know, when I met him, I wanted to hate him, but the more I was around him, the more he grew on me."

"Leading to now when you feel…?" she prompted.

"You're right. When I left him, it felt like a piece of me had been ripped out. Even now, I can barely sleep. So yes, if those are the signs, I love him. Feel better?"

"It beats being lied to," she said after another bite of her lunch. "It was obvious to me at the wedding."

"What?"

"When the maid of honor and the best man are mostly MIA at the wedding because they're off banging each other's brains out, it's hard for the bride to not notice."

And I thought we'd been discreet.

She pointed at my food. "So what are you going to do about it? About them attacking your man?"

I shrugged. "I have to stay away from him." That hadn't changed.

"You suck," she said, slamming her fork down.

I nearly spit out my water but recovered. "What?"

"Travis deserves better. You said he fought for you when Harry came after you. Now he's under attack. You should be in his corner, supporting him and fighting for him. Instead, you're letting this warped issue of which side of the river you live on get in the way. Why aren't you fighting for him like he does for you? Do you want to be right about Manhattan versus the outer boroughs that badly?"

I was stunned into silence.

"Do you?" she demanded.

I probably had been at least a little bit like that. "I thought staying away would help. I don't know how to fight in his world. I don't know anything about corporate boardrooms."

"Then you find someone who does. If you won't go to Travis, then who?"

Spencer would have been my choice. He knew the corporate world, but he was unavailable.

"Who?" she prodded.

The name that popped into my head was logical because he was also affected. "His father." As the words came out, they filled me with hope. From what Travis had told me, Victor Carlyle was a corporate shark, and who better to chew up the enemy than a shark? "Yeah. His father knows how to fight in the boardroom."

"You better start eating or it's going to get cold," she said, pointing at my plate.

I scooped a large bite to catch up, suddenly energized with hope.

As we finished, I had one more question. "You remember the rumors about Harry when we were at NYU, the ones about underage girls?"

She nodded. "And he's still disgusting."

I'd asked everybody I knew except Chelsea about this. I had avoided her to avoid the difficult discussion we'd just had. "Do you remember any names?"

She mentioned two that I'd already been in touch with and then added, "And Angela Ecker."

Hers was a new name, so I typed it into my phone. "Ecker with an E?"

"I think so."

~

AFTER LUNCH, I SPENT THE TIME UNTIL GEORGE WAS DUE TO PICK ME UP IN THE library. Unfortunately, I had no luck tracking down Angela Ecker. *Bummer.*

Things got worse back at my apartment—or rather I was reminded how my life was turning to complete shit when I ran into the super in the stairwell and he asked where my rent was.

No boyfriend was the least of my problems. No job and no savings meant moving back in with my parents and hearing every night how I'd been warned that moving out was a bad idea. Then there was the Friday disciplinary hearing as well.

CHAPTER 79

Adriana

Tuesday, I dressed in my best school attire and with my paperwork already stashed in my bag, I made the call.

"Hi there," Travis's assistant, Mindy, answered.

I was glad she hadn't mentioned my name. "I need a favor. Are you somewhere you can speak freely?"

"He's downstairs right now talking to his brother. How can I help?"

"I need you to get me into the Carlyle building, and I need an appointment with Travis's father. But it can't be under my real name."

"An ambush? It sounds juicy. What's up?"

I fidgeted and decided on the truth. "I need to tell him something he's not going to want to hear. And I need it to be behind closed doors."

"I'm sure Travis could get you an audience," she suggested.

"Travis can't know about this. You have to promise me that."

"I'll see what I can do and call you back with a time."

"Thank you." I made her promise again to not tell Travis.

THAT AFTERNOON, MY LEG SHOOK AS I WATCHED THE FLOOR NUMBERS ON THE elevator increase rapidly.

"Nervous?" Mindy asked from beside me.

"More like terrified."

"He's the kind of man you have to hold your ground with. Be firm. Don't let him sense fear."

I took a deep breath and willed my leg to settle down. "Thanks."

"And I sent his assistant on an errand, so you have about half an hour of uninterrupted time.

"Got it." I nodded, and the door dinged, opening higher up than I'd ever been in any building.

She walked with me until we reached the corner office. The assistant's desk was empty. Mindy knocked once and opened the door. "Your one o'clock is here."

"Send him in."

She swung the door open and backed out of the way, giving me a thumbs-up.

It was time to face the shark and save my man. I strode in and shut the door behind me.

"What are you doing here?" Victor Carlyle demanded from behind his massive desk. "You're not Andy Brown."

I strode toward him with my best imitation of confidence. "I get that a lot. Andy is short for Adriana." *Be firm.* "Now, we have to talk, Victor." I chose to stand behind one of the visitor chairs where my jittery leg wouldn't show.

His jaw ticked at my use of his first name. It bugged him. Good. "You have it wrong, Ms. Moreno. I don't *have* to do any such thing." He pressed a button on his phone. "Deena, get security up here."

Don't let him sense fear. "It's just you and me, Victor."

His jaw ticked again. "We'll see about that." He picked up the phone to dial.

Be firm. It was make-or-break time. "If you don't talk to me," I warned, "you'll lose the fucking company. Everything you fucking worked for."

He snorted. "Having to resort to four-letter words to express yourself—"

"Is a sign of weakness," I finished for him. "Yeah, I've heard that, so fucking excuse me for being from Queens."

His face reddened.

"It doesn't change the fact that if you don't listen to me right now, someone else will be sitting in that chair next week."

338

That got his attention. His eyes narrowed and his fingers tapped the desk. "Sit," he commanded. "You get two minutes."

As my leg trembled, I ignored the demand to sit. "Gordon Neville, Xavier Breton, and Harry Hornblatt are plotting to have you removed at the board meeting on Thursday."

"And how would a girl like you know about something like that?"

Ignoring the *girl like you* dig, I pressed on. "I overheard them discussing the plot last week."

"I don't believe a word of it." He leaned back in his chair and smirked. "What's your game, Ms. Moreno?"

"No game, Victor. They want to kick out all the Carlyles and take over the company. Personally, I don't give a fuck about you or Luca, but I do care about Travis and what happens to him. He doesn't deserve to lose out after all the hell you've put him through."

He bristled at that. "He's the oldest, so I expect the most from him. He has to toughen up."

"You should consider treating him more like a son and less like an employee," I shot back.

"I think you coming in here and making up a story is just an attempt to ingratiate yourself with my son and get him to take you back. Well, that won't happen, because you're not an appropriate match for him. I won't allow it."

I no longer had to worry about him sensing fear, because now all I felt was anger. But I was the one who had to toughen up here and ignore his insults. My mission was to save Travis, not have his father accept me. We were way past that.

He picked up the phone again. "We're done here."

I hadn't expected him to believe me without some proof. *Be firm,* I repeated in my head. "Several weeks ago, Xavier Breton gave you a file documenting what he claimed was embezzlement committed by your son Luca."

He put the phone down.

Didn't expect that, now did ya?

"How did you hear about that?" he asked.

"I told you, I overheard them plotting."

He leveled me with a glare. "I still don't believe you."

I glared back. "Neville called you Monday before last, while you were on vacation, and told you, and I quote, that he was 'done being Mr. Nice Guy', and he'd 'have your balls for breakfast' if you didn't cut Travis loose if he caused another PR problem for the company. And he told you Kwan, Parker, and Jenson would back him up on that. Now do you believe me?"

He nodded as the blood drained from his face. "Now I believe you." He took in a long breath. "And what do you want me to do with this information?"

"Travis shouldn't be a casualty in whatever blood feud you have with this Neville fucker. If we were on my turf, I'd kick him in the balls and stomp the asshole into the ground, fuck him up good. But he's in your world, and I figured you'd know to fight him."

"I do." He motioned to the chair again. "Sit, Adriana."

This time I accepted the invitation. "I prefer Andy."

"Andy, a boardroom fight is just like that, except with words and information. You punch hard with facts and make sure you're the last one standing."

"It sounds like wussy fighting to me. I'd rather teach the guy a lesson with a bloody nose." Saying that brought back pleasant memories of Travis beating up Harry.

"We don't get bloody or in trouble with the police. Making the other guy bleed money is usually the outcome. To do that we need facts. Tell me everything."

As I recounted everything I remembered from that night at the country club, he made a few notes.

Later, a single knock preceded the door opening. "I'm sorry, Mr. Carlyle, I didn't realize you had a guest," the woman said.

"It's all right, Deena," Carlyle said. "Come in."

Deena shot me a questioning look and approached the desk. She was probably the assistant Mindy had mentioned.

He pulled a folder from a drawer and offered it her. "Scan and send this to Knowlton Forensic Accounting and return it to me. *Nobody*," he said sternly, "is to know about this."

She nodded and took the folder.

"And get them on the line."

"Please," I added with a smile as she left and closed the door. Why did nobody in this family have any manners?

"I'd planned to look into this when I had more time, but now that you've warned me—" His phone beeped, interrupting him.

"Katie Knowlton is on line two," Deena said.

She sure was fast.

He picked up the phone. "Katie, Victor Carlyle here. I have a rush job for you and Nick. Deena is sending you a file I received alleging some sticky fingers that I suspect may be fabricated, and I need it checked out. Cost is no object."

Chelsea had been right. For this battle, I needed to enlist the help of someone who knew how to fight in the boardroom. Victor was that man.

"Yes, it's urgent, and I repeat, cost is no object," he continued. "Great. I look forward to hearing from you."

I silently mouthed, *"Thank you."*

Carlyle saw me and added, "Thank you, Katie," before hanging up. "They're the best in the business," he explained. "Now, what else do we have as leverage?"

I noted his use of *we* and started explaining what I'd dug up so far on Harry.

"We have business dealings with his father," Victor said, smiling. "Go on."

I told him the rest of what I had.

"Okay," he said when I'd finished. "We have two days to put this together." Once again, he used the word *we*. "This is what I want you to do…"

CHAPTER 80

TRAVIS

THURSDAY MORNING, I JERKED AWAKE AS MY HEAD LOLLED FORWARD TOWARD MY desk. I almost hit the laptop in front of me. I was in my office on day sixteen without my sweet Adriana. The lack of sleep was really catching up with me, and I wasn't sure I could make it thirty days without calling her.

I'd kept up the daily gifts, but hadn't gotten any response. The lack of a cease-and-desist message gave me some hope.

Rubbing my eyes, I stared at the laptop's screen, reviewing my presentation on the Towers project in Queens one more time.

The board meeting was in a few minutes, and from the way Xavier had reacted to the financial details, I expected a grilling from our twit chairman.

As far as I was concerned, Neville was a weasel. Sending Xavier to take notes at our meetings on the project because he didn't trust Dad was disgusting.

Mindy appeared in the open doorway. "The meeting—"

"Yeah, the highlight of my day." I shut my laptop and rose.

I entered the boardroom and took my usual seat to the right of Dad, two seats away from Neville.

Xavier positioned himself across from Dad, as he liked to do if he beat Luca into the room. Today, it wasn't a contest because Luca was out of town.

The other board members, Parker, Kwan, and Jensen, clustered near the other end of the long table, closer to the screen on the wall. After the door closed, Xavier didn't make his usual move to start his presentation of last quarter's financial performance, which always began the meeting. His was always followed by Dad's strategic presentation. I'd been told my remarks would be a part of that segment of the meeting.

"Before we begin with regular business," Neville said, "I think we should address some improprieties at the company that have recently come to my attention."

My blood boiled, because I knew where this was going, and I didn't like it one bit. I'd kept my dealings with Adriana completely professional.

"And what would those be?" Dad asked, rubbing his fingers along the stack of folders in front of him.

Neville lifted a folder and slid it to Xavier. "Would you pass these around, please?"

Xavier pulled out a stack of papers and did as he was told.

When I got mine, it was several pages of spreadsheets with a typed summary page at the back.

"Xavier, would you please run us through what you found?" Neville asked.

Xavier picked up his packet and turned toward the outside board members at the end of the table. "A few months ago, I started to notice a disturbing pattern in some of our building expense accounts. The details are in front of you, but the summary is what's most disturbing."

At their end of the table, the board members leaned forward, seeming to listen intently.

I'd guessed wrong. This wasn't about me and Adriana.

Neville smiled smugly. Not a good sign.

"You'll see that in each of these three accounts," Xavier continued, "expenses went up significantly starting last September."

"And you only just noticed this?" Kwan asked.

Xavier hesitated. "In the previous quarter's analysis, there was only one anomalous month. And after talking with Luca Carlyle, he didn't think it was of concern."

Kwan nodded.

"The concerning thing when I looked into these accounts," Xavier continued, "turned out to be that the extra payments went to companies controlled by Luca himself, and I suspect for services *not* rendered."

"To whose attention did you bring this?" Neville asked.

Remembering the meeting between Xavier and Dad that I'd overheard a few weeks ago, I guessed the answer.

"I gave this to my boss, of course, Victor," Xavier answered.

Next to me, Dad oddly didn't react.

"And how did he respond?" Neville asked the setup question.

"He said he'd get back to me later, and he never did. I suspect he planned to overlook the embezzlement because even after we became a public company, he always intended to treat this as a family business."

"Is that true?" Jensen asked from the end of the table.

"It's true that he gave me this report," Dad answered in a monotone.

"Doing nothing because it involves your family is unconscionable," Parker said.

"I agree," Kwan added.

Dad sat stoically. It wasn't like him to not fight back.

All I could do was silently blame Luca for everything. Luca was such an ass. I wouldn't have minded him being kicked out of the company, but his actions were coming back to hurt Dad.

"Let's leave that alone for a moment," Neville said. He was probably planning to ream Dad in private. "I'd like to hear about the disaster the Towers project has become." He turned to me. "Travis, proceed." His wording made it clear I was the one about to be reamed.

I connected my laptop to the projector and started the presentation.

To say the board wasn't pleased with the terms I'd agreed to for the relocation of the community center would be the understatement of the century. Each of them had criticisms, all aimed at me and the concessions I'd made.

With Dad, my defense had been that I'd followed his instructions related to getting it done quickly, but in this setting, with Dad already under attack for Luca's embezzlement scheme, I wouldn't say that.

"The numbers may not be pretty, but since you…" I looked directly at Neville. "…want us to avoid bad publicity at all costs, this is what it took."

Neville shook his head. "I never said that, and certainly not for this amount of money."

The other board members nodded in agreement.

Neville pulled a piece of paper out of his portfolio. "The really concerning thing to me is this letter I received." He held it up. "It says here that you negotiated that agreement with one Adriana Moreno, your girlfriend."

That drew gasps from the other end of the table.

"It's a lie. While I was negotiating—"

"Hold on a minute, Travis," Dad said, putting a hand on my arm. He pivoted to Neville. "Who is making that accusation?"

"Harold Hornblatt," Neville answered.

Fucking Harry. My fist clenched under the table. I was going to kill that lying asshole.

"May I see that?" Dad asked.

Neville handed the paper over.

After he looked at the paper a moment he asked, "How did you get this letter?"

Neville's eye ticked. "It came in the mail."

"Does anyone know this Harold Hornblatt?"

I raised a finger. "I do."

Nobody else said anything.

This was quickly turning into a real shitshow. Luca embezzling from the company, Dad shielding him, and me accused of sweetening the community center deal. A quick glance down the table showed we didn't have any friends in the room.

CHAPTER 81

Travis

Dad folded the paper, rose, and went to the door.

"What are you doing?" Neville demanded, his face red.

Dad pulled open the door. "Shedding a little light on the situation." He spoke to someone in the hallway. "Would you join us?"

"This is a closed meeting," Neville complained.

My heart stopped when I spied Adriana in the hallway. What the hell was she doing here? I rose quickly and closed the distance to Dad. "She shouldn't be here."

"I want to be here," Adriana assured me.

Dad pulled me into the hall with my girl. "It'll be fine. Trust me and don't say a thing."

"Do what he says." A smile crossed Adriana's lips. "Please."

Her request damn near melted me. I nodded and opened the door to the boardroom, though the last thing I wanted was for her to be subjected to the brawl I would initiate if one of these assholes insulted her in any way.

"What's the holdup?" Xavier asked in that grumpy tone of his as the three of us entered.

"Andy, would you please take a seat on the other side?"

Andy? How the hell did Dad even know her? I retook my seat, unable to guess what Dad's plan was.

She rounded the table and sat, throwing a quick smirk in my direction.

"Who is this?" Neville asked curtly. "And what does she have to add to the discussion of your son's malfeasance?"

"My name is Adriana Moreno," she said, addressing the board members and avoiding looking at me. "And I represent the Astoria Community Center that is being displaced by your Carlyle Towers project." She returned to looking at Dad.

"Andy," Dad asked, "is my son your boyfriend?"

I gulped and waited for the humiliating answer.

Adriana's gaze shifted from Dad to me, and the sweetest smile grew on her face. "Absofuckinglutely, and I'm damned proud of it."

That was my feisty girl, and she'd even sworn for me.

I took a deep breath as a hole in my chest was filled by her proclamation.

"There," Neville exclaimed. "She admits it."

"Andy," Dad continued, "did this relationship start before or after you negotiated the lease for the community center in the Plaza building?"

"After," Adriana said clearly. "While we were looking for a suitable building, I didn't even like him. Hell, I hated anybody with the name Carlyle for what your family did to my father." She spoke of and to Dad.

"Of course you'd say that," Neville hissed. "We can't believe a word you say."

I was about to intervene to protect Adriana when Dad put a calming hand on me and offered a quiet, "Hold on." I settled back in my chair. I knew that tone. Dad had something up his sleeve, and from the determined look an Adriana's face, she was part of it.

"You're the one who shouldn't be believed," she said, straight to Neville's face.

"And why is that?" Neville asked.

The hint of a smile on Dad's face said Neville had just walked into a trap.

"Because you and Mr. Breton here…" She looked at Xavier. "And Harry Hornblatt have been plotting to have the Carlyles removed from the company."

"Is that true?" Dad demanded harshly.

Neville reddened and pounded the table. "Of course not. This is outrageous."

"I heard the three of you plotting at Glenside two weeks ago."

Neville blanched for a second, but he recovered quickly.

Glenside? That had been the night she'd dumped me, saying she didn't fit in. She hadn't said anything about overhearing a plot.

"You're merely slinging mud to protect your new boyfriend." He waved a dismissive hand. "You can leave, little lady."

I raised my water glass to hide my smile. My little Queens fireball was on a roll and had really gotten to him. I glanced down the table and couldn't get a read on the other board members.

"Be quiet, Gordon," Dad said.

"I will not," Neville fumed. "Your son's conduct is what we're discussing here, and she has no proof of anything, only baseless lies meant to shield her boyfriend." His accusing finger pointed at me.

Dad rose from his seat. "Let's discuss proof then."

"We need to get back to regular business." Neville huffed.

Dad opened the door, letting in an older gentleman I didn't recognize. "Have a seat, August. Over there."

Xavier's face fell.

"What is going on here?" Kwan asked as August fell into a chair across from me.

"Hold on, Tom. You're going to want to hear what August has to say."

"I don't care who he is," Neville sputtered. "He has no right to be in here or to say anything."

Dad wagged a finger at Neville. "I told you to shut up."

Neville cowered.

"August, how do you know Harold Hornblatt?" Dad asked.

"He's my son," the man answered.

That surprised the hell out of me and drew a gasp from Neville.

"And what is your relationship to Xavier here?" Dad pointed.

"I'm married to his sister."

"Which makes your son, Harold, his nephew?" Dad said, focusing on Xavier.

"Of course."

"Xavier, you claimed to not know him. How is that?"

Xavier didn't answer or look up.

"We'll get back to that." Dad passed Neville's letter across to August. "And what did your son tell you about this letter?"

Regardless of what happened in this meeting, I was going to hunt fucking Harry down after I got out of here.

348

August's eyes darted around the room. "Uh, that it's a fabrication meant to get your son Travis fired."

Neville's eyes fell to the wood surface in front of him as he shrank a few inches. Everyone else watched August with rapt attention.

"And how did Mr. Neville come to have this letter?" Dad asked.

Apparently, Dad had known this ambush was coming and was prepared for it, much more prepared than Neville expected.

"He told me Mr. Neville brought the letter to him to sign," August said, clearly very nervous in this room.

Xavier had stopped me from applying pressure on the Hornblatts, but Dad obviously had.

Parker got in on the action. "You're saying the accusation is false, and Gordon authored it?"

August nodded. "That is what my son said."

Neville had had enough. "That's a lie. He's lying."

"How many times do I have to tell you to shut up?" Dad shouted.

Neville cringed.

I didn't bother hiding my smile. This was good theater, and my Adriana had a part in it. But that thought erased my smile. It meant Adriana had been plotting with Dad this whole time, rather than coming to me with what she knew. The realization soured my stomach. How could she?

Dad pulled a thick folder from his stack and slid it over to me. "Travis, would you please give everyone a copy?"

I went around the table, distributing copies to everyone. The header on the papers read *Knowlton Forensic Accounting*.

"You heard Xavier tell us I hadn't looked into the allegations he brought me regarding my son Luca." Dad tapped the first page of his copy. "That is incorrect. This is a report compiled for me by Knowlton Forensic Accounting regarding the allegations Xavier brought to my attention."

Xavier shifted in his seat and wouldn't meet Dad's eyes.

"I've heard of them," Parker said.

Jensen nodded as well. "I used them once. Good firm."

I glanced at Neville. He looked as nervous as Xavier.

"In here it agrees," Dad started, "with Xavier's assessment that money was siphoned out of the company and sent to an offshore account. The difference is that they've linked the offshore account to you." Dad pointed a finger directly across at Xavier.

"He told me I had to," Xavier sputtered, looking at Neville.

349

"Shut up," Neville spat.

"August?" Dad asked. "What else did your son tell you?"

August looked at Neville. "That it was Mr. Neville's plan to force the members of the Carlyle family out of the company. Harry said he knew the financial accusations against your son Luca were fabricated, and it was his job to be sure the other son was disgraced and fired so Mr. Neville could force you out of the company as well."

"Why would your son participate in this?" Dad asked.

"Mr. Neville promised him the CFO position, and that Mr. Breton would be promoted to CEO."

Neville looked ready to pass out.

Dad nodded to August. "Thank you. You may go."

The nervous man left quickly.

Dad didn't address Neville, but looked down to the other end of the table. "I think it's time for an executive session."

"I second that motion," Jensen said.

"Xavier," Dad said. "You're fired, effective immediately." Dad turned to me. "Have security escort him directly out of the building and revoke his access. Andy, you stay."

"Gladly." I followed Xavier out and closed the door behind me. I grabbed Xavier by the arm and pulled him to a stop. "Deena, we need security up here right now."

"But I have things in my office," Xavier protested.

"Later. You heard him. You're leaving."

Xavier wouldn't meet my eyes. "He made me do it."

At this point, I didn't give one shit about anything Xavier had to say. "Tell it to the judge." I hated that my Adriana got to stay in the room to watch the fireworks and I didn't. It wasn't right that she'd worked this plan out with Dad and excluded me.

"Judge?"

"Embezzlement is a crime, and you tried to hang it on my brother. You can bet we'll be wanting to prosecute. But what you should really be afraid of is Adriana finding you and kicking your balls all the way to Cleveland."

Wetness appeared at the front of his pants and leaked down his leg to his shoe. *Disgusting.*

"Deena, we're also gonna need janitorial to clean a urine stain on the carpet."

Her eyes went wide, and she quickly dialed.

Security arrived to escort the now ex-CFO down to the street.

"Be sure to cancel all his access immediately, including electronic."

"Sure thing," the shorter of the two guards said.

I waited around for them to finish the executive session. A janitor was running a carpet cleaner over the wet spot when the door to the boardroom opened again.

I stood aside while Neville scurried out and down the hall.

Kwan, Parker, and Jensen each shook Dad's hand on their way out, congratulating him.

Dad eyed the carpet cleaner. "What happened here?"

I shook my head. "Xavier peed himself."

"Figures," he said.

"So?" I nodded toward the boardroom, curious.

Dad beamed. "Gordon resigned, and I'm back to being the chairman."

"So, how did you figure all that out?"

"You can thank Andy."

Adriana stepped tentatively out of the boardroom. "It was all Victor."

Victor, Andy, what had happened?

Dad slapped me on the back. "You two should talk. She's quite a catch."

When he left, I held my hand out, and to my relief, Adriana took it. That was all the encouragement I needed to haul her close and snuggle her head against my chest. "You were brave in there." With Deena and others looking on, this wasn't the place. "Come with me."

CHAPTER 82

Adriana

Travis pulled me to the elevator at a rapid clip, not saying anything until he punched the button and the door closed. "Adriana, you are going to tell me everything."

I was elated to be with him again, but his tone carried an angry vibe. "Well—"

He stopped me with a finger to my lips. "In my office." When the doors opened, he towed me toward the corner.

"Hi, Andy," Mindy said as we raced up.

"You know her?" Travis demanded of his assistant.

"Sure," she answered. "How was your meeting?"

"Interesting," he growled.

"It went great," I corrected. Travis should be in a hell of a lot better mood after how things had turned out.

"No interruptions," he barked as he ushered me into the office and locked the door.

"What is your problem?" I demanded.

He huffed loudly. "My problem?" His exasperation was clear and very loud. "My problem is that you've known since that party what was going on, and instead of telling me, you pushed me away while getting chummy with my assistant and my father."

"That's right," I admitted.

"And now you show up after ghosting me for sixteen days and call me your boyfriend. I want to know why."

I amped up my volume to match his. "You want to know why?" I pushed at his chest and backed him toward the desk. "I'll tell you why, you big lummox." I pushed him farther. "Because you fell for it every time Harry pushed your buttons, and you almost got yourself fucking fired."

"I did not."

"Did too." I jabbed my finger into his chest. "And that was their plan. I had to save you from yourself. If I'd told you anything, you would have run straight at Harry and punched his lights out."

"Yeah, because he deserves it. I protect what's mine."

I poked his chest again. "See that right there? The overprotective instinct is what they were counting on. So I had to go to your dad instead."

"How did you even get him to talk to you?"

"I had Mindy sneak me in, and I threw f-bombs at him until he listened. Answer me this, big guy. Are you happy with the way things turned out?"

Travis took a long breath and started to laugh. "Yes, it turned out pretty well. You, my little wildcat, really put old Neville in his place. When I told Xavier out in the hall that you'd kick his balls all the way to Cleveland, he was so scared he peed himself. And now, I can go teach Harry a lesson he never forgets."

I gave an exasperated sigh. "No punching. Your dad is handling him in Manhattan rich guy fashion—you know, hit him in the wallet. Now, if you're done with the stupid questions, I have one of my own."

He paused.

I stuck a finger in his chest again. "When are you going to flipping kiss me?"

"When are you gonna tell me this time-out is over?" There it was, another battle for control. "Say it."

"I thought I just did."

He pulled me to him. Our tongues tangled, and our hands roamed at a feverish pace. This was the panty-melting kind of kiss that demanded to be followed by nakedness.

The instant hard peaks of my nipples threatened to cut their way through my clothes to reach his caress. The bulge in his pants pressed firmly against me. Yes, his anger had given way to a more primal desire that matched my own.

He broke the kiss. "I'm going to do a lot more than kiss you, Wildcat."

I liked the nickname. I palmed his erection and squeezed. "Are we going to let the dragon loose?"

"I'm going to fuck you so hard, you can't help but scream my name. And when they hear it down the hall, they're all going to know you belong to me. You're mine."

I worked his tie loose and started on the buttons of his shirt. "No, they're going to know that I caught you, and you're mine."

He attacked the buttons of my blouse.

"Don't rip anything," I cautioned him. "I want to walk out of the building with my clothes intact."

"So picky." He made quick work of my skirt and panties while I only got his belt undone. "The heels stay on," he said when I went to slip them off.

He spun us, and with a quick swipe of his hand, he cleared half the desk. Papers and folders hit the carpet.

I yelped as he lifted me and set my ass on the desk. He stood between my thighs, massaging my breasts, and lavishing kisses, sucks, and light bites to my nipples. "Tell me you're wet for me."

I leaned back on my elbows. "You have no idea. Check and see how much I've missed you."

He slid two fingers inside me. "Oh, yeah," he said, pulling away from my nipple for a second. "You're soaked."

God, I loved the feel of him pumping his fingers into me and playing with my nipples, but today, I didn't need the buildup. I'd fantasized about this all day. "I need you inside me," I managed between moans of pleasure.

His thumb found my clit, and I nearly exploded. He knew how to finger me in ways I'd never experienced with another—the circles, the flicks, the subtle pressure, pinches, tweaks. One after another, his movements sent electric shocks all the way to my toes. He knew how to play my body like an instrument. I did all I could to keep my moans from becoming screams that alerted the entire building.

"I feel you getting close, Wildcat."

"Oh, yeah," was as coherent as I could be. "So close."

He gave one more hard suck on my nipple, and with a crook of his fingers, I detonated. "Ohmygod, ohmygod, ohmygod," I said through the hand I'd clamped over my mouth. The blindingly hot orgasm rolled over me in a rush.

He continued pumping his fingers as I trembled out my release. *My God.* Panting, I yanked his hair. "I still want you inside me."

"Now that you're warmed up," he quipped as he stood and retrieved his wallet.

My eyes were laser-focused on the erection trying to tear its way out of his pants.

"Fuck," he said. "I don't have a condom. We used the last one on the limo ride to the party."

CHAPTER 83

Travis

After she left me, I hadn't needed to reload my wallet. There was no point.

"I don't give a fuck, Travis," Adriana informed me. "I got checked after Simon, and I'm on the pill."

"I'm clean too, but are you sure this is okay?"

She got off the desk, turned, and leaned over it, presenting me with that perfect pussy. She looked over her shoulder. "Does this answer it for you?"

I couldn't believe it. Not only did I get her back today, but I was going to feel her, really *feel* her, with nothing between us. She truly was my woman, and I was going to brand her from the inside.

I shoved my pants and boxer briefs down as she watched over her shoulder. Her eyes turned hungry as I fisted myself and stroked. When a bead of precum leaked to the tip, I wiped it off and brought that finger to her lips.

She licked it with a giggle. "Are you going to play with yourself all day, or are we going to do this?"

I pressed her shoulders down, positioned myself at her entrance, and slid in through the exquisite slickness. "You're so fucking tight, baby. It's so good."

She tensed, and the already firm grip her slick flesh had on my cock became even tighter. She gasped as I bottomed out in her. Pumping in and out, I knew quickly that I wasn't going to last, not since I'd dreamed of this every night she'd been away. Her moans became louder, urging me to speed up, to push in harder. The primitive instinct took over. There wasn't going to be any thought of going slow in this orgasm, as my lizard brain took over. My balls tightened, and tingles started at the base of my spine.

"I'm close," she mumbled between moans.

The words broke through my caveman instinct, and I pulled her back from the edge of the desk enough to reach for her clit.

Four quick circles was all it took to launch her over the top again. Modesty won out as she clamped a hand over her mouth to muffle her scream of my name.

The clenching of her orgasm triggered my own as I drove deep and tensed up, spilling my load inside my lovely Wildcat.

After a minute of recovery, I went to my bathroom and brought back a warm washcloth to clean up. "You're coming home with me," I announced as we redressed.

For once, she didn't argue.

When I opened the door, Adriana rushed to Mindy and gave her a hug. "Thank you so much for the other day."

That was my girl, piling on the thank yous.

"It was my pleasure." Mindy then glanced at me with a raised brow and a knowing smile. "You two kids have fun."

CHAPTER 84

A**DRIANA**

F**RIDAY MORNING** I **WOKE UP IN THE PENTHOUSE, WITH** T**RAVIS SPOONING ME.** Even before my shower, I was much more refreshed than I had been any morning since I'd retreated to my apartment. It was a testament to how miserable I'd felt without Travis next to me.

So I could get enough sleep to face Gleason and Luce at the hearing today, I'd insisted on no sex after ten o'clock last night. The soreness of my well-used muscles attested to how much we'd fit in before that deadline to make up for lost time.

"Good morning, Wildcat." Travis breathed into my hair as he pushed his morning wood up against my backside. "Ready for round nine, or is it ten?"

"Not this morning, big guy. I have to get to school, but I will be back tonight." Neither of those things was a lie. I did have to go into Hightower for the hearing this morning, and I would be back tonight. I hadn't told him about the suspension or the hearing. It was my mess to sort out, and I didn't want him to get involved.

"Are you sure?" He tweaked my nipple, not hard enough to hurt, but enough that my subconscious shifted to sexy times and my nipple to perk up into a hard little bud.

I pulled his hand away from my breast. "I'm sure. I take my job seriously, and I can't be late the way you can." I slid out of bed.

Travis showered with me, which was a temptation for both of us, but he adhered to the rules and didn't try to have sex with me.

After, Travis dressed quickly and headed to breakfast. He liked to eat slowly.

After drying off and blow-drying my hair, I looked through the closet and selected a conservative, navy-blue business suit—one I hadn't worn yet. When George had brought me clothes from the penthouse after the night of the party, I'd told him to leave all the expensive business suits Travis had paid for and only bring over the less expensive top-and-skirt sets. Hair in a neat bun and no more makeup than normal for work finished the look.

I knew the rule was always look your best for court, and this was the educational equivalent. Getting fired from Hightower would put an indelible black mark on my teaching career.

"Doesn't she look positively gorgeous today?" Travis asked.

"You're biased," I noted.

Katherine brought over a plate of ham and eggs, with toast on the side for me. "But I'm not, and I agree with him."

George raised his fork a few inches. "Me too."

Giving up, I sat. "Thank you very much." They'd both welcomed me warmly last night without any comments about how I'd treated their boss, which I'd actually worried about. This place and these people felt like home again.

"George will drive you, same as before," Mr. Bossy announced. His investigation hadn't yielded a suspect yet.

I cut into my ham. "And I'd love to have him drive me."

GEORGE LET ME OUT, AND I REGRETTED HAVING EATEN SO MUCH BREAKFAST AS MY stomach threatened to revolt. Toughing it out like a big girl, I walked into Hightower and started up the stairs to the room I'd been told we'd be using. I stopped one floor shy to use the bathroom. Breakfast didn't taste as good coming back up.

Cleaned up, and with a comfortably empty stomach, I climbed the final floor.

Harry was in the hall outside the room.

With an internal chant to *be calm*, I strode up with confidence in my walk. "Why are you here?"

"I wanted to see you get what you deserve."

Be calm. "I don't deserve to be slandered by the likes of you." I had to remember that his stock-in-trade was goading people into a reaction.

"It never would have come to this if you'd agreed to go out with me. And sending your boyfriend after me was a big mistake."

"I don't know what you're talking about." It was pretty clear that Travis's father had put pressure on Harry's dad, who had then turned the screws on Harry. But the less Harry knew, the better.

"Your threats don't scare me," Harry suddenly said very loudly.

A moment later, Gleason came up behind me. "What was that?"

"She warned me to leave and threatened me." Harry slid back a step like I was a physical threat.

From this distance, I could've kicked him in the balls like he deserved, but that would only have cemented his bullshit story. "Hornblatt, you're delusional if you think Mr. Gleason can't tell when you're lying." Playing on Gleason's vanity was the best I could come up with to defuse the asshole's accusation.

Gleason didn't react verbally, but his glance at me was scornful as he passed and opened the door. "You may join us in a moment."

My heart thundered. This was bad. Before the door closed after him, I spotted Luce inside, and a woman I didn't recognize.

"It's going to be a pleasure destroying you," Harry said before he pulled open the door and followed Gleason in.

A second later, I was alone in the hall. A check of the time gave me three minutes to compose myself, and I was going to take that time.

When the hour ticked over on my phone, I entered.

Gleason introduced the lady I'd glimpsed earlier. "Moreno, this is Mrs. Vera Bigheart, a member of our board of trustees. She'll be joining us as a judge in this hearing."

When he said the name, I finally placed her. She'd been a B-list actress and had married a rich, old banker in the city, a typical trophy wife. The guys had flocked to a few of her movies and called her Very Bigchest for obvious reasons.

Harry sat off to the side, while my three judges, Gleason, Luce, and Bigheart, were lined up behind a table, looking very much like my three executioners.

"Ms. Moreno," Luce began. "You have been accused of falsifying your employment application. Specifically, you did not inform us that you had been an exotic dancer, knowing that this institution cannot be associated with such conduct. What do you have to say for yourself?"

I'd thought about this. "The form specifically asked me to list my job title, and I did. I wrote down dancer. During my interview, I was not asked any questions to elaborate, so—"

"Are you suggesting it is our fault?" Gleason asked. "For not digging down into that misleading answer?"

"No, sir," I replied. "I have been accused, as Mr. Luce said, of falsifying my application." I pulled out the pay stub I'd found from that time period and rose to place it on their table. "My pay stub says my job title was dancer, and writing that on my application is not falsification."

Bigheart picked up the slip of paper and nodded. "That's what it says," she agreed.

As I returned to my seat, I sensed victory but didn't stick my tongue out at Harry.

Gleason looked pissed. "That does not change the fact that such a background brings disrepute to this institution."

When the other two nodded to his statement, my bubble of optimism burst. Gleason was determined to get rid of me.

Luce took the pay stub from Bigheart and set it down. "Then we have the second charge to deal with."

That got my attention. "What second charge?"

Gleason lifted a piece of paper. "I have a letter here stating that on a recent trip to the Caribbean, you offered sex for cash."

I gasped, and my heart nearly stopped.

Harry grinned. The fuckhead was behind this.

"Specifically," Gleason read from the paper, "that you told Mr. Hornblatt…" He pointed at Harry. "…That you were broke, and you suggested he pay you three thousand for a night of sex. When he refused, you asked for one thousand, and he refused again." He looked up, and his evil glare fixed on me. "Prostitution clearly disqualifies you as a teacher in our school."

"That's not true." I tried to keep my voice below a yell. "He was the one propositioning me, and I was the one who refused."

My stomach sank when Bigheart shook her head. Without her support, the vote on this would be three to zero against me.

My eyes drilled laser holes in Harry when I turned. Fucking Harry couldn't contain his smile. It wasn't fair. A Manhattan asshole had screwed me over again, and he was proud of it.

When he least expected it, I'd come down on him with a wrath he'd never known. I'd kick his ass and good. I wasn't one to take this kind of shit lying down.

When I switched back to the judges-turned-executioners behind the table, dread overwhelmed my anger. Nothing I did going forward would matter.

My stomach roiled as I realized my future. If I'd had anything left in my stomach, it would have painted the floor. Harry had won, and my career was over. Hightower would tell any school I applied to that I'd been terminated for prostitution. All because of Harry's lies.

CHAPTER 85

ADRIANA

I'D JUST CONCLUDED I WAS OUT OF OPTIONS WHEN THE DOOR OPENED BEHIND ME.
When I turned, it was Travis's father. I slumped in my seat.
"Sorry I'm late," he said.
A lump the size of a boulder lodged in my throat. Now Travis's dad was here to see my ultimate humiliation.
"Mr. Carlyle, we're just about to wrap this up," Gleason said. "I wasn't aware you were scheduled to join us this morning."
Victor walked over to the chair next to mine. "I thought I'd see how this process works. Is that all right?"
I almost objected, because Victor's opinion of me mattered, but that would make me look weak, and that was one thing I wasn't.
Gleason pasted on a smile. "Of course. This is Mr. Luce, our director of human resources, and you know Mrs. Bigheart, and with us, we have Ms. Moreno, a teacher under disciplinary review."
Victor nodded to Bigheart. "Vera."
She nodded back. "Victor."
"And?" Victor pointed at Harry.
"Harry Hornblatt, sir," my nemesis said.
"Mr. Hornblatt is one of our platinum-level donors," Gleason added.

Victor sat down next to me. "Morning, Ms. Moreno."

"Hi." I wished we could be back to where he was comfortable with Andy.

Victor pulled out his phone. "Just a second, I need to tell my son something." Then, he began typing a message. "What did I miss?"

Luce puffed up his chest. "Ms. Moreno is accused of falsifying her employment application and not informing us that she'd previously had a job as an exotic dancer. Today, she presented us with a pay stub…" He held it up. "That lists her job title as a dancer, but clearly we can't have someone who gets paid to take her clothes off associated with the school."

"Is that how you feel, Liam?" Victor asked. He was powerful enough to get away with using Gleason's first name.

"It is," Gleason said firmly.

"What do you have against Vera?" Victor asked. "I happen to think she's an excellent trustee of the school."

Flustered, Gleason sputtered. "Nothing."

Victor turned to Bigheart. "Vera, you used to be an actress. Did you ever take your clothes off and get paid to do it?"

"It was the job," she explained. "And it's in my past now."

He turned to me. "Are you currently an exotic dancer?"

I shook my head and smiled. "No, I am not."

"What's the difference?" Victor demanded of Gleason.

"I see your point," Gleason said, looking down the table. "Should we agree that on the first count, Ms. Moreno is innocent?"

The other two agreed, and I whispered, "Thank you," to Victor. It was the same argument they'd rejected when I made it.

"The second," Luce stated. "Is more serious. She is accused of prostitution."

I turned to Victor. "It's not true. Not a word of it."

"And who is her accuser?" Victor asked.

Harry spoke up. "I am."

"Do we have any evidence?" Victor asked, taking control of the meeting. "Or is this a case of he said, she said?"

"As a platinum donor and an esteemed alumnus," Gleason said. "I will vouch for Mr. Hornblatt."

"Is that so?" Victor pulled a folded paper from his jacket and opened it, but he was interrupted by his phone ringing. He held up a finger to pause the proceedings. "Yes. Bring them on up. Room four-oh-one."

Gleason tapped the table impatiently. "I think we should vote on the second charge."

"I'd like to read this first." Victor started reading from the paper. "My name is Angela Ecker…"

My heart leaped at the mention of Angela Ecker's name. Victor's detectives had found her.

Victor continued. "When I was twelve, Harry Hornblatt and I had—"

"Stop," Harry yelled. "That's slander."

"Shut up," Victor said with the same tone as he'd used to quiet Neville yesterday. "You are a vile excuse for a human. Preying on young girls is despicable."

The door opened behind me. My heart skipped a beat when Travis walked in, followed by two NYPD officers. "That's him," he said, pointing out Harry.

My three judges went slack-jawed.

"Harold Hornblatt, you are under arrest for sexual abuse of a minor."

Travis sat next to me and took my hand.

I zoned out as they arrested Harry and read him his rights. I had my man next to me, and that was all that mattered.

After they led Harry out of the room, Victor stood. "I can personally vouch for Ms. Moreno's character. She is actually the one who helped us locate the victim. Liam, are you going to believe her, or your platinum-donor scum?"

Gleason had turned pale. "I think we can adjourn this and agree that Ms. Moreno is a teacher we are proud to have on staff at Hightower."

"I think you owe Ms. Moreno an apology," Bigheart prodded.

It took Gleason a second to catch on. "Of course. My sincerest apology, Ms. Moreno."

"Thank you." I doubted he had a sincere bone in his body.

Outside, I clung to my man's hand and asked Victor, "How did you know about this?"

"As a trustee, it was on my calendar," he explained. "You didn't mention anything, but I didn't want you to face this alone."

I let go of Travis and hugged his father. "I can't thank you enough, Victor."

It took him a second to loosen up and hug me back. "Nonsense. And you should have asked for help, not attempted this alone."

I released him and went back to Travis. I'd been accepted, and nothing could have made me feel better.

Travis squeezed my hand. "She's stubborn that way. Keeps insisting on doing things on her own."

"Andy," Victor said sweetly, "we lean on family. It's the right thing to do. Nadia is back in town next week. How about the two of you join us for dinner?"

"We'd love to," I said, accepting for both of us. A month ago it would have surprised me, but my life had taken quite a turn since then. I was proud now to be associating with the Carlyle family and my amazing man.

CHAPTER 86

Travis

On Sunday morning, the sun broke through the overcast, shining brightly off the thin coat of fresh snow on the park.

"I think I should do this alone," Adriana said for the seventh time.

Yes, I'd been counting. "We do things together, remember?"

She rolled her eyes as if I couldn't understand simple English. "You don't understand how badly it hurt Daddy," she repeated.

"I get it, and that doesn't change a thing. I'm coming along to support you."

She kept up the argument, the same one we'd had for the last two days since I'd announced I was joining her for her Sunday lunch to meet her family. "I never even told them I was seeing you," she protested.

"I know."

"To go from that to *guess what, here's my new boyfriend and he's a Carlyle* is just asking for a disaster. I need to warm them up to it."

"Let me handle your dad," I said, repeating myself as many times as she had. "Are you going to break up with me again?"

"Shit, no. I barely survived that last one."

"Then it's settled."

She huffed loudly. "You're impossible."

"Determined," I countered.

"Ground rules—Momma doesn't allow swearing in the house."

"Good to know."

"And we're taking the train. No limos allowed in our neighborhood."

"George can drop us at the subway station, and we'll walk from there."

ADRIANA TRIED THE DOOR. IT WAS LOCKED, SO SHE PUSHED THE BUZZER.

A moment later, the door burst open. "Andy." A short woman, in her twenties I guessed, burst out and hugged Adriana. "Is this?" she asked in a more hushed tone.

Adriana stood back. "Jules, this is Travis. Travis, my sister."

I extended my hand to shake. So this was the sister she'd mentioned, seemingly the one member of the family who would accept me.

The girl lunged forward and hugged me with only slightly less enthusiasm than she had her sister. "Andy has told me so much about you."

I gave her back a pat. "Nice to meet you, Julia." That's when I saw him. The big burly man standing just inside the doorway.

"Somehow she forgot her parents," he muttered, extending his hand. "Travis, I'm Mario, this forgetful one's dad." First names only it was. He ushered us in and closed the door. "Your mother went out to get some horseradish. Can't have pot roast without horseradish."

Sergio appeared. "Hey, Trav." He didn't bother with a handshake.

I tipped a chin to him. "Hi, Sergio."

"How come everyone but me knows about this guy?" Mario asked Adriana.

"This is the first Sunday lunch, so it didn't come up," Adriana explained.

Mario's expression said he wasn't buying it. "We weren't expectin' guests, so her mother didn't prepare any fuckin' finger food. We'll have to wait for the roast."

"None expected, and the roast smells delicious." I shrugged out of my coat and helped Adriana with hers.

"Best in the whole fuckin' borough. Am I right?" Apparently, the no-swearing rule didn't apply when Adriana's mother wasn't here.

"You're right, Daddy." Adriana hung our coats in the closet.

Mario opened his arm toward the living room, and I followed. He took the wingback chair and pointed to the one across the coffee table from him. "Have a seat and tell me about yourself."

This was it, make-or-break time.

"Maybe we should go in the kitchen?" Adriana suggested. "And I can make us some appetizers," she added, clearly trying to avoid the conversation her father wanted to have.

I didn't run from problems, so I lowered myself into the chair.

"How did you meet Andy?" Mario asked.

Sergio decided to leave. Julia sat on the sofa.

"We met looking for a location appropriate to move the community center," Adriana said as she settled down next to her sister. She picked imaginary lint off her jeans.

"You like a real estate agent or somethin'?" Mario asked, crossing an ankle over one knee.

"I'm in real estate, but not an agent," I explained, getting ready to dive into the hard part. "My family company bought the property the current community center is on."

Mario's brows drew together as he tried to process what I'd just said. "I heard it was—"

"My name is Travis Carlyle," I interrupted. There was no avoiding this or sugarcoating it.

His mouth set in a firm line. Everyone was quiet. Forget hearing a pin drop, you could have heard an ant taking a shit outside.

The door opened. "I'm back," a woman's voice announced. "I had to go all the way to Dominicci's to get the good stuff."

"We're in here," Adriana called.

When she appeared, I rose to greet my girl's mother. "Travis." I offered my hand.

She shook enthusiastically. "I'm Elena. Mario and I had no idea. Let me prepare a snack."

Mario had other ideas. He pointed at the door. "You can get the hell out of my fuckin' house." *No, this was not going well.*

"Mario, language," Elena chastised. "You don't want to do that."

"The fuck I don't."

"Language," she said again.

He peeled a bill from his pocket and threw it down. "Put it in the swear jar, cuz I'm gonna tell this fucker exactly what I think of him."

I tried to defuse things. "We should discuss this. I'd like to offer my assistance."

He pointed at the wall. "The last Carlyle who wanted to help me took my fuckin' business and gave me that motherfuckin' check in return."

Adriana cringed. "Daddy."

"Don't you say a word, young lady. I framed it, cuz it isn't even worth cashin', and it reminds everybody in this fuckin' neighborhood what scum you Manhattan assholes are with your fancy suits and big words." He waved an angry hand.

This was exactly what I'd wanted to avoid and the animosity I'd hoped to defuse. It took all my willpower to breathe deeply and not yell back at him. "That wasn't me. And I really am here to—"

"Fuck you," he said, cutting me off. "Get out."

Adriana stood. "Daddy, if you throw him out, I'm leaving too."

"What?" Mario hadn't counted on my Wildcat coming to my defense.

"I won't let you treat him like that. I love him."

Her words floored me. *She loved me.* My brain stopped to appreciate the moment. My Adriana loved me.

"Mario." Elena walked in. Her sharp words brought me back to the bad situation. "You have to listen to him."

I breathed a little easier with the two of them on my side.

"Why are you gangin' up on me? He's the fuckin' Carlyle," Mario said, pointing like I carried a contagious disease. "I don't have to listen to another Carlyle liar, all big words and bullshit."

Hands on her hips, the little woman stared her husband down. "He stays. This is the man who saved our Andy, so you can darn well hear him out."

The man's jaw went slack. "What?"

"Have you already forgotten? I showed you the video. When our Andy got hit..." She pointed at me. "He came to her rescue and decked that horrible man."

Sergio rejoined us. "I saw it. That was awesome." He pulled out his phone. "Ya wanna see it, Pops?"

Mario waved him off and looked between me and Elena again. "Is that true?"

Maybe fuckwit Harry had a use after all. "I only wish I'd gotten to her faster, and that I'd hit him a hell of a lot harder."

He sat back in his chair. "You can say your piece."

I pulled the envelope from my pocket. "I understand that you lost a lot when the Plaza was built."

"Lost almost every fuckin' thing. Took me years to build the business back up."

"And you lost your repair contract with the city," I clarified.

He nodded. "Yeah, they license locations. You move, you lose. I got kicked out of the building, so I lost and somebody else got my slot."

I offered the envelope.

He eyed it suspiciously but took it.

"This is an invitation to bid on another slot, as you put it, to get your current location licensed and begin contracting with the city again."

"Don't fuck with me. There ain't no slots available. I know."

He hated big words, so I mirrored his blunt ones. "I'm not fucking with you. There is a slot." I pulled out my wallet and threw down some bills. "For the swear jar, Elena."

She scooped up the bills and smiled.

Mario gave her the evil eye and dropped the envelope on the coffee table without opening it. "I don't take charity, and you can't fuckin' buy me."

"Read it," I challenged.

He didn't.

Elena walked beside him and rapped a knuckle on her husband's head. "Now who's being stupid?"

He flinched. "Cut that out."

"I will when you stop being stupid," she insisted. "Now read the darn thing, or should I?"

With a sigh, he opened it and started reading. "This for real?"

"Fuck yes." I was on a roll with the f-bombs. "It's only a fuckin' invitation to apply. It does not guarantee a fuckin' thing. Your shop still has to pass inspection, and you have to go through the whole contracting process. This is not a fuckin' gift. This is a fuckin' chance. Pass or fail, it's all fuckin' up to you."

The big man's eyes looked a little watery. "That's all I asked for back then, and they said no." He swallowed hard. "Why?"

I gave it to him straight. "Because Adriana told me how unfairly you'd been treated by my half brother and the city."

He nodded and reread the letter. "Well, I'll be."

Then I added, "And because I love your daughter." I looked over to see tears in my girl's eyes. Julia was also crying and had a death grip on Adriana's hand.

"When are we eating?" Sergio asked.

"I think now is a good time," Elena said. "Don't you, Mario?"

"If Travis and Andy are staying."

Elena started for the kitchen. "It wouldn't be family Sunday lunch if they didn't."

Adriana had on her biggest smile as she took my hand and led me to the dining room. "You should have told me," she whispered.

I glanced at the framed check Mario had mentioned as we walked by. It was written on our corporate account and signed by Xavier, but only for a measly one thousand dollars.

Fucking Luca.

Today I couldn't let him bother me. I had a woman I loved, who loved me too, and she was back in her family's good graces. Nothing else mattered.

CHAPTER 87

Adriana
(Five months later)

Summer had arrived, and I'd made Travis's penthouse my home for half a year now. His father had relinquished the CEO role to Travis, and Luca had left the company in a snit.

Travis had agonized over it for a about a week, but in the end he'd decided not to try to get his brother back into the fold—a good decision, if you asked me.

Last night, I'd barely slept, and I'd left our bed early this morning, something I never did. But today was not a normal day. Today was a big day times about ten, and I was worried about my speech.

In the kitchen, I paced around the island, doing my best to burn off my anxiety. I'd read that exercise could burn off excess adrenaline and boost endorphins, two things I needed.

I stopped at the fridge, pulled out the OJ, and poured a quick splash into a glass. Sipping it, I looked around the insanely clean space and contemplated how things had changed for me.

We'd developed a routine, the four of us, if I included Katherine and George.

I'd convinced Katherine to allow Travis to cook breakfast for me on Saturday in addition to the Sunday she was off.

We now gave Katherine and George Monday night off as well, so I could cook dinner for my man. The concept of being waited on hand and foot was great, but we needed a little alone time.

Monday night was now our stay-in date night. It hadn't taken much to convince Travis to continue our Nassau experience and eat that dinner in the buff. It was date night, after all.

He'd bought a new glass dining table for us and had only turned a light shade of red and fumbled for an explanation when Katherine asked about it.

After dinner, we would crank up the popcorn machine and climb into sweats for a movie on the couch. With his killer eighty speakers or whatever sound system and the ginormous television screen, it was almost as good as a theater. Better when I figured in that we got to cuddle on the couch.

Without any idea if it was working, I set down the glass and picked up my pace again, scooting around the island in my bathrobe and bare feet.

My walkathon seemed to be working when Travis surprised me on my millionth lap. He leaned against the wall with a smirk. "What's going on?"

"Uh, I'm nervous."

"I get that. But what's with the?" He made a circle in the air with his finger.

"Burning off excess adrenaline."

He shook his head. "And I thought you had a college degree."

"I do."

"You obviously didn't read the paper very carefully. It only applies to aerobic exercise."

I swiped my hair over my shoulder. "Shit. Don't tell me I have to go for a run?"

A mischievous grin spread across his face as he advanced. "I can think of another way to get your exercise."

I shifted to the other side of the island and waved a finger at him. "Oh no you don't."

"Oh yes." He lunged around the island.

I made him chase me.

"You're being naughty."

"Oh, yeah? What are you going to do about it?"

It only took another half-dozen laps around the island to catch me, because this was one of our games, and it was better for me if I didn't wear him out too much.

Two minutes later, I'd been carried to the bed over his shoulder, flung down, and was naked under him, giggling with my hands held above my head, clamped in place by one of his.

His dragon dick was out and hung over me, ready to administer my punishment. "I love you, naughty girl."

"Love you more, big guy."

"Love you most, Wildcat."

My response became a moan as his mouth took my nipple in a long suck followed by swirling his tongue around the sensitive peak.

He released my hands and settled beside me.

I speared a hand in his hair and kissed him. What started as a tame reconnection became a heated and torrid struggle for dominance between us, tongues battling for control.

I gave in when he slid a hand down and trailed a finger the length of my slit.

He wasn't playing fair, so I retaliated by grasping his lower lip with my teeth and pulling at the same time as I grabbed the dragon and tugged.

Two of his fingers pumped inside me, and he lowered his mouth to my breast again, teasing, licking, sucking, and biting with that combination of tenderness and firmness that drove me crazy.

My back arched into him, and I began stroking the pull toy in my hand. Every stroke of his fingers inside me caused me to dig the rest of my nails into his shoulder as I tensed up.

His thumb found my clit, and the lazy circles interspersed with pressure threatened to undo me. "I'm getting close," I warned him between moans.

He switched to my other breast for a minute of torture before rising over me.

I spread for him, and he slid inside me, grunting when he reached the end of me and held me there. "I love how wet you are for me, and how tight."

"Not as much as I love how you stretch and fill me." I bucked against him to get some movement.

He stilled. "Greedy, aren't we?"

"Oh yeah. You said I need exercise…" I rocked my hips. "To burn off my excess adrenaline."

His breath hitched with my movement before he got out. "I did."

I yelped when he quickly rolled us and I ended up on top.

"Then you should be doing the work."

Eager to oblige, I pulled away, situated myself kneeling over him, and guided him back inside as I settled down on his length. Like this, he was dangerously long. Starting, I rose slowly and slammed down hard on him, then again and again.

Each of his grunts, combined with the faces he made, told me I had it just right and he wouldn't last long. I was in charge for a change and loving it as I rode him hard, pulling more of those delicious sounds from him.

He stopped guiding my hips and busied himself worshiping my breasts with both hands. Then he pulled my shoulders down enough to give his mouth access as well. "Oh, baby, you're torturing me."

I kept at it. "Come for me, big guy. You can do it for me."

He hated the idea of coming before I did, often giving me two orgasms before he took his own pleasure, but that wasn't what I wanted today.

The unbearable pressure inside me kept building with every delicious slide down his cock to rub my clit against him. When I couldn't withstand any more of the electric shocks that rocked my body, I slid a hand behind me and pressed up hard, right behind his balls.

His reaction was immediate. "Oh, holy fuck." He tensed up and spurted his release inside me, once, twice, and a third time. Then his thumb came between us and attacked my clit with a vengeance.

I hurtled over the edge. "Ohmygod, ohmygod, ohmygod." My channel convulsed on him, and my legs shook.

He kept up the pressure on my sensitive bud as I rode out the waves of my climax, eventually leaning forward and collapsing onto him.

Our chests heaved as our hearts beat together. When our breathing slowed enough, our lips came together as well. Him inside me was our ultimate togetherness.

When I broke the kiss, my "I love you," overlapped with his.

~

TODAY WAS THE DEDICATION OF THE NEW ASTORIA COMMUNITY CENTER, A PLACE we could all be proud of.

Travis had his arm wrapped around me. It wasn't cold. Actually, it was quite warm, but I shivered anyway. He leaned down to kiss the top of my head. "You'll do fine. This is the easy part. You've done all the hard work already."

It didn't feel that way to me, but he was right. Our new community center was finally ready to open, and the crowd outside the plaza was huge. Probably because we'd scheduled this on a Sunday when borough residents had a day off work.

I hip-bumped him. "Thanks to you."

"All I did was write the checks. You did the organizing and chasing down all the details. That's the real hard work."

While we waited, I spotted Momma and Daddy were talking to the Gomez family from a few doors down. Searching further, I caught sight of Serg chatting up a redhead with big boobs who I'd seen around, but whose name I didn't know. Some things never changed.

"Pretty big crowd," Travis noted. "I had no idea the mayor was this popular."

"It's not him." I laughed. "It's because we have free hot dogs and pretzels after this."

This was a community-bonding event and a good use of two thousand hot dogs—all courtesy of one Carlyle I was proud to call my boyfriend.

Eventually, two black SUVs pulled up at the end of the block. The street had been closed for this event. The mayor waved and shook hands as he and his security detail waded through the crowd.

"He seems to think this is a flipping campaign event," I said to Travis.

"To him, I'm sure it is."

After a while, the mayor took the podium and began his speech. It was blah, blah, blah until he finally said, "I remember a few years ago when there was some controversy about this building being built..."

A rumble went through the crowd.

"But today we are here to commemorate the opening of the new, larger Astoria Community Center. An improved center to serve the residents of Queens, which was made possible by this building behind me. This is a testament to us New Yorkers. In the end, regardless of our address, we all come together every day and every year to build a newer, bigger, better New York for all our residents."

The crowd gave him a polite but subdued round of applause. "And because I know you all would rather get to the food than listen to me any longer..."

That line brought more laughter and cheers than any of his previous ones.

377

"I'd like to call up the real hero here, the woman whose determination made this new center possible." His finger pointed at me. "Adriana Moreno."

It warmed me that the cheers that came after that were heartfelt ones from my neighbors. I walked up next to the mayor, shook his hand, and accepted the microphone. "I had a speech prepared." I held my note cards up. "But screw it. All I have to say is thank you, Mr. Mayor, and welcome, my friends, we're open." It took me two tries with the giant scissors to cut the big red ribbon. As it fell away, the real cheering began.

"Now," the mayor said, taking the microphone back. "It's time to do what we New Yorkers do best. Let's chow down and have a good time."

Travis enjoyed two hot dogs and a pretzel. I stopped after one hot dog because we still had my family's Sunday lunch to consume. There was no way Momma would allow something as silly as the community center opening to get in the way of family tradition.

A little while later, Travis and I wandered inside the community center, poking our heads in the various rooms and listening to the excited chatter. People seemed impressed with what we'd built.

When we came to the entrance to the room that housed the pools, the dedication above the doors made me cry. I'd lovingly removed each of the brass letters from the old building to remount here.

"Katarina would be proud of you," Travis said. "And what you've built to honor her."

I nodded. She would be.

Travis tightened his hold on me. "It wasn't your fault."

I nodded and repeated out loud the lie I'd told many times, "I know." The burden that had driven me for years was getting easier with time, but it would never be erased.

～

"Shoo! Get out of here," Momma screeched at Travis. "Nobody's allowed in my kitchen."

"But it smells so good," he argued. "Can't I have just a taste?"

It was a game Travis played with her every time he came over. He would try to break one of her rules, and she'd enforce it.

"You can taste it when we're all sitting down around the table. And not a minute before. Now scoot." She waved him away with an oven mitt.

"You gotta see this," Serg yelled from the front room. "We've got company."

"No way. Your aunt and uncle aren't back yet," Daddy grumbled from his recliner.

Travis ambled to the front room.

"Not them. It's a limo," Serg added.

In a panic, I rushed to the window. Victor Carlyle got out of the long, black limo. "Did you know about this?" I demanded in a hushed hiss, looking at my traitorous boyfriend.

"Don't worry. It'll be fine."

I hit his shoulder. "Why didn't you tell me?" My daddy and Travis's dad in the same room was a recipe for disaster.

"Because you would have acted just like this."

"Well, who is it?" Daddy asked, still planted in his recliner.

"I'll see." I huffed and marched out the door to try to avert the explosion.

"Ah, Andy, I must be in the right place. How did your opening go?" Victor asked, buttoning his coat. It was Sunday in Queens, and the man had worn a suit. *Clueless.*

"It was good, but what are you doing here?" I tried to not make it sound insulting, I really did.

"I came to talk with your parents." He retrieved a bouquet of yellow roses from the car before shutting the door.

"This is not the best time," I tried.

"Don't be worried," he said, correctly assessing my angst. "It'll be fine." When I didn't answer he added, "You owe me this opportunity to apologize."

He was right. Thanks to him, Harry was awaiting sentencing, and I still had a job at Hightower. He had done an immense amount for me.

"Let me introduce you." I led the way inside.

"Hey, man, sweet ride," Serg said, as clueless as ever.

"Victor, this is my brother, Sergio. Serg, Travis's dad."

"Hey, man," Serg said, shaking with Victor.

"Pleasure," Victor returned.

Travis nodded to his father. "Dad." The rat wasn't surprised by the arrival, and worse, he hadn't warned me.

As always, Momma beat Daddy to the door.

"Mrs. Moreno, a pleasure," Victor said, offering the roses.

"Oh, my, Mr. Carlyle," Momma gushed like she'd just been handed a dozen gold bars.

"Call me Victor, please."

"Mario, we have a guest."

Daddy ambled in.

"Mr. Moreno," Victor said offering his hand. "I'm—"

"I know who you are," Daddy said.

Victor withdrew his hand but kept his smile intact. "I'd like to have a chat, if you don't mind."

"You can fuckin' stuff it," Daddy snarled. The slack he'd cut Travis obviously didn't extend to the man Daddy figured had screwed us over the Plaza building years ago. It didn't help that he'd kept the insulting check on the wall all this time.

"Mario…" Mamma used her don't-screw-with-me voice.

Daddy whipped out a twenty and dropped it on the entry table. "For the swear jar."

Victor was undeterred. This was probably what made him good at business. "I really do have something to say, and some news that you might find encouraging."

Daddy stormed off.

"Well," Momma said. "You can call me Elena, and I'd certainly like to hear what you have to say. Serg, put these in water." Momma handed the roses off.

"This goes back a few months. Travis mentioned to me the paltry compensation you were paid when you moved out of the property that is now the Plaza."

"Paltry?" Daddy stormed back into the room holding the framed check. He shoved it at Victor. "Is that what you suits call it? This is fuckin' insulting is what it is. Motherfuckin' wrong." Daddy was a few seconds from busting a vein or something.

Worried, I glanced at Travis to see if maybe he'd jump in to stop the fight, but he was holding back a smirk. I knew that look. He was hiding something.

Victor took the framed check. "You're right, and this is wrong—criminal, in fact."

Daddy pushed an angry finger into Victor's chest. "Damned straight, and you should be locked up for lying and cheating the way you did, causing the destruction you did."

Victor stood his ground, just as I'd seen him do in the board meeting months ago. "Not me, my CFO at the time, and the news I came to share is that he was arrested yesterday."

Daddy stopped. "What?"

"The amount you were scheduled to receive was one million, one hundred thousand dollars."

Daddy huffed his indignation. "Does that look like a million bucks to you?"

"Our CFO at the time, a man named Xavier Breton, cut the checks to you and three others down to minimal amounts and sent the rest to an offshore account of his own. He stole from you, and us."

Daddy stood there dumbfounded for a second, then found his bravado again. "You telling me this now does me no fuckin' good."

Victor pulled an envelope from his pocket. "But this will. It's the money you're owed, per our original agreement."

My heart skipped a beat. A million dollars would be a godsend to my parents.

Daddy took the envelope and pulled out the check inside, his eyes going wide. "This is a hell of a lot more than a million-one."

"The original difference, plus accrued interest. I had it rounded up slightly." Victor smiled.

Momma shoved in to get a look at the check.

"You didn't tell me," I whispered to my traitorous boyfriend.

"Does this mean I can have a 'Vette now?" Serg asked, like a dummy.

"No," Daddy and Momma said together.

"This is real?" Daddy asked.

Victor nodded. "One hundred percent."

Momma lunged at Victor and hugged him. "Thank you."

Taken by surprise, Victor woodenly patted the tiny Greek woman on the back. "We always strive to do the right thing."

Daddy shook his head and then folded the check and stuffed it into his pocket. "How? After all this time?"

Victor laid his hand on Travis's shoulder. "You have Travis to thank for that. He saw your check and did the digging. It took a long time because offshore accounts are hard to crack."

I clung to my man, a man that I couldn't have been prouder of. I had to let go of him when Momma attacked him with a hug as well.

After a second she composed herself. "What are we doing standing around? We've got plenty of pot roast, and we're about to sit down to eat. I'd love it if you'd join us."

"I've got to get going," Victor said, backing up.

"What?" Daddy challenged. "Pot roast not good enough for you?"

"Dad, it's excellent pot roast," Travis added.

The gauntlet had been laid down, and Victor wasn't going to retreat. "I'd be honored to join you."

"Serg, set another place," Momma said as she marched off to the kitchen.

Ten minutes later, we were all seated around the table, enjoying a meal. The rift between our families had been healed by the work of the man I knew I'd marry someday.

I couldn't believe how far my life had come since the day I'd met the most wicked man on the planet in Benjamin's office and he'd told us the community center was being shut down.

My community center had moved to its new location. Xavier had been arrested, Harry was about to be sentenced for his crimes, Travis was now the CEO of the Carlyle family company, and that awful Neville character was out. Things were pretty freaking awesome.

And even if none of those things had come to be, I still had the man I loved, Travis, and best of all, he loved me back. It was all I could ask for.

"Victor, perhaps you'd like to bring your wife along and join us next Sunday?" Momma suggested.

Victor wiped his mouth with his napkin. "I'm afraid Nadia already went down to St. Barths. I'm supposed to join her on Tuesday."

"Is it as beautiful as everyone says? I've always wanted to go to the Caribbean," Momma mused.

"Better," Victor answered.

Daddy tapped his pocket and mumbled through his food. "Now we can find out."

"Perhaps you'd like to join us?" Victor suggested.

From there, the conversation started into discussions of the various islands, but when Travis slid his hand over my thigh under the table, all I could think about was getting out of this house to someplace private with the man who'd introduced me to Caribbean pleasures.

EPILOGUE

ANY MAN WHO CAN DRIVE SAFELY WHILE KISSING A PRETTY GIRL IS SIMPLY NOT GIVING THE KISS THE ATTENTION IT DESERVES. – ALBERT EINSTEIN

Adriana

George held open the door of the limo, and I climbed in.

He loaded my suitcase in the trunk for the weekend trip—the last weekend before the new school year started at Hightower.

For the last several weeks, Travis had booked a string of business meetings stretching into the evening hours. I was looking forward to having him all to myself for a few days.

I'd been in this decadent car a million times, but I still felt like an impostor whenever someone craned their neck to watch us go by. They probably thought it was somebody important behind the tinted glass.

We stopped at a light. Two women in maid uniforms exited the hotel on the corner. They stared at me, or more correctly, at the blacked-out window of the ostentatious car. One shook her head, speaking to the other. I was tempted to roll down the window and say, "Hey, it's me. I'm just a poor girl from Queens too."

The light changed, and we pulled away.

If I'd said that, and they'd asked what I was doing in a limo, what could I have said? *"I got lucky and landed a billionaire?"* Settling back into the seat, I decided it was true. I was the luckiest damned girl on the planet to have found love with Travis Carlyle.

This would be my first time at his place in the Hamptons. *Off to the Hamptons for the weekend* sounded so decadent it was almost obscene.

"George, I didn't see Katie this morning."

"She went ahead to get the house ready."

Having zero experience with a second house, I hadn't considered that. It also made sense that George and Katie traveled with us since they felt like family. "How long will the drive take?"

"Over two hours with this traffic."

I fidgeted. If we'd waited for Travis, at least it wouldn't be a boring two hours. But, oh no, *"You go ahead and get settled,"* he'd insisted. *"I don't know how late my meetings will go."* Always bossy.

I opened my phone and started to type out a message to Mr. Bossy. The voicemail icon glared at me. But it wasn't from him. It was a number I didn't recognize—probably the parent of one of my students for the coming year.

There were always one or two who called to complain about the reading I required students to complete during their summer break.

I played the message, and it wasn't a parent. "Ms. Moreno, this is Rebecca Sinestri. I'm sorry we won't be able to make the celebration today. My husband came down with chest pains, and we're at the hospital now getting him checked." Her voice was tremulous and distraught. "We so wanted to thank you in person. Maybe another time. God bless."

She must have been confused, because the only ceremony coming up was next Friday's lifeguard class graduation at the community center.

I decided against straightening her out on the schedule. With a husband in the hospital, she had enough on her plate today. I put the phone away, thinking better of nagging Travis to get the hell out of his meetings so we could get our weekend started.

After getting bored watching the city go by, I pulled my copy of *Trapped with the Bazillionaire* from my big bag and started reading, quickly getting engrossed in the story.

~

GEORGE'S VOICE PULLED ME OUT OF MY BOOK. HE WAS ON HIS PHONE. "WE'RE almost there," he said. "Love you too."

It had to be Katie. I closed my book and, for the first time, noticed water beyond the houses.

384

A minute later, George announced, "Here we are." We turned in to a gravel drive leading to not a house, but to a monster mansion on the beach.

The crunch of the tires and the view of the water beyond the house mesmerized me. It was like nothing I'd seen before. "This is his? He doesn't share it with like a half dozen other families?"

George chuckled. "All yours." He said that a lot, *yours* instead of *his*, even though I was just the girlfriend. Granted, a longer-term girlfriend than Travis had ever had, but still, just the live-in girlfriend.

It was a title I tried my best to deserve, and I was damned proud to call Travis my boyfriend. After his father's initial response to me, being accepted by Victor and Nadia was perhaps my biggest accomplishment.

I wasn't fighting the battle today, so I waited for George to open my door and rose out of the car, greeted by the warm sun on my face and the smell of the ocean on the breeze. "Thank you, George." I didn't even argue about who would take my suitcase after he pulled it from the trunk.

The door opened, and Katie appeared. "How was the drive?"

When George didn't answer, I guessed she'd meant to ask me. "Long, but I brought my reading." I held up my book.

"I'm so looking forward to this weekend," she said, holding open the door for us.

George brushed a kiss to Katie's lips as he passed inside, something he only did when the master of the house wasn't around.

Inside, it was a bit dark with the curtains facing the ocean pulled closed. Where the penthouse was decorated to be modern and elegant, this house was casual, almost historic—not a piece of chrome or a stitch of black leather anywhere.

Familiar delicious aromas filled the air. "Smells wonderful. What's cooking?" I asked.

"I'm trying a friend's lasagne recipe," she answered.

"I can't wait." Katie's cooking was always top notch, and with that aroma in the house, I didn't know if I'd be able to hold off until Travis arrived.

I stepped over and brushed my fingers along the top of the farmhouse-style table, then set my book down. Its worn surface spoke of decades, if not centuries, of use. "Where should I put my things?"

George leaped on the question. "I'll take care of that while Katherine shows you around." The switch to Katherine was odd.

"I have tea ready," Katie said.

That was Katie the Brit, always offering me tea.

385

"Thank you. That would be nice."

"Would you like to take it outside? The sound of the ocean can be so calming."

"Great idea." I shuffled to the French doors on the back wall, my legs still a little stiff from the hours in the car.

I pulled it open and froze. My breath stopped. It wasn't the Atlantic in front of me. Travis was here.

"Surprise."

My hands went to my face. There with him were my family, his family, and a crowd of others who also yelled "surprise" and began clapping.

Soft instrumental music began to play. "What's going on?" I asked when Travis moved forward to hug me.

He let me go. "Isn't it obvious? A surprise party."

"For?"

"For you, of course." A banner behind him read *Andy is Awesome*. "Because I'm so proud of you."

My heart squeezed at the sentiment, and then I was mobbed by Momma, Daddy, Serg, and Jules. Everybody was saying some version of "We're so proud of you."

"Why?" My single question went unanswered. That Travis had brought everyone here for a party for me made my eyes go watery.

"I've got to check in with Katie on the lasagne," Momma said as she went back into the house.

No wonder the smells were familiar.

"I'm so proud of you," Benjamin and Rachel and a half dozen others from the community center repeated when they got past my family. I was stuck in the department of redundancy department.

Victor and his wife, Nadia, had hung back. "Adriana, I'm sorry I treated you so poorly at our first meeting," Victor said, holding my hand in both of his. "I certainly wouldn't have if I'd known all this." He was the first one brave enough to not follow what I figured had to be a script Travis had insisted upon.

"Thank you, I guess."

"Our city needs more women like you," Nadia added.

The music stopped and was replaced by Travis's voice booming through the speakers. "Adriana's mother has slaved in the kitchen all afternoon, making us a batch of lasagne, so let's get this started and we can dig in."

A few people loudly agreed.

"First up," Travis announced, microphone in hand, "are the Garcias."

I was lost as a couple I didn't recognize approached Travis.

The crowd went silent as the woman accepted the microphone. "Thank you, Mr. Carlyle." Her eyes swung to me. "Andy, my name is Maria Garcia, and this is my husband, Fernando. When our young Mario's canoe flipped on Hempstead Lake two years ago, we would have lost him if it hadn't been for you and your swim courses at the community center."

Hot tears streaked down my cheeks upon hearing her words.

She sniffled. "We want to say thank you, Andy, for saving our son. You're awesome."

Another couple took the mic, and the Garcias came up to hug me.

"My name is Don Bindle, and this is my wife, Sarah." The woman meekly raised her hand. "Andy, our daughter Sonya wouldn't be with us today if you hadn't started the swim lessons at the center." His voice wavered. "We think you're awesome."

Travis kept his strong arm around me as I sniffled and sobbed, hearing story after story from the parents of children who'd gone through our swimming lessons.

I couldn't stop crying as eight sets of parents I'd never met before today shared their stories, eight families. I was proud to have helped them avoid the tragedy that had befallen our family.

With a ton of thanks and hugs accepted, I finally got control of my tears and wrapped my boyfriend up as tight as I could. "Is this what has kept you away from me the last few weeks?"

"It is," he said, pulling my head to his chest. "And I wanted it to be a surprise."

"Mission accomplished." I sighed as I gave him another giant squeeze.

The door from the house opened. Momma and Katie came out, each carrying a large tray. "Come and get it while it's hot," Katie said. "Momma Moreno's special lasagne."

After serving ourselves, we ended up across the table from Travis's dad, Nadia, Serg, and Jules, and next to Momma and Daddy.

Nadia hummed contentedly after her first bite. "This is just delicious, Elena."

Momma smiled. "Thank you." She nodded toward Daddy. "An old family recipe. A wedding gift from his mother."

"That's so sweet," Nadia cooed.

Victor had a forkful halfway to his mouth. "Until this afternoon," he said, looking at me, "I didn't understand your obsession with the community center having a pool. Andy, I grow more impressed with you every time we meet."

"That's cuz she's one smart fuckin' cookie," Daddy told him.

"Mario," Momma scolded. "Language."

Daddy elbowed Travis. "Your house, Trav. You got a swear-jar policy here?"

Travis shook his head. "No fuckin' way."

Both his father and my mother shook their heads in disgust.

We were devouring Katie's death-by-chocolate cake for dessert when Travis's hand slid over next to my plate, and he whispered in my ear. "For you." When his hand slid away, a keycard lay on the table.

"What's this?"

"The penthouse at the Plaza."

Fear gripped me as I narrowed my eyes, trying to get a read. "Is this your way of moving me out?" I whispered, though not quietly enough as the conversation at the table stopped, and all eyes were on us.

He nodded. "Moving back to Queens."

My heart stopped as all my worst fears came crashing down around me. I refused to cry. I'd known from the beginning that it couldn't last between us, and up until now, I'd beaten the odds. But why would he ruin such a wonderful day?

Travis pulled another keycard from his pocket. "We're both moving."

My heart restarted, but the emotional whiplash made my blood boil. "Why would you—"

He cut me off with a swift finger to my lips. "Because a husband and wife should live together, don't you think?"

Mr. Bossy was back in force, and I was pissed. "You can't just tell me we're getting married. You're supposed to ask, on a knee actually."

"That's right, I can't tell you. Are you telling me you don't want to get married or you do?"

The words spilled out quickly. "I do—of course I do."

A huge smile grew on his face. "That's the answer I was looking for."

I'd been tricked. "Shut up and kiss me."

His lips took mine, and the clapping started. It quickly faded into the background, as all I could focus on was my wonderful man and how he'd made me the happiest woman on the planet.

THE PARTY HAD MORPHED INTO AN ENGAGEMENT CELEBRATION. LIBATIONS WERE served, dance music played, and a good time was had by all. The sun had long set when we bid the last of our guests goodbye.

Travis's arm came around me as we waved. Then we were finally alone.

I turned in his arms. "Thank you for today. It was magical."

He rubbed his nose against mine. "I remembered when you told me that meeting just one set of parents whose child you'd saved would make it all worthwhile. I knew there had to be more than one, so I set out to find some of them."

"Thank you. Today was wonderful. It really has made it all worthwhile." In searching out these parents, my man, now my fiancé, had given me the best gift of all.

He squeezed my ass. "So you liked your gift."

"Loved it." I pushed away for a little space. "But your proposal skills suck."

"Really? I thought I did a good job of it. Negotiation one-oh-one."

I laughed because he was right. By agreeing with my argument that he couldn't tell me what to do, he'd gotten me to be the first to stake out a position on getting married. "Wasn't I supposed to get a ring out of this deal?"

"It's been upstairs on your pillow the whole time."

"Pretty cocky of you. What if I'd said no?"

He pressed the hard ridge of his erection into me. "Then we'd renegotiate naked."

I laid my hands on his chest. "How am I supposed to explain your proposal to our grandkids when they ask about it?"

"It doesn't matter. I got the answer I wanted. Win-win."

Win-win was right. I'd won the lottery in the man department, and life couldn't get any better.

"Grandkids? Don't we have to have kids first?"

"I'll throw out my pills right away."

I yelped when he scooped me up. "I hear it can take a lot of tries after you stop those." We reached the stairs in a few strides.

I giggled, ready for the next step our lives with my man—the wicked man who I'd learned was actually the best man.

Printed in Great Britain
by Amazon